Emma T

TRAVESTIES

The Bad Sister
Two Women of London
Faustine

ff

faber and faber

LONDON BOSTON

First published in Great Britain in 1995
by Faber and Faber Limited
3 Queen Square London WC1N 3AU
The Bad Sister first published in 1978
by Victor Gollancz Ltd, London
Two Women of London first published in 1989
by Faber and Faber Limited
Faustine first published in 1992
by Faber and Faber Limited

Phototypeset by Intype, London
Printed in England by Clays Ltd, St Ives plc

© Emma Tennant, 1995

The poem on page 36 of *The Bad Sister* is from *Marina
Tsvetayeva: Selected Poems* translated by Elaine Feinstein,
from a literal version by Angela Livingstone, © Oxford
University Press, 1971. Reprinted by permission of
Oxford University Press.

Emma Tennant is hereby identified as author of this work
in accordance with Section 77 of the Copyright,
Designs and Patents Act 1988.

A CIP record for this book is
available from the British Library

ISBN 0-571-17615-1

2 4 6 8 10 9 7 5 3 1

Contents

The Bad Sister

For Hilary Bailey

Let beeves and home-bred kine partake
The sweets of Burn-mill meadow;
The swan on still St Mary's Lake
Float double, swan and shadow!

From *Yarrow Unvisited* by William Wordsworth

EDITOR'S NARRATIVE

IN THE EARLY 1950s Michael Dalzell was a young man. He owned estates in the Borders of Scotland and a small house in central London, and when he decided to marry, as we can see from this photograph, he chose as his bride a fair-haired girl of the same class as himself. The newsprint is smudged with age, but she is pretty if prim. The caption says the honeymoon would be spent abroad – but another clipping from a gossip column announces they have decided to settle immediately on their Border estates. At any rate, whether the couple went abroad or not, a daughter was conceived, and born in Scotland. A quarter of a century later both father and daughter were murdered, victims of 'political murder' at the hands of a woman who seems to have been a daughter of Dalzell. This strange case – for the killer was never found – has been the subject of many TV documentaries and journalistic 'reconstructions', but until recently the original wedding photographs, and police photographs of the corpses, and bewildered statements from friends of the family have been all the evidence available. Now, two changes have come about. Several of Dalzell's old friends have been prepared for the first time to give an account of him at about the time of his wedding, and in the course of doing so have casually mentioned 'a collection of women in the hills'; and a friend of 'Jane' (the supposed murderer) has filled in a good deal of her life before the double crime. But, most important of all, a strange document, apparently by 'Jane' herself, has come to light. It now seems possible to understand these odd killings a little better, and it may protect the health of our society if we learn to do so. They are not, after all, isolated instances – murder by middle-class female urban

7

guerillas is ever on the increase in the West – yet it is also the case that 'Jane' may not fit easily into that category of person. I will only present what I know, or have been told, and 'Jane's journal' can supply the rest.

Michael Dalzell, in the days before his troubles began, liked gambling and staying out late. This he did on July 21, 1952, on the eve of his wedding, in his London club, although he knew he would feel far from well the next day when it came to flying up for the celebrations. While the marquee was being put up at Dalzell, and a bonfire was assembled on the highest hill, the young groom and his friends sat playing backgammon and drinking champagne till dawn. The bride's name was Louise, and she was toasted from time to time, along with other women friends. At five, the future husband was half-carried into a cab, and twenty minutes later he was fumbling for the key at his door. He was not in a good temper – he even, a friend reported later, felt 'rather jinxed'.

The evening at the club hadn't gone well. Dalzell lost two thousand pounds, which he could only raise by selling a wood on his estate, and he had the unpleasant feeling that his wife would stop him from gambling altogether once they were married. He dreaded the prospect, which Louise had also manoeuvred, of spending the rest of his life in the Borders. But most of all, in his gloomy drunken state, he felt uneasy at the way his 'stag party' had progressed. His friends agreed they had never seen anything like it. The backgammon dice were laughingly examined, as if the points could vanish or multiply in the hands of a skilled conjuror. They couldn't, of course! – but it seemed almost unbelievable, and certainly ludicrous, that a man could play the game all night and throw nothing but twos. 'Deuce Dalzell' they began to call him by the time the brandy and champagne had been succeeded by scrambled eggs and strong coffee and followed by champagne again. 'You'll be seeing double at the wedding, old boy!'

Worse was to come, though, when the young man finally negotiated his key and stepped into the house. He had left the hall and ground floor sitting room lights on, as he always did, to keep the burglars away, and even in his uncertain condition he could see that someone had turned the sitting room light off. At the same time, he saw that a shadow stretched from the half-open sitting room door onto the grey carpet of the hall. There was no grandfather clock, or similar tall piece of furniture which could have accounted for the shadow, and for a time Michael Dalzell stood stock still. It did cross his mind that tonight was as good a night to be killed as any. But, tonight at least, he was to be spared.

The girl who had climbed into the house from the rear and concealed herself in the sitting room – and whose shadow now betrayed her – had until recently been employed as shop assistant in a big London store. Her name was Mary, her mother was unmarried and Irish, and she was six months pregnant with Michael's child. Dalzell had seen her while buying white calfskin gloves for his fiancée, and had insisted she try on the gloves for him, telling her her hands were 'just the right size'. She had had to have them sprinkled with powder by the chief vendeuse and had rested her elbow on a velvet pad intended for customers. He bought six pairs. When the bill was signed, Mary was asked if she would like to go out later that evening, and she said she would. She certainly found him very charming, and although there were many evenings when Michael was invited to parties he wouldn't have dreamed of taking her to, they went to gambling clubs and nightclubs enough for her to feel he must be interested in her almost to the point of proposal. That this wasn't the case she discovered, inevitably, when she became pregnant. She had a difficult time, for her mother, who'd only a few years before come over from Ireland with her daughter, shocked by the news and already in poor health, working as a domestic in a big country house in Southern England, refused to see her. When she relented the mistress of the house, a Mrs Aldridge, made it clear Mary would not be welcome. Michael gave her a hundred pounds and suggested they didn't meet again. Social workers advised that the baby should be adopted. And Mary lost her job behind the glove counter when her condition became too evident. She was desperate, in fact, and having read in the gossip columns of her lover's impending marriage, decided to plead with him one last time before handing herself over to the hostel and the adoption society.

Michael Dalzell, of course, was adamant. He turned on the lights once he had come to his senses and realized who the owner of the shadow was, and he settled the girl on the sofa and poured a large brandy for each of them. He explained he had just lost two thousand pounds at backgammon and Mary found herself commiserating with him before she knew what she was doing. He said he had big expenses with his wedding, and had found it necessary to convert an upper floor at Dalzell into a nursery, which had involved the installation of central heating. He then went on to point out that the baby had the chance of a far better life if adopted, and that it was selfish of Mary to want to keep it and for him to pay for it. In the end, half-reeling from the brandy, which was new to her (whereas Michael's mind, after an evening's drinking, had been marvellously cleared by it), Mary let herself out of the house and stumbled a long way across London to the room in the shared flat she could no longer afford.

A few hours later Michael Dalzell was on the plane to the North. Events of the night before seemed already distant and unimportant. He remembered the unlucky gambling with more irritation than the episode with Mary – in fact he felt more sorry for her in retrospect than angry at her untimely visit – and it's clear that his conscience troubled him a little at the wedding, because he confided the visit to a friend and asked him to keep an eye on her in London over the next few months. By then she had moved and the friend was unable to trace her. But by then, too, Louise Dalzell was expecting a baby. By all accounts the young couple were excited and proud, and the last touches to the nursery floor had to be added in haste in order for the rooms to be ready in time for the baby.

As I was compiling these notes a letter arrived from a man named Luke Saighton, who had been a friend of Michael Dalzell in his gambling days and who had gone to stay frequently at Dalzell before the estate was sold. 'I can't remember exactly when the people of whom you inquire arrived there,' a part of the letter ran,

> but I think it was probably the summer of 1965. I do remember one or two incidents very clearly. Michael and I were standing on the track halfway up the valley – at a point where the track divides and one part winds downwards to run a couple of miles beside the burn before petering out, and the other climbs the hill – they used it to take shooting brakes in the summer and you could get the snow plough along it in winter, for the shepherds – when we saw a car coming towards us at a terrific speed. It was only a broken-down old Austin, but the track was narrow and rough and I honestly don't know how it managed to go at such a rate. It had been a dry, dusty summer and they were in a cloud of dust – it was like a typhoon approaching. Michael and I stepped pretty quickly out of the way, as you may imagine! Anyway, when the car had gone past and we had mopped some of the dust off our faces I saw Michael was looking pretty badly shaken. I'd only just managed to get a glimpse of the inside of the car, and my first impression had been of a huddle of women, long hair and what looked like gypsy shawls and skirts. But I do remember one of the faces. She was quite young but gave us the fiercest look I've ever seen on a woman's face. It was her eyes particularly – I'm afraid I can't describe them except to say they seemed to burn right through you. 'What's the matter, Michael?' I said. I really wondered if he was going to have to sit down for a while to

recover himself. 'It's nothing, must be the heat' – or something like it, was all he would say, but it sprang into my mind that maybe he knew the women in the car and would like his wife not to know about it. He had a bit of a reputation in the area for going after girls. (I hope, incidentally, that this will not be grossly exaggerated in your book, or documentary programme.)

Next day we heard that these women had moved into a semi-derelict cottage at the head of the valley. Michael was furious but he was very reluctant to go up there. In the end he asked me to go, and of course it was the last thing I wanted to do. If there has to be eviction I believe it is the job of the forces of law. Yet Michael didn't want to call in the police, in fact he flatly said he wouldn't. So in the end I went. It was an unpleasant business – they said they wouldn't move out – and the fierce-looking woman, who on second view wasn't as arresting as I'd thought – fairly ordinary really, medium height, brown hair, etc. – was actually holding a rifle! The other woman was more pleasant, and had very white skin and dark hair and blue eyes. She spoke in a quiet voice which sounded Irish, it stood out particularly in that part of the Borders, where the Lowland Scots is very marked. She said: 'We can't move, we're not going' over and over, while her friend stood behind her with the gun pointing straight at me! There was a little girl there, about twelve, she was standing with her head against the wall as if she couldn't bear the scene, so I couldn't make out what she looked like. She had dark hair, rather straggling, to her shoulders. Anyway, I told the woman I'd repeat what they'd said to Mr Dalzell, and they'd be hearing from him. 'Why couldn't he come himself?' said the armed woman, with a good deal of contempt. (I couldn't help rather agreeing with her.) 'No, no, leave all that out of it,' the nicer-looking woman pleaded. 'His time will come, Mary,' was the

THE BAD SISTER

reply. Then she turned to me and told me Mr Dalzell and I
could both go to hell.

When I got back to the house I didn't repeat what the
fiercer of the two women had said because I didn't want
Michael to get upset again. I now think perhaps I should
have. I stayed only a few days more on that occasion, and
he didn't go near the place. But I was to return a month later
in September for the annual shooting party, and I knew he'd
have to go up there, as you climb above that cottage to reach
the butts. I did however try to make him call in the police.
It seemed quite ridiculous that he should allow these vagrants to stay in his property. He refused again, though. I
began to suspect something, and I think Louise Dalzell did
too, so we kept off the subject.

In the event I went down with 'flu and missed the shooting
party. When I went again it was after Christmas. I remember
talking to the gamekeeper about the birds and how the September shoot had gone. I enclose a few of his observations,
and his present address, in case you would wish to interview
him.

At this point I stopped reading Luke Saighton's letter, which
had only a few more pleas, at the end of the page, that I try not
to hurt the feelings of the friends and relatives of the Dalzells,
and gazed out of my study window at the autumnal trees in the
street. After collecting accounts of that summer from a few of
Dalzell's old intimates, it seemed fairly certain that the arrival
of the women, early 'squatters' on the laird's land, had been very
annoying to him – and also, during all those months, he had
made no effort to get them out. Things only came to a head in
the spring of 1968 – nearly three years after they arrived; before
the thaw, when the rain was coming down but there was still no
let-up from the cold, he sent half a dozen farmhands up there
and the women were forced to move. It would have seemed more
humane to have done this in the summer months – yet it was

certainly odd tnat he had allowed them to stay so long. According to some eye-witness reports, it was because one of the women was doing her best to be aggravating that he finally evicted them. Here, as before, I can only piece together the few fragments I've been able to lay my hands on.

Michael Dalzell, after his marriage, soon settled down to become a typical landlord of those parts: Tory-voting, suspicious of change, and with a television kept in a back pantry, seldom visited either by himself or his wife. Louise Dalzell was a perfect complement to him and was popular in the village, in this neutralizing much of the hostility which inevitably built up for her lazy and wealthy husband. The daughter born to them was to prove an only child and both parents adored her. By the mid-sixties, when she was twelve years old, Michael and Louise, despite social changes more marked then in England than in Scotland, were planning her London début, followed by some years in a foreign university, and her eventual takeover, for death duty reasons, of the Dalzell estate. The arrival of the women in the valley, however, caused a certain strain between husband and wife, which was reflected in a rather maddening 'hoity-toity' manner in the child – and this manner was made worse by the daily conflict, at the village school, between the daughter of the Dalzells and the girl, the same age as herself, from the half-ruined cottage in the hills. They fought so often and so angrily that the teacher became used to complaining to the laird. But each visit from the teacher to the 'big house' was followed by a visit from the fierce-looking woman from the head of the valley. In summer she walked barefoot and wore long skirts, which had never been seen at that time in the region. She and Michael Dalzell stayed in his study for a short time and when she came out of it was always with the promise that he would do nothing about the situation. No one ever knew what was said. So – going on in this way – the strains began to show in the Dalzell family. It was as if a shadow had fallen over the happy household – this was the opinion of others as well as Luke Saighton.

These weren't the only troubles. Michael Dalzell, bored perhaps with rural life, and uneasy at home, began to gamble again. He took to meeting friends at the Black Barony, a remote hotel in East Lothian, and playing championships and drinking all night in rented rooms. It was at this hotel in fact that he gave a dance for his daughter in the New Year of 1968, and at the dance that the incident occurred which led to the expulsion of the illegal ménage from the Dalzell estates. But before we return to Luke Saighton's account of the party, it's worth quoting from the gamekeeper (not a man to have been on the side of the squatters, of course), and to record that Michael Dalzell started to sell portions of his land to meet his gambling debts, keeping this secret from his wife and usual lawyers by using a small firm of Edinburgh solicitors. He must have been in a fairly desperate frame of mind, for however hard he tried to prevent the modern world from coming into his kingdom, it came: a woman reporter from London appeared one day and said she had heard there was 'a commune of radical feminists' up in the hills beyond his house and she was going to write about them; several more women *did* arrive in the summer of '67, and Michael Dalzell could only look the other way; and there were reports of Revolution on all sides. Not that these factors in any way disturbed the Dalzell capital or landholdings – it seemed more that he was intent, at this histori- cally suitable time, on losing all his possessions himself. The gaming table was the most aristocratic and honourable method and the laird applied himself to the partitions of the backgammon board with more zeal than had been allotted to his fields.

It can't have been pleasant for Michael, or his wife and daugh- ter, to go out on a country walk in those days. Possibly, in his difficult situation – for as well as his backgammon losses Dalzell must surely have also been regularly blackmailed by the women in the cottage – he cared less about the gradual loss of his land now that it was no place to be quiet and private in. For, according to MacDonald the gamekeeper, wherever they went a contingent of women followed. There was a small shop in the village, where

Mrs Dalzell bought wool, and her daughter, now fifteen, went to look at the women's magazines; here mother and daughter would find themselves surrounded, in a place that was by no means large, by women in long black skirts and with scarves tied around their heads. The atmosphere soon became intensely claustrophobic, and the lady and her daughter had to leave. The villagers thought this shocking, but when it came to speaking openly to the women, something seemed to prevent them. MacDonald, who had no such scruples, was often shouting to them to get off the land – they disturbed the pheasants' feeding – and on one occasion suggested to Michael Dalzell that he 'take a shot or two, just wing them, sir,' but at this his employer only shook his head. As MacDonald pointed out to Luke Saighton, Mr Dalzell was 'too kind-hearted. Wherever he went, and the ladies too, over the moor or along the brae, they followed behind like a row of corbies.' Certainly it seems these women had the upper hand at that time, and that they almost invited the pitched battle with the farmhands which was the result of the party at the Black Barony Hotel.

Luke Saighton's account runs:

I don't know why Michael chose to give the dance for his daughter at a hotel rather than at home. I don't want to be 'psychological' about it but I think holding the party at Dalzell might have given him painful memories of his own wedding party, when everything seemed to be set fair, and it was glorious weather too with the light fading almost at midnight and a bonfire on the hill. He seemed deliberately to choose midwinter and another setting – on the other hand I gather he was in debt to the Black Barony and had promised to bring them a lot of publicity (they thought Michael was the friend of kings and multi-millionaires). The proprietors of the Black Barony must have been horribly disappointed when, uninvited of course, the party from the derelict camp arrived. I gather they thought Mr Dalzell had decided on a fancy dress occasion when they saw the gypsy attire – one or two neighbouring landholders went home to deck themselves out with plaids and mantillas before returning to the dance. At any rate, they let them in – and then there was the devil to pay.

Michael and Louise's daughter was looking particularly pretty that night. She had fair, curly hair tied up on the top of her head if I remember, and a new dress she was very proud of. All the young men wanted to dance with her, and there was quite a crowd round her most of the time. There were Scottish reels and a few ordinary dances – even at that time Michael wasn't going to have any 'pop' or rock and roll or whatever you call it. And it was in the middle of the 'Wee Drops of Brandy' which had always been a family favourite at Dalzell before the bad luck set in, that the 'corbies' walked straight across the dance floor and went for the girl. Just like that. The fierce-looking one – I heard the quiet one called Mary crying her name as they went into the fray – was called Margaret. There were two others, whose names I didn't catch, and there was the black-haired girl who was the daughter of Mary. It was extremely shocking to see their violence. Margaret had pulled the poor girl's dress off – and someone had lurched into a waiter carrying a tray of fruit cup, so that she was covered in slices of peach and raspberries and so on. Mary's daughter looked as if she was honestly trying to scratch her eyes out. And the others were all kicking and punching. When Louise Dalzell came running up they gave her the same treatment. It took about fifteen men to pull the women off. All the while the Scottish dance music went on because the band was in the alcove and couldn't see what was happening. I must say I shall never forget that evening. I needn't describe Michael's reactions. He was as white as a sheet, and although one shouldn't joke about a late friend, if anyone had had a few too many 'wee drops', he had. Frankly, he was quite incapable of coping with the onslaught. I think he knew if he came forward they'd go for him too – and he'd go down with the first blow.

He got his revenge the next day, of course. An army of farmhands went up to the valley to the cottage – they had sticks, and two of them were allowed to take guns – not MacDonald the gamekeeper, as he might have proved too keen – and in an hour the battle was over and the women were loaded onto a farm lorry and driven to the border. Michael wanted me to go up there and help with the eviction, but I really didn't have the stomach for it. And he was keen, too, for them to be deposited in England – I don't know why – perhaps he felt they'd be further away if they were in another country. I can't remember where they were dropped off, but it was somewhere south of Carlisle.

There was one odd thing about that day. Michael told me that when it came to loading the women onto the lorry there was no sign of Margaret anywhere. Departure was held up for a good time while they searched for her. Everyone knew she was the most dangerous of the lot, and well capable of going to ground and building up a new centre on another part of the Dalzell estate. But she had completely vanished. Mary'd obviously tried to go with her, but she didn't get far. They found her in a snow drift, in a deep cleuch below the cottage. They bundled her onto the lorry and some of the men, I believe, took trouble to wrap her in her shawls. She had a poor physique apparently, could never have lasted the course. Anyway, the other women swore Meg had left the night before, after the fight, cutting across country to the Yarrow, on to Moffat and then south. As Michael still refused point blank to call in the police, there was no way of making roadblocks and catching her there: it wouldn't have been easy anyway, with those great stretches of hill and heather, and the dwarf forests of pine trees as far as the eye can see. Two reports came in the following day – one that a distant figure, probably a woman (it had long hair, but then this was 1968 and so did many men), was seen running amongst the trees on a steep hillside near St Mary's Loch. It 'flitted like a shadow in the trees,' the onlooker said, 'zigzagging backwards and forwards as if it had no idea of direction'.

The other report was of a polite, well-dressed woman, never seen in the neighbourhood before, who walked up the drive at Dalzell, met Louise Dalzell walking there, exchanged a few words with her, saying she was going to visit relatives in the village, and then, when Mrs Dalzell turned round to take another glimpse of her, had disappeared. When asked what this mysterious stranger had looked like, Mrs Dalzell – who was still suffering from shock from the night before – said only that she was 'quite sure she had seen her somewhere before'. No, not last night, but the face was very familiar to her. She even felt it might be some distant relative of *hers* who, coming on her suddenly in the drive, was too embarrassed to declare herself. Well, of the two reports we could make nothing much. With the first, Michael and I concluded the running figure must have been a roedeer. There are a few left in the region, and particularly in the old trees of what was once the Etrick Forest, which was where the report came from (not so far across country from the 'commune' but it seems fairly unlikely Margaret would have run off in this way). With the second, we put Louise's 'hallucination' down to shock. We made a few inquiries in the village, and in fact no one had received a visitor that day. I wondered if she should see a doctor, but again Michael was adamant that no one from outside should interfere in this matter. A day later, I left. When I next saw Michael and Louise – when they had moved to London – the subject didn't come up, and I'd pretty well forgotten it too. I would of course be very grateful if you could let me know any developments that may crop up in your investigations. I feel, as I am sure you do, that the police have been very inefficient in this matter: surely this 'daughter' of Michael's, if this is what she really is, can't be impossible to trace. After the death of Michael and his daughter, I felt I should have given more information on the subject of the invasion of the women during those years, but at the same time, as you must understand, I couldn't see there could possibly be any connection between those women and the killings, and I was particularly anxious not to hurt Louise's relatives by dragging in even the shadow of a doubt of Michael's devotion and fidelity as a husband. I look forward to hearing from you if there are any developments.

I couldn't help thinking, when I'd read this letter, that Luke Saighton should certainly have told the police about the commune of women in the hills. But perhaps he was as shocked and disbelieving as Michael Dalzell: to them it seemed incredible that a humble, pregnant shopgirl, the classic recipient of a cash hand-out and abandonment, should in the course of twelve years have become an aggressive member of a large and growing aggressive army. If this was the present, they didn't want to know about it. They simply shut their eyes and ears.

Michael Dalzell sold his estate in 1970, to pay his gambling debts. His wife wasn't given the reason, and was simply told by her husband that he thought it was time they went back to London so he could 'go into the City'. He would have been quite unable to do this, of course, or to support his family, if a stroke of luck hadn't befallen him in the death of two uncles and the unexpected inheritance of a large fortune from the other branch of the Dalzell family. If the twos he had thrown at backgammon seventeen years before had brought him bad luck, lasting all that time, now things seemed to have reversed very favourably: within three months of the sale of house and land, Michael Dalzell and his wife and daughter were ensconced in a magnificent house in Hampstead. Plans were immediately under way for a ball – in the photograph here, taken from the society pages of a glossy magazine, all three, as they stand shaking hands in the reception line, look as happy and prosperous as might be expected.

As I said earlier, there would have been little point in recapping the story of the Dalzells, if it hadn't been for Stephen, the young man who came forward in reply to my latest batch of advertisements. His evidence, and the document we print here which is the journal of the mysterious 'Jane', have solidified the picture considerably – have made it possible, indeed, to reconstruct, as we have just done, Michael Dalzell's early escapade in London. But, until the girl is found, nothing can be certain.

Stephen came to my study one morning with a copy of the *Times* – my advertisement appeared in the Personal Columns that day – and he seemed nervous when I offered him a chair and asked him to introduce himself. He may have thought I was a detective, I suppose, and regretted his decision to come, but I felt a certain excitement, as if I knew somehow that I was getting nearer to the truth, as soon as I saw him there.

Stephen was plump, and middle-aged and fair-haired. He wore a dog collar, and gave me the name of his parish in South London. Altogether he seemed a most unlikely companion for the killer of the Dalzells – yet, as I said, I was sure I was on the right trail at last. With some mumbling and apology, he pulled a battered-looking manuscript from his pocket and handed it to me before sitting in the armchair on the far side of my desk.

I didn't read the MS there and then. Stephen, who said he would prefer not to give his second name, explained that it had been sent to him by a woman who was a mutual friend of his and 'Jane's' and that he felt more and more convinced that 'Jane' was both the daughter and the killer of Michael Dalzell. 'I don't know where Jane is,' he began. (Stephen has a very soft voice and I had to lean over the desk to hear him.) 'I suspect she's not alive, or she would have been found by now. But I'll tell you what I know. I met Jane first when she was about eighteen. It was at a Vietnam meeting and she was sitting next to a girl I knew slightly, who was at the LSE. We started to talk, after the meeting we had some supper, and then she took me back to meet her friends where she lived. It was a peculiar set-up. A big house in Notting Hill lived in exclusively by women. There must have been thirty of them – there was one room on the ground floor where men were allowed to visit – quite a lot of children around, and Jane told me they all had the same surname, which was Wild. She said her mother was somewhere there, and they had been in the house about three years – before that they'd been in Scotland.'

I found myself giving a little grunt of satisfaction. 'And did she introduce you to a woman named Margaret?' I asked in a voice as soft as Stephen's. He fiddled with his dog collar (it seemed more and more strange that he should be a friend of these Wild women, but then nowadays one must accept new mixtures, such as radical gay clergymen or the like) and frowned before answering, more tentatively than usual: 'Do you mean Meg? How could you know about *her*?'

I explained there had been a women's commune in Scotland, and the ringleader had been a fierce woman by the name of Margaret. Looking back through Luke Saighton's letter, I realized she had never been properly described, and was therefore unable to get corroboration from Stephen, except that he agreed the woman Meg was also indescribable. 'I didn't meet her often, but she always seemed to look different,' was how he put it. I thought for a moment of jokingly remarking that the days were long past when this changeability of appearance was known as being 'journalière' – you'd more likely get reported to the Sex Discrimination Board if you remarked on a woman's looks in this way. But I decided against it: he was of the protest generation despite his mild Church of England looks, and might decide to stop confiding in me. It was enough that this stranger had walked into my study and described what sounded very like the 'corbies', only grown in number – for he went on to say that Jane's mother was Mary, that she was Irish, and that 'Meg' was very much in control of the place.

'Did Jane ever refer to the name Dalzell then?' I asked.

'No. No, she didn't. Her name was Wild like the others, of course. But she did say she had met her father once, when her mother had taken her to his new home in London, demanding money. He wouldn't give it, but he offered to send Jane to a boarding school, which she accepted.'

'A private school?'

'Yes, the commune was up in arms about it but Jane escaped and went there for a couple of years. She hated the set-up by then, I think, and wanted an ordinary . . .'

'Bourgeois,' I put in, trying to keep a straight face.

'Exactly. She would have liked the childhood Michael Dalzell's legal daughter was having. Ponies, coming-out parties, everything. She was sick of the rhetoric and of being on the wrong side of the police. But in the event, the boarding school sickened her too. By the end, I mean. She found the girls limited and the teachers snobbish. So she returned to the fold. This meant that Meg's influence over her increased considerably.'

'And what was that? What did she do to her?'

Stephen laughed as if he was surprised, and then gave a loud sigh.

'I'm sorry. I lived for so long worrying about what Meg would do to Jane that it's difficult to imagine that you know so much about the whole background and yet you don't know that. Well, to go back to that first meeting with Jane and the evening in the women's house, the atmosphere there was absolutely terrifying. The room I was allowed to sit in, I remember, was dark red, and although it was very much out of context, I couldn't help thinking of the front parlour of a grim Victorian brothel. While we sat and talked, several women flitted in and out, and they all had the same expression on their faces – self-contained and dedicated, eyes to the ground, like nuns but with very different, striding movements. Jane's mother brought us some coffee. She looked tired and strained, and I had the feeling she had been taken over there without knowing what she was letting herself in for, and now couldn't get out. Then Meg came in. All the women present turned to her automatically, as if waiting for orders: the strangest thing was the way they turned, though, like votaries in a temple, swinging around, eyes half-closed and then standing completely still, waiting for Meg to speak. I'll never forget it.'

'And Jane?' I said, privately wondering if Stephen had gone into the Anglican Church as a reaction against all this. 'Did she swing round too?'

'No. Not really. She'd been away at school until fairly recently, I suppose, and hadn't got back into the habit of complete obedience to Meg. But I could see it was Jane that Meg was most interested in. Little did I know then, of course, what she wanted me *for*.'

'And did Meg give any orders?'

'Yes. Her voice was surprisingly light – almost chatty. It was her eyes that were frightening: grey and prominent and when they were fixed on you you felt it was your duty to do exactly as she said. She told them some place they were all to go to the next day – I wasn't really listening but I do have a vague memory of Islington being mentioned, and then seeing in the papers the next evening there'd been a bank hold-up there. I wondered if it could possibly be them. The atmosphere was like that, you see, nervous and evil, with a tremendous wall of control imposed from above by Meg.'

'Poor Jane,' I said after a while. 'Did she get away again?'

'Oh yes. She was fond of her mother, I think, and sometimes stayed for her sake. But she ran off a short while later, got a job and found a room . . .'

'What kind of job?'

'I think she started as a reporter. She went up quickly. She wrote about cinema, and in the last couple of years, before the . . . the relapse she had, she was film critic for a big magazine. Yes, she was doing well.' Stephen shook his head, like a disapproving uncle. I wondered how much he *did* know, whether he had known all along that Jane had gone to kill Dalzell and then his

24

daughter, rather than coming to the conclusion only now, on receiving the document. He must have read my thoughts then, for he leaned even further over my desk, and said in his soft voice. 'Until I read this journal of hers, I can assure you I had no idea of what Meg was doing to Jane. I knew she had influenced her a great deal in the past, but I thought Jane was a long way from all that by then. She was living with a boyfriend too. It was tragic.'

Stephen and I sat for a while in silence. He was clearly upset, remembering the gruesome events of ten years back, and I too was thinking of the evening, in March 1976, when Michael Dalzell lost his life. I opened the clippings file, and looked again at the photograph of the outside of his Hampstead House. I looked once more at a news picture of Michael Dalzell – he had grown plump and middle-aged by 1976, had taken on the features of a prosperous banker, which indeed he was – and then I flipped the photographs over until I came to the ones of him dead. There was a neat bullet wound over his left eye, which was open and round under it. He looked aggrieved and resigned at the same time. A black tie, sign that he had been at a formal dinner party, was tied very straight under his chin.

'The extraordinary thing is,' Stephen said, 'in this journal of hers Jane doesn't mention the affair of Mr Dalzell at all. It was the distorted version of getting the girl that made me first think . . .'

I looked up and nodded at Stephen, then went back to glancing through the clippings from the newspapers and reconstructing the night of the parricide. Michael Dalzell and his guests were half way through fillet of veal with wine and mushrooms when the butler went to answer the front door bell. Louise Dalzell, who had died a few years before, had been replaced by a succession of girl-friends, and one of these was in the hostess's chair, sipping wine and remaining quiet during the business conversation. (She announced later that she had thought of going out to answer the bell herself because she was so bored, and her decision not to had probably saved her life.) The butler returned and told Mr

Dalzell that his daughter was outside, and had a gift for his birthday. She would like to give it to him personally if possible, and was sorry to come at an inconvenient hour.

Now Michael Dalzell knew it was nowhere near his birthday, but in his slight drunkenness he became easily sentimental and imagined the visitor to be his legal daughter, who lived on her own now, much to his disappointment, as he had hoped she would stay on in Hampstead and care for him after her mother's death. He rose to his feet with a beatific smile. One of the guests said he tripped, but quickly corrected himself, on the rug by the dining room door. The next thing they heard was a shot. By the time they had run out into the hall, there was no sign of anyone – the front door was open, and Michael Dalzell was lying half in and half out – and they dragged him into the hall and closed the door (not that it would have made any difference to him), for it was a cold March night.

The butler was at first suspected of being mixed up in the Dalzell killing. He was a temporary, and therefore, having never met 'the real Miss Dalzell', could hardly be blamed for letting another woman convince him she was Dalzell's daughter. But his descriptions were very odd and contradictory and he was watched for some time, although it was obvious he would have been unable to commit the crime (after he had answered the door and called his employer, he had gone to the pantry and stayed with the parlour maid). He said at first that two women had come to the door, but one had been standing so much in the shadows behind the one who said she was Dalzell's daughter that he hadn't been able to make her out at all clearly. Then he said that as he had gone to inform the banker of the visit he had looked back and only the second woman was standing there, the first having disappeared. He described her as tall and brown-haired. When he was questioned as to why he went ahead to the dining room leaving the front door open and a total stranger standing there, there were no satisfactory answers. He only said the 'gift was now in the other woman's hands' and he thought 'Miss Dalzell must be behind her for some reason'. That was all.

I handed Stephen the clippings and asked him if this made sense now there was a chance that it had indeed been Jane, and Meg standing in front of her. Stephen shrugged. 'I don't think you were listening just now when I said it's odd there's no mention of the event in the journal. Jane could have been hypnotized, you know – either when she was there, and shooting her father, or afterwards into forgetting she had been there at all. God knows what new powers Meg had over her by then.'

'But you didn't know that Jane had been seeing Meg again? And what "powers" do you mean?' (I was conscious of feeling slightly uncomfortable: was Stephen going to try to persuade me that the killer of the Dalzells had been suffering from diabolic possession? That he had tried to exorcize the demon and had failed?) I felt this was going a bit too far, and said so.

'I did suspect that Jane was seeing Meg again,' Stephen replied. 'But you must understand that she was very much in two minds about the whole thing. On the one hand, Meg and her mother had brought her up to fight capitalism, to be in a state of perpetual war with the society they lived in, and she was a radical by temperament, and on the other she wanted peace and harmony, which it seems she could never find. As for the diabolic qualities of Meg, I don't know how else you would describe them. Have you never felt real evil?'

'Well, what were these powers,' I said again. No doubt Stephen wanted to protect his friend, whether she was dead or alive, and by believing she had been 'possessed' at the time of the crimes he could condone them.

'I began to grasp them when I went to see Meg shortly after the murder of Mr Dalzell,' Stephen said after a short pause. 'Jane had recently seemed very agitated and confused and all the newspaper reports of his Scottish background, etc. made me uneasy. I knew she had seen Meg again and I wanted to try to have it out with her. But – and whether you believe this or not is up to you – Meg threw me off course from the beginning. I rang the bell and one of the small (female – the boys were sent away) children let me in. It was quite dark in the hall and there were rows of bicycles stacked there. Then the door of the red room, the visitors' room, opened. I saw Jane quite clearly standing against the light. One of the bicycles was in the way and I couldn't see her legs and feet, but from the waist up it was definitely Jane. The only snag was that I knew Jane was at a film showing the other side of London. I'd spoken to her just as she set off, so as to make sure I *wouldn't* bump into her when I went to see Meg. Then she turned and went back into the room, and Meg's voice called to me to come in. I went – and there was Meg and no one else. I remember it was a very windy day, and cold, but the window was open at the top and some white blossom was blowing in. It had settled on Meg's hair, like confetti. But I can't think of a less likely bride! Well it's possible she was up to that kind of trick at Michael Dalzell's house and Jane wasn't there at all. It all depends on what you believe.'

'It certainly does,' I said. I knew I sounded cold, but I was beginning to feel that Stephen wouldn't be the ideal witness, as I had hoped.

'So what did Meg say?' I went on.

'It was terrible. I realized that she had spun a web round Jane from which she would never be able to extricate herself. There was nothing, no method of persuasion she hadn't used. She'd persuaded Jane, I think, that if she killed her father and her half-sister, the Dalzell money would go to her, as the natural child – and if there was any trouble she, Meg, would see to it that there'd be a big court case, and all the women out in force. (All this I worked out afterwards, wondering about Meg's motives, but once I saw it was the money that was wanted for the group, it was simple.) I don't know how she convinced Jane she wouldn't be found out but, after all, none of them ever were. It was only since the second killing that I began to realize all this and then they'd all disappeared. It was an extraordinary gamble, for Jane coming forward and claiming the fortune would certainly have made her a suspect. But there was no proper evidence against her for either crime. The butler in Hampstead saw either two women, or one woman, and was so upset by the disguise, or change, or whatever it was, that he refused to swear to anything. In the case of the second killing, the girl was found in a street bleeding to death from a neck wound, at the time where there were plenty of witnesses who saw Jane at a party. They would have pulled it off if the vital ingredient hadn't vanished into thin air.

'Meg's method was to trap her victim in a dialectic of madness. I'd never dreamed fanaticism could be carried to such lengths, and sound so purely and coolly lucid and convincing – once you'd been brainwashed, that is. I asked her if Mr Dalzell was in fact Jane's father because I worried about her, and about possible repercussions. "I don't believe for an instant that Jane knows or cares," Meg said. "This is a paternalistic society. Mr Dalzell was a symbol of the father of all women." "A symbol?" I said. "How can you see him as that? He's now a body in a morgue. Doesn't that make any difference to you?" "His assassination was symbolic," Meg replied. "It was a ritual killing. The left hand performs the act figuratively, the right hand performs it literally. There is no difference between the two. He was the incarnation of capitalism. We have incarnated our disapproval of him."

'I just didn't know what to say to all this. It's the modern evil, I believe, this jumble of Marxism and Tantrism and anything else thrown in, which is used to persuade people to kill each other. Meg went on to tell me that women had been defiled and degraded always, and particularly since the seventeenth century when they had been execrated as witches or elevated to virtuous wives. She said something about "taking one of each" and I should have realized Dalzell's daughter was in danger but I didn't, for once again Meg confused me, and I thought she was still talking about the "two-women-in-one" which she claimed was the root of the wrongs of society – the suppression of masculinity in women and of femininity in men. Had I thought then, too, that it was the money they wanted, I'd have been quicker.'

'So Meg told you nothing definite.' I was determined to get some facts, if I possibly could, but it was becoming clear to me that there was something quite unusual in the case. I knew I would have to hear more of this woman's crazy theories – the future, I fear, is on the way to becoming more and more like this, an endless display of a phenomenon I read somewhere described as 'evaginative pyrotechnics'. However, if only Stephen could remember Meg admitting to – or perhaps boasting – of the murders we could inform the police and mount a full scale search.

'No, no, she didn't say anything definite,' Stephen said. 'She said the power of the word would return through women, that it was when belief in the prophecies of witches and sybils ended that the word began to die.'

'Oh yes,' I said. I glanced quickly at Stephen. He sounded quite unmoved by Meg's wild ideas – I suppose he had heard them many times before. I flipped open the file and turned to the photographs of the body of the daughter of Michael Dalzell. They were a horrible sight. She was lying partly under a sheet but you could see her neck was badly torn. Her eyes, unlike her father's, were closed. She had what looked like a small tiara in her fair hair. 'So you saw Jane before this – you've seen these, I presume? – happened?' I handed the police photographs over the desk. Stephen flinched and looked away from them. It crossed my mind that he had persuaded himself by now, to such a degree, of some kind of magical agency at work that he had forgotten the brute facts.

'Oh yes.' Stephen put a hand over his eyes, then removed it again quickly. 'I saw her that night. She wasn't well, but she wanted to go to the party. We'd been going to some strange parties then, I remember, mostly through Jane's boyfriend who was in the film world. We went to a party given by some rich people called Berring . . . and then, a few nights later . . . on the night . . .'

'And you honestly think she was responsible for the death of Michael Dalzell's daughter?'

'I don't know if that's who she thought it was, by then,' Stephen said. He looked suddenly sad and tired. 'Or if you could call her responsible. She seemed to be living in a perpetual state of sanctioned irresponsibility – the state induced by Meg, of course. And she couldn't have done it anyway, could she? She was seen at the party at the time the girl was killed.'

'Unless it wasn't really her who was seen,' I heard myself saying. I stopped short, and avoided meeting Stephen's eyes. 'No . . . well,' I corrected myself. 'It was one of the gang perhaps – the point being that Jane lured her from the party to her death?'

'I just don't know.' Stephen glanced in the direction of the document, which was lying on my desk, and said: 'If I'd read that then, I would have done everything in my power to find her after that evening. Not that I would necessarily have succeeded. She was secretive about her movements. She never talked about her childhood. I wouldn't have known where to look.'

'No.' I stared down at the identikit pictures, all ridiculously dissimilar to each other, of the girl seen by passers-by in Hampstead, and the girl seen in the street where Dalzell's daughter was found. There were photographs of Jane in existence, of course, but it was hard to gauge anything about her from them. Her hair was blonde, but it looked as if it was probably tinted. Her face was curiously blank.

'What was Jane really like?' I said.

Stephen looked up at me, surprised. 'I couldn't describe her. At her best she was confident, but too often she was very uneasy with herself. I was fond of her. Being with her made me feel interested in things. Yet she often said she wished she was someone else.'

'Did she? This is a difficult era for women, I suppose.'

31

'Oh yes. She was always searching for some "missing male principle" or something.'

'Poor Jane!'

For a time Stephen and I sat in silence, thinking of the sad and messy lives of Jane and women like her. Then Stephen said: 'I think Meg's cleverness was in realizing she couldn't gain her ends by crude political argument. Jane had been away from her world too long.'

Again I hoped to steer the conversation away from this unprofitable area. I said:

'Would Jane inherit the Dalzell fortune if she were alive and came forward to claim it?'

'That I don't know.' Stephen rose. I saw that his patience had come to an end. 'Don't they wait seven years before you're declared officially dead? Then it'll go to a cousin, I suppose.'

I had the feeling Stephen was a little annoyed that I hadn't taken his descriptions of Meg more seriously. He made his way to the door, and I made a point of showing him out of the house and thanking him warmly. I promised I would read Jane's journal and would let him know my impressions. On the doorstep he paused. 'Meg was a kind of embezzlement,' he said. I was surprised at his use of the word, and couldn't repress a smile. 'An enravishment,' he went on. 'You must bear that in mind.'

Then he went down the street. Because he was plump he had rather a waddling walk. I glanced at the address on the piece of paper he had handed me, and wondered if I would ever see him again. Then he turned the corner and was gone. Somehow I knew he hadn't told me where he really lived. And when I looked for him it turned out I was right. The address I'd been given, at the end of a wide street in Battersea, was that of an abandoned and boarded-up church.

I now present the strange 'journal' of the girl Jane. The poem printed overleaf was found among the pages of the journal, and I presume must have been copied out by her: what it signified to her I don't know. I will make no comment on the pages which follow, except to say there can seldom have been so forceful an example of the effect a fanatical mind can have on an impression-able one.

Edinburgh, July 1986

THE JOURNAL OF JANE WILD

INSOMNIA
by Marina Tsvetayeva

In my enormous city it is   night
as from my sleeping house I go   out
and people think perhaps I'm a daughter or wife
but in my mind is one thought only   night.

The July wind now sweeps a way for   me,
From somewhere, some window, music though   faint.
The wind can blow until the dawn   today,
in through the fine walls of the breast rib-cage.

Black poplars, windows, filled with   light.
Music from high buildings, in my hand a flower.
Look at my steps   following   nobody
Look at my shadow, nothing's here of me.

The lights   are like threads of golden beads
in my mouth is the taste of the night   leaf.
Liberate me from the bonds of   day,
my friends, understand: I'm nothing but your dream.

I'LL HAVE TO tell you now of the night I first went on my travels . . . the night, most of all, that Meg gave me further signs of her power.

I left the Berrings' party and walked home through the streets where it looked as if it had never rained, I walked fast in front of the dust gardens and the brick walls to keep people in, I sent cats up trees to perch heavy as fruit in the foggy grey leaves. As I walked on I could feel myself falling apart. I was in a frenzy of impatience to become another person. My rump was soft and divided under my clinging silk dress as men photographers would have it divide: ripe, ready for a mouthful to be taken out. My legs were thin and perched in high-heeled sandals, the pale tights making them all the more ridiculous and vulnerable. My breasts, unshielded, nosed the air for potential attacks like glow-worms swimming always a few inches in front of me. And yet – somehow – I got home! The streets had been very silent; tonight the menace hadn't come out in a humped back in grey gaberdine, or a gaggle of youths flying low like crows; it had lurked there, the urban forest, waiting for something impossible to come about.

I let myself into the house-converted-into-flats where I live and think every year will be the last. Look at the lino! That purple and cream scum whirling and foul smelling on the floor, dead blood and feathers. And the walls! Who made this elephantine pattern of chandeliers on a mango background, what grandeur did they think they were instilling there? As always, it is chilly in the hall and on the stairs. The overhead light, resplendent though it is, goes out after a minute with a popping sound from an odious black plastic button by my door. I am never at my door on time. I have to fondle this excrescence, caress it into being, so it will click on again and let me in through total darkness to my flat.

There are all the signs in the flat of Tony and I having gone out to the party in a bad mood. Once up the three stairs carpeted in hard cord, lights on and standing on the landing, I can smell us there together: from the sitting room, where we drank cold Stolichneya vodka before we left and Tony complained at me spending too much of my money on it; in the bedroom, which is just on my left, I can see the dresses and skirts I tried on and then threw on the bed in despair. The whole place feels both over-occupied and totally empty. Perhaps I never will return.

I can imagine how Tony is doing at the party. He has a small affected smile on his face and he is pretending he isn't working his way ever nearer to the daughter of an American film producer who might make his life a little more exciting for him. Although he's a screenwriter, the editor of a literary quarterly has just asked him to write on the new Spanish cinema. Tony is secretly more pleased by this than by an offer to write a Hollywood blockbuster. He can't forget Cambridge, and the poets and writers in old tweed jackets who give a short surprised laugh when they bump into Tony now. Or perhaps he has been trapped by Fay Langham. She is telling him about feminist cinema. His eyes are wandering, his tongue suddenly becomes dry. 'Let me get you a drink, Fay.' I laugh as I go into the bedroom and then into the tiny bathroom beyond.

There was no time to lose. The familiarity of the flat had deflected me for a moment, and had reconciled me to my skin – I sat in both uneasily for so many years that it was hard to imagine I could change. But now it was happening. I sat down on the bed because the floor seemed to be moving under me. Over the pile of discarded clothes, the scarlet flowers on black background, black roses on white nylon crêpe de chine, layered skirts and flimsy tops, I reached for the scissors that lay on the table beside my bed. I picked them up and my hand brushed the soft dresses: I thought of Meg – Meg whom I had seen again tonight, her dress of gypsy handkerchiefs and the eyes that had made me turn on my heel and leave the party as if I had immediately read her command. I hadn't expected her to follow me. But I knew that she knew tonight was my first real chance to escape.

With the scissors I started to hack at my hair. Long pieces of blonde hair, high-lighted every three months and slightly curled for the party, fell onto the rumpled clothes. I almost immediately felt calmer and more peaceful. I wandered to the bathroom, and watched my face look out as naked and surprised as a sheep at shearing. Aren't you trying to cut it properly? my eyes seemed to be saying back to me from the mirror. This is a terrible thing to do. *Think* how long it'll take to grow out again!

I shrugged at the reflection and strolled this time to the bedroom window, still hacking away with the scissors, which seemed to have taken on a determination of their own despite the protests of the owner of the hair. I pulled back the curtains, leaned on the window sill and looked out. I had often imagined myself flying on my broomstick from here – as my mother flew on that icy night after the brawl – but she fell, even the strength of her beliefs couldn't keep her in the air, and when they took her from the bank of snow to the lorry she knew the battle was lost. I would fly so as not to be with Tony any more, so as not to be me. Yet Tony could go if we decided it wasn't working out. We didn't have to marry. I didn't even have the risk of pregnancy: an I.U.D. like a computer gadget lay inside me, with a thin cord for removal if I decided to 'start a family'. How many times had I dreamed of launching myself from that window sill, floating into the black night until I banged up against the stars! And now I was going, but by a different route, and into quite another Universe.

The scissors had reached my fringe and decimated it, little spikes of straw stood on my head and it was quite rough when I ran my hands through it, like stroking a pig's back. For the first time since childhood I could see by looking straight ahead, instead of shaking my fringe to one side, a gesture which, over the years, had become apologetic and feminine, as if I had to admit it wasn't my right to contemplate the world. I laid the scissors on the sill and looked down into the street – for the last time, I thought. A sort of rage came over me, and the night air, with an abrupt coldness, gave me the sensation my body had shrunk.

Down on the right, near the junction with the High Street, is the house run by the kind woman with big brown eyes, the house for the battered women of the neighbourhood and their children; but the most successful lesbian nightclub in London, Paradise Island, is next door to them, and the men who pass smile and shift uncomfortably at the mixture of misfits: the women who had the foolishness not to stop themselves from being beaten up, the great lakes of blue bruise on their faces and arms in unaccept-able disfigurement, and the women who want each other, whose breasts meet like soft pillows as they dance. In the mornings the bottles come out on the pavement in front of Paradise Island. They look desolate: empty tonic, empty bitter lemon, hundreds of empty litre bottles of wine. Somewhere, scattered in their different flats, the women are sleeping it off. But when it's hot in the street, and the old man further down away from the High Street puts his parrot out on the door-step, and the parrot calls out with a sound so alien that you feel there is no chance, ever, of one human being understanding another, and the smart young Persians opposite turn up their record players in their sunflower-papered rooms, then it's time to wonder what happened, to shut the window before you fall, and make, as far as possible, a construction of a day.

Now I did close the window, for some of my fear was still with me. I went back to the bathroom and re-examined my appearance. Women and mirrors; mirrors and women. My face seemed to have grown much smaller and my eyes were round and rimmed with exhaustion, black as the underside of a moth. My hair stood in tufts all over my head. I would have smiled but my mouth, which looked thinner, was clamped together. I wondered if my teeth were different underneath.

I could see the foot of the bed in the mirror. My heart missed a beat: a pair of legs in blue jeans was lying there! Then I saw that it was blue jeans alone. And a straight jacket, also made of denim. I went towards them. I looked down at my body before I pulled off the silk party dress. My breasts were tiny now, and the bra that had once contained them looked large and empty. Like a shroud, I thought, as I stood there paralysed a moment, unable to move. Although it was ordinary modern gear that lay there on the bed, to pull on these trousers from an unknown world was like stepping into death.

The first thing that happened as I changed my clothes was a complete reconstruction of the party I had just been to with Tony – it flashed before my eyes, colours muted, but with cast complete. First I saw the people I liked there: Gala, Stephen. Then I saw Tony, being patronizing with a literary agent, frowning down into his glass as if an important truth was to be found at the bottom, like those mugs with a frog. I saw the hostess, rich, American: her walls hung with brown silk, shit silk money. Her hair was rich brown curls; her head was tilted back; she liked mixing people. There was a man who ran a famous gambling club talking to an ex-socialist historian. A Chinese-American hooker who said she had just come from Brando. Then I saw Meg. Meg's eyes were fixed on me. I felt the floor moving under my feet and the hostess's splendid pink candelabra went dim.

By this time I was ready. I was narrow-hipped, not too tall. There was a gun in the pocket of the denim jacket. I went out of the flat, shoved the black plastic button and was over the petrified lino steps three at a time.

I am out in the street, I think I can see Tony coming towards me, a little drunk from the party, weaving slightly as he walks. Yes – we passed – three feet apart. He didn't even give me a glance.

WHERE WAS I going? My new body seemed to know. I was walking fast, but smooth and controlled, and I was heading for the High Street. The street where I lived looked already like a ruin excavated a hundred years ago: as if the houses had been built with their deformities, crazed pipes, broken roofings, ghastly follies in the worst of Victorian taste. The light from the slit-eyed lamps was lunar. Women stared at me as they went into Paradise Island. They hesitated at the sight of me: I was unplaceable perhaps, a new genetic pattern like a neon sign in cuneiform, something ancient and known and at the same time infinitely strange. I didn't smile at them, so they remained unsmiling back. Their lips were hard, the colour of prunes.

And I passed the house of the battered women. There was one light on at the top of the house. It was a bedside lamp, with a pale blue frilly shade. This pale blue light showed up two heads, and two bodies in black jumpers and skirts. The room behind them was dark as a cave. They sat immobile there, in this distant, parodic memory of the primeval beach – the blue light thin as water around their scarcely breathing forms, the cave an illusion, four walls in reality, property of the Council, dark, stretching back to the days of their birth and the first astonished burst into the sunshine of the untouched beach, four walls of crumbling lath and plaster, a temporary refuge, a mock womb before it was time to move on again. One of the women was knitting. She looked down on me with less concern than the women who had gone into Paradise Island. Her options were closed. She had copulated with the wrong man. She had been sterilized now, as a punishment for her mistakes, and she sat quietly, drawn to the

42

artificial light below, its stern lack of mystery resembling hers. Her eyes were empty and black, like a moonless sky. And, to reassure myself, I looked up beyond her at the moon. It was there tonight, whether people would have it or not: wisps of black cloud danced over its face. Whether man had climbed on it or not, it still smiled sardonically. And I smiled – thinking of the facial twitch, the smirk, which would send them off into unending space, like swatted flies.

I was at the end of the street, by the corner supermarket, the compound for the women who are neither battered nor dyke. The channels are narrow, and iron gates, like automated warders, bang against the knees. The women smile at the cheerful goods. Who knows but one day, unwrapping the bright tartan package, mile on mile of paper, some crinkled as corrugated iron, some transparent and horribly soft, membrane, caul, out will fall the wax doll with the pin in its heart, the scapegoat for all this. Then it will have been worth it! Until then, the Pandora's boxes hold vertigo and fear, and fear of closed spaces and fear of open spaces and a drowsiness while operating machinery. In the dark corners of the boxes, the still unwrapped portions, under the Free Gift Offer, lies the forgotten past. The women pull and tear at the little white worms of paper that make the wadding. Then the box lies open and shallow. It has revealed nothing at all.

Tonight there are only representations of these women in the supermarket, for the supermarket is closed. Cardboard women, shown to be beautiful for their sojourn there, and in their cardboard surrounds, at least, bathed in colour. Some of them hold boxes of objects to eat, others boxes of objects which will absorb their blood, some hold a pink drink. I bow to them as I pass. Hi! I feel sympathy for them: they can reign at night, when their alter egos aren't bustling and shopping in the compound, but unlike me they are locked in with the darkened goods. They can contemplate the shelves. They love the boxes, they gaze at them in total self-absorption.

The High Street is wider than I remembered. There is no traffic. The islands look as if they would sink if boarded; glacial mannequins wave from distant shops; in all this, which is like a muted cruise, a secret departure at night for Purgatory, I am walking several feet above the ground and with my hand firmly on the pistol in the pocket of my coat. This time others are at risk, not me. I am looking for someone to kill. And as I pass the fluorescent reds and yellows, the prayers and exhortations to eat and sleep and breathe for the sake of the manufacturers alone, I exult in my new power. I might fire a bullet at the perplexed, wrinkled brow of Burt Lancaster as he struggles on the poster level with my head. I might blacken the teeth of the housewife suspended in the vapours of her pie, her smile moistened in the wreaths of animal fat coming up at her like winter breath. Or I might shoot at the steeple of the church, which is encircled by motorway now: if the elastic were pulled any tighter it would snap and fall. But I'll save my fire. I may need it later on.

There is a strong smell of the sea at the end of the street. Dead, flat sea trapped in walls, sea heavy with driftwood and speckled with the white bellies of dead fish, a scum of sawdust by the gangways to the ships. I can see the masts standing in the port. The smell quickens my step. I am bringing the smell with me. The moon rests at a cockeyed angle to the highest mast, string slipping, clouds bob over like streamers and are gone into the night. I arrive at the port. So this is where I will disembark for another world! On one of these great liners, filled with orange light and soundless activity. Dancing on the deck, sailing into warm, opaque waters so deep they seem to balance the sky above them like a plate. Going up in a cloud of spray to pierce the ether. But first, I must find my prey.

The first thing I see is that I am in the centre of the port. Its wide arms embrace the ships, the strips of pavement and the shadowy cafés with lights and onion-braids of sponges hanging by the doors and blue round sailors' hats thrown down. There is no movement in the water at all. Not even the smallest boat nudges the jetty. I can see people walking about inside the big liners – it looks as if they're making ready to cast off any minute – and more people in the cafés. But not a sound. Are they all dead already? Have I come too late? I pull the gun from my pocket and make my way along the right hand tentacle of the harbour. I will go into the first bar. I will accomplish my mission, as they say in Men Talk on TV. And then I will be free to go.

The bar is stained with green light when I go in. Bars of green on the sailors' faces, like shutters hiding their eyes and distorting the curve of their jaws. Pools of green on the surface of the bar where there are half-drained glasses and plates of crumbling, soft nuts. I cock the gun and point it at the room. Green smoke comes down steadily from the roof, as if expelled from the mouth of an amateur theatrical dragon. It blows into my eyes. I fire the gun at the first sailor in my range, who is sitting with his chin cupped in his hands at the nearest table. He slumps to the ground. But the shot was noiseless, and so was his death. It's not what I had hoped.

Now the sailor is dead all the others crowd round and beg me not to kill them. They clasp at my waist, and we dance without sound. When I drink, the green liquid scorches my throat, and when I see myself in the glass, through the verdigris and the smudged filth from the sailors' hands, I see why they want me so. In my perfect androgyny, my face round as a mermaid's, my mouth black and slit like a wound from a knife, my legs like a young stevedore's – with the rime of green under my fingernails that tells how long I have been under the sea, hair growing upward, sucked by the bubbles, waving like weed in the cold green current – like a treasure long lost at sea, embedded in nacreous green rock, shifted here and there on the sandy floor by shoals of spotted fish, I am for them the dread of their seafaring days: the siren with a cracked voice who lures them to the bottom of the sea, the forgotten woman and half-man who make up the Angel of Death. In the deep, sub-aqueous silence we dance on,

for I know now they will never let me go. In sea years, they are
a long time dead.

In the port, the biggest liner pulls out. No sound, just the
orange lights in the cabins – and I can see a Latin American band,
all orange satin frills and soundless maracas on the forward deck.
A steward ushers guests aft, to wave us all goodbye. Champagne
corks are forced from bottles, silently they fly up to the sky.
Everyone waves. I am whirled faster and faster round.

My hand lay curled on the floor by the bed. Blood had gone
down into the fingers, and they were bunchy and red: they felt
as if they had been trussed by the butcher and then cut apart
again. The palm looked up at the ceiling, mottled, the lines of
destiny like faint pencil marks on the flesh. On one line, which
marched across the hand and disappeared over the other side in
a delta of fainter etchings, a strong, adventurous exploration of
the upper side, the side it never could see without taking the
inexorable step, I had walked for a while last night. But I had,
literally, missed the boat. I was to be kept here a while yet, on
the inner track.

Tony's back faced me on my left. I pulled up my hand from
the floor, and before the blood crept down my fingers I felt it for
a moment make an independent movement, in the direction of
the door, as if the invisible body to which it was attached had
decided to go out. No such luck for me! I was still only half in
myself and I must lie still until things were right again or I might
vanish altogether. I must contemplate Tony's back. Shoulder
blades, freckles. Matrons, soap, thin shoulder blades in sports
blazers, white aertex shirts open-pored over freckles, like tiny
molluscs living on the skin that must be allowed to breathe.
Thick white clouds over too many dark rhododendrons. Tony's
beautiful feet in white plimsolls, which hardly seem to anchor
him to the ground as he runs over the grass. I think of Tony like
that because that's where he's stuck: twenty years later still the
prep school boy: charming, eager to get on but tentative; would

the effort of becoming a man break him up and turn him to dust? No, he need never change.

Bells were ringing in the church at the end of the street. I had forgotten it was Sunday – a day to pray for good, to pray for strength to fight the evil world into which I would soon be abducted. But a pleasant laziness came over me at the thought. Who said that where I was going was evil? Why make out that the present world had anything good to say for itself? In this godless street only the old man with the parrot went to church, leaving the parrot haughty and outraged in the window of his front room. And some of the old women, shoe-horned from attic rooms at the sound of the bells, their heads grey as winter cabbages, flesh in bulges all down their bodies under their coats. Did they pray to go into the next world just as they were now? Or did they think it would be something quite extraordinary, a real shock, but well worth getting down on stiff knees square with pain to ask for, one eye on the vicar's pointed black shoe under his skirt.

Tony moved, and the shoulder blades went down under him as he turned on his back. No matter: I was myself again now, I could deal with his sleeping profile. Ageless in sleep, I saw that he belonged to another century, a time when the important thing for a man was to go away and then to return again, a long crusade, a dusty journey home in a column of armoured men glinting like fish scales under the foreign sun. Once home, he could enjoy his tomb, and the placid skies of Southern England beyond the crypt. But now, poor Tony, with his script conferences in Rome and Zurich and the rubber corridors of the airport: he was always setting off and returning, to no avail.

Tony's eyes opened. It was a melancholy sight, for as the lids lifted I felt his uncertainty, and his depression with the world, and his puzzlement at the wall opposite, as if he had never been here in his life before. Then I felt annoyed. I had been a long way, further than him. I even despised his dreams. Yet his foolish frown at the wall, with its Victorian oil of a pig he had bought in the market a year ago and a Paris May '68 poster I had once put up (it was a dark bilious yellow, de Gaulle's powersaw nose had been ripped at the edge), suggested he had no real desire to be here at all. It was as if he had come for a one night stand and stayed two years, after a drugged potion, an uneasy sleep.

'Do you want coffee?'

I always address Tony as a guest, although we share the bills of the flat. In fact, he has made almost no impression on the flat, which is as hard and gloomy – in the ridiculous red brick building with the artificially grand hall, the syringa bush outside and the irritating unmown grass by the gate where cuckoo spit collects in summer and brushes my bare legs, and then is gone again – as before he arrived here. What difference *could* he have made? Sometimes I think, although Tony may imagine he's returning from these journeys to me, it's really his mother he yearns for. Ah, Mrs Marten! When will her next visitation be? Her thin legs, her jerking arms. The flat is mine in name only, she is the white magnet that draws him and me and the rooms we live in, she controls us and burns us dry. He leaps like a mouse to the sound of her voice. Yet, as if it's too unbearable to marry a son and mother in this way, I often think instead of his past life, in another flat, with another girlfriend. I imagine him transformed, radiant: the girl is pliable and dark. What do these words mean? That I want him to have been capable once, at least, of being the other side of himself? And is my vision of the girl just another escape from my own skin into the opposite? I suppose so. Tony and I – as we are – are not very convincing.

He noticed my hair. He asked me what the hell I'd done that for.

'I don't know. I just did it. Last night.'

'Obviously. It wasn't like that at the Berrings.'

'Why? Does it look so awful?'

'Of course it does.'

'But men cut their hair off like that. Why shouldn't I?'

'Suit yourself.'

48

I went into the bathroom. What was the point of going on like this? Certainly my face looked odd, but it was what I felt like at the moment rather than a picture to please someone else. I was in a transitional stage. The strawy spikes standing on my head announced my state of siege. I brushed my teeth and looked around for the jeans and denim jacket on the floor. There was no sign of them. My heart sank.

'I'm making scrambled eggs,' Tony said from the bedroom.

I heard him walk past on his way to the kitchen and I stared at myself intensely in the mirror. Sometimes his movements in the flat were like the stealings-up of an enemy spy, sometimes an outright military takeover. I could never tell where he would be next. I dreaded meeting him in the passage, as if our passing there only underlined our meaningless lives in which we were anyway going in the opposite direction to each other.

'Do you want scrambled eggs or not?'

'Have you by any chance seen a pair of jeans anywhere?'

I had given myself away. If they weren't there I didn't know what I could do. I thought of the outside of the building where I lived, the pretentious façade that made it, the only block of flats in the street, the kind of building where people scrawl insults in chalk on the lower walls. I saw myself going out, in jeans and jacket, walking on air, and coming back in the clinging silk dress. What had happened? Why had the other world rejected me like this?

'Yes. I put them in the washbox. I'm making the eggs now.'

This brought me out of the bathroom. I had a bath towel round me, which emphasized my fatness and my sloping shoulders. I went along the passage to the kitchen, already a victim for Tony, unable to wait for what he had to say.

'Why . . . why did you put them in the washbox?'

'They're not yours, are they? They looked far too small. I thought you must have got into some tangle with someone.' He looked at me oddly. 'What the hell's going on, Jane? With your hair and everything?'

'But why were they dirty. They didn't have . . . blood on them, or anything?'

Tony forked the eggs onto plates. He set his marble profile above them and began to eat.

'No, they weren't dirty. They had a strange smell. Like burnt matches, rather.'

I went back to my bedroom smiling. So the other world smelled of sulphur, did it? I would have to consult Meg on this. And I put on my 'normal' clothes with a light heart: a cotton skirt that had gone at the waist so that the zip had to be dragged up to the waistband and stuck there, a green T shirt and floppy white sandals. I wouldn't be needing them much longer, if my other outfit was really lying in the washbox; and they felt already like a dead woman's clothes, neither in nor out of fashion, slightly embarrassing and poignant. I pulled back my shoulders and walked at a quick march to the kitchen and the scrambled eggs. One of Tony's virtues, which went with his low expectations of life, was his lack of curiosity: he would almost certainly fail to ask me what I really *had* been up to the night before. He didn't like surprise, which he treated as if it were sudden pain, backing away from something unforeseen, however pleasurable, with a hurt, blinking stare. If – which he must have suspected – I had picked up a youth, played with lighted matches, fallen with him in waste ground somewhere beyond the refinement of our street and shopping precinct, Tony didn't want to know about it. And, sure enough, we had our coffee and eggs in silence while the brimstone-tainted jeans lay, carefully covered with the lid, in the straw box in the corner.

'There's a press showing today,' I said at last. We either talked about the films I went to and wrote about, or the progress of Tony's script. Tony, with his gloomy standing invitation to bad luck, was involved in a script of Conrad's *Chance*, and had already announced that there was a jinx on Conrad in the film business, things never worked out as they should. Secretly I didn't blame

Conrad for cursing people like Tony. Why couldn't they leave his work alone?

'It's a West German film,' I said to Tony's half-questioning look. 'About two men who wander the roads on a lorry.'

'*Easy Rider*, German style,' Tony said. 'Why're they showing it on a Sunday?'

'The Schroeders always do. Don't you remember, you came to one.'

'No lunch then?'

No lunch.

I got up, feeling vaguely guilty as always. Sunday lunch was supposed to be a cementing thing for couples: you could see the woman fingering bleeding meat on the Friday, frowning over the joints as if the secret of their future happiness lay in the grain of the flesh. Yorkshire pudding solidified relationships too, producing a drowsiness after the meal, a soft acceptance of everything. I would be sitting watching the screen instead of preparing all this. And Tony would be hard and distant as a result. All for a portion of an animal. But offerings were important. Without the smell of roasting meat from the beaches below, the gods might have turned away from the world.

'I'll do the meat,' Tony said. 'I'm only juggling around with the script this morning. Did I tell you, it looks as if Susannah York might be Flora de Barral.'

'It's not true!'

'You think she'd be right for the part?'

I tried to give an encouraging smile, and failed. What on earth did it matter? I certainly wouldn't be going to a press showing of *that* one. And at the moment, because I knew I would be leaving soon, travelling to places where, in a million years of searching, Tony would never find me, I felt a great warmth towards him, an affection filled with regret that I would be losing him too. I went over to where he was sitting and put my arms round his head. I brought my chin down on the top of his head. There was no parting in the thick brown hair, which smelled of toast. How would he manage without me? Perfectly well, was the answer as I straightened up again. He would hardly notice I had gone!

'It's just that I don't want lunch today,' I said. 'I'm thinking of going to see Gala after the film.'

'Oh.'

'You don't mind, do you?'

'Of course not!'

'Very well then.'

After this exchange, in which I apparently conveyed total heartlessness and from which Tony emerged downcast, I went with too buoyant a step to the door of the flat. He was watching me as I left, but there was no way to present my physical departure acceptably. If I walked like a woman cowed by thousands of years behind the veil, eyes down, erect, shuffling gait, there was no reason for me to be allowed out at all and I would be unable to get as far as the main door of the building. If I went 'ordinarily', as Tony would go, simply walking out of the flat with a quick wave, it would be selfish, uncaring. If I were coming back for the meat, of course, I could make a quick apologetic dash of my departure for my job. But I wasn't. So I went with an energy that was clearly provocative. Tony's sulky glowering face came out with me into the darkness of the stairs and hung in front of me like the after-image of a violently bright light as I groped my way towards the black plastic button. I heard his silence affect the whole building, and it hung over me like a hood until I was halfway down the street.

There is a wind blowing today, the air in the street is milky white, and scraps of white paper float along at first floor level. The street is as different today from the black stillness of the night before as I, in my cotton skirt and plodding step, am changed from the creature who flew down it. Since then, the full bottles that went in to Paradise Island have been emptied and are set out on the pavement for collection. The supermarket, still closed because it's

Sunday, reflects in its plate glass windows the ghostly figures of the women who will go in and become enclosed there tomorrow. A noise comes from the wives' shelter: children, pent up, and suffering from the misery of their mothers, pelted, like the street, with mysterious scraps of words, nervous in the hot wind which also blows white dust into the open windows and flaking paint of the surrounds. I walk up to Notting Hill Gate, where the press showing of the film is being held. The flowers in the sloping gardens are smothered with the fine white dust. One householder, rich and proud, has a sculpture six feet wide and twice as tall in his front garden – it looks like the head of a white tulip, two of the heavy stone petals peeled back to reveal the empty centre. In a poorer street, where the railings of the houses seem to press against them, allowing only a mantrap-size descent into the basement, someone has propped a flying figure in white papier mâché at the top of the steps: one leg and one arm are flung out into the street, the eyeless face, like the face of a victim of an accident, swathed in white plaster bandages, gazes at the houses across the strip of grey concrete. I feel a sudden fear, as I walk past, that this is someone like me, someone who tried to escape, punished by the world, frozen into a ludicrous figure, not even made of hard substance but ready to melt into shreds of pulp at the first burst of rain. Or is it all that is left of the Snow Queen, this white, artificial, sexless thing, after her splinters of ice had gone out into the world and she had fallen from her cold throne? The rich smell of Sunday dinners cooking, the red meat spitting in this white bottomless world gives me nausea. I have to cling onto a railing, at the end of the street of the arrested, flying figure, before I go on up the hill.

I know or recognize most of the film critics standing outside the cinema. They have tired, blank eyes from seeing too much of other people's fantasies, and are annoyed too at having their Sunday morning taken away from them. One or two nod to me. 'Yes, but did you see that other Fassbinder?' 'He comes in at the end of this – the Wenders, you know.' 'I know. But I mean, did you see that very early one?' They seem to be mouthing the words, the door of the cinema is shut, and they are agitated and anxious, longing for the film to be over and for Sunday lunch. What is the film going to show us? Life in contemporary society, it says on the hand-out. The apathetic, passive, alienated life, an odyssey without any point of return. I would rather watch a pearl grow in an oyster! I stand amongst the velvet trousers in the small crowd, and wonder if Meg will really send me away from all this. She once said, cryptically, that she would show me everything, all that was inside me, and all the different regions that can be reached without taking a step. I believed her. I stand thinking of tomorrow, when we will meet. Already, last night's journey seems far away, like a flash from a distant meteor. 'Jane!' One of the critics, a short man with a frown, comes towards me in the white air. 'Tell me, what did you think of the Skolimowski? They showed it again the other night. And I wondered if you'd seen it when it first came out . . .'

'The best foreign film to be made in England.' I hear myself offering this stupid remark, but I remember the film well. It is violent, obsessive, surprising: as if a whole layer of England had been peeled off, the whiteness scrubbed away, and the underside, people's real passions and feelings, pushed up into the light. The critic nods as if I had said something interesting, and we begin to file into the cinema.

It is as we pass into the first dusk of the foyer that I see the girl. I stand for a moment, clutching my press card, waiting for her to turn and see me. So Meg answers me when I think of her! She has sent me this girl. And yet . . .

The girl turns. What is it that is so familiar about her? She has something of mine. We have been bound in an ancient story, of bitterness and revenge. Yet I feel I have never seen her before in my life. I can see that she recognizes me too, for her eyes flicker and the message from her skin is one of familiarity. A small triumphant smile compresses the corners of her mouth. What did she do to me? Or was I the victor and is she, at peace now while

I suffer, regarding me with pity and contempt? I move slightly in her direction, with a stumbling movement as if my knees have forgotten how to function while I walk. She stiffens at this, and glides into the cinema, but her stiffness is an invitation. Her head is full of pictures for me. I follow her into the dark red darkness, and sit down behind her, in the second row.

The film begins. In black and white, it says on the screen. But it's not the real blackness, nor the real whiteness: it's grey. A grey motorway stretches out on the screen above our heads. As it soars upwards, making us, the audience, like tiny creatures at the side of the road, my eyelids bisect it and come down halfway over my eyes – and through my lashes, which are trembling slightly with the effort of staying in that position, the first flickering blobs of colour begin to appear.

My mother was in the kitchen. The kitchen door led straight out onto the hill: there was no yard, just the grass that was always wet, either with rain or heavy dew: it went up in furrows to the line of Douglas firs planted as a windbreak by the grandfather-of the laird; it was humped, long bolsters of grass which seemed to move on the steep hill when the rain swept into the valley from the west. On the grass were small white mushrooms, exhumed every morning from the deep, stony land, and sheep, fleece yellowing with rain and faces oddly patterned as if with their markings they could signal something to each other. Beyond the line of firs and the half-broken stone wall grew the scratchy heather. I went up the cleuch sometimes, to search for cloudberries, those strange fruit which look like a drawing in a medical student's textbook, of internal organs stitched together: their taste is acrid and they grow only above the cloud line, tinges of red on their pink fleshy surface suggesting a faint scorch from the few moments when the clouds part and the sun comes down on them. But my mother used to like to make cloudberry jelly. I took a basket and I would pick blaeberries too, but sometimes the laird and his party were on the hill above our cottage, shooting from the holes in the ground burrowed out for them, or collecting the dusty purple blaeberries, and then I would have to slide back down the hill over bumps of heather and harebells to the grass and the kitchen back door.

What had my mother done? When the laird poked his head round the back – he always tried the front door first, forgetting that cottagers keep their front doors locked and the front rooms like small mausoleums behind them – she would go crimson, as if he had caught her stealing some of his property while he looked on. He had given her the cottage. He often referred to this as I stood at the door between the kitchen and the escape to the hill behind. She always thanked him, but went on looking guilty. Why was she so uneasy, fingering the old black skirt she wore, gazing past me at the hill as if she was longing to run for it and disappear into the white mist that came down the cleuch at midday every day and stayed there until rain and dark cloud brought on night. She had been his mistress, of course: some part of me understood that even when I was very young. I was his daughter. That was why she was allowed to live in the cottage. The way he looked at me was furtive and eager, like the stare of a man searching for evidence of disease on his own body. He never touched me if he could help it. Yet he and my mother often looked vaguely at me and through me at the same time, as parents do when discussing ordinary matters in front of their children. Sometimes I felt I belonged to both of them, and then the cottage and the kitchen seemed to grow – and I did too, suddenly seeing into some bright space where there would be infinite possibilities. Soon, though, my mother would catch herself out in this relaxed attitude, and so would he – and Meg would be seen, walking up from the Burn Wood in her long skirts – and they would return to a combination of embarrassment and resentment, and the gloom, the stone floors, the stone sided sink, the thin wooden table with the gay plastic cloth seemed more oppressive than before. When there was sun, it was all right to go out the back: the light blue sky over the hills looked as if it could be reached in a minute, peewits and larks were everywhere, the gurgle of burn sounded loud as it slipped down out of sight to a hidden loch. But there was so seldom sun. The valley was steep. It looked, on a black day, as if its contours had been drawn with slashing lines on rough paper, and as if the lines contained our sentence, my mother's and mine. For our sins, we should stay here forever. And as it was clear she had practically no money, there seemed no way of getting out at all.

I'd seen the girl several times, the laird's real daughter. I'd been up the narrow mud road that led to our exile's cottage, and stared down at the large white house where she lived with her father and mother. She had a thin, bony, Scottish face, with grey eyes and fair hair, and always a slight smile of self-satisfaction at the corners of her mouth; she bounced an old red rubber ball against the wall of the kitchen garden as I watched her from the moorland above; sometimes her hair was tied in bunches and I knew it went a little frizzy in the rain. I was completely and obsessively jealous of her. I was her shadow, and she mine. By the time we went to the village school together, for we were almost exactly the same age, I think we both knew we were sisters. We fought in the school playground, which was a small stretch of concrete slung high in the hills, on the outskirts of the laird's small village. I went up on the seesaw, which was made from the thick trunk of a felled tree, and she went down; she went up, her eyes excited, grey as the drizzle that fell continually on us, her hooked, bony nose and thin mouth hovering over me, while I was down on the ground. One day she got up and walked away when I was up in the air, and I came crashing down. The teacher looked the other way.

My mother called to me from the kitchen to come in. It was the summer holidays: long, empty, grey days. Today the jeep would come along the mud track, over the top of the hill, and the laird and his party would spread rugs out in front of our cottage, on the sloping grass by the overflowing burn. In the gentle rain, watched by sheep, they would eat pies and hard-boiled eggs and drink beer and wine, leaving the cans and bottles for my mother to collect. Then, flushed, they would go slowly up the hill to their holes. I was never allowed to be there. But if the daughter was with them she would twist on her rug and gaze at the windows of the house. Her mother, fair-haired as her daughter, and self-contained, also with an expression of secret amusement on her face most of the time, never turned to look at the cottage. When she walked back to the jeep with the picnic basket after lunch, it was always head down, eyes on the thin grass by the track, and the sheep droppings, and the ugly colt's foot that grew there, yellow and darkened with rain.

'Can't you see it's raining?'

Of course; it was always raining. My mother was using it as a pretext to get me in from the grass in front of the cottage. She came halfway towards me from the back of the house. Her head was jerking in the direction of the track; she must have heard the jeep. I saw she was crying. My mother's eyes were blue. When she cried they were like the water of the burn, bursting its banks. I went stiff, with anger at the life we led here. I stood my ground.

'You'll be soaked. Anyway, they're coming. Jane! Hurry up!'

My mother scurried up the bank and disappeared round the back of the house. In the past she would have dragged me with her – perhaps a part of her now, exhausted by the repressions of the past years, wanted a showdown of some kind. Indecision as to whether to move or not kept me rooted to the spot. And the jeep reared up on the crest of the hill. The engine was roaring, in first gear, the wheels were coated with mud.

'Jane!' My mother tried calling me one more time, from behind the window of the front room, and her voice sounded distant and resigned. I turned to face the jeep. Rain ran down the windows and the faces of the other mother and daughter were distorted, like the sound of my own mother's voice. Ishbel, for that was the name of my sister, looked as if she had been painted grotesquely onto the window, in thick white paint, and yellow for the streaks of her hair down her face. I made no movement, but watched them park the jeep, and push the doors open, and from the back two Labradors sprang out so there was an instant movement of sheep on the side of the hill.

On the screen in front of me the men are wandering the roads with their lorry. They are passive, looking for meaning, resigned to the fact they will find no more than the half-buried roots of their own childhood. They are lonely, but have blocked off their hunger and loneliness behind expressionless faces and obsession with technology and film. They can't live with women, but they can't live without them, for their wandering seems so absurd, so unlike any real journey of exploration of the past.

The girl in the row in front of me – Ishbel – looks at this sad whining end of the age of the conquistadors in silence. When the audience laughs she remains silent. The music is sad and persistent, not unlike bagpipe music I used to hear coming from inside the white walls of her house when her/our father gave a party. I sit tensely behind her. She had what I wanted. She had what should have belonged to me. What is she doing here now, what of mine has she got her hands on now? She is an omen. And there above our heads, on the grey flat roads of the over-discovered world, the men neither of us want go aimlessly about their lives. What shadow battle will she and I fight next?

I knew what I was going to do. I leapt the burn while the pale stockinged legs of the laird and his party were still coming out of the jeep, and I ran up through wet bracken to the wretched line of trees by the wall at the top of the hill. These firs, straight and black, with wispy branches at the top hardly strong enough to support a wood pigeon, had no doubt been planted to protect the shepherd and his sheep from the terrible winds, the snow drifts that came at the speed of wind, the rain that was like having a bucket emptied in your face. But they were our bars. They surrounded our small prison, our patch of sheep-nibbled grass – in the long Northern evenings, when the sky went dim behind them and I was sitting out on the collection of rough pebbles that made up our front garden I would reach my arms out to them sometimes, prise them apart and squeeze them together again. Wherever you looked, there they were, except for the cleuch, of course, and what was the point of thinking you could escape up that boggy face that led to nowhere? Stumbling to the invisible horizon, clamped under mist, walking on dead legs deeper and deeper into the peat. It was fifteen miles to the next crofter's cottage, and much further to the town.

I would hack my way out, and take my mother with me. I stood thin behind the tallest tree on the hill. My hands clasped the wet bark. It was scaly, unpleasant, like some sea animal which has struggled to shore and grown a thin fuzz of fur. The soft, wet wood dug in under my fingernails. I thought of the school, and Ishbel walking along the road to the school. She always looked confident and happy. My mother never used that road – the few times she left the laird's land to go shopping in the small store beneath the school she walked along the side of the hill on a sheep track. They were treating her like a sheep. I was some animal they would never even look at, although the law insisted I should go to school. I looked down at the jeep, and saw Ishbel climb out, stand exposed on the grass, yet blurred by the constant rain.

Suddenly I felt something watching me. I turned round: the track, planted on either side with a bristle of young firs stretched in a straight line across a wash of grass and heather to the white house, down in the furthermost dip, which was wrapped in cloud. There were eyes on me. Then I saw them. They were no more than three or four yards away. They were set close together, in a hare's face, brown, bright, almond-shaped. There was no intelligence in them. I felt they were my eyes, staring down at Ishbel, concentrated with an evil energy, and yet they were staring at me. I felt as if the hare had sprung onto my chest and was crouching there with heavy feet.

While the eyes were on me I saw myself holding Ishbel under

the water. The brown water of the burn made partings over her face, like waving hair. Her face was very pale. Her eyes had slipped out of her face and there were only white circles, like snail slime. She didn't move, after the first flutterings. A small trout darted from a round hole under the bank. There were wild nasturtiums growing above her head, bright orange and yellow, with their spotted, orchidaceous lips, and they made a crown over her head. The trout lay as if stunned by the giant's face under the water, then it went quick as a blink back under the bank again.

But all I did in effect was throw a stone. The hare went off on a slow bounce as I stooped to reach for a three-cornered stone from the crumbling wall. The hare looked quite domestic from behind, hindquarters low and rather fat. It didn't turn once, to give me the brown stare. I stepped out from behind the tree, raised my arm, and threw the stone as hard as I could at Ishbel.

> Take me to the station
> Put me on the train
> I got no expectations
> To pass through here again

The men are singing in the film. It's a desolate countryside, on the border with East Germany. It looks like most industrialized countries now, as if it's been made for passing through – yet where to? Piranesi's dreams have been realized, in an infinite complex of overpasses and autobahns. One of the men leaves the lorry and squatpees on a mound of industrial waste. Water trained for our uses sits in a square tray, about one hundred feet long, beyond the mound. Soon they will travel on, holding the only unchangeable thing left to them, reels of edited film. It's a country of loss, where there's no point in mourning.

The stone hits Ishbel on the side of the face. Immediately several things happened. My mother ran out of the back of the house, skidded on the wet grass and threw herself at Ishbel, as if trying to shield her from me, too late. Ishbel's mother, who has just extricated herself from the jeep, stood back with a terrified expression, gazing up at the fringes of trees where I was hiding. The men, who were slithering down the bank to the picnic quarters, noticed nothing. It was only when they looked back – where was the rug, where were the women and the food – that they saw Ishbel still on the same spot with her hand held to her face. Her/my father climbed up the bank to comfort her. She pointed at the bracken at the foot of the tree. Yes, she was right! Ishbel knew where I was. Only she would know the exact place. Her mother, who had recovered herself by now, patted her cheek with a handkerchief. Was there blood? The bracken was too thick for me to see. Would they hunt me? I lifted my head a fraction in the hard fronds. Now I saw my mother and her mother together. What had I done? My mother was standing with her head to one side and she was pulling, pulling at her hair as if she was trying to get it out by the roots. Ishbel's mother was staring at her, for the first time she was taking a really good look, she could even afford to have her hands on her hips like a caricature of a fishwife, for my mother's child had thrown a stone at hers. And as she stared, my mother tugged at her hair and stood silent.

In the end, they did nothing. They ate the picnic, and threw the wine bottles and the beer cans down the bank, and packed up the greaseproof paper in the hamper. They went up to their holes in the side of the hill. Ishbel and her mother drove home in the jeep. But by then I had crawled through the bracken all the way along the hill. I was miles from where they were shooting, shivering and frozen, lying by a cairn on the highest, barest mountain above the loch which was fed by our burn. I could hear the shots. It was nearly dark by the time I limped home.

The film is over. I leave the cinema, knowing Ishbel is just behind me. In the foyer I turn quickly, to catch her there, but she is too quick for me, she has gone. I walk out into the real street. The buses are painted silver for the jubilee of the monarchy, the streets are as grey as the film I've just seen. Images from the real world superimpose on the film, and on Ishbel my shadow, who must be following me somewhere – or I am following her?

GALA LIVES IN a messy ground floor flat in North London. There are wooden steps going down off a shaky wooden platform into the garden, the wood is grey with damp and age and the whole construction looks like some kind of underwater gallows, the packed, dense greens of the bushes and grass rising up to meet the feet of the suddenly falling victim. Cats with magpie markings prowl the low brick walls. There is nowhere less private than these gardens, which are overlooked by all the rear windows of all the houses in the street, yet oddly enough the patch of rough grass behind Gala feels completely secluded, as if she had cast a spell of invisibility on her minute portion of land. Because it was a warm day, and most of the families in the street were inside eating their Sunday meat, we took rugs out into Gala's garden and settled on the grass. I immediately asked her what she thought of my experiences of the last twelve hours.

Gala took some time to answer. She is a sculptor, her face is long and high-boned at the same time, like a stone face, a face from the desert, and her black eyes swim fiercely towards each other but at a downward angle, carried by a strong current for they flash and leap, even when her face is at rest. A part of Gala has for a long time been with Meg. She lives in fear, I think, of losing touch with the spirit world, the world she needs for her work, and of finding herself on the surface again, condemned to tread endlessly the flat plains of accepted reality and received ideas, her idea of hell as I suppose it would be mine. But this doesn't mean she is incapable of being realistic: her boyfriend Paul, who has a wife and children in the country and is also a sculptor, is seen very clearly by Gala: she is caustic and affectionate, and good at keeping a distance in a situation in which she might well feel miserable. Sometimes I think she does feel miserable more often than she admits – but she has a good, strong laugh and a love of the absurd. Also Gala, with her brittle bones and her thin hands that look as if they could be unscrewed at the wrist, is strong and tough. I know she may well be stronger than I am. For the first time since she took me to see Meg again, and I saw the first avenues of my escape, I began to wonder if I had been right to go. It could well be that Gala could cope with these other worlds as well as the one in which we were sitting now – where the black and white cats were jumping along the tops of the walls, and a man in a short-sleeved shirt was standing heavy with concentration at his kitchen window in front of a tin and a tin opener, and his arm, thick with reddish hairs, turned like a torturer's above the tin, and a plane above us left a gap of white smoke on the sky – I couldn't. What horrifying, uncontrollable regions might I find myself in – perhaps forever? I told Gala of the waterfront at the end of the High Street, and of my instant knowledge of Ishbel. I was afraid. My hands were twisting on the edge of the rug, and I saw Gala see them.

'You're looking for something,' Gala said in a very quiet voice. 'It's not as simple as escape.'

Gala gave a sudden smile as she said this. I wondered how her voyages had affected her way of seeing her life. She didn't seem very calm as a result of them: in fact she was often nervous and agitated. But perhaps she would have been unable to survive without her strayings into the first circles of the outer world.

'Let's go in and have something to eat,' Gala said. 'I'm hungry. No, Jane, it just sounds to me as if you've got to do something about this sister Meg seems to have given you.'

'Do something about her? What do you mean?'

We were standing in Gala's kitchen now, after coming up to the wooden platform and stepping from the damp green garden into the clutter of indoors: enamel pots and pans with half the enamel scraped off, an angular sculpture by Paul, cushions and basketwork chairs. It was a relief to be in. Gala took ham and some gherkins from the fridge and reached over my head for plates.

We sat at the kitchen table. Gala was also a teacher, to earn enough money to be independent of Paul, and exercise books were scattered on it, as depressing somehow in their anonymity as faces of the unknown dead in Eastern cemeteries: all the effort, the desperate upright writing, and the feeling of seeing something that's not meant to be seen. Gala pushed them to the far end of the table. We began to eat.

'I hate correcting their work,' Gala said with a half nod, for she must have known what I was thinking. 'If I give them bad marks I feel low for days.'

'And how's Paul?' The effect of the ham, and thick slices of white bread was to make the shadowy other life more doubtful, more distant. Gala shrugged.

'He's feeling old. He tells me that if his wife had been a more organized person he would have been a sculptor of the first class instead of the second. Presumably he tells his wife this too. It must be very irritating for her.'

'It does sound very irritating.' I laughed. 'But you feel free of all that kind of thing, then?'

'Only because I never married or had children. I think it was because I can't bear criticism! It was built into the puritan idea of the family, I suppose. The head of the family may criticize the wife and the children. He may morally disapprove of them. Now why should anyone morally disapprove of me? I would lose my nerve as a sculptor if I were under a constant barrage of criticism!'

'Quite right,' I said. I felt cheered up. Sometimes Tony's disapproval of me was as strong in the flat as the scent of a fox. It half choked me, I had to get out. It was strange, I thought, that Gala had two sides like this, and that I always forgot one when she turned to the other. But now she was reversing – after her loud laugh and a swig from the bottle of red wine on the table she fell silent again.

Her everyday thoughts began to be submerged and a parallel track shot out ahead of them, going at a dizzying speed. I looked round the kitchen, feeling trapped. I wanted to go home. I would make it up to Tony, by cooking an evening meal, sitting in front of TV and watching old movies. But the thought of that was trapping too: they were eerie, the old, unageing stars acting out the fantasies of their long-dead scriptwriters. And the documentaries on 'thirties fascism, the faded goosestepping and deafening noise juxtaposed with brightly coloured food and bouncing pets, were more of a dictatorship of my mind than the travels imposed by Meg or Gala. I wondered how Tony could stand it. But he did more than stand it, he consumed it and helped to produce it. He moved freely in those wildly fluctuating zones of time and space.

'Give Meg a chance,' Gala said. She got up and I followed her into the sitting room next door, which gave out onto a balcony too narrow to sit on and a low wrought-iron railing and the base of a thick tree with new green shoots sticking out from the bark. I saw that Gala was tired. When she sat I stood, my eye on the door.

'I think she'll help you to eliminate that bad sister,' Gala said. She yawned suddenly and briefly, like a cat. Her eyes closed. She could sleep like that, anywhere and in front of anyone. But her expression, even when sleeping, was sombre. I wondered where she had galloped off to now. 'Goodbye, Gala,' I said in a whisper. I let myself out of the flat. And I went into the street feeling dejected and alone. All the excitement of last night had evaporated, and I wanted only to sit at home and think of nothing at all.

I wasn't really surprised to find her in the street. She was waiting by the corner. I had already passed several girls who could have been her: white face, empty eyes, dark hair. Now she had no name. She followed me to the bus stop and when I got on she hopped on last, as if she had only just made up her mind that this was where she wanted to go. She sat two rows behind me. I only dared to turn once, when asking for my fare. She was half obscured by a large African woman with carrier bags in a mountain on her lap. Was this half-hidden girl what Ishbel had looked like? She seemed a complete stranger, and utterly familiar at the same time. Her face gave no glimmer of recognition. Yet when we were there, at my stop, she got off ahead of me and I had to follow her all the way down the street to the block of flats.

As I went in I could feel my heart pounding. She had gone off down the street a little way and stood watching me with her back against the area railings of the house next to Paradise Island. A man came between us, heaving a crate of soft drinks. I ran into the cold, numb smell of the lino hall and jabbed the light button. I prayed that Tony would be in. I heard no steps as I scratched round my purse for my key. If she was there, she had come in silently and was standing still in the entrance to the hall where I couldn't see her.

The door opened. I pulled the key out clumsily and banged it shut behind me. The lights were on. TV voices spoke earnestly and then with laughter from the sitting room. I thought of the room empty, and the voices speaking to the empty room. I couldn't feel that Tony was there.

He was. He hardly looked up as I came in and threw myself down beside him. He was merged with the set, part of the antique dramas dancing in front of his immobile face.

I took his hand. I strained for noise other than that noise which seemed inescapable but could be cancelled at the click of a button. I wouldn't be able to turn this girl off at the switch. But it seemed that she hadn't followed me in after all. I could sense the complete silence in the other parts of the flat which always seems to reign when TV is on and claiming our attention, as if, transported somewhere else by the pictures, we are really no longer there and it can relapse into the silence of emptiness.

Tony gave me a quick glance. He asked me how I was. I said I was fine. Later he would ask me about the West German film, in two programmes' time probably. Slowly, sitting beside him there, I grew calmer. But it was always with the sense of being a victim that I went through the rest of the evening: I cooked dinner guiltily, I smiled at Tony too much and felt already that he had abandoned me, gone off – and rightly – to someone else. I was no longer the triumphant predator, I was persecuted and at fault.

The evening seems to last forever. Tony, who is good at suppressing his feelings but unable to prevent himself from showing triumph, came into the kitchen as I cooked the joint we should have had for lunch and ran his fingers through my hair. I saw us reflected in the window – it was growing dark at last – my hair standing up in hedgehog prickles and him behind me like a husband in an ad. They'd never let a woman with hair like that on the screen. And what were we advertising? Certainly not the quality of our life together – it was a long time since either of us had made the effort to understand what the other wanted. It was as if there was a limited space in our minds that was open to the other's mind, and the space was gradually closing.

'Hair still looks funny,' Tony said. He tweaked it again and I winced. I made myself smile. Now! I said to myself. Go to the window and look. While Tony's here. Go on.

I went to the window, half-pulling Tony behind me, as if in an affectionate, playful mood. There was my face, coming up closer to me in the glass. There was the street, which only last night I thought I had left for the last time. I saw a straggle of women going into Paradise Island. Their jeans made a clot of darkness against the pavement. The moon was full but not yet strong. It hung above my reflected face: two round, foolish faces staring down blandly at the women below.

'Are you looking for the pots of herbs that used to be on the window sill?' Tony said. 'Because they died. I threw them out this morning.'

He sounded friendly and co-operative. It probably had been a boring day for him. I didn't answer, but opened the window and leaned out. He was still holding my hand, and he gave a surprised squeeze at my behaviour.

She was under the street lamp opposite. I couldn't see her eyes because they were in shadow, a shadow so deep that it looked as if she had empty sockets, as if the blackness on the upper part of her face were really night. She stood, as Meg had stood under the thin birches behind the cottage on Dalzell land, defiant and still – but this shadow owned all the world round her, by throwing her darkness over it . . . Margaret . . . my Meg . . . and my mother, is this what you've given birth to? She was like a woman who has been drowned in daylight, the lower part of her face as white as the day that saw her go. She was one of the women on the raft of the Méduse. She was gazing at me apparently sightlessly, with utter anguish.

'I didn't throw them out,' Tony said, with good-natured impatience. 'Is that the kind of thing you think I get up to when you're not here – throwing pots onto the heads of harmless passers-by?'

I drew back from the window and shut it. I was trembling, but Tony didn't seem to notice. When he was using his bantering tone he was particularly impervious to me.

I made the onion sauce to go with the meat. Tony stood at the sink, peeling potatoes. The meal would never be ready. It would never be eaten. I didn't know how I would make my body ingest it – and if I did, wouldn't it just sit there like a lump, for if time was refusing to move then the functions of the body would refuse to move too. How was she there? How did she dare to be there? The sky outside remained the same uncertain blue. We were in a perpetual twilight.

'So how was Gala today?' Tony said at his most jaunty. I knew he hated Gala. He suspected her of conquering me, colonizing parts of me that couldn't be his. Not that he wanted them for himself, but it was irritating for him not to be complete possessor all the same.

'She was fine.'

'Talk about anything interesting?'

'Oh, I can't remember . . . just the usual.'

I wished suddenly that Tony *could* answer the questions I wished I had made Gala take more trouble over. What did she mean by my sister. My bad sister? How did she know about her, if Meg hadn't described what was going on? Or had she been there, watching me and Ishbel from behind a tree, shaping words out of our violence to one another?

'It must be lonely, being a sculptor,' Tony said. I glowered at him: I was in no mood for fatuous remarks tonight.

Yet I laughed. The meal was before us at last, and Tony was eating with satisfaction. He put a blob of redcurrant jelly on the edge of his plate. He unscrewed a jar of mint sauce. He beamed down at his food. At last, as a recompense for having to wait for it, he was getting his Sunday lunch.

I glanced towards the window. It had grown darker after all. We were tilting away from the sun, we were spinning just as we always had done. The moon had grown stronger and more assured. I thought of Gala's face, pale on the cushions in her sudden sleep.

'It's time men were prepared to become more psychic,' I said wilfully. 'Then we'd be able to talk about the really interesting things – you know.'

'I'm sorry, I'm sure!'

The lamb had put Tony in a benign state of mind. He cut himself another slice. The gravy was wrinkling already in the pan. The clock was ticking. She was standing out there, trying to jam the world into reverse. But it raced on without her, she stood under the moon like a sore finger. Would she be there when it was day? Day was waiting somewhere for her, a grey dawn standing in the swirling lino hall of my block of flats.

'Some things are too important to say,' Tony said. 'I wouldn't say them for anything.'

TV. Coffee. I wouldn't wash up, in case I was tempted to look out at her again. Tony felt that by peeling the potatoes he had done enough. I felt his surprise when I sat beside him in front of the TV: he had unconsciously allowed himself a space on his own while I cleaned the kitchen. I was smiling at him, I was holding his hand, I felt his unease.

'Why haven't there been any great women composers,' I said. 'Why wasn't James Joyce a woman? Why are we so narrow in our minds and wide in our hips?'

The documentary was on Thailand. How did they manage to flatten the place like that. The people smiled despairingly at the camera, as the Americans had taught them to do. They knew they were revealing nothing, they glanced round uncomfortably, feeling the packaging coming down round them once more.

'Shall we catch some of Film Night?' Tony said.

The Thai vanished. I went into the kitchen after all. The night was still dragging. I poured out a glass of wine. I toasted my reflection, and the figure beyond, in the dark street. Idly, I opened the drawer of the kitchen table. The moon was shining right in at me now, and in Paradise Island they were dancing to revamped Elvis. Everything comes round twice, there's nothing new under the moon. I rummaged in the drawer, beyond the string and a worn ovencloth: my fingers were searching for something now.

It was so slow. After I found the photo I went back in to Tony with it. So there she was. The dark hair, the pale face. I recognized her straight away. The programme showed a clip from a Spanish movie – a woman was slaughtering a fox in a deep green stream by a millhouse. The green celluloid waves spurted jets of red.

'I've no idea how it got there,' Tony said.

'But it's the one who was your girlfriend, isn't it?'

He sighed wearily. We were in a motor station in the States. There were two funny guys in the car. It was a comic film. Tony's stern mouth lifted in a smile.

'She's outside, waiting for you now. You never stopped seeing her, did you?'

'What on earth do you mean?'

'She's standing under the streetlamp. I recognized her at once.'

Tony got to his feet. It was all so slow. He went to the kitchen, he opened the window and leaned out. Later he chewed the back of my neck as we lay in bed. He came into me, but his body was dead. Had he really not seen her there at all? As in slow motion films, his cock moved in and out, paused, shuddered in an exaggeration of slowness, and released spray. The night was right over us now. Day was unimaginable. We lay breathing self-consciously, as if trying to catch each other out in some demonstration of lack of feeling. Had he really not seen her at all? Yet I knew she was waiting there for me.

I SLEPT AND I woke. The walls of the bedroom and the humps under the covers that were our bodies and the dim piles of our clothes on tables and chairs that looked as if they had come adrift from the floor were like characters in a forgotten language: if we could understand them – the four walls which man had for so long constructed for himself, the two bodies welded together by Nature's relentless urge, the familiar, perishable things which are kept for comfort – we would learn the world again, read the signs. But we've thrown down our blots. The image is more important than the real. The world swims beside its own satellite photograph, uneasily. And even in that room, where I had slept for years, there wasn't only myself and Tony. There was the photo of the girl. It lay two inches from my nose, on the thick shadow of the bedside table. I could see its white edges: she was preserved in four walls of white, as we were. I was sleeping between them – from time to time I turned to stare at the outline of Tony on the pillow and then back at her again. I picked her up delicately, by her corners, so as not to put my thumb on her face. Even in the dark I could see her, only her face looked paler and her eyes even more profoundly obscure.

I ached with loneliness. Tony's reptilian movements had done nothing to stir or assuage me. I jammed my fingers up against my cunt and pressed on the soft flesh. I wanted to make a gate there, never to feel the desolate openness again. My hand made a five-barred gate over the entrance. I saw the girl in flashes, riding Tony in a sexual frenzy, her pale composure gone. I saw them at a table, eating – outside was a green river and trees, they were enclosed in their privacy. Sometimes I saw her alone, and

74

this was worse. She was quite self-contained. There was nothing in her screaming for a wild ride through the night. She fitted in the world like a glove. It protected her as he moved through it. She was quite complete in herself.

Jealousy. All this was quite untrue, of course. If she was half of me then she was incomplete, the half that was me she yearned for, her dreams of me were as much an invention as mine were of her. We envied and pitied each other, we begged for our fullness. Yet the joke in the whole matter was that these two halves were quite arbitrary – Tony, by needing us both, had split us in this way.

It wasn't a difficult thing to do. The Muse is female, and a woman who thinks must live with a demented sister. Often the two women war, and kill each other. I thought of the male Muse – or the male counterpart who is needed to make a woman complete in herself: he is yet to come. And as I lay hating the girl in the photo I wanted to expel her too, to throw her from my body. She had tormented me in childhood. She was always there, as she is now: with her secretive, slightly self-congratulatory manner that also suggests a passionate nature smugly concealed. She, my shadow who waits still in the street, is the definition of that vague thing, womanhood: a pact made with the eyes, sig-nalled to men, that suggests women should pretend to enjoy a subservient position while ruling the men with 'an iron hand in a velvet glove'. Men like her because she is so finite. She never dreams, there is no static around her head – this is reserved only for me, only for the other sister, and in the terrible competitive-ness, it's a battle she will always win.

The night shifted slightly, a grey bar showed under the door, but it would stay there a long time before it advanced. My mind moved too – through dates, meetings, moods: when had Tony last seen her, why had he placed the photo in the kitchen drawer? How long had it been there? I thought of my face hanging over the kitchen table, as I was chopping, skinning, peeling, plunging hands in flour only a tiny distance above that quiet smile, that dark head and white face. Did they do this together too – cook in her flat: did Tony stare at her hands kneading and wringing and coiling and straightening as dispassionately as he glanced at mine?

I crept up to Tony and touched his back, which was turned to me as always when he slept. He gave a grunt, a sigh. He had knowledge locked in him that could never be extracted. He was like a sealed pyramid: I wandered, lost in the labyrinth of speculations that lay around his inner knowledge. Yet, if he were really brought to account, Tony would probably be surprised at the idea he might love her more than me or the other way about. There were as many strands to him, as there are to all of us, as veins in the body. Why did I feel I had to be the other half of him – or, for that matter, of the girl? Why this terrible need for joining, unless we were all perhaps two creatures once.

The restlessness couldn't go on. I knew from the implacable appearance of his back that Tony wasn't going to turn and hold me. I hated myself for only wanting him so ferociously because the existence of the girl had come to light again. I wondered if Meg had sent her, as a challenge. And I thought of Gala's words, that I should get rid of my bad sister.

It drove me mad, that she should be standing so patiently out there, waiting for Tony and me to come to an end, waiting to take him calmly from me. Only a short time ago I had been dreaming of my escape from him. Now she was there ... she could wait as long as she liked but I would never lose either of them. Now – if I didn't let go – I had them both in the palm of my hand.

I got up and pulled on my skirt. I went to the kitchen, took the jeans and jacket out of the washbasket and substituted them for the skirt, which I threw in on top of Tony's musty-smelling shirts. The jeans went on without difficulty: as I lay in the dark bedroom I must have gone through my metamorphosis. I found my sandals in the corner of the kitchen. It was a warm night – warm in the kitchen, at least, with the cooker and the feeling of safety from the food, bread and spaghetti on the shelves. I didn't go to the window and look out, at the moon and the street lamps. Anyway, the moon had gone, risen, tugged away to a higher part of the sky. The light from the streetlamp came up at the window in a blue haze. I was going down the stairs, into the terrors of the hall, and out.

How bright it is. Even before I open the door I feel the brightness, which is trying to burst through the keyhole, and in at the hinges: a strong, white brightness, almost blinding. Day as it might be constructed by beings from a lightless planet after hearing descriptions of the phenomenon: a force nine laboratory daylight. I half close my eyes before stepping out. This is day as you must remember it when you are lying dying in the night. Day as white as ice and without shadows.

There are no signs of the street around me. I feel the block of flats at my back slip away like a heavy liner going down the estuary into the sea. Grass at my feet. Fields. Little flowers, yellow and white, which also look more invented or remembered than real – they are too neat, somehow, too well placed. I might be in a painting, or in a housewife's embroidered tea towel of the 'thirties, for a house with Jacobean chimneys, and a garden with dark red roses, and a reddish cow are all arranged straight on in my line of vision. There are no hills, and the width of the white sky is oppressive: it's like being under an eyeless head. Clumps of trees make an impressionistic fuzz behind the house. There is even a plume of smoke from one of the tall chimneys. What a comforting scene! How peaceful! I know I live there. But I hate it. I am afraid of it. Why do I have to live there? Why do I have to walk over the field, on a path conveniently stretching to a low stile, and then across the long grass of the outer garden, before sneaking through the roses to the back door. What crime have I committed, or am I about to commit?

I look down with dread at my body. The jeans and jacket I put on in the flat have disappeared and I see instead a black dress, about mid-calf length and of very poor material, and two impossibly white, floury legs, with mud marks on the ankles. My breasts are large, and in no way contained – they swing under the horrible dress at every step I take. I feel like a felon, a convict, a laughing stock. Have I just been publicly humiliated, pelted with rotten fruit in the village square, raped by the village idiot with froth at the corners of his mouth? I know I am reviled, hated. There is a great void in me, an O that drips and aches, a round sea with rancid tides that slap against me at the pull of the moon. But it's not a man I am looking for. I came out here in search of the pale girl with dark eyes. She is the only one who can save me. Without her I am too alone in this smug, tapestry world: I might die. She was waiting for me before. Now, when I need her so badly, she has gone.

In my cheap canvas shoes I can only walk slowly through the grass. It springs round my ankles and then back again, like a succession of feather traps. One of the strangest things about this landscape, I begin to see, is that although it gives an impression of such opacity it is in fact threadbare in places: there are tiny suggestions, as if the tea towel had got wet, worn thin, of the street where I live in London. For all the weight of the richness of the red land, and my body pulled like a sack to the well-settled house, and the woolly white sky, traces come through of the familiar pavements where I had gone in my jeans to seek the girl. Sometimes, underfoot, there is a fleeting glimpse of tarmac, a hardness through the thin shoes of broken concrete. In the fresh, untainted grass there lies a soft-drink can, such as are consumed at Paradise Island. And if I lift my head suddenly, a row of windows seems to appear in the sky, like an after vision from staring at a bright light: they turn to empty rectangles and are gone again. It feels, here, as if I have arrived in a place which is both the past and a piece of the future superimposed on the present. What I have done – what I am about to do – has been done, and until the balance of the world is restored it will be done again.

The uncertainty of the world where I am walking, despite its appearance of enduring stability, makes me feel more nervous and desperate than before. My thighs, fat and moist from the permanent, needing leak above them, smack together as I try to run, to reach the house. Surely she must be in there. She must be waiting for me there. But as I run I feel myself watched, pointed at, there is laughter. My breasts! My blubbery cheeks! To them I am an animal. Hardly worth feeding, let the fat sow lie on its side and die. But my arms at least have developed muscle. I have worked for them. I have heaved and hoisted. My thick back has a permanent pain from carrying for them. After the drunken dinners they come up the back stairs from the smoking room and into the bachelor quarters, and they rattle up into the attics, they want to stick themselves into my black swamp. But we have pushed the narrow brass beds against the door. We pant there, eyes bright with fear in the darkness. They go away from our pigsty muttering, to release themselves under plaster ceilings. They hate us, they see us as pigs.

Now I know why I have the feeling of being seen. I have reached the low stile and my legs open as I climb clumsily over it. They are playing tennis on a court just a few feet away, kept in by wire netting, running and leaping like prisoners in a cage, but it is they who are the jailers and those wandering outside who will never be free of their rule. One of them guffaws and points – specifically at my cunt, knickerless, exposed to them as I pant and clamber over the stile. They all pretend to drop their rackets and come after me. But the game is more important to them. I am over now, I head like a beast for the long grass, which parts to take me in on all fours, I run stooping through the moving flanks of grass. What will I do when I come to the rose garden? There is implanted in me already a memory, a prophecy, of punishment among the stiff roses, the violent movement of my body under a flogging beside the stiff, espaliered roses. I pause, my breath comes in short gasps. Kneeling in the furthest extreme of the long grass, I see my white, fat breasts heaving under the dress.

Of course! We're not allowed in the garden, my sister and I. Not in the formal garden. We would bring chaos, a bad smell in the place of the polite handkerchief smells this garden has been trained to produce. Yet sometimes we have to run through it – to deliver a message, to take food and drink at a sudden command to Master George, who makes a black pinch with finger and thumb on our legs. If we're caught, we're beaten. Even if we went the long way round, the gate from the drive is usually kept locked. So that's one of the ways they trap us – they'll beat us just for the sake of it. They whack out at us if they see us there with their flowers, they lash at us before the hedges clipped to the shapes of peacocks and chessmen – sometimes Master George is on the sitting room balcony and he laughs.

Still, I have to do it today. If I stretch my hand out I can touch the mown grass, the rolled lawn where we must not put our cheaply shod feet. It hardly looks like grass. It is so compressed it might be the filling of a sandwich, with the earth they own below and the sky which is also theirs, fitting down neatly from above. All the daisies have been shaved away. I must go onto it, with my filthy legs and my unkempt, slobbering cunt, and crawl the length of the roses to find my sister.

The woman is coming down towards me from the direction of the house. She has a wide basket for flowers, secateurs and a hat tied down with a blue scarf to keep out the glare of their indigestible sky. Her eyes are tiny, triangular and blue. I know the coils of white hair she makes me brush at night. I know her artificial mouth, which she draws over the thin, unforgiving line of her own. There are dabs of rouge like pink sugar on her cheeks. But she is a death's head. In her stomach lie the small, permitted quantities of pastry and chocolate mousse and good meats served at their table in the light of white candles. She sees me, or rather she sniffs me. I can see her small, thin nose going up in the air and a small, detestable smile. I stay like an animal, resting on my hands on the mown lawn, which seems to melt, to dissolve under my weight. She comes up closer and stops.

'What are you doing there, Jeanne?'

'I was looking for Marie, ma'am.'

'And why should Marie be in the rose garden, I wonder?'

'She was taking a cool drink to Master George, ma'am.'

The woman looked down at me in complete contempt. She was tired today, there would be no floggings. But she leaned down with the secateurs and nipped my ear. I let out a scream. It sounded like a pig's scream. At the same time, through the woman's legs, I could see Marie coming. She was running down the path, her black hair out behind her, her horrible dress, exactly the same as mine, beautiful on her body. I moaned for her.

The woman turned and shouted at Marie to get off the path. So Marie came the last hundred feet plunging through the waving grass. She was electric, the grass hissed as she ran.

'Irish sluts!' the woman said. She left us, wandering down the path to the deepest red roses. Her hat was at a saucy, arrogant angle. I could have run behind her like a Japanese warrior, I could have jumped her from behind. She was so frail, half my size. But they owned everything. We were cramped, slave giants in their small, perfect world.

At last we were together. There, in the concealing grass, I searched her face anxiously. She was my sister, all my dark sisters. I had never needed her so much. I had never known her so well. We would never be enemies. We never had been. With our love for each other we would keep the rest of the world away.

We went the long way round, and climbed the locked gate. We crept in the back door, by the dark box hedges which smell of urine. The cook shouts at us – vague abuse.

Then we are up the back stairs, up and up against the brown paint worn to a shine by the backs and buttocks of beasts of burden, footmen and chambermaids and all those who wait on Mr and Mrs Aldridge and Miss Sylvia and Master George. All who serve the Manor and the enduring tapestry, although here and there it is wearing thin.

Our room, white and pointed, crammed under the eaves like a house marten's nest spattered with white shit, has two beds narrow as shoe boxes and a round window that looks out onto the central courtyard. Marie and I are in the one bed now, and our black dresses, which we never take off, even to sleep, are up around our waists. With our fingers we give each other comfort. We are kissing and biting. Her black hair is in my mouth. I will die, float, never let her out of my sight again.

MONDAY. TONY HAD a quick breakfast in the kitchen. I lay in bed. My body was aching, my back and thighs with pains like contractions, as if the expansion and shrinking they had undergone had simulated the labour pangs of my birth as another. I was more at peace. Tony had removed the photo of the girl while I slept, and I knew no one was waiting outside for me. Day takes away these shadows – sometimes at least. And my jeans and jacket were folded neatly on the bedroom chair, as if I had gone nowhere at all. These magic garments, which make you invisible because everyone wears them, which transcend sex and wealth and individuality – who had folded them like that when I came in?

Tony brought me a cup of tea in bed. I looked at him, wondering if I might ask. He sat down on the chair, on top of the jeans, and my heart missed a beat.

'Looks as if we might get the girl who plays Emmanuelle as Flora de Barral,' Tony said. 'She's very small and thin. It might be good.'

Poor Flora, whose life was recounted by three men, all equally determined on her helplessness and fragility. If she had had power, she would have turned their words into meaningless gossip by taking matters into her own hands and doing something so unacceptable they would have been unable to recount it. But she was impotent: while they inveighed against the feminism of Mrs Fyne she meekly followed the destiny laid down for her. I smiled at Tony and nodded my head. He saw I was laughing, and frowned.

'Will she strip in the film?'

'Don't be silly. Of course not.' Tony leaned forward and put his hand on my foot under the bedclothes. 'Well . . . I've got to be off really. And I'm going to Milan tonight. For a few days. It's to polish up the script. It's just come up or I would have told you before.'

'With her?'

Tony looked at me with what seemed a purposeful stupidity. His eyes were like a cow's – or I could see that was what he was aiming for. They were shallow and vague, pupils wandering, smooth as polished veneer. She was for a moment reflected in them: a minute figurine of her, she was standing with a hand on her hip, in a 'fifties skirt, and she was smiling like a hostess in a TV ad. I winced at her and looked away.

'Did you take her photo from the table here while I was asleep?'

Tony's voice was blurred in his new stupidity. 'Honestly, Jane, I don't know what you're talking about. What photo?'

'The photo that was in the kitchen drawer. For God's sake, Tony, don't start pretending it wasn't there.' I sat bolt upright. My thighs, stretched as bows made from wet wood, ached beneath me. I was weak today. Why did he have to go like this? My eyes filled with tears.

'Oh, that. I'm not pretending it wasn't in the kitchen drawer.'

'Well, never mind.'

What did it matter? I had my film review to write. I would go and see Stephen when I had finished it, he would calm me like a familiar blanket. For if Gala travelled sometimes too far, to the dangerous limits of her mind, Stephen remained always within the same ground. His ground was less tenable than hers – he was training to take Holy Orders, he 'believed', and Gala would never understand what that could mean. But his madness was sanctioned, worn as cloister stones. Paradoxically, his belief in something unprovable and unseeable only seemed to confirm the reality of the palpable world. When I was with him I drank tea and whisky and ate biscuits and felt the small comforts and irritations of childhood. One of his rugs was scratchy to sit on.

His mugs were chipped. When I thought of him these things returned to me intensely, physically.

'I won't be gone long.' Tony smiled and patted my foot. I moved it away clumsily, it felt as heavy as if it were wrapped in plaster. 'Jane, give us a kiss, then. And I hope your hair grows!'

How charming Tony could seem! He stooped over me like a handsome doctor and his lips made a bulbous shape as they came closer. His eyes were still blank, and his lips were like the magnified image of an insect's eye, popping pink membrane, blind but feeling, probing. I met them. They were warm and opened up further, to a shelf of saliva and then blackness. They went into a final smile before he left.

'Don't see too much of Gala! OK?'

Then he was gone. Tony wasn't as much of a fool as I – and he when it suited him – thought. He knew something. Just as surely as I knew the girl was still in his life, still part of his flesh, crawling in his arm hairs, moving in the packed cranium which must contain so many memories of her. I would always know this, however much he denied it. And now he knew about Meg. Perhaps he thought of Meg, but he had only seen her once. And for a time I lay back in bed, thinking of the girl, and killing her atom by atom inside me, tearing and fading her image until she was no more than a floating negative print in a pool of developing liquid, black as dark red blood. The dim light went out and I saw nothing. For a time I slept. When I woke, it was to realize that Tony had properly gone, and that I was alone.

I posted my review on the way to Stephen's. I was glad to be out of the flat. Once the feeling of Tony had gone, the shadows made themselves felt everywhere: Ishbel behind the doors as I opened and shut them in my nervous hurry, Marie in the kitchen, sticky and warm. And the girl, Tony's girl, was mocking there somewhere. They had taken over the place – it was as if, since my first journey and thwarted escape, they considered me out of this world and themselves, my ghosts, the legitimate heirs. I thought I wouldn't go back until Tony returned. I would stay with Stephen – or with Gala perhaps. Then I thought of Stephen's spare room, its absolute colourlessness, the sense when confronted by the faded chintz bequeathed by his calm mother of a nothingness in the world filled by polite chatter, herbaceous flowers, newly baked cakes which already contained the smell of their staleness, and I knew I would go and see Meg. In Stephen's world, so much had been brushed under the carpet that although he hadn't lived the life of his parents for years, some of it was still his: sudden moments of embarrassment with him would come from the rush of involuntary thoughts, which all this concealment in his past made inevitable. The deadly, 'good taste' Persian rugs brought pictures of women of fifty struggling to keep their heads above water, their blouses buttoned at the wrong button over rasping, red chests. The stiff Dutch tables were his father in the bathroom, a rustling newspaper, a bad gut, the lawn mower going outside as a life of dividend-supported, uneventful failure went by with the shit. Stephen was unaware of the climate of his house. But I couldn't sleep there now. And at Gala's it was trying to lie in another's spoor. There was no inch that she hadn't protectively covered with reminders of her worldly, and other-worldly identity: letters from solicitors, poems, childhood journals in different-coloured inks, hats with poppies stuck in the brim, long, spotted scarves. I would drown there. So I knew, by the time I got off the bus and walked up Stephen's street, that I would go and see Meg. I calculated I had three days before the next viewing of a film, and before Tony got back. In three days I might rise again. I could lose my shadows, and walk alone.

Stephen was in a white silk caftan, with bobbles swinging from the sleeves. He stood to greet me in his pale blue hall like a plaster madonna in a niche. He was plumper, and his gingery hair grew forward onto cheeks plump as a pigeon's breast, like pale flames threatening to consume the face. He was smiling, his small eyes were nearly shut. Stephen might be eaten, or licked, and he moved as if he knew this, like a tempting piece of food being jerked always just out of reach by an unseen hand. He gave

off a smell of orange water. It was three or four years now since
the conversion – when Stephen had decided to study to join the
Church. He was horrified by pain and injustice, and it was true
that in his presence it seemed impossible to believe in such things.
Perhaps that was why he added so greatly to the physicality of
objects and surroundings – when one was with him he and
everything round him seemed the only reality. Yet he led a spiri-
tual life, as well concealed as the crimes and sadness of his
parents' life: he prayed, and fasted, and felt the existence of God.

'Have you been seeing that woman again?'

Stephen put his Jesus-robed arm round me and we went into
the sitting room together. I flinched as I always did at first at the
square chairs, the horticultural covers nibbled by long-dead dogs.
I went to a sofa and went down with a bump. The ancient springs
creaked beneath me. I had told Stephen about Meg, but some
time ago. Now I regretted it. Since then, I had travelled. He
would be horrified by my journeys, though.

'Yes. At a party on Saturday night. She's sent me all over the
place, Stephen. Don't ask me to give it up.'

'Why should I ask you to give it up?'

Stephen looked surprised. There was a plate of cakes on the
table, and a pot of tea. In heaven Stephen would have cakes and
tea, as if resigned to an eternal station waiting-room.

'Have some tea,' Stephen said. 'But Jane, I'm not laughing at
you – I'd like to know where you went. I've tried often, you
know . . . to get somewhere, *anywhere* that would help me to
understand the Divine mysteries. As so many doubters have said:
just one glimpse of God and I'll be faithful for the rest of my
life.'

'This isn't about that,' I said. 'This is about believing something
different.'

Then I stopped. It seemed already that another voice had
spoken from inside me. I mustn't find myself at war with Stephen
now, when I no longer knew what I believed.

'You can hardly tell me you're going in for the fashionable

demonology,' Stephen said with a laugh. 'An emancipated woman gives birth to the Devil! I've seen the movie.'

Stephen was pink and fluffed when he was annoyed. I was frightened to see him like that, for it seemed I must have brought something in with me, a cobweb from the nocturnal branches of my walks. Did I seem changed to him, or utterly different? I had only seen Stephen like that once before, when we were in the park and a big boy had knocked a smaller one to the ground and stamped on his head.

'My clothes stink of sulphur when I get back,' I said. I laughed – it was worth the risk. But I could feel my dark sister, my Bad Muse, stir inside me and object to my flippancy. However much I wanted to keep Stephen as a friend, I must not betray my new path. Of course – and here my heart sank – she was only speaking like that because she knew Stephen was one of the few people who could dissuade me from the course before it was too late.

'You might be possessed,' Stephen said. He hadn't laughed at my reference to the sulphur. He looked serious. It occurred to me suddenly that he believed in all this kind of thing far more than I did, with God and Heaven and Hell. He might even think I had been to Hell. Perhaps I had.

'Can I have a cake? Listen, Stephen, I really don't think all this is to do with religion at all. I think it's to do with people having power over others – I think Meg can control the lives and thoughts . . . and invisible movements, if you like . . . of a lot of people. I think . . . that she wants people to learn about themselves, to see the world below the surface.'

'I see,' Stephen said. He watched me as I ate the cake, with his head to one side like a large bird. 'And what are you supposed to give her in return?'

'Well . . .' I said. I felt uncomfortable. 'Nothing as far as I know.' I finished the cake, and looked at the last crumbs fall onto the Persian rug with the same fascination as I always felt at all the small manifestations of the ordinary in Stephen's flat. There was a silence between us, as I thought of Meg again. She was reversing science, translating the known into the unknown. With her power, the old magic that people had known would pour back into the world again. Because she believed so completely in her words, what she believed would come true.

'Are you still thinking about that girl of Tony's?' Stephen asked. I felt uncomfortable again: Stephen was too close on my heels today. Yet I should confide in him, tell him how the shadows were always there now, one of them the girl, and the others . . .

'Most of the journeys I've done have been penances,' I said to Stephen. 'Don't think I've been *enjoying* myself.'

At this we both burst out laughing. It seemed ridiculous, even in a discussion on the possibility of a Second State, Another Reality, or whatever it might be called, that I was still anxious to give assurances of a bad time. The Puritan instinct is the hardest to die. And I wanted it to die, one of the reasons I would follow Meg wherever she sent me, for one day soon I would reach regions far removed from the Puritans and the black, clayey soil in which you must lie in unending suffocation for your sins.

'No, I don't think about the girl all that much,' I said. I saw Stephen blink, he didn't believe me. 'Tony doesn't see her any more, anyway.'

'Oh, I thought you said he did.' Stephen looked hurt. The last time we'd met I had told him so much, and now I was curt and offensive. Despite his enjoyment of our laughter he was sad again now. He took another cake, predictably.

'Why is the sea always connected with crime?' I said. I was thinking of the waterfront, where Meg had given me the first glimpse.

'And madness,' said Stephen, giving me a quick glance. 'The mad were put out to sea and they wandered rudderless. The ship might nudge into the coast of Holland and go up a canal. Think, if you were sitting in your garden . . .'

'Surrounded by tulips,' I said, beginning to laugh again.

'And one of these ships came along the canal a few feet away.'

'With men with striped caps and bells, and people whose bodies had quite gone and only eyes and hair remained . . .'

'The sea, mad and female, the criminal's punishment.' Stephen shrugged. 'An inspiration to kill, perhaps, from the depths of the irrational, from the waves that hide all traces. I don't know. Seriously, Jane, is that where she sent you?'

'Maybe.'

Again I felt another voice had answered. Our enjoyment died away. I suddenly saw very clearly the sea on the South coast, when Stephen and I had gone on a daytrip once: a sea with blue ruled lines like a child's exercise book, not the sea I wanted, very short grass on the cliffs, flowers too painfully small, birds chirping. Stephen had brought the picnic. There were thick sandwiches, with slices of tongue. We had talked about nothing much. This would never happen again.

'Do you think I'm mad?' I said.

Stephen sighed.

'No, I don't. But I don't think you have any idea – either of what's going to happen to you or of what you're really looking for. Do you think the world is that bad? Do you really feel you must leave it?'

'I'm not going to leave it. I'm just going to understand it in another way.'

'And another thing, Jane. You don't know what Meg is going to exact from you. You must be prepared to think about that carefully.'

'My soul?' I smiled. 'I haven't got much of a soul, Stephen, but she's welcome to it.'

'Jane! That's a terrible thing to say.'

All Stephen's recent conversion appeared on his face at that point. His eyes went upwards, his cheeks went a deeper pink, in his martyrdom, cake in hand, he gazed at the ceiling. I got up, fighting back a smile.

'I must go, Stephen. Thank you for the tea. That was nice.'

'But you know it wasn't!' Stephen was on his feet, very agitated.

'You've never been like this with me, Jane. You seem quite . . .
you seem totally translated!'

Translated! It may have been a slip of the tongue. But that was
what was happening to me. I was being translated into another
state, without death to intervene. I was going from the known
state to the unknown. I went up to Stephen very contrite and
kissed his soft cheek. 'I'm sorry,' I whispered at him. 'I'll see you
soon. It'll be better then.'

'Wait a minute!'

Stephen went to a cupboard in the corner of the sitting room.
He rummaged about inside, his back large and womanly in the
white robe. There were boxes of stationery and rolls of gift wrap-
ping paper. He pulled something out and turned to come towards
me with it.

Soon I saw what it was, although at first I couldn't make it out.
It seemed to look like a rhinoceros's horn. But it was a crucifix,
of course. It was made of imitation ivory and a small, faintly
coloured-in Christ hung from its arms. There was a gold chain
attached.

'Put it round your neck,' Stephen said. He put the chain over
my head. The crucifix dived down the front of my shirt and came
to rest between my breasts. The coldness brought a shudder
through my body. I looked down and saw the tiny Christ jigging
there, cupped by mammary flesh.

'If . . . if you're frightened, Jane . . . why not use it?'

'Thank you, Stephen. You're very sweet.'

We kissed. I walked down the blue hall to the door. I looked
back once, for I knew Stephen would be standing there, his eyes
rushing upwards and back again in anxiety. He gave a pretence
of a light-hearted wave when he saw me turn. But he couldn't
keep up the façade. By the time I had opened the front door, he
was safely inside his sitting room again, wrapped in the wings
of his robe, in his favourite chair by the cakes.

The air is very bright and pale outside Stephen's door. There are his front door steps, which have been scrubbed and rained on until they look like slabs of hard, dirty sugar. The bottom one dips in the middle. The maid-servants in their long black skirts wore it down as they trudged, in and out, out and in, the black pendulum of their labour and their unrequited lives, the pall-bearers wore it down as they carried them out, the householders in their stiff hats pressed down firmly on the step: it was the boundary of their territory: it might go down under them but it would not move.

And yet the step is not so respectful as it was. The cement is cracked at the side, which makes the step unsteady, no longer so firmly anchored to the black railings, and this seesawing has in turn cracked the step itself. The fissure runs with violent twists and turns the length of the step. It's not very wide, but moisture has gathered there from past rains. I put both my feet over it and feel the tilt. The thin lips of the fissure are directly beneath me, and the globules of moisture like spit. I imagine that if I were sucked down into this aperture I would sink into the centre of the earth. There, in the hot brown earth along with the bowler hats and the dead maids and the starched aprons laid out in boxes, I would wander forever. I can see the labyrinth of passages, none more than a foot wide: like buried Rome, no elevation of the spirit after death but a dragging down into the bowels, a narrowing amongst the broken games and smashed mosaics and balloons hanging like young boy's painted faces in the leaning streets. I would go down into the world that had produced Stephen and his kind. The people and the prayers and the secret lives, layers of rich coal under the decaying house. From this hell there would be no escape. I would brush the earth walls of those terrible subterranean streets with wide skirts, bleeding onto discreet rags, giving birth in agony in mud caves hung with rich hangings, dying with my child on linen bedding – I would never rise away from it. I would be remodelled when I was needed again – prostitute or maid or wife with bombazine and keys. There was little sound down there. No one would hear my cries.

So I stood on the step a while to gain my balance. It rocked gently beneath me. I closed my eyes. I could see the haunted eyes of the people as they came and went on the pavement. What happened to them? Did they go out of their houses one day and find themselves seized by eagles, carried to an eyrie from which they could look down on the wickedness and deceit of the world, see it written in the serpentine rivers and the ranges of mountains like gnashed teeth, and the swamps and rain forests that dragged you in and left you there – had they returned without their illusion, with starved eyes? I could hear a bunch of children coming in my direction along the street. At least they didn't know, or care. They were jumping over the cracks in the pavement, while I still stood on the crack in the step. Perhaps it was the origin of the game: they knew hell was waiting for them between the paving stones.

The step, very gradually, increased the seesawing motion. It was pleasant, like being in a boat going at a stately pace across a lake. The fine white light came down on my face and my upturned, closed eyelids. If only life was always like this! I had all the time in the world. When I was rested, I would go and see Meg.

I thought of my life, and the surface where I live with Tony, and the hard, bright entrances to the modern cinemas where I go to watch the mushy, coloured dreams of the future. Those mirrors aren't worth walking through. I thought of Stephen and the vision of Heaven he carries in his head. I thought of the crucifix he had given me. But I could no longer feel it against my skin: it had assimilated itself with me, and wherever I went it would have to go too. I wondered, standing there, suspended in time, what Meg would do for me when I saw her. I could feel, now, that my shadows had been removed and that I was allowed to sample, for a while, the feeling of completeness. It was as if she had given me something else in place of the bad sister, something that made me as strong and round as the beginning of the world. For this feeling, I knew I would give her anything she asked. I was an addict already, dreaming on the white-grained step, emptiness blocked out. My sisters had been nightmares. Meg would help me to drive them away, black bats of uncertainty and loneliness and despair. I would walk on my own and in my own place so that not even the strongest wind could blow me down. I knew Meg wanted to take, in return for this, everything I had: my salvation would be paid for in blood, but never hers: she was an anti-Christ, she would take where he gave, the wooden cross on which he hung, a passive victim, she would plunge into the heart of her prey. That was the first time, as I stood swaying there on the tilting step between the two worlds, that I understood what she was and where I was going. I understood the meaning of the sacrifice, that I would be a living shadow, a walking living being without a shadow, a drinker of blood, a nightwalker in perpetual and thwarted search of day, a white skin without blood, a dark predator, a victim. I knew I would be lured to this by the promise of the journeys, and the final ecstatic completeness: I saw that Stephen and Gala both knew it and were afraid for me. But I could no more turn back now, with one foot stretched forward into the magic, invisible current of air that would carry me on, and the other on the fissure in the step, holding down the bone-meal of the past, than make myself forget the journeys I had already undertaken. I was committed. I had never been committed before. The people on the pavement, with their starved eyes and their TV, believed in nothing. Yet there was an irony in believing that I would be happier, or superior to them, when I had gone over to Meg. For my eyes would be starving too. I would hover over them in my endless quest for the feeling which Meg would occasionally allow me. A junkie with no eyes flitting behind trees. They would shrink from my touch, from my gravebreath. An upright shadow, draining life. Still, I wanted to go on. The white light bathed my senses, in my absolute happiness I swore I would go on.

The step broke off the seesawing movement, and the abrupt stopping sent me down onto the ground. It was like walking off a merry-go-round at the fair, I felt dizzy and the ground spun as I opened my eyes.

Stephen's street had disappeared. I was in a forest, which was dappled with light and shade, so much so that the proportions of darkness and light seemed exactly right: small clouds raced over the portions of the sky that were visible, exactly corresponding with the delicious patches of shade on the ground under the trees; pale gold and green grass was as light as wheat in the sunlight, and cushions and banks of moss as deep green as if they had been saturated with water from an underground spring. Birds were flying about in the forest. They were black and bright blue and their song was harsh. Where they flew the forest changed, into a blue metal forest, without the light and the shade. In those parts of the forest where they flew I could see wolves, and sometimes a movement like a figure in the trees. In that part of the forest the trees were as straight as metal, and without shadow. The wolves never stopped pacing, under a sun unfiltered by leaves.

Where I was, however, seemed to me the most beautiful place I had ever seen. The black and blue birds never flew into the part of the forest where I was standing – they stopped short, always, on the other side of a small round clearing, a kind of fairy ring, some distance away. There was a stream a few feet in front of me, and it too was dappled evenly, like tortoiseshell. White flowers – Solomon's Seal and Star of Bethlehem – grew under the light, graceful trees, which had bark spotted dark and light as a leopard's back.

I sat down by the stream and picked some of the white, bloodless flowers. I felt balanced, contained by the shade as if this place, this forest, was the most perfect combination of the world's beauties, at the same time bright and obscure, warm and cold, concrete and hallucinatory, like the forest on the other side of the clearing, the hard minerals at the core of the world, and the hunger and evil walking the streets. The world was all around me, in its unchangeable balance. I looked down at my body, and

95

saw how the chameleon dappling moved to accommodate the white flowers I held against my dress, and the dark shadow made by my head tilting down. The light and shade flowed endlessly, like film, the essence of illusion, positive and negative light.

When I looked up again I looked directly at the clearing. There was something there. The sun and the leaves had become agitated in their patterns on the ground. The symmetry of the carpet was disturbed. And the walls of the clearing, the silver birches tainted with gold, knobbles protruding on the bark like bruises on the moving, swaying trunks, seemed to have closed ranks behind the clearing, to be shutting out the hard forest beyond. I rose and walked slowly towards the clearing.

The figure in the middle of the ring was hard to see, for the light and the goldness and the darkness played over him continually. He seemed to be wearing a coat made of shadow and light, of reflected leaves and pinstripe of bark, a patchwork of sylvan colours. His head, blindingly clear at one moment in the flashes from the sun, would vanish, and then change again. He was tall, but only as tall as the bolt of the sun that fell over him – when the leaves overhead rustled and changed he disintegrated into an autumnal chaos before reassembling in the mossy ring.

I walked up to the edge of the circle. A thin haze of light like a mesh wall kept me from going any further. I saw him as he stood before me, as he melted into striped and filmy air and came back into split second focus. He was extraordinarily like me. I felt that sense of recognition and disbelief which jars at the sight of an unexpected mirror: the thing before you that is too familiar and too strange. But I knew him. I reached out my hand, and the light and shadow fell evenly on my arm, making gold bars on the dusky, dim skin. He smiled: I saw him clearly then. But before I could speak a wind that soughed like an evening wind came down over the trees around us. The branches were tossed as if a hand had come up from below and squeezed them into a broom to scour the sky. They sighed and rattled, and as they divided, the evenness of the light and shadow was gone, and he disappeared. He might have flown up one of the shafts of white air in the parted trees. Or he might have gone into the ground, like a fox. The light in the ring was flat, and tired – round a tree stump there was a slight enhancement, from the dying goldness of the day, and a sense of shadow on the moss. I went to sit there. I was disconsolate.

Some time passed, which could be seen as a gradual blindness, for as I sat on in the abandoned circle the range of what was visible grew less and less, and I felt the light as it faded was coming directly from my eyes. It was twilight: the balance of two lights – the grey surrender of the day to the pounce of the night – but the balance I had known in the bright gold of the forest was gone. I felt completely alone. Where had he gone? What had he meant? And how would I ever reach Meg, now that strips of black cloud as wide as shawls were coming down on the deepening grey over the trees? The silver birches were becoming white. The bruise patches on the trunks looked like the faces of small animals, tucked into their sides for the night. My body ached with loneliness. My fingers and toes tingled like quicksilver, as if some message from somewhere were urging me to run before it was too late.

In the metal forest, a melodramatic Disney-movie night had set in. And I could see her waiting for me there, under a hard moon bright as a sequin, by the straight trees which looked as if they had just been sprayed with aluminium paint, her head to one side and her eyes as always in deep shadow. He had gone, and she had returned to me. She was my curse, my bitter dragging-down weight that would keep me out of true all my life, pulling one side of me down in grief and rage, snapping my heart. The wolves walked round her, but they didn't turn to look at her. She was all mine, she was for no one but me.

I rose and walked out of the ring. I left behind the twilight, the uncertain time when the world might turn and go in the other direction. Meg had sent me the vision. I thought of it as I walked straight into the metal forest. I walked past the girl, who was leaning against a tree, her lips blue in the unnatural light from the moon. I went on, through the lines of trees as straight in rows as the crosses of dead soldiers. I looked back once and she was following me. Meg had sent me the vision. I would lose her in the end.

There was no way of measuring time in that artificial forest. My heart beat as if it could hardly beat any longer. My legs felt nothing. After a time, through the last rows of the trees, I saw the lights of Meg's house.

MEG'S HOUSE WAS in one of the streets allowed to remain 'pretty' in Chelsea. The houses were low, and flanked by magnolias. The doors were painted fruit colours. Rock music on summer nights was subdued here; the crowds, the mixing of the races, the energy and the corruption and the optimism and despair of modern London were kept out by a system of one-way and dead-end signs more potent than written language. This timelessness – chi-chi is the word that would have been used to describe it a quarter of a century ago – was odd and disconcerting. Even the young people seemed to wear deliberately dated clothes. Posters of the Queen were on show in several windows. There was an air of slightly self-conscious well-being as if the residents knew they were exhibits, perhaps: last traces of a vanishing way of life. My shadow, with her shoulders hunched in a black coat, and her sallow face and her black, sightless stare, was horribly out of place here. She turned the corner after me, and leaned against a low wall as I rang at Meg's bell. She looked like a murderer, or a rapist. As I waited for Meg, I watched women cross the street rather than walk into this sudden chilling patch of shade.

The patio in front of Meg's house was whitewashed, and there was even a grape vine climbing a neat canopy of trellis over the porch. The windows had muslin sash curtains, tied, Bo Peep style, with shiny blue ribbons. The house looked blind, and white, and innocent – a nest for an old woman with fleecy hair, a retreat that was at the same time a fashionable and expensive investment. It had all that disingenousness. That was why, I remembered, I had shuddered at it when Gala took me there –

for finding Meg inside was like opening a mother-of-pearl box and finding inside a jet of fire.

Meg opened the door. Along the street, my sister moved rest-lessly. It was a bright day, and she wanted the unmitigated black of the forest, or at least the two lights of evening, to help her creep up on us. A light wind stirred the flowers and leaves outside the neat houses. And a sweet smell came off them – it may have been lime – it was the sweetest I had ever known. I wondered, when we were in Meg's narrow hall, why she chose to keep it out and burn the inevitable incense sticks. The heavy, Eastern smell closed us off from the street more effectively than thick curtains. I could sense my shadow moving closer, pressing up against the impenetrable scent.

Ah, it was a relief to be in! To be in there, in the red glow. Meg kisses me on the cheek. She looks amused. She is in a long gown of deep red, slashed at the bosom to show a white neck like a column going up to support a Roman head. There is a band of cherry velvet round the middle of the column, and a white rose pinned under her left shoulder. Her lips are carmine, and glisten under the soft red lamp from the hall ceiling. She doesn't take my hand, but leads the way to the first floor sitting room. It is redder than I remembered, the light so red that it becomes grains of redness, like African sand in a sandstorm. You can almost touch it. We sit on the pile of cushions, by the claw-legged table with the red baize cloth.

'I've shown you a great deal,' Meg says. 'How have you liked it, Jane?'

She must know. She must know very well why I am here. Yet I hold back, as if afraid to answer. Meg's head is tilted to one side, like a statue decapitated at the cherry velvet band – down one side of her face runs a shadow of the deepest red.

'I . . . I want to go back to the waterfront. Why can't I go back there, Meg?'

'The waterfront?' Meg chuckles. 'You want to leave on the ship, you want to go there again?'

'No . . . I . . .'

I am becoming confused now. Meg's tones are distant and rather affected, as if I had disturbed her in preparation for one of the soirées common in the area. I see there are candles – red of course – burning on the card table at the end of the room. A scarlet-headed Tarot card lies on the top of the pack there. Perhaps she really is planning to entertain. I came at the wrong moment. I can feel my triumphant shadow stir outside in the street, just under the trellis of vines.

'Of course you shall go there again. But perhaps not quite yet, Jane!' She reaches out both hands, and places them over mine. As happened when she did this last time, I feel astonishingly refreshed: my fear begins to slip away.

'That's better,' Meg murmurs. 'My poor Jane! What you've been through! My poor Jane! And that girl such a tiresome nuisance to you . . . inside you day and night, enemy or friend, enemy shadow . . . or sister . . . I've seen her . . . she dogs you day and night. Oh yes . . . I know. And only when you are rid of her will you go to the port again . . . and see the man . . . the man in the clearing in the forest, you know . . . Oh yes, he'll be there, Jane. How would you like to be with *him*, instead of *her*? Ah, it's hardly a question, is it?'

Meg breaks off at this point and looks with such intensity in the empty grate that I fancy she has started a fire flickering there – for a second I see the orange, leaping flames and a face, a face of forked flame, a face that is my own and looks straight into my own – then it is gone and the stifling red of the room closes in on us once again.

'Certainly you can't live with them both!' Meg gives a short laugh, rises, and pulls me up with her. 'It's so easy, Jane. Get Tony's girl, bring her to me, and I'll do away with the rest of them, I promise you!'

'Get Tony's girl?'

All the while, with her light hands, Meg is pulling me across the room and out onto the landing. I see the door into another room I had never noticed before is open to receive us. A slice of reddish brown light comes out at us on the gloom of the landing, like the blade of a rusty knife. I hang back, heavy as a stone, afraid.

But Meg drew me through the door into the room. My palms were ice cold now, and wet, but Meg's touch was unchanged. I looked round the room, which was as dim as the sitting room, and small, although it was difficult to tell the proportions in the infra-red glow. There were glass cabinets, and files; in the far corner, pushed up against a heavily curtained window, was a divan covered with a patchwork quilt in diamond scarlet and white pattern. Meg slid open the top of one of the show tables and pulled out two squares of glass with a coil of hair between. I turned to search for the door, which had closed behind us and was now invisible in the small, square room the colour of dried blood. I was in panic. Meg held the twist of hair up close to me. It lay inert and brown as a long-dead caterpillar between the miniscule panes of glass. I shrank away from it.

'You know what this is, Jane? This is hair from the head of a woman struck by thunder three centuries ago. Now, we all know it's impossible to be struck by thunder. But not really, Jane, not really. It all depends on what we believe and how we say it. Now, Jane, you want to lose that wicked sister, don't you?'

'But why . . . how . . . can I bring you Tony's girl?'

I pulled the crucifix from the chain, wrenched it from my bosom and broke it in two. Why had Stephen given me this? A man handing a woman the effigy of a tiny man on a cross! I feel my fear recede once more. And Meg's demanding tone had changed and she was smiling. I noticed how familiar she suddenly seemed to me, as if in some way she was a part of myself, as if I had known her for a long time. She reminded me of something, of myself . . . of the figure in the clearing in the forest, who was perhaps a part of herself for she had sent him . . . I felt a balance return, as light and easy in that forbidding dark red box as it had been in the even light and shade of the forest ring. The snapped cross lay on the floor between us, Christ's head and body at right angles to his feet.

'I'll show you how to bring her here.' Meg was looking down at me through eyes as slanting, mocking and clear as those of the elusive figure in the fairy circle. I saw suddenly that they were one and the same: if I brought Meg what she desired he would indeed be mine. She had only to conjure him from air, from leaves, from atoms, from water and fire ... Meg put her hands on my shoulders and I felt him there. There was a violent lurch in the pit of my stomach as my shadow struggled outside, beating her head on the walls in an effort to get in and take possession again.

'Who is he?' I said.

Meg's face was close to mine. Her eyes were shining. Her lips parted. In the depths of her mouth the teeth were as long and white and pointed as stalactites.

'Whatever you care to call him. He may be my brother, he may be yours. Use the initial K for him, if you wish. A bent line that comes in on a straight line and shoots it to pieces! Or Gil-martin, that's my name.'

From under the cherry red choker at Meg's neck two drops of blood appeared. They stayed a moment defying gravity on the stately white neck, then, leaving a tearful trail of pale red, went down to the edge of her dress and the white rose pinned there. The rose took the tinge. I stood fascinated. Meg was very pale now and her cheeks drawn, mouth open and wet and red behind the needles of white, upper lip arched as a rainbow. She pulled me to the corner, to the divan pushed up against a window – the divan covered with the white quilt and the scarlet diamonds of blood. She pushed me so that I fell backwards, and lay on the quilt, head butting the red velvet curtain that covered the window a few feet above my shadow's head.

'Jane!'

Meg's face had become huge above me. It blotted out the light, anonymous as the memory of a mother's face. From the sides of the vast head sprang her snake locks, and the rest of the room, the glass-topped tables with the strange relics from the days before science, the filing cabinets – God knows what she kept there: the names of her victims, the addresses of the invisible regions they would be permitted to visit? – lay beyond her without perspective. From the angle where I lay crushed, the objects and the dim red room seemed painted round her head, like detail in an icon, like stilted representations of figments of her imagination. As she leaned further over me, the redness became more interior . . . it was the redness of a bloodshot eye, it came from within me, particles of red spattered out in the dark room. I felt a total guilt . . . the weight of the guilt was Meg . . . I could do no right, I was the eternal victim. I floated in the horror of the guilt . . . but she pinned me down there . . . if she was going to kill me now, I wanted it. I was at one with her: she was completely accusing, and I completely guilty. And as I half-fainted, in the room which seemed encompassed behind the lids of my eyes, of red membrane and buzzing dots of blood, I saw the witches Meg and I had been: I saw us in the villages, in the mud streets, hounded in the open country, with our chums, and old hands with webbed fingers, and the gaze of self-righteous accusation straight into our eyes like stakes. I felt the hatred. I felt to blame. And yet . . . somewhere beyond that . . . we had been happy together, in another country. We had been whole.

'Jane! Open your eyes and look at me now!'

I did. I began to struggle, but I soon stopped. Meg's white bosom lay over mine. In her throat the wounds shone like a ferret's eyes. Beneath us, my sister beat her head – slower and slower, like a collapsing heart – against the door of Meg's house. I could feel he was somewhere in the room, for Meg lay very still and as mine opened, her eyes closed. Somewhere, over by the door to the red landing, or in the far corner by the dark cupboard, he was standing. He was made of red light, and dancing particles of dust, and all the magic relics, amulets and cabbalistic papers of Meg's collection. He had come as suddenly as a flame when two sticks are rubbed together, and he was as suddenly gone. But I felt his warmth, at the side of Meg's cold white body.

The pain – ice splinters of pain for a second so intense that I thought I heard my own scream, but there was no scream, for it was there that the pain came, at the side of my throat, and my larynx closed – threw my sister outside onto the ground, and there was a thumping, and then silence. Meg's eyes were shut. Her teeth were still extended: her canines, her eye teeth which took blood and gave sight, jutted over her lower lip – my blood was on her chin and on the quilt, where it ran down into the scarlet lozenges as if they had been sewn in there for that purpose. Her face looked smaller again, a normal size: as she drank, perhaps, she bloated, or she needed that vastness to stun her prey. Her hair, free from the blood, lay in damp coils over the side of the bed. She was like a woman who has given birth, where there is exhaustion, and blood and sweat. Her breath was noisy, and fast.

I lay in a limbo. My sister was dead. My guilt was gone. I was as empty as if a hand had gone inside me and pulled out my guts. I had felt his presence, and Meg would bring him again. I felt such gratitude to her that I lifted my arm, which was as heavy as lead, and stroked the dark hair that hung over the side of the bed.

'Jane!' Meg's eyes opened.

'I'll do anything for you.'

I was sure I had never said those words in my life. And as I said them, I knew she would make sure I still had my side of the bargain to fulfil. But she had given me the means to do it! I would bring such power to Meg, that she would be like a great Buddha on my blood.

Meg was smiling up at me. Her lips were together now, a faint red, bow-shaped.

'So you will bring me the girl?'

'Yes I will,' I said.

TONY'S MOTHER WAS sitting in the flat, on the sofa where Tony and I sit as far apart as Martians and watch TV. She was doing several things, all of them characteristic: she was smoking, and waving her second and third fingers up and down with the cigarette between them, as if to admire her painted nails; with her other hand she was opening and shutting her bag – click! – and taking out her compact, which was white and frosted over with a goldish sheen; she was flicking open the compact lid with her thumb and raising the round mirror to her face, and making a strange little moue into it, as if she was trying to shrink her face down to fit the lid; and with her foot, in a pointed and high-heeled shoe, she was tapping to some fast and silent rhythm on the floor. I stood for a while and watched her from the doorway, but she knew I was there for she must have heard the front door slam, and I knew she knew she was putting on a performance to prove that Tony could give her the key of the flat whenever he liked. I wondered if she had put her overnight bag in the spare room without even asking me. It was probable. What terrible event had she come up from the country for this time? A 'delicious play', perhaps – but plays were getting too rough these days for Mrs Marten's delicate tastes. 'As long as it's funnee,' she would say with a sigh. 'All I want is something fun-nee.' She had walked out of nudity and agitprop, bewildered but still dignified, all the way to the Savoy. Or a 'dinner': perhaps there was a ball gown in my spare room now, bulging like an uninvited guest against the back of the door. The 'dinners' were in flats in Eaton Square, and there were hired footmen and gold chairs, vases of sweetpeas and lilies which were described afterwards

107

with an odd laugh, as if they were in some way more significant to her than the people. She had seldom dared to stay more than one night. But now, with Tony away, I had the feeling she had come for longer. There was a bravado to the small shoulders in the perfectly cut coat. The chignon of flaxen white hair nodded, as the foot tapped and the little made-up face, hardly bigger than a gibbon's, stared at itself, rapt, on a far journey but still perfectly conscious of me there. Her hair was like the wool on the distaff of the wicked old woman who puts a castle to sleep for a hundred years – her whole person was the spindle, which pricks you through and through. I went towards her warily: I was tired and all I wanted to do then was to sleep, and after to speak to Gala. Her sharp, miniscule frame swung at the sound of my step and the curves of her lips followed the smile which was already painted on.

'There was no one at the Bartons. Do you know Lady Lucy Barton? Oh. So I came on here. There's a "do" this evening, Jane, at the Belgian Embassy. Do come!'

No sign of apology or explanation for being in my flat, I noted. I gave her a stiff nod, no smile. Mrs Marten seemed further away than ever now. Her cosmetics, her concealed terrors of death or solitude were as poignant and distant as the rigidified body of an unknown woman preserved in lava. Her lifespan seemed tiny, concomitant with her body: a butterfly span, a scarf. I felt I could see her flutterings, her crumbling to chalk. She was smiling still in my direction, eyes glinting from a bed of green mascara and imitation lash.

'Jane dear, would it be awful to ask for a G and T?'

Oh God, I thought, Gala, where are you? Meg, come soon and make a spell over this ghastly woman. But I went to the drink cupboard at the other end of the sitting room and took out the gin and tonic. Without asking, I went to the kitchen for ice, and found half a mouldy old lemon. Mrs Marten wanted her drinks with 'all the trimmings', as if they weren't alcohol but instead some sort of gay, childish drink, harmless and refreshing. I scraped off the grey-green mould and put a slice of lemon in the glass.

'How heavenly! Then I simply must have a bath. I do hope my dress hasn't got too crumply! Well, Jane dear, tell me all your news! Lots of exciting things been happening?'

I smiled. I sat down on the armchair next to the sofa. Perhaps I should tell her I was going all out to 'get' Tony's girl – or the girl who had once been 'his', at least. If I confided in Mrs Marten, would she suddenly tell me something I didn't know: that Tony was indeed still seeing the girl, for instance. Would she break his web of lies, if he was in fact at the centre of one? No, of course she wouldn't. She would protect Tony for all she was worth. From that frail, expensively suited chrysalis Tony had come: his head had appeared between her legs to stare anxiously at the reversed order of things. She would guard him against 'predatory' ladies like me; she would have preferred me, but for my useful ownership of the flat, to have been an out-and-out victim. But little did she guess quite how predatory I had become! So I smiled again.

'Busy seeing films all the time? I really don't know how you do it! I find they've become so dreary, recently.'

Privately I rather agreed with Mrs Marten, but I decided against saying so. The slightest mark of encouragement and she would move into the flat for the entire 'season'. As it was I was prepared to let her stay one night, then she could find friends, or go back to her home in the hills of Surrey where the woods and belts of trees looked like curtain on a swish rail, pulled across the sinister, semi-rural countryside.

'Yes, I've been seeing quite a few. Nothing I could recommend to *you*, I'm afraid.'

After this blatantly snobbish remark on my part, we fell silent. The evening was beginning to come in the windows, there was the sound of the soft drinks crates being thumped down on the pavement outside Paradise Island. The parrot gave a squawk or two to greet the pale, untropical evening and Mrs Marten rolled the ice in her glass and tapped her foot and grinned like a skull in front of the blank TV. I reached for the evening paper she had brought with her, to see what programmes were on later – I might not sleep. I might watch instead. And I felt the faint dampness on my legs, from the plants outside the main entrance to the flat, the residue of rain showers and the cuckoo spit which collected there. I brushed my leg dry with the back of my hand, while Mrs Marten looked with surreptitious horror at the lack of stockings or tights. If only she could know how far I had been! Yet for her, to go outside bare-legged would be an unimaginable step into the unknown.

While I was thinking these thoughts – tired, increasingly irritated with her presence – the telephone rang. Mrs Marten was on her feet before I could move. What was this? Had she left the number here already to a host of social secretaries? Were we to be *poste restante* for summer invitations? It was because of Mrs Marten that Tony and I had gone to the Berring party – she was a 'close personal friend' of the Berrings, and Tony, pretending enthusiasm, had insisted we go (who had summoned Meg there? Had she simply followed me?). Were we now to be subjected to more of this? I decided to tell her, as soon as she was off the phone, that she must leave by tomorrow morning. Friends were coming to stay. And I thought – what a good idea – Gala could come and keep me company, and help me in case I became afraid thinking of Meg.

Mrs Marten was speaking low and fast into the receiver. She presented her back to me as she did so, as trim as an airport doll with its topping of nylon hair. Her left hand waved a perpendicular cigarette and the scarlet nails danced about like fish in an aquarium. 'Yes. My dear, I wasn't sure ... Yes ... Yes. Look, Miranda, why not wait ... no, not for two days more I think ... Yes. Yes. I quite agree. But this is the trouble, Miranda ...'

I felt a slow coldness, first in my stomach, but there was a wriggling and a fainting in my stomach too as if it had become a sack of fish, packed and anaesthetized by ice. Nerves jingled in my fingers and toes. Miranda. Of course, that was her name. It would be Miranda. She was smiling out at me from the photo in the kitchen drawer. At night she pursued me on my journeys, and chained me when I was about to escape. She stood under my window ... Meg had stunned her, but only for a while ... She was on the 'phone now to Tony's mother. And who better? The woman who must for every psychological reason detest me more than any other human being, was conniving with the other woman enemy. These two women – one who had carried Tony as a water creature, a nail-less monster, a blind, puckered parcel of flesh attached by a crusty yellow cord to her bag of food, who had finally pushed out into the world a man responsible for her future comforts, her Surrey home, her electric blanket and holidays abroad, and the other with whom, having crawled from between the legs of his mother, he had finally found refuge, plunging in again between her legs for safety – formed a wall against me, a society for my end. They would drive me mad, extinguish me, remove me. I had no place in Tony's unbearable trinity. And yet they wouldn't get away with it as easily as that! I gritted my teeth as Mrs Marten spoke, and thought of Meg. She was right in saying I could only do good by bringing the girl to her – that I would purify women's legion souls.

'Yes, dear, well why don't you come? Of course they won't mind. It's a buffet ... but I'll tell them and I know they'll be thrilled. It's the Belgian Embassy, at eight. Well, I'm wearing long, but at your age ... lovely, dear. Goodbye.'

Mrs Marten rang off. She turned in my direction with what was, I thought, a guilty smile. But no – as she came nearer she seemed actually triumphant. Her face looked even smaller, like a shrunken African head painted white.

'Who was that?' I said. I heard myself sound blunt, manly: somehow between them the mother and the true love had excluded me from their sex.

'Oh Jane darling, I don't think you know her. I'm so pleased to have someone to take to the Belgian Embassy party . . . I was simply dreading it alone . . .'

'Is she a friend of Tony's?'

'Well I suppose she *knows* him. As a matter of fact I think she's in the film world a tiny bit. She said something about the film . . . is it one of the books by that marvellous Joseph Conrad?'

'*Chance*,' I said.

The phone rang again. This time, while Mrs Marten still stood in a mock-abject attitude before me, I rose to my feet, almost pushed her out of the way, and went over to answer it. Thank God, Gala's voice was loud and clear, strangely grating as it always was when she had been on her own for a time. She had guessed, of course. 'Are you all right, Jane?' Gala said. 'I was worrying about you. Where did you go today?'

'Come over,' I said. 'Can you?'

'Yes, but not for very long. I will though. I'll see you.'

'Good,' I said.

It was my turn now to face Mrs Marten from the other end of the sitting room. She was still directing at me her primitive-mask smile, her small eyes shone from the thick white pancake.

'You were asking about Miranda. Rather fascinating . . . it's an old theatrical family of course. No . . . she said just now they were going to ask Janet *Suzman* to be the heroine in the movie . . . Isn't that rather exciting? I don't know how she knew of course . . .'

No I bet you don't. She's been with Tony, or she's been speaking to him. I nodded at Mrs Marten as if I had received important news on the telephone and failed to sit down, which left us standing awkwardly, like people at one of the cocktail parties Mrs Marten loved so much.

'Janet Suzman as Flora de Barral,' I said. 'Yes, that sounds very interesting.' Inside me, at last, a great wave of laughter was coming, and with it the strength to abolish the woman who brought me so much pain, who stood in my way. (Gala was coming. She would help me.) 'I'm afraid I have a friend coming to stay tonight unexpectedly,' I said. 'Her husband has just died. So I can't invite you to stay after all!'

I had never behaved like this before. I saw Mrs Marten step back from me as if I had just announced a leprous condition, then, with infinite care, she approached me again and put her arms on my shoulders. Her eyes in the buried face looked up at me with a passable but exaggerated show of sympathy.

'Jane, do you know you're looking a little pale today? I'm feeling ever so slightly worried about going out and leaving you here. And I couldn't help noticing, when your scarf slipped . . . you seem to have hurt your throat. Is there anything poor old Mother can do?'

'I'm sorry. This is really the situation.' I could hear the firm gruffness of my voice, I could see Mrs Marten's ball dress being bundled into a suitcase and away to a cheap hotel, I could feel Mrs Marten's terror. 'There won't be time for a bath, or time to change, I'm afraid,' I said. 'She's coming now, you see, and she needs every care.'

Why was it that it appeared more cruel to treat a woman like Mrs Marten in that way than to do far worse to a person really in need of care? She was so outraged. The monkey face began to gibber. I took her stick arm, with a sense of revulsion, and led her through the hall to the spare room where she had made herself at home.

'Now pack,' I said.

'Well, Jane, I don't know what Tony will say!' Mrs Marten stood in the centre of the room, arms akimbo, like an expensive scarecrow. 'You aren't well, Jane, I fear!'

'I'll call a mini-cab,' I said.

Five minutes later, Mrs Marten and the ball dress, which lay in a polythene bag like a slumped body, and the suitcase, and even the smell of her scent that made me think always of the chintz armchairs in her Surrey house and the sickly roses that grew outside, had left the flat. I went to the sitting room to wait for Gala. I was weak, and my heart was pounding. I prayed she wouldn't be long.

Waiting is painful because it is an eternal present. The past is frozen, the future atrophied. And objects become lifeless too: the armchair which a short time ago contained Mrs Marten, had been an indispensable part of her maddening pose, is square and stiff as a chair in a hyper-realist painting. The cloth on the round table goes down to the ground in folds that could never be disturbed. On the table are a half-dead geranium in a pot, a tubular straw container which was made to put a glass in, in a tropical country where sweat and heat make glasses drop from hands – it holds broken fibre tip pens, and out-of-date postage stamps – and a pile of books and papers, all covered with a fine film of invisible, immoveable dust. I sit like an object myself, one leg crossed over the other – it would be as hard to part them as to roll two tree trunks in opposite directions. My left arm is firmly down on the arm rest of the settee. My right hand holds a glass of white wine, which is from time to time raised to my mouth. In this state of permanent suspension, I wait.

Night has come down on the street now that Tony's mother has gone. But I am distant from it, hanging in a cage of light above dark pavements and the slow tread of battered wives who go out in threes for safety, and the beginning of the pounding hum from Paradise Island. I am a rectangle of yellow light, and tonight there is no round moon sailing in on me. I am empty and square as a windowpane. Only my throat aches. What will Gala say to that? And what will happen now? As the room shows no sign that Gala will ever come, I can think of no answers. The only objects that seem to move in my mind are the clothes I wore for my first journey – the jeans and narrow-shouldered jacket still, I suppose, in the washbasket in the kitchen. I can see them more clearly than the things round me in this room yet it may be I will never put them on again. How can I 'bring' this girl to

Meg? How can I do it? She will have me stuck here like a fly if I don't move.

The thought only paralyzes me further. I see Tony and Miranda together in a car, they are travelling fast through rain while I am glued here, they are smiling at each other like people in a film and there is the red glow of a cigarette level with her face. They are talking but I can't hear them. There are such big rainspots on the window that her face seems to have run a little, to have grown lopsided: but she is still beautiful. She is an enigma, she is deep. I am shallow, one white plane.

I see Meg. We are at the limit of a wood and beyond that is ice which is very crisp under the moon. We climb onto a sledge. We go fast over the ice. We are at war – we are chasing or being chased – but the ice wind is so cold that my face is frozen and I can't hear what Meg is calling to me. When the trees disappear, I am in terror: there is only the expanse of white ice as far as the eye can see. If it could crack, even! But it won't. There will be no black, ice-cold, welcoming gush. Just the ice, and us going fast over it like witches in our sledge.

I try to see him again. Of course this is impossible. He is the void. Meg won't show him again until I bring her what she wants. I am frozen because he isn't here. The lack of him has chained the objects in this room to their places, and has stopped the clocks so Gala will never come, and has filled the world with somnambulists who turned the world upside down, walking themselves one-eyed, Cyclopean, seeing from the eye in the ass the mess they made of it all. When it's night they say it's day. I sit in this artificial day without him – not even able to make the expected clucking noises, not able to produce what I'm expected to produce. Soon they'll get rid of me perhaps – sterile, expendable. But what could I have done to please them anyway? Strut for a few years, push out unwanted babies, find part-time 'fulfilment', take the blows or the eternity ring, die?

From under the table with the telephone a bright green triangular edge of cardboard – a part of Tony's address book – is sticking out on the carpet. A blob of Mrs Marten's cigarette ash lies on it, and it's because the colour of the book so resembles the colour of the ash that I start forward in my seat and then freeze again, this time with my arms out in front of me in the air. I had only imagined that bright green – in reality it's grey to me! So – it's happened already. And I almost feel relief. Until Meg frees me . . . yet the thought is too horrible and I turn away from it. Deuter Jane, who can see no green in the real world, who must leave the world to breathe. My palms, which are still stretched out and a foot apart from each other as if I were about to clap, begin to run with sweat. I am the bad throw of the dice. I am the double, now it's me who's become the shadow. Where I was haunted, now I will pursue. And the world will try to stamp me out, as I run like a grey replica of my vanished self – evil, unwanted, voracious in my needs. I will be outcast, dogging the steps of stronger women, fastening myself onto them at nights, trailing as their lying shadow in the day. Unless . . . bringing the world to rights . . . bringing to Meg's red altar the essential sacrifice . . . I am restored to life and greenness and in tearing out the simulacrum need no longer live as one myself. I can feel my legs tense as I prepare for the journey across the room to that triangle of grey board. My hands go down on the settee and give a push . . . slowly, deliberately, I go through the ever-greying room.

I never knew Tony knew so many people. A lot of them seem to have moved several times since he first inscribed their names, there are crossings-out and rehousings on every page. What does he do with these people? There is something ridiculous about the address book – it makes me laugh to think of Tony's serious face as he copies them out. Does he 'go through' the book to discover whom he feels like seeing? It's true we gave a party once, and he used the book with an air of triumph, but the party wasn't much of a success. Nobody seemed to know what they were doing there: perhaps they felt they had walked straight out of Tony's address book and couldn't wait to get back in there again.

My hands are clumsy and the pages turn over in clumps as I look for her. M . . . why should she be in under her first name anyway? But I have a feeling she is. M for mother, for murder, for Meg. M for her. She made me a shadow, discarded by Tony before he had even met me. I am in Meg now, for Meg has my blood, and soon, M, you will be. We'll both be there. Together again! But this time I'll be the strong one, you'll see.

Monica . . . the name in faded pencil and no surname . . . I smile in spite of myself at the idea that Tony went to prostitutes. But how can you tell anything about people? I see Monica in a flat in a redbrick mansion in Chelsea, opening the door in a clinging black sweater and tossing her head. Tony makes a foolish face. They go in and the door closes behind them. No. Monica, it's not you. Margaret . . . Margaret has changed her name and address so many times that her different married names pile up to the right of her like the corpses of flies – in the end Tony must have decided she was simply Margaret. Oh, Margaret, why did you marry so often? Did you believe there was going to be happiness and content? Didn't you see the world in grey sometimes, didn't someone come and take your substance away? How optimistic you must have been, every time you left the Registry office and went off to buy a new casserole, material for comforting curtains that would screen you and your new mate off from the outside world! Did you tire of them quickly . . . or did you kill them perhaps, like Bluebeard, and leave them in a small room with their congealed blood? For you must be quite rich, Margaret, you live in an expensive area. Did they marry you for your money and your casseroles and then play a double game? They two-timed you, there seems little doubt about that.

Miranda . . .

Now I've found her I don't know what to do. I was right, Tony had simply put in the first name, for him she has no second name unless it's his. She is a part of him. She lies right on the middle of the page in the middle of the book. M the thirteenth letter, the centre of the alphabet, the centre of his world. She is written in a careful sloping hand, as if every letter was stroked as it went down, and she is in a strong black ink he doesn't seem to use otherwise except for the addresses of solicitors and doctors. This makes her official somehow, and obedient to him – for although the ink is strong the curve of the letters is feminine and submissive. Maybe she wrote her name herself? But there is something of Tony in the writing: together they entered her in his life.

Miranda lives at 114 Albert Drive, the other side of the river. Albert Bridge which is strung with coloured lights at night – on a dark night they make a red and yellow and green road above the bridge – leads to Miranda. I can see Tony walking the aerial road, arms outstretched in the artificial faery glow ... dropping down into the blackness to take her in his arms. But this time, Miranda, it's me that's coming to see you. I'll go over the water and I'll bring you back. And I almost laugh, squatting there on the grey carpet by the grey TV screen, with Mrs Marten's cigarette ash scattered on the floor. This is Caliban calling, Miranda ... When I've delivered you where you belong, I'll be myself again.

At first I misdial the number. My fingers are numb, and for some reason I don't feel like sitting down properly, so I stay in squatting position and it makes me unbalanced and shaky in my arms and legs. Then finally I get it right. As it rings I stare across the room at the window ... ah, I'd like to fly out there now and not make this call. Or ... why didn't I close the curtains? Suppose there's a wave of laughter and singing from Paradise Island or a fracas in the wives' home at the appearance of a drunken husband – I won't be able to hear what Miranda has to say.

In fact, a silence seems to fall on the street as Miranda answers. There are no footsteps, the parrot no longer fills the puncture it has pierced in the air, the clink and thwack of the Schweppes bottles has entirely stopped. I can hear Miranda breathing as if her throat were two inches from mine.

'Is that Miranda?'

'Yes?'

'This is Jane.'

In Miranda's silence, the street begins to come to life. Right under my window, from where she used to stand, a man gives one of those shouts that are meant to communicate nothing, that are just a man's shout, like a dog's bark. But the shout hangs in the street: in response a wooden crate drops and a window goes up with an ear-splitting yawn.

'What do you want?'

'I thought . . . I thought you'd gone out this evening with . . . with Mrs Marten. You didn't?'

'What? With whom?'

'To some embassy . . .'

'What Jane *is* this?'

Now that's a good question! You know very well, Miranda – but perhaps you're not being so disingenuous after all. Have you also dreamed of me? Do you know you follow me wherever I go?

'With Tony's mother,' I said. 'I'm sorry, it must have been another Miranda.'

A pause. Miranda is thinking. I can feel her think and I can see two blue veins in her throat, pulsing.

'Yes I did go actually,' she says. 'Earlier.'

My first thought is prosaic. Whatever time can it be now? How long did I sit waiting for Gala? Then I freeze. The bitch! How cool and collected she sounds! What on earth is she doing with Tony's mother? I refuse to accept that she must have had a relationship with Tony's mother long before I met Tony. Tony, after all, only existed for me when I met him – Miranda too through him. It has always been impossible to imagine Miranda sitting in Mrs Marten's home in the Surrey hills, flipping through magazines and making plans, quite unaware of my being in the world.

'I think I'd better ring off,' says Miranda.

She thinks I'm drunk, hysterical. She knows, from what Tony has told her, that he can't wait to leave me and be with her again.

'Miranda! I'm only ringing to ask you to a party. As we've never met . . . it seems so silly really . . .'

'A party?' Miranda sounds suspicious. Tony has probably told her by now, on the phone from Rome airport or a Geneva hotel where he lies groaning for her at night, of my obsession with her photo. So why am I asking her to a party? But I'm good at this. I didn't get my job for nothing.

'I just think you'd enjoy it. And it seems a bit ridiculous that we can't ever meet . . . as if Tony was standing between us like the sword of Damocles! No . . . it's a party the day after tomorrow at Miles Alton's house . . . yes the man who makes . . . exactly . . . And as I know you're doing sets at the moment for that film . . .'

'Where is it?'

Miranda's voice is still very cool but I can hear the excitement, buried under layers of ice. How clever of me to remember that Miles Alton's party is in fact the day after tomorrow . . . is that Thursday . . . yes it is . . . and consciously I haven't given the matter a thought since the card came weeks ago. Of course she'll want to meet him, he's one of the few good film directors. Of course she'll want to be asked to design his next film. Can't she just see herself doing it – in Hollywood with any luck – she'll wear black, with a V neck. I can't help smiling at my vulgar jealousy. But I know I've caught her, fair and square.

'14 Sloane Gardens,' I say. 'All one house, one bell. About eight onwards.'

'I'll see if I can make it. Well thank you, Jane, for asking me.'

We say goodbye and ring off. For a long time I stay crouched on the floor. Two more days, before Tony comes back . . . before the party . . . before seeing Meg again. We were in my bedroom, Gala and I. Where Tony lies, on the side of the bed nearest the window, his shoulders hunched and his back to me as if in a state of perpetual shrug. Gala sat and smoked, her spine up against the wall. She was late because her sculptor had come to see her – they'd gone out to supper then he'd had to go back to the country again – and her eyes were bright, her movements sudden. She had embarked on an evening with him, and I felt that only a part of her was with me. I lay diagonally from her on

the end of the bed, with the big square ash-tray between us. Her
legs swayed as she spoke, in a secret dance, and her arms
swooped and circled. Her energy crept into me, through my veil
of tiredness and confusion.

'Were you afraid then, Jane?'

'Yes. Yes I was. I can't believe that's what she wants me to do.'

'Oh I think you do believe it. You do believe it's right.'

Yes. Gala, as always, could recognize a past feeling spoken in
the present, smell its wrongness. I did now believe Meg. But
why? How? I was in two worlds, and slipping into the abyss
between them. My actions showed my growing belief. My spoken
thoughts were firmly in the world I lived in with Tony, and work,
and that muddle of hope and defeat which everyone drags with
them through the day. But if I were really to go after Miranda . . .

'You realize you were very lucky to be chosen,' Gala said. 'She
must see the potential in you, Jane. There are only a very few
people like you, you know . . . Don't you think you *are* fortunate,
Jane, to be one of us?'

I stared at Gala, who was more animated than ever now. She
seemed to be speaking to someone else as well as to me; her eyes
were fixed on the wall opposite and in her persuasiveness I
almost felt the street move and stand to attention beneath her.
With her will she was pulling the world into her hands . . . But
the bump of rock music from Paradise Island went on, and a car
stopped with a screech at the pedestrian crossing outside the
supermarket with the cardboard dolls.

'But, Gala, do you know the answers?'

'Where do you think my sculpture comes from, Jane? It can
make no difference yet, but Meg has sent me on journeys where
I can gather it up. She's shown me the way. I can't do what you
can do, though – I can't bring Meg what she needs for the next
stage. Come on, Jane, you've given her your blood. Now bring
her that shadow to destroy!'

The hair of the head of a woman struck by thunder. I could
see it, coiled between the glass slides, terrifying symbol of Meg's

power. I felt weak – my body was numb – only Gala's current kept me conscious. I found myself nodding though the rebellion was in me still like a small fish struggling to swim upstream.

'Why should it be me, Gala? Surely . . .'

'Perhaps it corresponds with your external situation,' Gala said briskly. I knew she was uninterested in my life with Tony, in my exasperations and jealousies. In fact, she seemed to have little belief in my external life at all. She and Meg together had translated me into this new zone and for them it was my sole existence. Was I to be their guinea pig, going from the known to the unknown and changed at their will?

'You remember how you felt about the first trip Meg sent you on,' Gala said. 'Don't you want to travel again?'

Ah, of course I did! The walls of the room where we sat were straining to be rid of me. Down the corridor, long and winding and grey in the eye of my exhaustion, there lay the kitchen and the washbox and the small, battered clothes and the door out onto the fire escape and the void. And all I had to do . . .

'We'll be proud of you,' Gala said. 'Jane, you look very pale. Are you all right?'

'I'm a bit drained,' I said, and we both laughed. 'No, I think I'd better get into bed. Don't worry, Gala, I've already made the first moves for what Meg wants.'

'Have you? Have you really?' Gala leaned across the bed and gave me a sharp stare. 'Ah!'

'Tell me about K, though, or Gil-martin – I don't understand.'

'You will!' Gala motioned to me to get under the covers. 'I'll bring you some tea now. Jane, he can only be insubstantial at present, for you haven't rid yourself of your double female self yet. You could call him the male principle, which you lack . . . or . . .'

'Yes,' I said. 'All right, Gala. All right. I'll wait. I'll go to sleep now.'

I lay under the covers, and listened to Gala taking cups out of the cupboard in the kitchen. She came with the tea, and biscuits that had gone soft with age. I ate and drank, although I hardly had the strength to lift my hand. When we had finished, Gala brought the TV in from the sitting room and we watched the last hour – Richard Nixon, as he explained away his past.

Gala was smiling, my eyes were half-shut but I could feel her pleasure and excitement.

'You see, Jane! No one could believe his language, the language of Watergate! It remains to us to lose our evil selves and speak again!'

Through my lowered eyelids I stared at Nixon's face. It may have been the effect of a reddish blur from the inner lids themselves, or it may have been my imagination, but his grey face seemed every moment to become more pink. A roseate blur surrounded the set, and slowly filled the room. I closed my eyes altogether, into a red nothingness.

'Everything looked so grey earlier,' I mumbled to Gala. 'And now it's turning red. As for green, I can't see it at all.'

'We all have that,' Gala said. 'We must suffer it until the day comes, as you say. And you must rest, Jane, as you're the one who will bring it about!'

I slept then. Gala stayed the night in the spare room, where Mrs Marten had tried to introduce her ball gown. She said she would come to me early in the morning, with more tea and a boiled egg. I must rest. She advised me to rest as much as I could. I must be healthy, and there was a great deal of preparation ahead.

I WOKE THE next morning feeling extraordinarily well and happy, as if I had been purged of all the miseries of the grey street outside, and the grey shadow that used to live inside me, knocking against my ribs in her effort to get out, and the weight of my own double face in public places. I was bled of it all. I was free. I knew I must revisit the old haunts again, that Meg would make me do this so that I could settle my scores with my sisters there before settling once and for all in this world with Miranda, but I no longer felt any doubt of my future . . . the journeys . . . K or Gil-martin: they were all mine and I would leave on my ship soon to enjoy them. I felt even frivolous: memories of Tony's mother – another Mrs Marten, but how different from Meg! – made me smile as I lay in bed waiting for Gala. Poor Mrs Marten! Had she had a good time at her Embassy dance? How could she know, setting off to meet her dear Miranda, that it was the last time they would go out together? But, when you added up what there was in it for Mrs Marten, would she really care? She would lose a daughter and gain a son – no, she would lose two daughters, for no doubt she saw me as a daughter too, an unwelcome one – and yet, when her grief for Miranda was over, she would after all have Tony for herself. She would imprison him in Surrey while he wept for Miranda and told her again and again that he couldn't understand how I could have brought myself to do it. She would marry him, fill his fat, disconsolate body with suet and lumps of meat and potatoes, sew his feet into his socks, sometimes take him out to look at the autumn trees that were so disconcertingly like curtains. He would play bridge, and give up his film career. Or would he go on with the script of *Chance*, year

124

in, year out, playing with the concept of two narrators, two male 'voices over' discussing the pride and shame of poor Flora de Barral. I would be a long way away by then, of course. I, who had recounted my own life and taken my own decisions rather than have them recounted or taken from me, would he think of me sometimes, in his chintzy eunuch's bedroom, as I sailed the high seas? I doubted it. Mrs Marten would put an opiate in the tea from Jackson's. I would be blocked from his mind for good.

These enjoyable fantasies were broken by Gala's appearance in my room with a messily made up breakfast tray, a cracked egg and a slice of burnt toast. She had made coffee instead of the promised tea, and the smell was strengthening: I realized that however well I might feel I was still very weak. I thanked Gala and took the coffee with a shaky hand.

'Did you sleep all right, Jane? How are the colour problems?'

'Still a little rosy!' I smiled up at her – Gala seemed very grey still, while the rest of the room was bathed in the red spots Meg had bequeathed, like the dots in a comic. I raised myself to look out of the window – sure enough, the tops of the sparsely leaved plane trees in the street had lost their dull, London green. A slight wind shook them, and they danced like spirals of smoke against the grey houses. It came to me that in my memories of Mrs Marten in Surrey, the colours had all been normal. And despite my happiness I felt the shudder of the premonition of death. Where I walked, the colour of life was drained away. There was life only in my memories. I was already the walking dead, a shadow, drawn to my old life in search of the green.

'Don't worry,' Gala said. 'You're between regions, Jane. You're about to embark. Now eat your egg! I'm sorry it cracked, but it's a battery egg, it must be. Thank your lucky stars you weren't born a battery hen, my dear!'

I laughed, and felt some of the new frivolity return. If my new powers were beginning, what tricks I could play on the world before I finally bowed out! If my words became truth, I could literally destroy the film I disliked or disapproved of: under my acid gaze the celluloid would turn to muddy water and run away. How I could tease poor Stephen, by substantiating his Christ on the cross for him, right in his sitting room as he handed out his sweet cakes to young men with burning cheeks! How it would torment him ... what would he do? Go down on his knees by the bleeding feet ... seize the dark emaciated legs? I laughed aloud. And Tony, I could set him dancing with Miranda and make sure they never could stop. I would hire them out on a cruise ship to South America, as dancing lovers, allowed only to pause for a few moments and refresh themselves with champagne. I would call the tune faster and faster, until Tony fell on his back and was pushed to the side in ignominy, and Miranda ... ah, Miranda ... I would call Taranta! ... and what could she do but obey me, she the woman in a sexual, hysterical frenzy, the spider-bitten woman trembling and shaking in the poison of her wants. There! She tries to slow but she can't: in *her* marathon there'll be no dragging steps.

'Jane!'

Through the open door of my bedroom I saw Gala's legs coming from the kitchen. I was disappointed, I felt moist with excitement at Miranda's humiliation, I saw for a moment the posters in the Underground where I had passed, every day as a woman child, the alluring figures of other women, whom I must become or emulate but was forbidden to love. I felt the bitter sting of my own defeat then, when I had first felt the other woman stir in my breast and point to the beautiful and impossible breasts of others. I saw the eyes of the crowd on Miranda, as her silk dress was ripped from her and she danced naked, screaming with pain. There was laughter on the ship, as the rich men savoured the sight. And I had tried to be the woman of the posters and yet not to love her ... to be myself and her, and to please the world. My hands slid between my legs: I waited upright for Gala to reach my room.

'It's bad news, I'm afraid.' Then Gala saw my expression. 'Now,

Jane, only two more days to go before you're whole again! Wait. He's waiting for *you*. But in the meantime, I have to tell you the unfortunate news that Tony is back. And his mother seems to be with him. They're coming in the main gate at the moment. D'you want me to go? I could use the fire escape in the kitchen, couldn't I?'

Dear Gala! I jumped out of bed, kicked the door of my room shut behind her, and threw my arms round her thin body. Where would I be without Gala? Still going off with a sinking heart and a sense of duty to my job, still bored and jealous with Tony, still trapped in a greyness far worse than the actuality of the state of the world provided by Meg. I would have no prospect of becoming whole at all. And there I was, in my miserable state of the past, when I should have been preparing for the great deed of tomorrow night. How did I imagine I was going to bring it off, after all? Did I think it would be easy, to kidnap Miranda, who would have no desire whatever to go with me? And in front of two hundred people. I trembled with agitation, standing there in my nightdress and listening to the horrible clang of the main door and the scrape of suitcases on lino.

'Well . . . which do you want me to do?'

'Stay, Gala, for heaven's sake!' I clutched her arm. 'I feel . . . I feel afraid.'

Gala pushed me away and looked at me severely. 'You don't seem very rested, Jane. What are the plans, then, before they come?'

'At the . . . at the party.' I was stuttering: I could hear Tony at the flat door with his key, and the shrill, self-consuming laugh of his mother.

'At Miles Alton's party . . .' Had I already told Gala or not? I felt confused, almost as if the party were already over and the deed done. As so often when there was about to be a confrontation with Tony, my colour went up, and my head throbbed; but this time it was worse, as if Mrs Marten's opiates had already been at work.

'Don't panic!' Gala hissed at me. 'It only helps them. Now, can you make this party a fancy dress party, do you think?'

'A fancy dress party?' I thought Gala must have gone out of her mind, when there were more important things to do than prance about in borrowed clothes.

'Try!' Gala said. 'Go on, think about it hard. Try!'

As Tony and Mrs Marten came up the haircord stairs and stood exchanging unnecessary remarks – they didn't know whether or not I was there and they wanted to test the atmosphere, to sense if I was iying in wait for them, hostile – Gala took hold of me roughly and pushed me into the corner of my room by the window. Struggling to be free of her, I pressed my head up against the pane: through the layer of dirt I saw the Persian students in the house opposite, with reflected sun from my windows striking their gold sunflower rooms . . . A succession of old women on the pavement below going past as if on a conveyor belt, motionless and lumpy, carrying parcels . . . Two women in jeans brushing up broken glass from the steps of Paradise Island and then standing back, hands on hips, to enjoy the sun. A lovely summer day! The first real day of summer! And it was sparkling crystal grey to me, while the light summer breeze tossed leaves and ruffled grass the colour of black and white film. I stared through the frame of the window, as if from a million miles away. Gala's grip was still tight on me. Tony and his mother went into the sitting room and sat down, still keeping up an artificially loud conversation.

'Just do what I say,' Gala said. 'You'll understand when the time comes!'

I closed my eyes, and reluctantly I thought of the party where the conflict would be resolved. First I saw Miles Alton, whom I hardly knew. He was taking ice from the icebox. His hair was long and golden. There were candles everywhere, and guests were coming up the stairs. I sighed at the banality of the vision. What on earth did Gala want? Perhaps to introduce Meg and Gilmartin, by way of disguise. My interest quickened. They would be there then, would they? We would carry the drooping body of Miranda together to Meg's house. K would come towards me with a smile I could almost see. So, in fancy dress . . . I closed my eyes harder, shutting out the movements of the street and the unbalanced, reddish room where I stood with Gala. I saw a man dressed as a monk, with a cowl pulled over his face. I saw a twist of full taffeta skirt as the stair was turned. I saw a face that had become detached from a face . . .

'Jane!' Tony was rattling the doorknob, as if the door was locked. 'Are you there? I'm back, you know!'

'Well?' said Gala softly. 'What do you see, Jane?'

'The face has slanting eyes,' I said. 'It stands on a stick. But there's no soul behind the eyes, Gala. What does that mean?'

'Jane, why did you lock the door? I hear you're not terribly well and I want to come in. Come on now, Jane!'

I turned to Gala, who still had me by the arm. I opened my eyes. Irritation . . . the red-dotted room was the colour of irritation . . . my vision was broken just as it began.

'Why did you lock the door, Jane? For God's sake open it!'

Gala went to open the door. I sank on the bed. I felt at a disadvantage, still in my nightdress with Tony there coated with the dust of International Airports, and his mother, who must have been up and covered in cosmetics for hours. I gazed down at my arms, which looked thin and white. How could it be me who would save the world, bring about conjunction when there had been so great a fissure? I was no more than a fragment myself. How many broken corners of humanity did Meg lure to her web in this way?

'A most disappointing trip! Rome was far too hot! And the worst bit of miscasting for years. Woody Allen as Captain Anthony. Really!'

Tony was sitting on my bed. I had the unpleasant feeling he had been there for some time. He had a hand on my leg and his hand was warm: the nylon nightdress was beginning to sweat under his touch. I saw that Gala had gone. There was the sound of voices from the next room. What could Mrs Marten and Gala, inhabitants of universes as remote from each other as the stars from the earth, ever find to say to each other?

'But, Jane . . .' (For I still made no move: I knew I was 'acting catatonic' and there was nothing I could do about it) 'I heard worrying reports from Mummy! Were you . . . did you really have to be so rude?'

This shifted me of course. I pushed Tony's hand away and stood up. Then I turned to face him, as if the bedroom had become some kind of tribunal. Tony's face was at least as red as Nixon's had been last night, I noticed. It was splotchy, as if the colour needed adjusting, and went into a vivid orange by his receding hairline. 'Do you honestly believe that it's my duty to put your mother up whenever she feels like coming to London?' I said. We had had this row so often that I saw Tony's features relax into spectator folds. It was my part to play the Japanese Noh theatre, and his to sit and growl from a distance.

'But you might have been a little more polite,' Tony mumbled.

'And so might she! She was just sitting here!'

'And where had you been?'

Ah, that's a good one! In the metal forest, my dear Tony, in Meg's white house with the red heart. In the forest clearing too, betraying you!

'I don't like the way she sees Miranda, and asks her to parties, and expects me not to mind!'

'Miranda?' Tony looked surprised. He glanced with a worried expression at the bedside table, to see if the photograph had been resuscitated there. We never normally call her by her name – that's why, too, he seemed particularly uncomfortable. I saw him wondering if I'd been to see Miranda: what I'd been 'up to' now.

'She's welcome to see Miranda, as long as she doesn't sponge off me,' I went on unnecessarily. 'Surely, Tony, you can see that?'

'But Miranda means nothing more to me . . . to her I mean . . . than an old friend . . . really, Jane . . .'

'Please ask your mother to leave the flat!'

I wasn't to be allowed that, though. The bedroom door opened – just as Tony was coming towards me in an attempt to remonstrate and give a kiss at the same time – and Mrs Marten put her head round it. Her body, which was in a white summer two-piece and very high white shoes, followed.

'My dear Jane, how are you this morning? Tony, don't you think . . . Jane looks so terribly *pale*. I *do* think you ought to have a holiday, Jane dear! Tony – be gallant! Take Jane away somewhere for some air!'

I saw Tony looking at me in the way he always did when he had decided I was menstruating. This would account for my rude behaviour, and also my paleness: I had discovered, in fact, that it could account for anything and therefore removed any proper claim I had to identity, as pre, post or current bleeding was always at the root of the problem. The same thought clearly went through the mind of Mrs Marten, and mother and son carefully failed to exchange glances.

'If only I could get this film settled,' said Tony, with the very definite air of a man who has no intention of going on holiday. 'But then we will . . . Mummy . . . Jane!'

'Gala your friend was telling me about the party tomorrow,' Mrs Marten went on. She crossed the room as if she had been invited to feel at ease there, and glanced out of the window. From where I stood I could see her profile in a buzzing orange that looked as if the colour overlay had been badly applied, and beneath her in the street a battered wife with her child making for the supermarket and the tanned cut-out women guarding the goods. She stared at them, oblivious of their existence. I turned angrily to Tony, but he was unpacking a small bag on the end of the bed and pulling out a dressing gown.

'I love fancy dress parties,' Mrs Marten said.

'Who said it was fancy dress?'

'Oh . . . I . . . I don't know. I just assumed it was. Did your friend tell me? I can't remember, darling. Why? Didn't you know? Haven't you got an outfit?'

Even Tony was beginning to be annoyed now, I was pleased to see. He clearly thought the best way to set me right again was to spend some time alone with me, and the presence of both Gala, whom he detested, and his mother, about whom he felt constantly guilty, was getting on his nerves.

'I want to have a bath,' he snapped. 'What is this party anyway? Do you mind, Mummy, I want to change and so on?'

'Dear, I'm so sorry and tactless!' Mrs Marten turned away from my view, having raped my private knowledge of the street from that angle, taking with her in the retina of her eye green trees and grass I couldn't see, and went girlishly to the door. 'I'll chat to your friend again, Jane! So fascinating to talk to artists. I used to know dear John Masefield, you know! But we'll all have a wonderful time at the masked ball, I'm sure of that!'

A masked ball. Of course, a masked ball. I saw the faces without eyes, floating in the dark rooms. Behind one of them was Meg . . . behind another was my dark, unknown enemy. The faces walked on sticks . . . I had to tear them from their owners' heads. I pulled the eyes through the holes in the white paper heads.

Tony had his arms round me. He always wanted to make love when he came back from these trips, as if it was the only thing that could ground him properly again. So he was concerned about my condition.

'Have you got the curse today?' he whispered. His tongue shot into my ear. I shrank from him, then pretended to succumb.

'No. But I've lost a lot of blood,' I said.

Tony made a satisfied, clucking sound – I was OK, now, then. He pulled me over to the bed. I lay under him. It was true, I was weak from loss of blood. There were red spots in front of my eyes, and whiteness, like when you are about to faint. I thought of the ball. Behind a mask on a long stick, prowling the dimly lit rooms, was Gil-martin, his shadow falling over me and replacing mine.

Tony's eyes were closed as he did his thrusting. Mine were open,

132

my head was to the side of him, and his mouth was fastened in a sucking shape a few inches above Meg's bites, of which he was as yet oblivious. I stared up at the ceiling at the naked light bulb. There had been a shade once, but the paper had cracked and it had fallen, and I had never bothered to replace it. The bulb swung slightly, from the draughts that always manage to penetrate the flat, even when the windows and doors are shut. It swung above me, on a brown flex. It swung back and forth, globular, growing in size, bursting from the ceiling like a giant droplet of dew. I saw faces there, and as Tony sawed into me I saw clouds in its full roundness, and the street in miniature upside down. Mrs Marten and Gala were talking next door – or at least Mrs Marten was talking to Gala, constructing an identity for herself, turning it around for the customer to see in the light, like a new mink coat. Tony drove on, powered like the planes which roar in and deposit him in different corners of the world. I divided for him, but my new emptiness made me slip away. I was no longer truly under him, a match of his own making. I was oblique, I was half-filled, I was diagonal. And as if he felt me disappear, he gripped all the harder until the bulbs above me dissolved, and the faces and people spilled into the room.

It's strange, to lie to the side of Tony and slightly above him, and see my own body still in his clamp, I can feel that people are searching for me . . . but they don't look there. I don't care to look down on my face. Suppose it weren't my own! And part of me still holds the sheet, so it must be me. Am I naked? No, I seem to be in a skirt like a little girl's skirt, so where are my jeans and jacket, if I'm to leave now on another journey? I am floating almost up to the level of the light bulb – can the Persian students opposite see me, flying without a carpet? The thought makes me smile. Am I taking this light-headedness with me to the other world? And the shopping women, some of whom look up into the sky on their return from the supermarket – will it rain today, wouldn't it be good to put the washing out for once? – do they see my weightless state under the swinging bulb?

In the crystal ball that hangs just beyond my reach I can see Meg in her red house, eating at her round table with a man. Below me in the room, Tony and my body are still locked, but there are other people there now, and a feeling of airlessness and suffocation as the room fills up. The red glow has disappeared, as if drawn back into the bulb, into the filaments of Meg and her companion. Above the crowd, which makes no sound at all, I swim fascinated a few inches from the bulb. Meg has a red and white spotted scarf on her head, like a gypsy scarf. Gil-martin – for I know it is him – is staring into the fire. In my peace and emptiness, I circle over him. He doesn't look up, but I have no need to see his face. We had rough times together when we were children, he and I! Then I lost him. He looks the same, a little sadder perhaps. For his sake I'll bring the shadow woman Meg needs, I'll drag her like a dead vole to their front door.

Meg is saying something. K leans towards her to listen. Both their faces are distorted in the rotundity of the light bulb, like funfair faces. I can see myself in him, though: K is I divided by $<$. And now I am alone and empty, with only a few mundane chores to carry out before we can be joined, I hover near them, separated from them by thin glass. A girl comes into the red, rounded room. She is Jane. I never saw her before like this. Was this the way Jane talked and moved? Against the sides of the swinging bulb I see Jane's life pass in flickering characters. She looks a fool there with Stephen, giggling . . . a colour that sums up a whole year of her life passes, scratched on the glass like a Chinese ideogram . . . a stone, next, that is the house where she lived as a child. And Tony. He stands, last in line of her worldly lovers, while the others, ahead of him, look at her without recognition, and jostle for a place to show off their importance. Poor Jane! She is in her own street now, which is still showing as tiny as when she was lying in bed, and she, as small as a witch's doll, is walking along it. When she turns into the garden of the block of flats, and the cuckoo spit on the already browning grass washes over her thumb-high legs, will she walk up and right into me?

Yet at the same time I can still see her, in the semi-transparency of Meg's room, sitting large as life beside Gil-martin. Below me, in the room where Tony and my body lie, it is dark and stifling. There is a smell of sweating flesh. In the red room, as my shrunken figure crosses the glass, Meg is speaking in a low, intense voice, and Gil-martin nods his head but still doesn't look at me.

'You can rest assured that society will thank you, will praise you for your bravery,' she is saying. 'For, just as society is responsible for the creation of such monsters as Mrs Marten and Miranda, so, when it is purged of them and reconstituted, it will exonerate you of any blame for violent acts performed symbolically. You are leading the way, Jane.'

I can see Jane nodding, although she looks afraid. What are they leading her into now? I wish I could break through the glass and discover how she feels. For it must be extraordinarily wonderful to be with Gil-martin like this, as close as if they met every day . . . and yet I can feel nothing, shut off out here. I'm not ready yet, I know, to find my wholeness but all the same . . . the scene in the red room is as frustrating as a romantic movie, with all those feelings nothing but dead celluloid. In my cut-off state, it's hard to imagine that I'll kill Tony's mother . . . but for Meg . . .

Jane gets up, she is ready to leave. I see that, like me, she is wearing a skirt that is too short and too tight for her. She looks like an overgrown child who has forced herself into her younger sister's clothes. Gil-martin turns in his chair and smiles at her. Meg goes to open the door. And the bulb shrinks and swings, glowing in a last, bright red as Meg and her companion turn to burning fibres once more. I am alone. I am Jane, or what remains of her. Like a heavy fish in an aquarium I float in the dark, confining room.

The room is smaller. The window has gone. Round my head, as I struggle downward to the cluster of people now obscuring the bed, are long dresses smelling of mothballs and scent, and skirts bunched on hangers, and ghostly ruched shirts. I know it is Ishbel's mother's cupboard. I can feel her in the clothes. We're hiding in the cupboard, all the children from the village, and Ishbel, and me – my annual invitation, along with the village children, to go to the big house. So it's Christmas. I remember walking along the road on the side of the hill. It wouldn't snow, although the clouds were heavy with it. I was in a best dress made of scratchy wool. And my mother stood at the gate to wave me goodbye. Her hand was the only thing that moved. There was no wind, just as there was no snow: the valleys and the sky were paralyzed, the slightest tremor would bring the storm, and obliteration. And all the colours were raw. It was almost January – the place needed the snow poultice. Then some of the terrible cold would go. I walked quickly, keeping my eyes on the frozen crevices in the road. When I broke out of the valley, and the next one opened up in front of me, I would see the house, which sat there as if it had always done so, smugly, in a square garden protected by hills.

Ishbel's mother and my father gave us tea at a long table in the main hall. It was a cheap village tea, and we ate slowly and politely. The food seemed to stick in our throats. The crackers only made a sound of tearing paper. My father made a speech. He said he was glad to see us there. He must remind us again that upstairs was out of bounds for games after tea. Now he was going to put out the light and we could see the Christmas tree. He would call out our names, alphabetically.

Yes, I remember that. I am down amongst the other children now, and a very faint light from under the door shows shiny, scrubbed faces and, in the case of the girls, hair wrenched back into bows for the party at the big house. How have we disobeyed my father like this and come up into the most forbidden place of all, Ishbel's mother's bedroom? My heart begins to race. It's my fault. It must be. I led them here, and we'll all pay the price for it – except for Ishbel.

The lights in the hall went out and the Christmas tree lights went on, as they did every year. The small children were pleased at the blue and the red and the green. I sat looking at the big windows in the hall, which stood as straight and bare as the branches beyond them in the garden. There was an early moon. Where did I come 'alphabetically' in the list of names this time? Some years my father avoided the embarrassment of my namelessness by calling me last as if I were an afterthought, or a guest, or someone who had turned up at the party by mistake – sometimes he got it over by summoning me first, before the children had settled and taken in what was going on. The girls always got dolls, the boys dinky cars. My row of dolls from past parties stood on the top shelf of the dresser in my mother's cottage. I never played with them.

The child next to me in the cupboard nudges me hard in the stomach. They can all hear someone coming but my heart is too loud for that. There's little air in here. The breaths are sweet, a mixture of cake and bread and paste. I think I can make out Ishbel, on the far side of the cupboard from me, leaning against the door. She looks excited and frightened. More of her vicarious thrills! For Ishbel will be only mildly punished for this. She came after all from the skirts which are draped round us, and we are from the outer ring, the squat houses which produce manpower for the big house. We have no right to be under her mother's skirts. Downstairs her motherly role is a farce. She would rather die than foster us.

This year my father called me last, so I had to wait with my hands sweating on my lap while the children were led up by their parents, and curtseyed or bowed and were led away again. When it was my turn to go to the tree I realized how much bigger I was than I had been the year before. And Ishbel's mother saw it too: she looked at me with hatred as she handed me the neatly wrapped package with the doll inside. I was big and awkward standing there, but she saw me as a woman no doubt, as my mother again. I was blinded for a moment by the lights from the tree and I blinked at her. She turned away abruptly. Usually there was a scatter of applause after each presentation, but now there was silence. I stumbled into the bench on the way back to my seat. The main lights went on. Now that his job was done, there was no sign of my father. I knew he had gone to his study, to take a drink.

Ishbel has edged her way through the crowd of children and is at my side at last. She looks up at me with teasing eyes. Yes, she engineered this! I remember now. We all played in the big hall, and there was some half-hearted thumping on the piano, and while the parents of the village children huddled round the fire and nervously turned down offers of cigarettes and tea, she made us climb the stairs at the far end of the hall. We had to go on hands and knees. We were on the first floor landing before we knew how we got there. And we ran down the dark passage as if we were trying to bury ourselves right in the centre of the house.

The steps are in the room now. It's my father, but there are other men with him as well. Ishbel is so close to me we could have been sewn together. The teasing look has gone and she is worried. But there is still something triumphant about the set of her shoulders and her round, spoilt face. By standing so close to me, of course, she is both protecting and condemning me. They won't strike in our direction, for fear of hitting her. But she will point the finger at me, and I'll be marched away. My ribs are tight with fear. One of the children begins to sob. And my father pulls the cupboard door open, our side first, as I knew he would.

What I hadn't taken into account is the torch. It hits me straight between the eyes, and Ishbel too, so that she whimpers aloud and claps her hands to her face. The game isn't funny for her any more. The other children file out miserably into the room. I hear my father ordering them to go downstairs, find their parents and go home. And as Ishbel and I instinctively edge backwards from the light into the depths of the cupboard, my hand clasps a dress and brings it down round my shoulders. Now I am really caught! The dress is light, and highly scented. I am standing in the bright light in the act of stealing Ishbel's mother's dress. My father, and Ishbel, and Ishbel's mother's dress, and I. There is absolute silence. My hand flies to my neck, to disentangle myself. It comes across something hard . . . a pin, a brooch . . .

'I'm so terribly sorry to disturb,' Mrs Marten said. 'But I feel the most *gnawing* pains of hunger. I know you're tired after the journey, Tony dear, but . . .'

Because our room was dark – Tony had pulled the curtains together before getting into bed – Mrs Marten appeared in the door in a fantail of light, her small body thrust forward and a gin and tonic sparkling in her hand. She stared greedily at us. 'Your dear friend is still here, Jane. Shall we all lunch together? I've discovered rather a sweet little Italian place round the corner.'

'Oh, Mummy!' Tony was on his back with his eyes closed. 'Do you really have to?'

The door opened wider. The light swelled to the shape of a bowl and began to encroach on the bed. I shrank from it, under the sheet, into the recesses of the cupboard where Ishbel still stood guilty and trembling, down to blackness. Even so, I could feel the stretching daylight on the top of the bed and round the room. When it saw me it would strip me bare. And I, white flesh and hair, crouching by the warmth of Tony under the covers, would be reduced to X-ray, gutted.

'If Jane isn't well she could have some soup here and we could go.' Mrs Marten's voice was muffled, but strong. 'Come, Tony, there's *nothing* in the house, you know!'

Then there was Gala. I was in the cupboard still. I heard Ishbel's mother's voice, her sharp cry of alarm when she saw her trampled dresses. I tore the pin from the thin folds of the dress that had got enmeshed around my shoulders. I fought with it, hung with the sweet-scented silk like an animal caught in a trap of leaves. I lifted the glinting pin, silver with a single bright blue eye.

'Go on,' said Gala. 'Now!'

'You'll come to the restaurant, I hope? I had such a lovely cannelloni there. And, you know, there's never *anything* here!'

Oh, I don't know how I could have done it! Ishbel was looking at me suddenly with such frankness. I could have trusted her with the rest of my life. She was very close to me again, crouching on shoes in the very back of the cupboard; there were discarded dresses there, neatly bundled but worn and old: in the skirts of a black dress we squatted like sisters, hiding from our mother the enemy. Her gaze was very soft ... very appealing! Her eyes seemed to have grown lighter, even in the gloom there, but her mouth and chin were ugly still: there was nothing she could do about that. She was quite unlike my mother. Why was she so close to me? I could feel her breath on my neck. And her shoulder looked as if it had sprouted from mine. I had to lean forward to press the pin home. Right in the middle, between her breasts that weren't yet breasts. It went in very easily, leaving the eye shining on her chest.

'Now run,' Gala said.

Ishbel fell as heavily as a dropped doll when I left her side. I dived under the beam of light from the torch. My father's legs were running towards me, but I dodged them. There ... to leave the house ... lighter already ... the great square house in the square garden was behind me when I was on the hill, in a total darkness. No snow. Thank God, no snow as yet.

'Perhaps I'd better book a table,' Mrs Marten said. 'He's a sweet man. Used to be at Da Lorenzo.'

Tony's legs were moving beside me in the bed. 'I'll get up then,' he said in the tone that suggests he is doing a lot of women a great favour. 'What's the time?'

'Well, that's the point! It's nearly two!'

'All right, all right. Come on, Jane ... aren't you hungry?'

Tony kicked me under the covers. In my darkness I knew Gala and Mrs Marten had left the room and closed the door. The light had gone. I saw the end of my race to my mother's cottage, but only in the dull reds and blacks of the dark room. That was all that was safe for me now. I must not be exposed. I could merge in the infra-red light, a shadow, half-developed, visible one minute, gone the next. But to go out into the street . . .

Tony pulled back the covers and gave me a quick glance. He dressed quickly and efficiently, snapping into his pants and trousers as if he wished he'd never taken them off. 'You look all right! You must be hungry, Jane, aren't you? Don't imagine I'm going to have lunch with Gala and my mother without you!'

It was certainly a strange party. It was true, I had to go. As always, I felt it was my fault for having Gala round there, rather than Tony's fault for having a mother like Mrs Marten. If I covered my head, stayed close to the wall . . .

Tony pulled back the curtains. I groaned again. The light pulled at the skin of my face. My eyes ached, as if the daylight would pull them out.

'You must have got a migraine,' Tony said. There wasn't a trace of sympathy in his voice. He pulled the quilt up over his side of the bed, and left the room. I lay there by his pristine side of the bed and wondered if I was even there. Had he been beside me; had we made love? I looked up at the bulb on the brown flex. It swung empty over my head. I pulled down Tony's cover and stared at the sheet. His stain was there, a grey mark shaped like a fish. I pulled the cover back.

Gala called me through the door. 'Get up, Jane! It'll be OK! You must eat, you see!'

They got me out with difficulty. I had to find a scarf for my head, and ended up with a black Greek scarf with gold sequins stitched on it that I had once bought on holiday in Delphi with another boyfriend – only to discover too late that the scarf denoted widowhood, death. I tied it under my chin and followed Mrs Marten and Gala and Tony out of the flat and onto the swirling lino. Mrs Marten's stiletto heels went down into the rubber with an airport sound and Tony trudged beside her: they might have been leaving, meaninglessly, for an international destination. I thought of the way they took and squandered and consumed the world, as if it had been laid out for them like a tray of hors d'oeuvres. Once, Mrs Marten would have been considered a sinner. Now she merely slimmed. I thought of Meg's instructions, in the crystal ball in my bedroom. And I could see Mrs Marten as disposable. The only sign of her non-existence would be an inscription on a board in her upholstered shrubbery: *For Sale*. It had been her motto, now it could be her epitaph.

We reached the street. How easy that sounds! Gala knew what I was suffering and hung back with me. The main door was open and Tony and his mother were passing through; I could see the patch of grass, grey of course, and by the gate the long uncut grass with the cuckoo spit, grey on grey now like an arty photograph. Beyond, the lumpy old women were walking, and a couple of grim youths in clerical 'fifties-style suits and steel-rims, conspicuous austerity. It was a brilliantly sunny day. The colourless trees cast deep shadows on the pavements. Broken glass outside Paradise Island glinted like coal in the shadows from the houses. I stood in the hall with my back to the grandiose mango wallpaper and my hands spread out on the walls by my side. How could I go out there? Had I really killed Ishbel? Or would she be waiting for me, always fleetingly behind me or ahead of me, blameless, triumphant, with a fixed smile on her lips above the stabbed heart? It was hard to believe she was gone. I had felt freer while anticipating her disappearance than I did now. Perhaps this was an omen – I would in no way benefit from the end of Miranda.

'It's only round the corner,' Gala said. 'Walk quickly and it'll all be over.'

I went out, still holding her hand – Tony hadn't waited for us and we had to pull the door open again: it had swung shut while I hesitated. Now we passed the long grass and opened the wrought iron gate, and we were in the street. Tony and Mrs Marten were quite a way ahead: just passing the battered wives' home, in fact, and I saw Mrs Marten look up at the building and give the little wrinkle of her nose which she considered a charming and rueful expression in the face of something unacceptable. I watched one of the women come out, with a two-year-old child in one arm and a bag of washing for the launderette in the other. She looked at Mrs Marten, in her white suit and her high white shoes and her white hair in a cascade of ringlets, as if she had just landed from the moon. Then she came along the street towards me. Her face was tired and her breasts drooped. She looked at me once, and then down at the pavement. Then she looked up at me again. Her eyes went wide. She pulled the child into her so that it wriggled at the tight grip.

'Keep walking,' Gala said. She spoke in a low voice. 'Don't stop!'

Why did I now feel the fear too? The woman wasn't Ishbel, after all. Or was she the first to notice that Ishbel was really dead at last? I watched her shadow approaching in ripples on the bars of the railings that guard basement steps and areas. It ran towards me, snaking on the bars, as large as a mother goddess, with the child fused into the body of the mother and the two heads rising and dipping as they came.

'Jane!'

Mrs Marten was standing outside Paradise Island now, in her 'model pose', stomach well in and head back, a tiny provocative smile on her lips. 'Do hurry, dear!' Behind her a powerful woman was cleaning the windows. She looked at me with impatience. What did she see? A sad woman in a black scarf, walking nervously near the railings as if she might have to cling to them for support, a sad woman accompanied by another woman with a singular lack.

Mrs Marten saw, at the same time as the woman from the wives' home was giving vent to her anxiety by literally breaking into a run, screwing up her eyes as if the sun had suddenly become too strong, dashing past me with a sort of muttered grunt of apology. Mrs Marten dealt with the phenomenon with a good deal more elegance, as she would certainly have expected of herself in the circumstances. She took Tony's arm – he too was standing impatiently at the junction with the main road, as if Gala and I were not to be trusted in a public thoroughfare – and went graciously up on tiptoe to whisper in his ear. I saw him frown. She didn't point, of course: that would have been bad manners.

It was then that Gala and I began to laugh. I was afraid still, and the laughter ran through me like electric current. Here, in the hard, bright street with the summer leaves that looked as if they had been sprayed with silver tinsel, and the sharp white paint on the houses, and the crooked black shade, and Mrs Marten standing upright and ridiculous in her white outfit, at the end of the street, were Gala and I walking without shadows, vulnerable in the extreme, shadows ourselves, spreading terror as we went! We were invisible except for our laughter, our nervous systems, our X-ray spines. If we had no shadows we couldn't be alive. And Mrs Marten, like a figure in a cartoon, frozen with disbelief, awaited us there. Outside Paradise Island, of all places! O women who love women, take heart from us! We drove away our shadows, and look at us now!

Gala still had a hold on my arm, as if to show we would be stronger together than apart. I felt my feet very light, I might float off the ground altogether, but not as I was when I flew at the command of Meg. I was weak, my body barely obeyed me. And now Mrs Marten was only a few feet away, with Tony at her side wearing an expression of utter incredulity. Our laughter seized us once more. What did this mother-and-son team want from us then? Respectable ladies with proper, well-dressed shadows, and bank cards in our handbags? Sorry we couldn't oblige! By the time we were at the corner of the street, the same mercury flowed in our veins. Whether we still belonged to this world or not, we would give the Martens all they deserved. And part of me marvelled at the way Gala could give me such empathy, as if the condition was hers for the first time too. Without her I might have been seized – exterminated – in the overpowering light of this day.

But the extraordinary thing was that neither Tony nor his mother referred to what they had seen. Tony nodded at us and said briskly: 'Funny we never noticed this place before, Jane. I wonder how long it's been going?' He indicated the restaurant canopy, which jutted out in the main road just beyond the super- market. And Mrs Marten, twinkling at Gala, said: 'Normally it's vitamins and a salad for lunch for me. But – I don't know why – I feel so *ravenous* today! It must be the party at the Belgian Embassy last night. Do you know, the food was virtually uneatable!'

Gala and I exchanged glances. The laughter turned warm and pleasant inside us. So the Martens couldn't face the confrontation! But we knew we were in a position of power now, and it was they who were afraid at last. Who and what did they think they were going to lunch with at the trattoria? Did they sense their hour had come? Tony, even, smiled in friendly encouragement at me as we went into the clean, Italian interior. He had seen me looking at the supermarket as we passed, perhaps, and as always had misunderstood my reactions. 'Look, Jane, if you've not been feeling too well in the last few days since I've been away, I'll get the shopping in this afternoon. Mummy says there's nothing in the house. I mean, I'll just get the basics, if you like!'

Eating and buying, shitting and dieting, the Martens stumbled towards their allotted places in the cemetery in the Surrey hills. That was expensive too: Tony's father was buried there and I had heard all about the cost. I shook my head, allowing myself a beatific smile. It was good, to feel the power of his fear. Mrs Marten was bending over backwards to sit Gala in the best seat at the table. She would do anything to postpone the hour of her death. Gala and I laughed again as we settled ourselves in the bright restaurant. Here, because of the bustle of people, and the moving light and shade from the low lamps which swing back and forth as customers come and go, our absence of shadows would hardly be noticeable. Perhaps that is what relieved Tony and his mother: unpleasant and embarrassing scenes could be avoided, for the moment anyway.

I WRITE THIS as the hour draws near, and in such confusion that I can't tell exactly what took place since yesterday . . . whether I dreamed . . . or if Mrs Marten put some drug in my wine at lunch . . . or how much I saw or imagined. Certainly the lunch went 'ordinarily' enough, with Tony and his mother discussing the prices of property in Central London, and the possible dates for shooting *Chance*, and summer holiday plans until, looking up and across Gala, who was eating quietly with her eyes fixed on her plate, I saw Meg sitting at a table opposite. There was a man with her . . . it was he . . . but he had his back to me. Meg smiled at me and waved. I stared. Mrs Marten noticed, of course, and, ever eager for social contacts, whipped an eyeglass from her bag. Then she turned to me and nodded. She still held the eyeglass aloft, and it was between Meg and me now, so that I could see her, magnified in a third eye, still smiling and very close. I flinched. Meg winked at me. Under the table I found Gala's foot and kicked it hard.

'Meg Gil-martin,' said Mrs Marten. 'An old Scottish family! I can't see who the man is, though!'

'Wasn't she at the Berrings' party?' said Tony.

Gala took my hand under cover of the tablecloth. I felt drained, half-alive. Between them, the Gil-martins and the Martens would crucify me, tear me from the material world into the outer regions, and back again. I saw land, I saw heaving seas, I saw a ship leaving a calm port, and a black cave in which I flapped without hope of escape. My face flamed. I looked down at my sitting body, polite by the white table, and the sun that fell in over the white tiled floor, and the hard white place where my shadow should have been. I looked up again. Meg was talking and laughing with her companion, as she had when she appeared in the glass in my bedroom. Had she come to give me moral support, to ensure that Mrs Marten would be dealt with as she ordained? I glanced from one woman to the other. Mrs Marten was preening herself in a compact mirror now, and Meg – or a slice of Meg – was reflected alongside her. Why did they seem suddenly so alike – I could hardly tell the difference! Or did I see resemblances everywhere, now that my own double was so near her end? I stared fascinated at the twin reflections – Mrs Marten was dabbing her nose – but Gala pulled at my fingers under the table and muttered to me to stop.

Some waiters went by with a trolley, and when they had passed and the space between the tables was clear again, Meg's table was empty. I heard myself gasp, and Mrs Marten's voice, from a great distance, asking what the matter was.

'Jane isn't herself,' Tony said succinctly. And so the rest of the meal went by, with Gala's and my high spirits somehow dampened by the reminder of Meg, and Tony and Mrs Marten at the zenith of their powers, their imposed vision of the world, their roundness and sureness in the face of our terrifying insubstantiality all the more crushing and oppressive as the pasta and veal-in-Marsala and crisp salad and chocolate sweet came and went.

I didn't go home after that. But I don't know what I did. It seems to me that I went to see Stephen . . . Gala must have helped me to get there . . . I remember his sitting room, with the curtains drawn. I must have asked him for darkness and closed them myself, for I can still see his large, comforting figure in the armchair and the outline of his face. He didn't seem surprised. But he couldn't help me either: my force was stronger than his, and slowly I disrupted the atmosphere of mild, complacent expectation of sanctity in which he lived. We sat in silence. From the corners of the dim room a cold wind got up, and there was the sound of rustling leaves. I closed my eyes. I knew the forest had pursued me here. After a while Stephen put his head in his hands. He was beaten, and we both knew it. But his fear made me uneasy, for I felt nothing but patience and resignation, a waiting for the night.

It came at last. I left Stephen without a word and went out onto the pavement. I was strong now in the cover of night, and I had a raging hunger. I was going to the house where Miranda lived, to reconnoitre, to plan for the next day, and my other sister walked with me but she, too, would soon be taken away. I knew that and I held her close. We walked through the dark streets, which were full of people as soundless as ghosts, and soon we were in the garden of that terrible house – it was a winter evening again and bright with stars – and we went in at the back door and up the uncarpeted servants' stairs to our room. What had we done? What crime would we pay for now? There was a note pinned to my pillow. It was from the mistress of the house. It said £2 each was to be deducted from the wages of Jeanne and Marie to repair the iron broken that morning. That was all. We stood and faced each other in the narrow room with the sloping ceiling and the dead flies that accumulated every day on the window sill. In the past, my sister would have sobbed. But now we just stared into each other's eyes. Four eyes – dark – fringed with black.

It took me some time to arrive at Miranda's house. It was a house that had been converted into three flats, and I knew she lived at the top, also in rooms with attic ceilings; she would have made the flat 'sweet', though, and there would be bunches of flowers in the wallpaper. I saw her at once, outlined against the window, staring straight down at me as if offering her throat. She was pale, her eyes were black, and there was a slight smile on her lips.

Marie took the note from the pillow and scrumpled it into a ball. She was the strong one now. I had never seen such hatred in anyone. She turned to me and her eyes told me to follow her. So I went back down the stairs, but on the landing where the baize door to the bedroom floor stood closed, we stopped as if we knew that this was where we must stay. We stood there, by the door which was there to muffle our sound. We looked down the well of the poorly lit stairs, and we smelt the dinner for the rich Aldridge relations. Pheasant and breadcrumbs and green beans. We were meant to be there, handing it. Instead we had fled across the frosty fields and tried to escape but, as always, we were driven back by cold and hunger and we had failed. What would they do to us, now we hadn't turned up? My God . . . they were helping themselves . . . we could hear chairs scraping and heavy footsteps, and the popping of a cork.

Miranda opened the window and leaned out. She wore a black silky top, which showed her white breasts as she leaned towards me. I thought I could see behind her a kitchen exactly like my own. Yes, even the white enamel drainer was the same, hanging on a peg over the sink. She was still smiling, but without any gaiety, as if she was expecting me to come up and take over her kitchen there and then. But I wouldn't! I hugged Marie to me. I wasn't ready yet, and neither was Meg. Poor Miranda, she would simply have to wait.

Marie and I were still very close together when the baize door suddenly opened and Mrs Aldridge and her daughter appeared on their part of the landing. They must have left the dining room, come in search of us, keener on vengeance for the broken iron and our truancy than on their own rich food. Behind them the soft colours of the main passage glowed, red and gold in the Persian carpet that ran the length of the passage, orange in the walls hung with oils of horses and loved dogs. Mrs Aldridge's scent was strong that night. I tried to step back, pulling Marie with me. It was then I realized she wasn't going to come.

If you don't retreat, you must either stand still or go forward. I felt the pull in me as Miranda, perversely, as if she half-hoped to plunge to her death in my arms, leaned further out of the window, and Marie, unrecognizable in her strength and determination, stepped forward until she was within a few inches of our employers. Now that Miranda was poised like a swimmer about to push off from the bar, more of the kitchen was visible behind her. I saw the black and white jars, labelled 1, 2, 3, 4, in which I keep coffee and sugar and old herbs I never use. I resented her having these too! Did Tony buy two sets then, furnish two kitchens at the same time? But as I stared at the numbers on the jars, I felt my hands going up – as if I wanted to get up there, to take hold of them as my property, to unstopper them and take the contents – and my hands were on Mrs Aldridge's daughter's throat, twisting, unscrewing, squeezing the porcelain neck. Marie had pulled out her mistress's eyes! They lay on the landing, one on the rich Persian carpet and the other nearer the edge where the bare boards began. Louise! I saw her distracted gaze as I knelt on the hill with the sharp stone in my hand. My mother . . . my Marie . . . generations of cruel mothers in rich corridors fell under our blows. When they had gone we would be whole. Well, we had the women so close they couldn't make a sound, except for a choking fighting for breath that sounded like wind going through the winter branches of the trees outside.

Still, Miranda was smiling down at me. I was horrified at her. Couldn't she see what she was doing: condemning Marie to death, and therefore herself too? For I saw now for the first time that Marie had put scissors in her pocket before running down from our room – and a length of piping which she must have always had concealed on her from the beginning of the afternoon when we tried to run away. The piping was thrust into my hand. How did I follow suit and hack them to pieces like that? The blood began to flow quite freely, sinking into the carpet without any difficulty, but running thin over the wooden boards, leaving erratic stains which leapt in front of my eyes as I struggled with my prey. Oh, we were grunting by now, Marie and I. And I had the daughter's eyes out too: I threw them down the passage with a shout that brought the men running. But Marie had never been so close to me. It was my last day with her, and we were half-drowned in blood!

Miranda took herself back into her kitchen. She drew across a curtain that flowered in pink and white, quite unlike mine. I stood on the pavement beneath her window, with the streetlamp shining on me and my eyes in deep shadow, as she had once stood beneath me. But I don't know how I got home. The streets were empty then of the silent crowds – I must have walked again – and this time there was no Marie at my side.

The men found us in our room, where we had fled after my shout. There was such a smell of fresh blood in the corridors, so many hacked limbs lying there, there was almost an instinct in me to tidy it all away before I ran. But Marie grabbed me . . . we stripped off our clothes . . . we lay deep in the narrow bed. Then the men came and wrenched us apart. Their sobs were loud and hoarse. I knew, as they carried Marie's unmoving body from the room ahead of mine, that she would die in a prison cell far from me.

'Jane, my dear!'

Mrs Marten's voice comes through the door. It must be late, there is sun behind the curtains and Tony has got up and left for work. Someone has hung a ballerina dress of pink net with a spangled bodice on a hanger on the outside of the cupboard, and beside it my dusty jeans and jacket. What can this mean . . . where did the dress come from? . . . and who has been interfering with the clothes I will wear when I finally go? It's Mrs Marten, of course. This is intolerable! I spring out of bed, but the glare from the day gives me a headache and I sink back again. I can hear her stepping about in the passage, as if she's trying to make up her mind to come in.

'I do think you should have some coffee! And what do you think of the outfit?'

This gets me to the door and I pull it open with a violence that obviously surprises her because she titters and waltzes away from me in the direction of the kitchen.

'What is that dress doing in my room?' I can hear my voice

still thick with exhaustion from the night. 'And where did you find those jeans?'

'My dear, do they belong to a younger brother? I didn't know you had one!' Mrs Marten stands in the doorway to the kitchen, arms akimbo and eyes blazing with malice. Over her arm is what appears to be a harlequin costume. One blue leg and one red dangle against her thigh. A cap with bells is suspended from the kitchen door-handle. I feel a chill . . . a terror . . . I will certainly never be able to despatch Mrs Marten into the other world! She will haunt me forever, bells ringing softly as she moves . . . divided, lozenge-patterned body thin and nimble as a cat.

'The ballerina dress belonged to my poor dear sister,' says Mrs Marten. She must guess at my thoughts, for she is backing slowly into the kitchen as she speaks. In my panic I know Tony is miles away: she may have sent him away forever. I must be on my guard now, for it's a battle to the end between us. Yet I have never felt clumsier, less alert.

'I just felt I would love you to wear it, you see! Do, Jane – it would make me so happy to see her again in you. She was quite promising as a ballet dancer, you know – but then grew a teeny bit too tall. And then . . . I thought I'd told you all this before but sometimes, you know, one is too upset to talk about these things . . . she died. Mummy and I were . . .'

I walked along the passage, monstrous in size compared to her. My nightdress sucked at my heels. 'I'm sorry to hear that,' I said. 'What did she die of?'

'Too tragic. Leukaemia. It often takes the young and gifted, I fear! So, Jane, will you? But I'm being too awful when you haven't had your coffee yet. Look, I've got it ready for you!'

I'm at the kitchen door. I reach for the handle, but the little jester's cap repels me. I step in. My kitchen is less familiar to me than Miranda's. Is it just that I can no longer stand the light? Even the white enamel strainer on the peg by the window looks somehow like a copy of the original. But there's something else . . .

'It may seem banal to you that I should want to go as Pierrot! But do you know it's always been a dream of mine . . . ever since I was a child.'

Now Meg's voice begins to sound in my head. The rosy glow, which always intensifies when she comes to me, dots the strainer over with red and makes a sunset on the white lino floor. I take another step forward.

'She's Mrs Aldridge, Jane! Think of your and Marie's bravery last night! And think of the great deed that lies ahead. But first, Jane, before she destroys you . . . take her . . . with the knife!'

'I must say I'm rather grateful to have been invited to this do!' (Why is Mrs Marten apparently intentionally leading me on, drawing me further and further into the kitchen, she is almost by the window now, where Miranda leaned out so perilously last night.) 'I spoke to Miranda this morning and she said she'd been invited too. She says she knows the film director *very* well . . . she's known him for years. It's extraordinary how many people Miranda knows, don't you think, Jane?'

I'm sure I've never seen this knife before. It's smart and has a French name on the handle. Did Mrs Marten buy it for the purpose? Will she spring forward, wrench it from my grasp?

'Jane, do you want to cut some bread with that knife? If so, I've moved the bread over here, near the window. I thought the bin was in *such* a fusty place! And that's when I came across that rather dirty pair of jeans, and jacket. I hope you don't mind me popping them in your room, but I thought if you looked at them you'd be bound to decide to give them to Oxfam, or something!'

Mrs Marten has become quite breathless. I am advancing on her, which she seems to have willed, but as I walk I feel my feet drag on the floor, and a wave of faintness come over me. Oh, not now . . . the faintness takes part of my vision, so that I see only segments of the room, and the window, and small chips of Mrs Marten like a mosaic with missing pieces. I can feel my legs give, and bring me down to the floor . . .

'Jane, I *told* Tony you weren't well. I think we should call the doctor! I don't think you should go to the party at all!'

Meg, where are you now? I lie on the floor and stare up at the ceiling. I begin to choke. The white bulbs hang together as thickly as fungus growing on a tree. They are hung on wires, and the wires are nailed in to the corners of the ceiling. They are round and white, but their skin is flaky, like paper. My mouth opens, but I can't even retch. And as I lose consciousness I know Mrs Marten can't have fixed them up there on her own. So Tony helped her! They know how to make me disappear! My eyes close, as the bulbs swell, and come down on me . . .

I am in bed. So I'm ill. It must be late afternoon, the light is comfortable to the eyes, but how weak I have become! Did Meg know the battles I would have to survive in this world before she let me into the other? Crash! There go the soft drink crates outside Paradise Island . . . it must be even later than I thought . . . it's strange, but now I can't see the street and the trees that are dead to my eyes, and the generations of women on the pavement, I miss it . . . I don't really want to leave. I'm afraid of catching Miranda, and going to the new regions. Suppose I could become a part of this street and walk every day to the supermarket and dance with the women at Paradise Island, and talk to the bruised women, and grow old with the women with their parcelled bodies, wouldn't it be better, more accepting than what I have in store? But Meg tells me I will never suffer. I'm sanctioned, so she would have me believe.

I look round the room. Certainly they're treating me like an invalid! Stephen is sitting in a chair at the end of the bed, and Gala is cross-legged on the floor near the window. Am I as ill as all that? They've brought grapes, and bunches of sweet peas and roses. The sweat peas are right by my bed, on the low table where Miranda's photograph once lay. They look like moth's wings, only in the colours of an early sky. I don't like them . . . I try to move the jug, but my hand is trembling and misses it altogether.

Stephen is smiling reassuringly at me. Am I going to die then? What have Tony and his mother done?

'Where's Tony?' I say. 'And ... what time is it?'

'It's six,' Gala says. 'Tony'll be back in a minute, won't he?'

'What happened to me? Am I ill?'

'Mrs ... Mrs Marten rang *me*,' Stephen says. 'She said you were ill. And Gala too I suppose ... what did she say to you, Gala?'

Thank God, they can understand my anxiety. Has Mrs Marten formed a plan to stop me from going to the party? She suspects, perhaps, that I was going to follow Miranda from room to room and – how clever! – she's pinned me here with my friends instead.

'She said she'd been worried for some time,' Gala says. 'Had been particularly worried at our lunch!' At this, Gala burst out laughing and I tried to smile – but the vile substance from the kitchen was still in my mouth and to move my lips was painful.

'She even went so far as to suggest that you had a disease her younger sister died of ...'

'Yes,' Stephen puts in. 'She told me the doctors thought you had leukaemia.'

'But it's unbelievable ...' I struggle to sit upright. Now I see that both Stephen and Gala are looking very upset. Am I so pale, then? Is Mrs Marten going to finish me off so easily?

The door opens. Tony comes in. The draught from the opening door ruffles the curtains and, as they blow apart, for an instant I see the grey leaves on the top branches of a tree and a new moon, cruelly small and thin, hanging in the sky. The parrot gives a long whistle. Tony is followed by his mother – of course: I stare at Gala and Stephen, willing them to stay, dreading that they will go now or just disappear into the ether.

'I agree we should get the doctor,' Tony is saying to Mrs Marten. 'If we can get him to come quickly ...' He leaves the sentence unfinished. What he means is he can get the doctor's visit over and still make the party. Tony wouldn't like it very much if he had to give that up while sitting here with me! And what would he tell Miranda, waiting in her black dress for him to come?

'We can stay with Jane and wait for the doctor,' Gala says quickly. She knows, I'm sure, that she can make me better in time to get there myself. She'll get Meg over – anything.

'Oh I don't think it would be right for the family to leave Jane!' Mrs Marten says, and gives a low laugh that is supposed to be self-deprecating and compassionate. Instead, there is the chill of terror in the room again. Tony catches his mother's eye and nods.

'Luckily, I prepared rather a delicious meal,' says Mrs Marten. 'And of course if Jane shows improvement we could probably leave her for a minute and pop off to the party. It's your favourite, Tony darling!'

'What's that?' Tony has settled himself on the end of the bed in a husbandly way. I know he dislikes Stephen as well as Gala, and he keeps his eyes carefully away from both of them.

'Why, lobster with aioli, of course! Don't you remember when we went to Avignon and you ate *so* much of it you were nearly sick!'

'Hmm,' Tony says. (Yet I know he must have hung the garlic there, that it was really all for me.) 'Well, Mummy, it sounds delicious!'

'Gala, would you like to come in the kitchen and see the little feast I've prepared?'

What extraordinary behaviour! In all my weakness I can only gasp at Mrs Marten's cool insolence. But Gala knows only too well what would happen to her, even though I haven't had a chance to describe the wicked bulbs suspended from the ceiling. She shakes here head.

'I'd rather stay here with Jane, if you don't mind.'

'I expect you would!' Mrs Marten gives her venomous laugh. But she seems too much in control of the situation. Where has she found her new power? She stands a moment longer in my room, with the Pierrot costume still swinging on her arm. Tony switches on the lamp, from which I recoil – she has never seemed so white, from her hair, to the dead whiteness of her face, and the white chiffon at her throat and the neat little suit and white shoes. Her eyes look out from sockets dark with eyeliner and mascara.

'I'll go and ring the doctor now, Tony dear! And then we'll eat. See you in a moment!'

There are so many people on the stairs. It's strange how the women are dressed: about half of them are witches and have black robes and pointed hats – some of them have even stuck on big, curved noses and their eyes are bright – and the others are courtesans, seductive and tempting, with beauty spots on their breasts and flounced, pretty skirts. When they look at me they smile openly. But I press on, waiting patiently to get to the top. There I will find Miranda. Every minute my strength returns.

Stephen tried to stop me from coming. He told me I should go with him, and he would help me to find Life. He had a handkerchief he kept taking from his pocket. He mopped his face with it. It's true it was oppressive in there, with the curtains still closed and the evening sounds coming in from the hot street. Every few minutes he put it back in his pocket and pushed it down before pulling it out again. Gala told me I must go. I lay listening to them, still very weak – Tony had muttered an excuse and gone to help Mrs Marten with the presentation of the aioli in the kitchen – and at one point I could have sworn Gil-martin came and joined my friends in that room, sitting on the end of the bed where Tony had sat and looking straight into my face. Yet I still couldn't describe him, if I tried: I only know I was relieved and happy to see him there, and promised I would pay no attention to anyone who tried to prevent me from carrying out my task. I would be with him later that night. I would find him when it was time.

The doctor came, a doctor I had never seen before. He said I was tired. I remember the syringe he held up to the light, and Gala knocking it from his hand. He left after an angry consultation with Mrs Marten and Tony in the passage. Then Tony came in and said supper was ready. I said I had to get dressed and

they all left the room except Gala. That was how we escaped –
but look at me now!

All my clothes had gone from the cupboard. Mrs Marten must
have taken them. All she had left me were the jeans and the
jacket, and the ballerina dress: the tulle skirt was pink, and bulged
out into the room from the tin hanger, on the bodice was an
assortment of tarnished sequins. And of course the jeans won't
fit me till later, I'm on Miles Alton's staircase in the ballet dress
and that's why people smile. It's none of me, as they say. They
must imagine it's some buried fantasy of mine! But I don't care.
I look up and down the staircase; some of the women are in
masks; there are even one or two Pierrettes, holding the little cat-
grinning faces in front of their own. None of them is Miranda, I
think. If only they would go up faster! Some of the men, who
know me slightly, are laughing at me openly now, and my mood
of defiance won't last. Gala is beside me, as always, and a stair
higher up. She is pushing with her shoulders and her face is set.

We left the flat so easily it amazes me they hadn't thought we
might run when we had the chance. Stephen is too greedy – he
was exclaiming with pleasure at the scarlet lobster and the great
bowl of pounded garlic paste. Tony was being ordered by Mrs
Marten to try and find 'good knives and forks, if such a thing
exists in poor Jane's flat', and was bustling to bring up chairs.
Their sense of politeness and taste and good living let us get
away into the night in search of our prey! It will always be
possible, in the end, to defeat such people, because if you choose
the middle of dinner their defences will be down. We simply
went down the main stairs and out onto the lino of the hall. I
was carrying the jeans in a bag. We shut the main door and went
out of the gate into the street. It was a dark evening. The new
moon had gone higher up into the sky. We looked back once and
there, sure enough, were the three of them in my kitchen window,
smiling at each other rapturously. Gala had put her coat over my
shoulders so that no one in the street, at least, could stare at

my outfit. This time ... it was the very last time ... I knew I would never come back.

When we get to the top of the stairs I see that all the rooms have been draped with material, as if Miles Alton is trying to persuade people they're in the Arabian Nights. There are some real Arabs in evidence, no doubt he has his eye on them to put money into his films, and some stupid young English journalists wearing Arab headdresses. On either side of Miles, who has long golden hair, two chins and a stomach gently pregnant in a striped caftan, stand a 'beautiful lady', thoroughly enjoying herself in her period costume, which pushes her breasts forward and makes it possible for her to wink and flirt behind a fan, and a tall, raven-haired witch with a false nose and a mouth under it as thin and red as a gash. What happened to women, that they were forced into these moulds? At least there are no 'wives' here, that would be too boring for a fancy dress ball! Unless ... I grab hold of Gala's arm. At the far end of the room where we're now standing I see a figure in grey chiffon flitting about in front of a large candelabra. Her hair is dark. She is quiet and grey as a moth. I think she has a mask on, but at this distance it's difficult to tell. Surely ... only Miranda, the rightful wife of Tony, the quiet, dark wife, would present herself at this gaudy occasion in such a way. Yet of course I had envisaged her in quite another way! Scheming, anxious to 'make' it in the film world, willing even to be taken up by a rich Arab and have money to spend. Why should I suddenly be convinced that this was she? Ah, Miranda ... she changes and dissolves as I do ... and as my force comes back to me now, fed by the night and the hunger that is beginning to return, she melts into softness, a wedding ring, a veil.

Gala is nodding at me in response. She says we must go in search of Miranda. We begin to push our way through the crowded room. Some film critic in lemon shorts and a tank top comes up to me and asks why I wasn't at the showing of the Francesco Rosi this morning. How hot it is in here! The incense is too strong, the heavy sweet smell of dope is rising above it and there are broken clouds of smoke on the ceiling, on the loosely hung, theatrical material which comes down in a clumsy swag in the middle of the room like a tent. There are arum lilies. Why are there so many mirrors, enclosed in swirls of bright gold, all the length of the room? I can see the reflections of the fancifully dressed, faded as ghosts in the antique glass. Some of the people are already lying on cushions the size of small boats. And suppose it isn't Miranda, or I fail, as I failed with Mrs Marten earlier on. What will be my fate then?

'About power, as all his movies are,' says the film critic. 'I thought you'd be there, actually.'

I grin at him – he is too polite to make reference to my ridiculous *tutu* – and press on, pulled by Gala. I look round once. Horror! There is Mrs Marten already, prancing in her Pierrot costume in front of Miles Alton at the door. The little gold bells on her cap are jigging with her. I can see three of her, positioned as she is within the loom of three mirrors. In each she grimaces and gesticulates and turns her head wildly, as if searching, like me, for someone in the room. Stephen is behind her. He must have gone home in order to dress up in purple ecumenical robes: it seems strange that he should parody his faith in this way. And Tony, of course, has made no concession at all. But he looks just as irritating in his suede jacket and white polo neck as the other guests in their wild gear.

'Come on! If you go on looking at them you'll lose her for good!'

Gala is right. And now I find, as I reach the far end of the room by the big candelabra, that she has disappeared too, losing faith in me perhaps as I stood gaping in fear at Mrs Marten and her son and my friend hung with his gold crucifix. Gala is nowhere to be seen. I know none of the people standing round me. There seems to be a preponderance of beauty patches, and a scarcity of witches. One of the men had decided to come as a vampire: he has fangs of white card down to his chin, and strokes of black eye pencil on his face to suggest wickedness. He looks at me and then quickly away, as all the men do when they see the obscenity of my ballerina dress. If he could know . . . My mouth, which had been dried, revolted, by the horrors of the garlic in the flat, is rosy and juicy inside as freshly killed beef and my teeth, which will be so urgently needed tonight, are beginning to grow. They ache slightly, but not painfully, as they descend over my lower teeth into my jaw. How am I to find her? It must be soon. Yet this end of the room seems to be a dead end. The walls are covered with plum silk and oil paintings of men in breeches and long coats.

One more glance over my shoulder. A waiter passes and I nearly knock him over. I take a glass of champagne. I can see Mrs Marten making her way towards me. Her white face looks more of a mask than the real ones, some of which are on sticks, as I dreamed, and waving animatedly in their owners' hands. Her face is blind and intent and terrible. A smile is set on it. She is threading her way through the crowd, horrifying in her harlequin suit. I back up against the wall at the end of the room . . . my glass swills round and the champagne spits out on the ground . . . three beauties turn their backs.

It's then that I see the hairline crack in the plum silk, neat as an incision and following the contours of a low door, but where . . . without daring to turn and face the wall I seek the handle under a long picture of a lady in a crinoline dress. There . . . my hands are sweating so that they slip from it as soon as it is found. A protuberance of metal on the silk . . . my fingers close over it again, and twist and push.

Mrs Marten is nearly on me. First a red leg and then a blue prances forward, like an illusionary army. Some way behind, I see Stephen's face, very flushed over his purple robe. There is no sign of Tony. I duck down under the picture and go backwards, half on my back, through the hidden door. I land on my bottom, on a parquet floor, and kick the door shut with my ballet-slippered foot. I crawl forward, see the gold bolt on the door and pull it across. There! She can't get me now! But someone must have slid the bolt the other way to let me in here at all.

The room is just as I imagined it would be. It is small and square, and empty except for two small tapestry settees and a tall mirror framed with antlers of gold. The curtains are dark velvet and are tightly drawn although it is a summer night. There are candles, in a glass chandelier. And Miranda is standing in front of the mirror quietly contemplating herself. Her dress is grey and fragile. Her eyes are grey. She has added a Spanish comb to her dark hair now: it is studded with moonstones which are too dim to shine much in the light from the candles. Her expression is serious. Has she seen Tony yet? Or did they plan to meet in here? Was it for him that the door was left unbolted? What a disappointment for her that I should come instead!

I come up behind her. Did she ever keep a photograph of me? Does she know, secretly, what *I* look like? Or will she guess at once, and turn as if she's been struck in the back?

But she can't see me. I'm not there! I stand so close to her now that the slightest movement of my hand would touch her back . . . I look up and into the mirror . . . my terrible absence is there in the glass, which shows the trim settees and the bottom half of the chandelier with the candles burning fierce and upright without a flicker. My non-existence there is almost concrete . . . unreflected I feel heavier, as abandoned as a new corpse. My limbs are paralyzed. I keep on staring at her. Her eyes are dim as the moonstones in her hair. And though neither of us can see me she senses me there. Her mouth opens to call out in fear.

I close in on her . . . My teeth go into her smooth neck. Miranda . . . these are my hours . . . when it's so dark outside that I can fly the streets without dread of the stake, ravenous, insatiable! You knew I was coming! You welcomed me almost. You give me your blood!

It was strange to hold Miranda in my arms like that, while Tony and his mother battered on the door behind the picture, and Stephen called to me to come out in the name of God. The blood gushed from her neck like a spring. As I drank she paled. And when the grey irises of her eyes went up into the whites and she fell backwards into my arms, I knew she was ready to take to Meg. I knew, too, how I could escape the room without going back the way I came. I pulled open the velvet curtain nearest to me, pushed up the window with one hand, and stepped out onto the parapet. There were iron stairs, just like the fire escape at home. And Gala was waiting at the foot of the stairs, with a black cab. How easy it was! I carried Miranda down without difficulty, and together Gala and I laid her on the back seat. We sat facing her on the way to Meg's, in the bucket seats.

As we travelled I looked at Miranda, and I saw the cupboard and Ishbel, and the stairs and Marie, and I saw the small, square room fill suddenly with hiding children, and the iron stairs of the fire escape, which dripped with Miranda's blood, turn to the wooden stairs in the servants' quarters of the mansion. I saw myself, in Mrs Marten's sister's ballet dress, sisterless now and ready to go. Poor Miranda! I felt sorry for her. In her own way she enjoyed life, and she made Tony happy. But in the end I was the more important of the two.

And now . . . after taking her to the red house . . . Meg delighted with me . . . I've changed to my other clothes and I walk or fly to the port. I can see the green glow from the port long before I arrive there . . . and for sentimentality's sake I take the route past the hoardings and the supermarket in the main street at the end of my road. Yes . . . as I go past so much higher than they, I see the women crowding into Paradise Island . . . husbands hanging about outside the home . . . cardboard cut-out women holding their painted Lil-lets aloft in the sodium glare. I don't look back at the flat where I live, or the glowing rooms of the Persian students opposite . . . I'm pulled by the moon, although it's small and new.

There are the sailors, there is the ship. The gangway is down.

I go straight on board. And as soon as I'm there we begin our voyage. There is music, and the green lights are reflected in the oily sea.

We go out into a night that is quite black and starless, with even the moon gone. I think of Meg, as I strain my eyes in the darkness. She was so happy! I gave her what she needed! I turn to go down into the ship. But they've put the lights out here too. And that's best for me . . . for in the absence of the light I can begin to see him . . . I know he is there . . . as we sail on, with the music silenced and the waves hardly more audible than the sighing of grass on a hill, I see him standing there, by my mother's cottage on the hill . . .

Gil-martin comes towards me. The ship sails through the deep folds of the hills. I knew he would be there waiting for me!

EDITOR'S NOTE

A FEW WEEKS after reading this 'journal', some interesting new discoveries were made as to the whereabouts of Jane. In the interim, however, I had shown the document to the chief psychiatrist at the ——— hospital in London, and he and his colleagues prepared the following report. If the new discoveries seem to go rather against the findings printed here, the latter may still be of some worth to students.

Psychiatrists' Report

Jane is a schizophrenic with paranoid delusions. She is an example of the narrow border-line between depth psychology and occultism: in her case the alternation of the rational and the irrational is particularly stressed by the introduction of the supernatural. There are clearly acute problems of sexual identity, but we would suggest that there were never any such people as 'Meg' or 'K' 'Gil-martin', and that these are projections of the patient's lover Tony Marten and his mother Mrs Marten, who were unsatisfactory in their relationships with the patient, and therefore appeared to be threatening. 'Jane's' mother seems an example of the schizogenic mother, on the one hand encouraging belligerence and independence in her daughter, and on the other demanding her attention and care.

So how are we to sum all this up? The psychiatrists went on at some length about the nature of Jane's illness – I have omitted to print this as I feel the combination of the recent discoveries, with the fact the psychiatrists showed little interest in the 'political' factor involved in her conversion (or coercion), largely invalidates

the report. Is she a victim of the modern resurgence of the desire
for the old magic of wholeness, for unified sensibilities? Is she
really an example, as some women would have it now, of the
inherent 'splitness' of women, a condition passed on from divided
mother to divided daughter until such day as they regain their
vanished power? As the reader will have gauged, this is not my
territory, though as a field of study it appears to be expanding
fast. I can only marvel at the cleverness of Margaret, or Meg,
who appears, to borrow the words of a friend of mine to whom
I recently showed the journal, to have 'used Freud and Jung to
achieve the aims of Marx'. (In the event, of course, she lost out,
and the Dalzell fortune is now in the hands of a second cousin,
another Michael Dalzell. I sometimes wonder even, if Stephen
was correct in his conjecture that it was the money only that
she was after, but it does seem the most likely motive.) The odd
fact that there is no mention of the killing of the father must keep
the identity of Jane as his killer uncertain; but I am now more
of the opinion of Stephen than I was: that a state of hypnotism
prevented her from remembering that evening in March 1976.

After my failure to find Stephen, subsequent to reading the 'journal' – and on my trip to London in July I made exhaustive and
unrewarded enquiries in the Notting Hill area as to the existence
of a community of women by the name of Wild, I returned north
convinced that if only I could find Jane and Meg (Gala too was
untraceable: it seemed she had left shortly before for Egypt and
had no plans to come back) I would be able to solve the crimes
and demonstrate to the public the increasing dangers of fanaticism. But when, three weeks ago, I saw the following announce-
ment in the *Scotsman*, Thursday, September 4th, 1986, I sensed
that my searches might well have come to an end. It ran as
follows:

'Disturbances' Reported Above St Mary's Loch
'Strange noises and intense gusts of cold air at irregular

intervals' were reported yesterday by men employed in the investigative drilling of —— Law (formerly part of the Dalzell estate, now Government property) above St Mary's Loch. The drilling is one of several in the area for a suitable site for the burial of plutonium, the Cheviots having now received the maximum quota under safety regulations. The 'disturbances', which caused men to down tools at midday – some say they won't return to work until the area has been thoroughly searched – seemed to emanate mainly from a circular clearing in the remains of the old Ettrick Forest. Conservationists had put forward a plea (unsuccessfully) that these ancient birches should be spared the axe, and it seems that it was at the felling of the first tree that these noises – 'wailing, shouting' and cold air prevented the workmen from going any further. There had, according to Mr B. Elliot of Tibbieshiels, been some kind of a history connected with the place, and the clearing was thought locally to be haunted. The origin of the haunting is considered to be a young woman who had come to the village one night in the late 1970s, asking for bed and board. She was clearly tired and agitated, and was covered in mud. Although she had no money on her the proprietor gave her a room at St Mary's Arms. When he went up to the room in the morning she had disappeared. A child in the village saw her heading for the hills towards the old birches. Ever since, there has been fear and distrust of the clearing, although it was very infrequently visited, of course, being very high in the hills. All those who had seen the young woman said there was 'something funny' about her, and some described her as 'like a walking corpse'. However that may be, the Ministry intends to continue drilling on the site on Monday.

Two days later, on the Saturday, I was walking up the steep hill above St Mary's Loch with the Mr B. Elliot mentioned in the newspaper report. He refused any remuneration, and when I said I knew probable relatives of the deceased he became very sympathetic, and after his wife had packed up some sandwiches for us we set off.

It would be hard for me to describe the effect that lonely walk had on me after all the long months of searching for my quarry. The purple heather, which gave off puffs of a dusty pollen as we went along, and the rather dark, low clouds which were occasionally broken by an early autumnal sun, seemed all the more dramatic for being concentrated on what was formerly the Dalzell estate. Mr Elliot wasn't much of a talker, and after he'd told me he hadn't even seen the girl who, ten years before, had come in such a wild state to the village, we walked on in silence.

The clearing was right on the edge of a young pine forest, which the Forestry Commission must have planted within the last ten years. On the other side, though, was a great stretch of moor – on a clear day you might be able to see as far as Peebles – and a circle of ancient silver birches, probable remains of the Forest of Ettrick. One of the biggest trees had been felled, and there was a strong smell of the sawdust in the damp air. Some instinct led me to the far side of the clearing where the men had been too frightened to penetrate, evidently, for the fine green grass, so unnatural an occurrence in rough heather terrain, was untrampled; and there, hardly discernible in the uneven ground, was the long mound I had been half-hoping and half-dreading to find. The only sign that some hand had sculpted the mound rather than the shifting earth was the presence of a stick, a simple ash such as shepherds use, driven deep into the hardly noticeable protuberance. I motioned to Mr Elliot – I had asked him to bring a spade – who came over to my side and, after throwing me a quick, perplexed glance (I think he knew, too, what kind of thing we would find there), we started to dig. Below us, on the outskirts of the man-made forest, was the drilling machinery, out of use now at the weekend. There was a good deal of sphagnum moss growing on the mound, and the stubborn roots of heather, before we could get down to the soil.

The first surprise was to discover that the stick wasn't, as would normally be supposed, at the head of the grave. It appeared to go right through the centre of the body which, as we lifted it carefully from the shallow trough, was in good condition still and was clothed, strangely, in blue denim trousers and a pink top, strapless, such as ballet dancers wear. The stick – or stake I suppose one might call it – had pierced the body just above the ribs on the left hand side.

We laid the body on the heather, and stood back to see it better. I must say, I felt a strong discomfort in the air which I think came from that unease experienced in the face of a sudden realization of the uncanny in ordinary people – amongst whom I count myself, of course. There was no way (and the uncertainty was not caused by the results of decomposition) in which it was possible to tell the sex of the corpse. There was something completely hermaphroditic about it, but I can't explain what that quality was. The face was completely blank and smooth, and the eyes were closed. A small bosom seemed to be discernible under the pink top, but the shoulders and upper arms, although small, were muscular. The hair added to the anomalies of the body. It was black for about three inches – it had grown that length in the grave, I suppose – and yellow for another three, suggesting the wearer, at the time of death, had had extremely short dyed blonde hair. As all these facts tallied with the facts in the 'journal', I began to grow excited. I said nothing to Mr Elliot, of course, other than I thought this person was almost certainly the missing relative of these friends of mine and that I would apply directly for permission for the body to be moved to a morgue where they might identify it.

We replaced the body in the ground with care, and covered it with the earth again, in the event of rain. Then we went back down to Tibbieshiels to phone the police and report the discovery of the body. On reaching base, we realized that our sandwiches were still uneaten. I think Mr Elliot had been shaken by the apparition, as I had been. I thanked him, and drove back to Edinburgh.

It was only when I was safely in my flat that the significance of the stake through the body came to me. Jane had surely not done this to herself. I am in no way psychic or superstitious, but the suggestion of my psychiatrist friends, that there had never been any such people as Meg or Gil-martin (I knew better than they on the first score, anyway, as Meg must certainly have been Margaret), seemed to me more than inadequate. I was forced to wonder: if Meg did indeed have these powers, had she perhaps summoned up a certain personage, well known in the Ettrick area for many hundreds of years, called Gil-martin, who, if I remember, had plagued a young man in the seventeenth century, and whose memoirs were discovered by James Hogg. Once she had called him up, to give her the powers she needed to coerce Jane, he had become too strong for her. And he had claimed another soul . . . But these were of course the over-tired and agitated wanderings of my mind after the drama of the day on the hill above St Mary's Loch. Some passing shepherd had thrust the stick into the mound, unaware of what was beneath. I decided to make an early night of it, and went to bed.

By Monday the body had been identified by Mr Tony Marten and his mother, and 'Jane' was lying in Selkirk morgue. I went to see her frequently, with the kind co-operation of the police. Although they listened with some show of interest to my tentative theories on the long-unsolved Dalzell murders, I believe they were more intrigued by the TV programme which I would shortly be presenting and in which they would appear.

I am now practically convinced that Jane Wild killed Michael Dalzell and his daughter. But it seems I will never furnish enough proof. For a time I was so taken in by Jane's jealous descriptions of Miranda as her boyfriend's past love that I felt the woman who had written this could in no way have been describing her half-sister. The psychiatrists say, though, that this type of transference is perfectly common in such cases.

There is nothing further to report, except that I went south last weekend, three weeks after the discovery of the grave, to discuss the programme and I decided to ask Tony Marten for an interview. He has of course been interviewed many times on this subject. He is now forty-five, and lives with his mother in Surrey. With some weariness he agreed to my going down to see him. Only one coincidence – and one finds plenty of those in this type of research – came up, and this was supplied by Mrs Marten, whose mind is beginning to wander, I think. I was talking of the discovery of Jane's body in the borders, and she gave a little laugh and an odd look. 'Yes, poor Jane wasn't terribly well. She'd spoken to me sometimes of her love for the Scottish hills, you know, and in the end it was me who had to get her a ticket and a sleeper north. She seemed to have become quite incapable of managing things, you know!'

I could get nothing more out of her. Neither the date, nor the circumstances of the visit. Perhaps by then I was becoming superstitious and irrational myself. But as I turned to leave, she came with me to the gate and waved goodbye. She was wearing a small white petal hat, and as it was windy outside, the petals ruffled in the breeze. I don't know why, but I couldn't help remembering Stephen's description of his visit to Meg, and the white petals blowing in from the window onto her hair.

Edinburgh, October 21st, 1986

Two Women of London

For Karl Miller

A MAN LIES DEAD in the gardens of Rudyard and Nightingale Crescents.

The gravel path, which was raked only this morning by residents and members of the garden committee, is disarranged at the point where it curves round to run alongside Ladbroke Grove, to the east: the hair of the dead man, brown-grey and thin, lies across it like a weed.

As night grows deeper and the noise band of the City drops, leaving a pink glow in a sky that seems permanently overheated, lamps go off in houses either side of the gardens. Chandeliers snap out, like dead stars. In apartments and private dwellings, frosted glass dims softly, children in nurseries turn in their cots and look out through freshly painted bars at the moon.

Below the moon and shining just as bright, the naked light-bulb in Mrs Hyde's kitchen stays on until all hours. It sends a white blade of light over the body of the dead man – and comes into the bedrooms of the Crescents' children, so that they reach out to pull their curtains closer together.

In the morning, the residents will decide to complain about Mrs Hyde's light, in the tatterdemalion house that shouldn't be part of the gardens at all, butting as it does the thronging, littered thoroughfare of Ladbroke Grove. But by the time they have grumbled to each other on the telephone Roger the gardener will have seen the corpse. Skirting the new saplings, in crinolines of wire netting to protect them from Mrs Hyde's children – and others on the 'wrong end' of one of Notting Hill's most desirable quarters – he will run through Nightingale Passage and bang on Ms Eliza Jekyll's door in the Crescent. Ms Jekyll is kindness itself, and always up early to work on her accounts: Roger has used her telephone before, when his wife was at the hospital.

Today no one comes to the door. As it is mid-February – 8 a.m. on the twelfth, to be exact – the only sign of daylight is the fading of the bar of filmy red across the sky and its replacement by an all-pervading, mottled grey.

Roger rings the bell twice and when he gets no answer he crosses Nightingale Crescent and starts to make his way up Ladbroke Grove, past the vandalized callbox, to the police station. An owl hoots in the gardens as he goes.

The brokers and interior decorators and solicitors and architects who live in these Crescents frown as they reverse their cars from off-street parking areas and set off for work. The cry of the owl, feared by their wives – feared by young, single women who live in basements of elegant mansions – feared by old women in unheated rooms – is no sweet, rural dream here. It is the cry of the prowler, as he makes his way through trees and shrubs to his next victim. Today, under clouds that are like bruises on the dirty, tender pink of a London sky, he will strike again.

Roger the gardener, however, knows better. Going slowly on legs bent from years mowing the lawns of the gardens – and leaving swathes as neat and straight as the lines in a bank book, deposits of grass regularly spaced – he reaches the top of the Grove and begins to make his way down the other side. The crenellations of Notting Hill Police Station come into sight. Roger will report the murder of a man in the Rudyard/Nightingale Crescent gardens.

All day excitement will spread. From the police themselves, who have spent so long trying to track this man down. From the press, who will interview past victims; from TV which takes the victims and sits them blindfold in the studio to make them talk of rape and violence. And in all the streets and crescents of the neighbourhood excitement makes women throw open doors into back gardens and stretch up to unsnib windows locked for so long against possible invasion that they give grudgingly when tried.

Everyone knows the dead man is the Notting Hill prowler. It is strange that this as-yet unidentified man – in track shoes, jeans and a battered sports jacket – is more intimately known than any neighbour or acquaintance. Nobody knew his face; and yet, as the police vans arrive and the TV cameras beam their hot, white light in the February darkness, those who run out and catch a glimpse of him as he lies there on the path seem to feel they have lived closely with him for years. And, mixed with uneasy jubilation, is a sense of loss. The man had inspired fear; and to some there is a sudden vacuum now it has gone.

Yet no one fears for Mrs Hyde, who killed the man and must answer for the crime.

WHEN I WAS asked by the Executors of the late Dr Frances Crane to try and come up with some kind of an explanation for her sudden illness and death in the summer of 1988 – her peers in the medical profession seeming all equally baffled by the rapid demise of a GP both happy and successful in her career and showing no signs of incipient mental instability – I can say in all truthfulness that if I had had an idea of the frustration (and sheer horror) of the task, I would not have taken it on.

We are surrounded daily by evidence of violence, poverty and misery in this city. The media leave us in no doubt that rapaciousness and a 'loadsamoney' economy have come to represent the highest values in the land. Crime and unrest are on the increase – as, so it seems, are fear and insecurity, which go hand in hand with great wealth and its companion, deprivation.

For all this – and the sad and shocking stories which arise from a society in thrall to greed are many – I would find it hard to believe in the existence of an example stranger or more alarming than the case of Ms Jekyll and Mrs Hyde. And I would go so far as to say that it was by delving too deep into the facts of this distressing episode that Dr Frances Crane met her death. Not physically – no, the cause of her death was coronary thrombosis – but (unproven though it must remain) psychologically: it was as if, on the last occasion before her hospitalization and collapse, she was unable herself to believe what she had discovered and was still, as she admitted, 'in two minds about the possibility of the whole thing'. Her heart gave out, I think, under the strain of trying to reconcile opposites; and, just as we have been told that the holistic approach to medicine may well be our only hope of survival on this earth, so we may find ourselves to blame when it comes to the treatment – manifestly unsuccessful – of the late doctor. No one understood the mental agony she suffered in her last weeks.

Perhaps I am beginning to understand that torment now. I will complete the task of attempting to reconstruct the terrible history of that summer in West London, the summer of '88. Where possible – and for reasons of speed and economy – I have 'described' events – see above – as a writer (presumably) would. Otherwise, in the many significant areas which were, as my friend Robina Sandel of Nightingale Crescent, put it, 'a closed book' to me, I have borrowed extensively from the journals, taped interviews and even, in one case, video film of witnesses and participants in the crime and its consequences.

I think it right, also, to give a list of the 'cast' of this perverse drama. These people have made their names available from a sense of public duty, and in the strong hope that mass hysteria, wrong judgements and other only too human failings may be, if not corrected, at least understood. Let it be remembered, too, that the neighbourhood in which these characters live and work had at the time of the act – Murder? Manslaughter? Execution? – been five years under the threat of a rapist's random violence.

CAST LIST

ROBINA SANDEL, *fifty-six*
Lives at No. 19 Nightingale Crescent, which has been her home for over twenty years. Came to Britain from Austria at the outset of war. Runs her house as a boarding-house-cum-club for women. Her 'Mondays' have long been famous for the conversation, wit and good companionship of women – lawyers, doctors, architects, sometimes a visiting researcher with a Ph.D. thesis – and if some bear a grudge against Robina it's because the club is considered

too exclusive and 'middle-class'. Those who do gain admittance speak highly of the Viennese *torte* – and of Robina's niece TILDA, who brings in Hock and seltzer just when it's needed.

MARA KALETSKY, *thirty*
Artist, film-maker, poet. Has an itinerant way of life, spending much of her time travelling (South America mostly, with troupes of actors and film crews) but at the time of events related here is staying at No. 19 Nightingale Crescent: ROBINA is an old friend, responsible some years before for saving MARA from a drugs bust in the notorious All Saints Road.

JEAN HASTIE, *thirty-four*
Was at school (Holland Park Comprehensive) a decade and a half ago with MARA and the two have kept in touch ever since. Latterly a practising solicitor, JEAN retired to look after husband and two small children in Scotland in 1984. At MARA's invitation she is spending a short time in London, at ROBINA's. She has research to do on the Gnostic Gospels; at the British Library and the Fawcett Museum, for an illustrated book due for publication in 1989. She has also received a missive from a woman she knew slightly when she lived and worked in London after leaving school.

ELIZA JEKYLL (*age uncertain*)
Lives at No. 47 Nightingale Crescent. Has had various jobs (researcher for BBC, art publisher's assistant, etc.) and has now been appointed manageress of the Shade Gallery at 113a Portobello Road. The Shade Gallery has recently opened, and its first show, of photo-montage and oil-on-board artworks, is by MARA KALETSKY.

DR FRANCES CRANE, *forty-two*
Was a paediatrician at Great Ormond Street Hospital, now a GP. Specializes in diseases of the throat. Lives in a garden flat in

Rudyard Crescent, on a long lease. DR CRANE is a frequent visitor to ROBINA SANDEL's house at No. 19 Nightingale Crescent. For an evening visit she is inclined to cut across the communal gardens and bang on ROBINA's back door, rather than go the long way round, via Ladbroke Grove.

MRS HYDE, *fifty-ish*
Lives in 99f, Ladbroke Grove, at a noisy junction, in a flat (basement) for which she has paid and continues to pay rent of £26.50 per week. The flat gives out on a small garden of its own, much neglected, which in turn gives out through a narrow passageway on to the gardens of Rudyard and Nightingale Crescents.

SIR JAMES LISTER, *forty-eight*
Financier and, amongst many other interests, proprietor of the Waldorf Gallery in Bond Street – and, latterly, the Shade Gallery, Portobello Road.

LADY LISTER
His wife.

TILDA
Niece of ROBINA SANDEL and working as a part-time *au pair* at No. 19 Nightingale Crescent while also attending an English course in South Kensington. She has recently arrived from her parents' home in Austria.

ROCK BOLT
Ex-rock star and recent purchaser of the freehold of 99 Ladbroke Grove.

ROGER
Gardener to the Rudyard/Nightingale Crescent gardens. Despite twenty-five years' work there, the residents take very little

interest in him – with the exception of MS JEKYLL, who sometimes asks him in for a cup of tea and has given him permission to use her telephone.

I

THE FOLLOWING RECONSTRUCTION of events must begin on Monday the ninth of February, at the Shade Gallery in the Portobello Road.

Mara Kaletsky has been kind enough to let me view her video of the gallery opening party at noon on that day. The camera used is a Video 8, which has sync sound; unfortunately, though, as the camera was not functioning properly (a friend had lent it to her) Mara was not always able to obtain sound successfully, and some – possibly crucial – speeches are inaudible. The film, nevertheless, is worthy of inspection for two reasons:

1 It is one of the rare occasions when Eliza Jekyll can be seen without knowing she is seen, and may lead, therefore, to some insights into her personality useful to the examination demanded by the Executors of the late Dr Frances Crane.
2 The ensuing footage of Mrs Hyde may well prove invaluable to the case.

Mara Kaletsky's taped comments on her film are included here.

MARA KALETSKY'S VIDEO (*Voice-over*)

At first you'd think it was the wrong film.

Mahogany book-cases . . . pillars of something that looks like Roman marble . . . a fireplace wide and high enough to burn a Yule log . . . all Heritage stuff in fact, and the funny part is that it's not two hundred yards from the most nefarious drugs den in all London, as well as the no-go area of All Saints Road, where the police have been clamping down on the blacks since anyone can remember.

Looks as if it's been there forever, doesn't it? But you could unclip that fireplace off the wall and stick it up in the hallway in any one of the new 'period' developments: it's a sort of instant respectability. Underneath . . . there's just a hole in the wall and on the other side of it the Indian shop where the incense smell is so strong it seeps through and turns Sir James Lister's face quite purple with rage.

That's Sir James over there. He owns the gallery. He owns the massive new supermarket up by Kensal Road. He has houses all over the world and has just bought a country estate in Dorset. Yes, he is that colour, naturally, and there's nothing wrong with the film. Maybe it's port: he's limping slightly, as you can see, and perhaps he's got a simulated Heritage disease like gout from drinking it.

That's not the reason, though. I know why Sir James Lister limps. Now look at my canvases. I shoot film of all the women and I intercut the stills so I get the ultimate woman. You don't like that one? Who is it? It's the Face of Revenge. Look in the catalogue. No. 41. Two hundred and fifty pounds. Dirt cheap at the price and Sir James takes thirty per cent of that!

Very well, then, here's Eliza Jekyll herself. Here's the official version, as the gallery is declared open by Sir James.

She looks lovely, doesn't she? If you fell for nothing else you'd fall for Eliza's hair. Thick . . . glossy . . . shining black hair. But everything about Eliza is pretty lovely. Her figure, for one thing . . . and her beautiful mouth with that cherub's bow taken straight from the old movies and those Ingrid Bergman eyebrows. Here she is, smiling up at Sir James. And she hardly stiffens at all when the dirty old man slides his arm round her waist . . . in that crêpe de Chine dress from Ungaro . . . and keeps it there for the remainder of his speech. He looks like a toad opening and shutting his mouth like that, doesn't he?

Here's Robina Sandel, whose house I'm staying in.

Robina says she doesn't like my pictures. 'Mara!' (imitation of a German accent) 'Why you put so much *hate* in your work? A pretty girl like you . . .' And I say, 'But Robina, I'm only showing what so many women feel. Under the designer décor, if you know what I mean . . .'

And this is her niece Tilda. Poor Tilda, who actually witnessed the dreadful deed. And worse, later. Don't these women understand that unless something is done, any man can feel free to be a rapist? How can she speak of love and hate, when things have got as bad as this?

Here the tape of Mara, as I recorded her on the subject of her film, breaks off. The camera, hand-held and wobbling violently, zooms in on a woman who looks distinctly out of place here: she's of medium height, wears a fawn mackintosh and has very short, curly hair that looks as if it's put into rollers at night. She's talking, surprisingly, to Eliza Jekyll – and they seem to have something very earnest to say to each other, as even without sound it's clear they're whispering with a good deal of urgency.

The camera, as if impatient of this acquaintanceship, veers off now to the main panel of pictures at the far end of the gallery. As it goes, there's a lurch and a sudden close-up of a red patch of fabric – and then it pulls back, having been handed to someone else to control while Mara grabs a bit of the limelight for herself. The woman in red, clearly no expert with this type of machine, succeeds in filming the skirt of her scarlet dress for several seconds before the exhibition and the gallery opening become once again the focus of the film.

Immediately it's easy to see why Mara 'puts people's backs up' – as I have heard Robina Sandel, loyal but disapproving, say. There's something provocative about her – it's almost as if she wants to invite some scandalous action and then draw attention to it. Though at this moment it's clear she's doing her best to show off – to attract any of the meagre number of men at the opening: perhaps she thinks Eliza Jekyll's immersion in conversation with Jean Hastie (as the curly-haired woman turned out to be) will leave the field free for her.

Not for the first time one is reminded of how frail – and how vulnerable – very small women like Mara can be. Possibly some of that vulnerability accounts for her pictures. They have a quality that is mesmerizing because it is, literally, indescribable: no single woman has those cheeks, that Cyclops eye, the turned-up nose that adds a note of macabre humour to the Face of Revenge. And the unknown woman is herself spread over multi-panels so that a portion of her brooding, bruised face looks out with sudden ferocity from a corner of the gallery – or, again, a curtain of gold-silk hair with a gash of red torn flesh for a mouth looms from a suspended raft. There is too much pain to allow for an easy judgement – but two art critics (male) are staring up at the pictures with something very like fear and scorn – while Mara pirouettes, desperately craving attention.

Eliza Jekyll comes into frame here. She's laughing, stimulated by the party – though her manner does seem rather artificial – and on leaving her companion she comes up to Mara, smiles down at her small, twirling head and walks on, to disappear through a door marked Private at the rear of the room.

And now the film takes on a surreal tone of its own. Just as the camera is handed back to Mara – or she seizes it, impatient with the party (and thus, paradoxically, disappears from it, as far as the viewer is concerned) – the glass door into the Portobello Road is flung open and a crowd of women push in.

A flash; the sight of a plate-glass window smashing silently. Shards on the floor, large and bright like the tears frozen on the cheek of Mara's 'Madonna of the Gardens'. Chaos: a waitress drops a tray. Triangles of ham and smoked trout lie like skin debris after a bomb attack.

Then there's a burst of sound. I suppose at that point Mara, quite accidentally, must have got it to operate on the Video 8; and as the camera is wobbling all over the place by now, the screams of the guests make the scene all the more disturbing.

Now a voice, louder than the rest, authoritarian: Sir James Lister trying to control the mob. To no avail, though. It takes a woman's voice, quiet with a Scottish burr, to restore order to the gallery. 'I ask you all to stand by the door, please,' Jean Hastie says. 'And wait until the police arrive.'

A groan goes up. While the lens, uncertain still after the sputter of glass into the room, wanders over the faces of the women, it's possible to make out a feature here, a turn of the head there, an incline of the neck, which seem suddenly recognizable. Mara, who is by now leaning over to switch off the set, laughs at my perplexed expression. 'That's right,' she says. 'That was the Face of Revenge.'

The women were each one a part of her composite portrait, she said. And each had been a victim of rape.

'By the same man?' I asked.

'Oh yes.' Mara got up to stroll across my sitting room to french windows leading to the patio garden. She stood looking out at the white-washed walls and hanging baskets of geraniums and then moved restlessly away again. 'They were protesting . . . but not about my pictures, you understand. About the police and their attitude to the rapist. About a rich man like Sir James Lister and his ownership of their image . . .'

I interrupted to ask if the women had planned the smashing of the window of the Shade Gallery in advance, or if it had been a spontaneous action. Mara burst out laughing again. 'What difference does it make? She was there . . . she always knew she was going to do it, probably.'

'She,' as Mara Kaletsky explained as she picked up her equipment and slung everything into a dark blue bag, was Mrs Hyde. 'I saw her running away from the scene,' Mara reported, with another of those flirtatious laughs which seems to sum up her contradictory and puzzling character. 'She told me – she'd go and get the rapist herself next!'

AT ROBINA SANDEL'S

Robina Sandel was in the third-floor walk-in linen cupboard in her house in Nightingale Crescent when reports started to filter in about the gallery opening smash-up. Jean Hastie had come up the stairs and asked her some questions – mainly about Mrs Hyde, Robina remembers, who had apparently been the perpetrator of the outrage. 'I didn't know Jean Hastie before – she's an old friend of Mara Kaletsky's and Mara asked if she could come and stay here for a week while she was doing some research work or other – but what I do know is that she seems a bit too interested for my liking in what's going on round here. You'd think she was researching Communal Gardens rather than Original Sin!'

This reference to Jean Hastie's academic work (she is indeed preparing a book on Gnostic interpretations of the Garden of Eden) is typical of Robina Sandel's sharp, scathing sense of humour. People say it's a pity she didn't do as so many of her compatriots did – go to America – Hollywood – and make movies about contemporary mores, dressed up as comedy or melodrama. 'Like Billy Wilder – or Douglas Sirk,' says Mara, a passionate admirer of these directors. 'But, of course, as a woman, how could she?'

All of which is probably true; but for my own purposes Robina, with her combination of voyeurism and Brechtian indignation, makes a perfect witness to the horrifying events of that February. Her inner eye, accustomed from childhood to the art of Grosz and the Expressionists, was the first to see, I believe, the logical outcome of an impossible political and psychological situation and its manifestation in one individual; and all that seems strange in retrospect is that an onlooker – more, a participant in these events, such as Jean Hastie – should have been oblivious to the underlying dangers of the situation.

Robina said she'd hardly known any two friends more unalike than Mara and Jean. It wasn't just that one was big – plump, even – and with those tight curls that were just about as far from Mara's rough, shaggy mane of dark hair as Jean's 'court' shoes were from the espadrilles Mara wore night and day on her small feet; it was the manner of thinking: the approach to life. 'Mara is sorry for everyone, you know.' (Robina does have a German accent, but not nearly so pronounced as Mara makes out in her mimicry.) 'Mara would take any lame duck that comes up in front of her. And – my God – there are plenty of those around nowadays.' Jean Hastie, on the other hand, seemed unmoved by the obvious changes in London since she had last come south of the border, several years ago. 'She's got a happy family life, I suppose,' Robina said, with a sigh that was immediately succeeded by a warm, enigmatic smile – most of Robina Sandel's family had been lost to Nazi Germany; and she had never married. 'But they've nothing in common – she and Mara. Funnily enough, they seem simply to like each other's company.'

That this was the case was proved by Mara's and Jean Hastie's late return from the gallery opening. Jean Hastie calmed Mara when she was in one of her 'states' – Robina Sandel conceded that – and after the smashing of the window and the arrival of the mob of angry women, Mara had certainly needed a gentle touch. 'She's torn both ways,' Robina said shortly. 'On the one hand, Mara wants people to buy her paintings – and to appreciate her as an artist. On the other, she's chosen to paint a very sensitive subject: the victims of the local Ripper. She wants the approval and patronage of such as Sir James Lister. Yet she would like to send him to the guillotine.' Robina chuckled in a manner, I thought, that would irritate Jean Hastie intensely, if she was truly lacking in pity and indulgence for others as had been described. Friendship, however, is an imponderable thing; and certainly, when the two women came back from a walk round Holland Park, Mara had recovered herself and was able to laugh at the whole thing quite good-naturedly.

'I was just sorting the sheets,' Robina said. 'I'd told Tilda to give Frances Crane – who'd just come across the gardens for a drink and a chat – she visits us about three times a week – a malt whisky from our supply. I had to make the bed up for Jean Hastie in a hurry because the other spare room has a young architect friend of mine – she's been in Brasilia for the past six months and she needs a good rest here and some nice food . . .'

Robina Sandel is inclined to get side-tracked in this way when it comes to domestic arrangements. It's almost as if, Mara pointed out, she has made the running of the house, the serving of meals, and the secrets of the linen cupboard a whole State, with all the importance and changes of policy which Government requires. Whether this was really the 'tragedy' that Mara claims, of the loss of a brilliant talent – so common a fate among women – and its submersion in the mundane details of everyday life, I wouldn't be able to say; I only know that it took some time to return Robina to the subject of the evening of Monday the ninth of February. It wasn't, as she was eager to explain, because there had been so many guests since then that the occasion had dimmed in her mind. 'No – if anything, that week burns itself all the time more deeply in my memory,' Robina said.

Nor was it just that the search for Mrs Hyde, as notorious by now as the absconding Lord Lucan in his day, was a part of the national consciousness. It was, Robina said, her own sense of shame – blame others though she might – at having been unable to predict the day of the murder. 'The Zeitgeist is not to my liking,' she said, rueful but with an intimation once more of the enigmatic look and smile. 'I don't like the priggish Jean Hastie – and I don't like the viragos poor Mara has got caught up with. All the fault of men. I cannot believe that. However – ' Robina became her sharp self again and delivered one of her fatally glancing comments. 'A snoop is always a snoop. That is what I thought of Jean Hastie.'

Apparently Frances Crane, already ensconced in Robina Sandel's shabby 'through' room overlooking the gardens, got on well with Jean from the start. Frances, as a doctor – and a specialist in the ailments of children – had enough in her working day, I suppose, of an 'immature' approach to things, to find Mara a little trying and Jean Hastie a welcome relief. Whatever the reason, the two women were soon settled on a battered leather sofa by the window. It was a horribly dark night, as Robina Sandel remembers, and she had gone so far as to light a candle and place it on a low table by the new acquaintances. It was one of those fat Christmas candles – her niece Tilda had brought it over from Austria when she came – and the flame, reflected in the window, showed up the gloom of a February afternoon only too well, the bare chestnut tree and forked ash outside groaning and straining in a deathly parody of the leaping light inside. There was a lot of rain – Mara remembers that because later she tried to film in the gardens and was blown back in again, soaked – and a wind that seemed to be trapped in the stretch between Rudyard and Nightingale Crescents, howling round, as Robina said with that Germanic, ghoulish humour, 'like a woman or a lost soul.'

Jean Hastie was asking Frances about Eliza Jekyll, whose gallery opening she had just witnessed. (Robina says that at this point two 'regulars' of No. 19 came in and made themselves comfortable at the street end of the room, with a bottle of claret produced by Tilda.) These details are essential, I believe, as the new arrivals, one a stockbroker who had lived in her ground-floor flat four houses down for six years, and the other a landscape gardener only recently arrived to take up a studio flat with private garden on the far side of the communal expanse, in Rudyard Crescent, were witnesses to subsequent events. Robina remembers that the stockbroker, Monica Purves, lit up a cigar and pulled one of the giant brass ashtrays Tilda has to keep polished close to her on the coffee table between them. Jean Hastie, who seems to have had a particularly strong sense of smell, wrinkled her nose at this, despite being at the far end of the room from them, and asked if a window could be opened somewhere.

'I suppose,' Robina said, 'that that was where the trouble

started. Two factions, if you like, declared themselves at that
moment and stayed implacably opposed until they were forced
to part – by the lateness of the hour, the necessity of getting up
and going to work the next morning – or the sheer weariness
that overcomes an argument when it finally becomes clear that
neither side will budge an inch.' It was then, Robina emphasized,
that grounds for her suspicions of Jean Hastie were first properly
laid; and though she could never have guessed, as she was the
first to point out, the exact nature of Mrs Hastie's mission in
the south, there was something of an air of espionage about her.
And Robina didn't like that at all.

The inevitable subject of the local rapist having come up (the
four women were sitting together, now, since Monica Purves's
offer to open the side window at the rear end of the room, with
its pitch black view of boarding and sodden shrub, had brought
them all to the garden end of the room) it soon led on to the
topic of women in general; and the change (if any) in society's
attitude to physical violence and social discrimination against
them. Monica Purves, still puffing on her cigar, put her legs in
pinstriped trousers up on the brass fender (another of Tilda's
polishing tasks) that guarded the fine old wooden fireplace at the
garden end of the room. There was a log fire burning, Robina
said, because a number of trees had blown down a few weeks
ago and Monica had sawn them up and brought them round. it
was about the time, as she remembered very well, of the rapist's
last attack in the area. Someone had grabbed his sleeve – they'd
got as near as that to catching him! – and he'd got away all the
same, dodging through the copse of silver birches on the western
side (where the land was boggy and wet, this time of year, and
residents didn't let their children play) and out into the street,
somehow. A shred of a bomber jacket had been left behind,
Robina added, on a branch of an ash that had gone down later
in the storms. Monica had enjoyed ceremonially burning it in the
fireplace of No. 19.

The conversation, as if drawn by a momentum of its own, now

moved to the nature of Ms Jekyll, followed by a heated appraisal of the nature of Mrs Hyde. It was strange, Robina reflected, that the characteristics of these two women, barely known to anyone present, should have brought a civilized talk almost to boiling point; but that it did was incontrovertible; it was as if, she said, these two not particularly newsworthy characters stood for all the divisions we are in the midst of suffering in this country. 'I don't know who really began it,' Robina went on to say, 'but you can bet your bottom dollar it was something Mara said that got someone's hackles up in the first place.'

As far as one can make out, the argument was well under way before the incident, as poor Tilda, frightened out of her wits, termed it, of 'the ghost in the garden'. Mara had spoken with derision of Eliza Jekyll – typical of Mara, as her friends will say sorrowfully – for her contradictory character likes to bite the hand that feeds it. 'Eliza is the kind of woman who gives women a bad name,' Mara said. She was perched by now on the leather top of the fender, Monica Purves's black expensive-looking lace-ups crossed beside her. 'She's the kind of woman who believes she is a post-feminist. Whatever that means. Except I'll tell you what it means – getting what you want in the old way while pretending you care for equality and other old-fashioned concepts. A fink, in other words.'

Robina put in a word here, before things got heated (or rather, she hoped to deflect the confrontation). Already the young landscape gardener, Carol Hill, was shifting restlessly in the upright chair next to Jean Hastie's and Frances Crane's armchairs. Jean herself, catching the look in the gardener's eye, was shaking her head vehemently.

'I don't agree,' Monica Purves said. 'Eliza Jekyll is an example of a woman achieving in the world without losing her basic feelings of compassion towards humanity. Did you know, for example, that Eliza is a sponsor of the local Homeless Women Trust? She organizes meetings for Legacy for the Homeless, where an elderly person may will his or her house to the Foundation, and benefit from tax relief in the meantime – '

'Yes. And personally as well,' Carol Hill put in. 'Since I moved into my flat here I've heard the children these homeless women bring round, playing all day in Eliza's flat. Surely that counts for more than just attending meetings?'

'Soon you'll be telling me she's running a Green Investment Trust, where the rich can put their money in wild flowers or butterflies or something,' Mara snapped at the stockbroker. 'Capitalism is the cause of Eliza Jekyll's prosperity. And capitalism will continue to bring her prosperity while others starve.'

It was at this point that Jean Hastie spoke up. Her voice, with its quiet burr, wasn't easily audible at first – and Dr Frances Crane, who had been sitting back during this exchange with a slightly worried expression on her face, held up her hand to stop the next bass outburst from Monica Purves. 'Jean came down from Scotland to see Eliza, I believe,' Frances Crane said, 'as well as researching for your book, isn't that right?' And she turned to her new friend with an almost apologetic expression on her face – as if the state of affairs in London was indeed very different from that obtaining in the fresher air north of the border.

'I haven't seen Eliza Jekyll for many years,' Jean said quietly, when Mara, too, had been persuaded to hold her tongue. 'We were at the same digs once – at Headington Hill, outside Oxford – '

'Digs!' Mara couldn't restrain a snort of laughter. 'That sounds pretty antediluvian to me. So you didn't know her when she was married, then?'

'Married?' Jean Hastie turned in her chair. 'I didn't even know – '

'It didn't last long,' Frances Crane put in quickly, as if already trying to protect her recently found ally. 'He – the man she married, I mean – has been living out of the country for years.' And, with a disapproving glance in Mara's direction, she said, 'I

202

really can't see what Eliza Jekyll's marital status has got to do with this conversation.'

'I agree.' Monica Purves tossed the end of her cheroot into the fireplace and stood up. 'A friend of a friend of mine did her divorce, as a matter of fact. The trouble was, she said, that Eliza Jekyll was a lot too soft on the bastard. Let him get away with murder, old Kate said.'

Robina's account is that she went at this point to replenish the drink tray and to call Tilda in the kitchen. Robina is proud of the mini-pizzas she hands out to those who drop in at No. 19; and if they dig a little deeper in their pockets for the extras, all the better. Certainly Monica Purves had no lack of funds, as Robina rather shamefacedly said. With London the way it is nowadays, you can do with every bob you earn. And as if unconsciously to underline a 'decent' way of thinking and talking that had, like Jean Hastie's memories of a distant past when Eliza had been studying art at a school in Oxford and Jean had been studying law, long disappeared, Robina added apologetically that No. 19 did, after all, need a new roof. You couldn't tell these days if you were always going to have a roof over your head, when it came down to it. The house might be hers – but for how long could you borrow against its very fabric, eating into walls and foundations as you struggled to stay on?

When the reasons for the providing of tasty snacks and charging for them had been gone through – for Robina was a hospitable character and didn't like to charge her regulars at all, when she sat and drank with them as well – the rest of the story of that evening was permitted to proceed. She'd found Tilda in the small room off the basement kitchen where she'd been temporarily housed since the arrival of a paying guest, Jean Hastie, who would take Tilda's room in the mansard extension at the top of the house. Robina's niece was packing up her things in a big hold-all and choking back tears as she did so. A tray of pizzas gave off a particularly pungent burnt smell from the oven next door, Robina said, and at first she imagined the girl was crying because she was guilty at having neglected them. Then she saw that matters were more serious than that. Tilda was afraid, she said. It was that woman Mrs Hyde who had frightened her. And the other woman, too – Mara Kaletsky, with her wild talk of revenge and her gruesome descriptions of the methods of the rapist. She said Mrs Hyde was going to kill the man. It would be soon, Mara said. At the time of his next attack. She had told Tilda to be very careful. 'But even if you're not in he cuts up your things,' Tilda sobbed. 'Your photos ... your underwear ... everything.'

It next turned out that Tilda had come down to the basement to fetch the appetizers when she had seen, through the open door of her bedroom, a pile of old clothes in a tangle on the floor. Heightened imagination – fear – 'well, they can do a lot to the way you see something,' as Robina, no innocent in these matters, remarked drily. She added, remembering perhaps the country she had left and the growth and easy acceptance of fear there when she had been a child younger than Tilda, that she'd thought then how good it would be if something – anything almost – would just remove the menace of the rapist from their midst. 'It's been a long time,' as she told the newspaper reporters when, inevitably, they came to prise a 'story' from her three days later. And – as if her niece's accommodation had anything to do with the whole grisly affair: 'I wouldn't have put Tilda downstairs, you understand, if a friend of Mara's, Jean Hastie, hadn't been coming to stay. Tilda was upstairs all the time since she came to England. I just moved her down until ...' At this point Robina Sandel's voice, or the transcript obtainable from the *Recorder*, dies out altogether. Did she really think she was in some way responsible for the events which succeeded the evening of the ninth of February? Everyone knew, of course, that she was not. But guilt and hysteria, brought back in one long gulp from Robina's childhood, made a confession of a simple domestic transfer of rooms. (It's possible, some say, that it was the presence of Tilda – the sight of her in the basement room, maybe, when she stood

204

by Robina's cheap pink unlined curtains, that brought things to a head that week. But how can it ever be proved? And, if Tilda's stay below stairs was indeed the catalyst, wasn't some kind of action exactly what was wanted then . . . as Robina Sandel had been the first to say?)

MARA'S FILM

Maybe it was because everyone seemed to be against Mara Kaletsky that evening – with the possible exception of the landscape gardener, Carol Hill, seen to be moved by Mara's vehement defence of Mrs Hyde – that the young film-maker and artist decided to go ahead with her 'project', despite the appalling climatic conditions, claiming afterwards that she had known all along what she would find out there in the garden.

The door leading from the passage to the flight of wooden steps outside had blown open in the wind; and this caused, as far as one can make out, a quite uncontrollable sensation of panic and hysteria among the women. You could practically feel the fear, Robina said; and Mara going out through that door, leaving it to bang behind her in the wind, didn't help matters at all. It was as if a collective terror was brewing, and was responsible, perhaps, for turning the ordinary sight of an ordinary woman into a vision of particular horror.

In Robina Sandel's opinion, the phenomena undoubtedly witnessed could be laid fair and square at the door of her niece, Tilda. Not necessarily known as a superstitious woman, Robina was soon talking of poltergeists; and if Dr Freud had been brought into the picture as well, he would probably have been the first to agree with Robina's other diagnosis, that Tilda's psychic state was due to her recent shock in the basement (where, it went without saying, she had left her clothes untidily herself, the mess being in no way the responsibility of the prowler or other invader) and that the state in which she now found herself was in all likelihood due to an innate guilt on the subject of untidiness, imbued in her by a mother who suffered from 'Housewife's Neurosis'.

However it was looked at, Robina stressed, Tilda came up those stairs from the basement as white as a sheet and shaking. Robina followed with a few of the pizzas she had been able to rescue. It was as if, she said, Tilda's shaking whiteness had been translated to some denizen of another world – for as she came in, the candle flame swerved wildly and went out (the electric lights had been extinguished by Monica Purves at an earlier point in the fireside chat) and a 'white thing', as Tilda screamed on first seeing it, appeared outside Robina's long windows overlooking the gardens of Rudyard and Nightingale Crescents.

Mara's film shows us at this point the appearance of Mrs Hyde – on the evening of Monday the ninth of February at 6 p.m. at least – and should prove an invaluable aide to the police in their search.

Mara's desire to film Mrs Hyde, and, as she said, some kind of weird instinct, led her to go out in the gardens at the most unpropitious time and aim her Video 8 at a path and shrubbery turned almost upside down by a seemingly unending squall. Her hair was standing on end, she admitted – and the sight from the garden of the women in Robina Sandel's drawing room, wide-eyed and open-mouthed – clearly seeing something she had not seen herself – was hardly reassuring. She'd heard, though, that Mrs Hyde on certain evenings would make a tour of the gardens in the hope of catching the man who had for so long held the neighbourhood in terror; she would avenge her sisters, Mara had been told; and this was an essential face for a new photo-montage devoted to women's resistance to oppression.

If Mara hadn't seen the woman approach, the camera had.

Robina Sandel, I believe, best summed up the responses to the apparition of Mrs Hyde on that stormy evening, and perhaps it's because they're so much at odds with each other and with what the viewfinder actually saw, that we should listen to her.

Tilda, of course, saw a ghost. This white 'thing', which humped round the gardens in a drench of rain so fine it was almost a steam, came straight from the subterranean world. Clinging to her aunt, she cried that she wanted to go home.

There was certainly nothing homely about the sight of Mrs Hyde that evening. Disgusted, possibly, by an unwelcome combination of the familiar and the unknown – for the 'thing' wore nothing more alarming than a white mac, one of those plastic, half-transparent coats with a hood that sell in millions – Jean Hastie commented that 'it was odious that a woman should disport herself in a respectable area such as this' – and was oblivious, apparently, to the unsuitability of the weather or the possibly unhinged state of mind of the walker. For Jean, the sartorial appearance of Mrs Hyde – for she wore nothing, it was true, under the diaphanous white plastic – was alarming and all-important, blinding her to anything else.

For Monica Purves disgust and alarm are expressed in economic terms. Her view is that women like Mrs Hyde could easily support themselves 'if they really wanted to': that 'making an exhibition of yourself' by parading in cheap and common clothing on a night such as this is done to draw attention to your straitened circumstances. If her wish was to catch the rapist, Monica Purves said, she would be unlikely to succeed. He would hardly be tempted out in a storm of rain by Mrs Hyde's unattractive get-up, to pounce in full view of other residents of the gardens.

Carol Hill's response differs drastically. She has heard from Mara that by now Mrs Hyde is shortly to be evicted from her premises in Ladbroke Grove. Her two small children are frequently ill (all this information passed on to the susceptible Mara by 'the *tricoteuses*', as Robina Sandel nervously describes those women who have banded together in the wake of the rapist's attacks to express their rage and dissatisfaction with society). Carol sees a woman hounded to the limits of her sanity by the brutality of everyday life.

Only Frances Crane and the camera are equally silent on their view of Mrs Hyde that night; both, perhaps, are equally revealing in their silence.

The lens shows us a face that seems almost to have stopped being a face altogether. It's as if a once wide-boned, generous face, a beautiful face, even, to go by the high bridge of a slender nose and the curve of the jaw, has in some indescribable way been pulled sideways and downwards – so that an evil, spiteful face, a nose hooked like a witch's in the old pictures, eyes baleful and peering in a cloud of rain that's like the rising mists of a Hell that lies always at her feet – looks back at us in Mara's version. Robina Sandel is right, I think, when she says that the extreme unease experienced by all the women in their different ways when confronted by this spectacle is due to there being something 'unnatural' about Mrs Hyde. Possibly, as a doctor, Frances Crane feels that comments on physical appearance due to evident malnutrition, stress and (although not proven) advanced alcoholism or drug-taking, would not be ethical in the circumstances.

It was after Mara Kaletsky had come inside once more that the argument resumed – its subject having gone round the gardens for the last time and disappeared in the direction of Ladbroke Grove.

The weighing of the disadvantages of this woman's situation against the advantages of a woman like Eliza Jekyll, in present-day society, went on until the small hours, for the simple reason, Robina thinks, that the women in her house that night were ashamed of their earlier fear and wanted to exorcize it with a strong, political discussion.

As Robina commented, it would be hard to know quite where Jean Hastie stood in the dispute over the 'new values', for, while she appeared to disapprove strongly of Mrs Hyde and the predicament in which the 'feckless' woman had placed herself, the solicitor from Scotland seemed almost equally disapproving of some aspect of another kind relating to Ms Eliza Jekyll. As the argument raged, the storm moaned outside with a tedium that made Robina think – and here she is wandering way off track again – of a reputedly haunted room in a castle in Jean Hastie's country, where card-players, gambling till dawn with the Devil, are all of a sudden whisked off to eternity, the sound of their laughter and revels remaining behind on wild nights to frighten poor sleepers. She would gladly have locked all her women guests in her sitting room until such time as the Evil One came to get them, Robina goes on, laughing. But, however that may be, there wasn't a soul there – professional, independent, self-reliant though all (with the exception of poor Tilda) indeed were – who had not been scared out of their wits that evening.

To discover further some of the reasons for Jean Hastie's ambiguous attitude to her old friend of student days, Ms Eliza Jekyll, it is necessary to read some at least of that good woman's journal for her stay in London while researching a book on the Gnostic Gospels and the origins of sin.

JEAN HASTIE'S JOURNAL

Tuesday, Feb. 10th

I consider myself a feminist. And I hope to contribute, with my work of gynocriticism *In the Garden*, to the controversy surrounding the very roots of the phallocracy in which women have been forced to live since the beginning of recorded history. Painstaking historical research, I believe, is the only sure path away from prejudice and towards a new state of equality at all levels between the sexes.

I must say here, therefore, that I am quite painfully shocked by the atmosphere and general behaviour of old friends and acquaintances as I have found them in London after a period of five years away. A combination of emotional insecurity and extreme aggression appears to be the norm here; and as for the possibility of efforts being made in a balanced manner to redress the economic-social disadvantages which remain, for women, all traces of an attempt at this appear to have been replaced by my own particular bugbear – monomania.

I hadn't met Monica Purves before – and it's possible that I'm simply out of date when it comes to lesbian activists, their aims and means of expression. And Carol Hill, the youthful Capability Brown of the Crescent Gardens, seems as easily swayed by one opinion or the other as she would be if offered varying fashions in the laying out of a parterre or pergola.

But Mara! – I am sad indeed to see the degeneration into bathos of one of the brightest sparks one was ever likely to know. I was literally horrified yesterday to see the outpouring of hatred and desire for vengeance in the canvases at the Shade Gallery. What can have overcome her? (There are still traces of the old Mara there, of course, and on our walk in Holland Park after the fracas at the gallery I was briefly allowed to savour them. She and I were reminiscing about the old days, when we shared the big flat in Elvaston Place – Mara was experimenting with colour then and great daubs appeared on the walls – 'That's a Rothko and that's a Frank Stella,' Mara would say laughing, before sponging them off again. And we had a laugh remembering Andy, who used to come round too often in pursuit of Mara and one night got drunk and ate the dog's bowl of Chum before passing out.) There was something more innocent about those days, I suppose . . . anyway, we were having a good time remembering all this until we got to Robina Sandel's and last night's chilling and absurd little melodrama was played out.

No doubt I am extremely fortunate to have a kind and loyal husband in Fife, two happy children, and a good income coming in from Paul's work in Edinburgh, where he commutes every day. And I know, from Mara's letters over the past few years – and sometimes we've gone a whole year without corresponding, Mara caught up in the internecine politics of Women's Agitprop and Art of one sort or another, and I sampling the exhausting but rewarding fruits of childbearing – that I'm considered by now a bit of a fuddy-duddy. Mara's view is that because I trained as a solicitor I should practise still as a solicitor, whether I have a young family or not. I should be helping women in their legal battles – against absconding, non-maintenance-paying husbands, against wife-batterings, in rape cases and the like. I'm seen to have let down the side, I fear, and Mara's letters, friendly but increasingly exasperated, accuse me of being a Women's Institute type who makes home-made preserves and crochets table mats for the Church sale.

Mara is right there and I'm sorry to say I can't feel apologetic about it. I prefer to raise my children in the calm, sane atmosphere of the countryside rather than in the frenetic drug-ridden inner cities. And I can't see anything wrong with making our own produce: both Karen and Allan enjoy our bilberry-picking expeditions and enjoy it, too, when covered with purple stains at the time of making the jelly.

Paul was quite happy to make arrangements in Edinburgh so that I could come south to visit the British Library for a week. I miss the bairns, of course – but I would feel that I was not making my contribution to the women's cause if I allowed the contingencies of motherhood to take me away from my work more than absolutely necessary.

Then, too, I have to admit that I was intrigued to receive a letter from Eliza Jekyll just a few weeks ago.

It really is centuries since I last saw Eliza. Those days in Oxford seem to belong to another age altogether. So it was particularly surprising to be asked a favour – as Eliza put it. She hinted that my legal training would in some way come in useful. But I was mystified as to what a woman in the centre of metropolitan life – and a woman who, as I heard last night, had married and divorced (and all without my legal aid) – could want of me when solicitors, barristers and influential friends must abound in her life.

I was most concerned when, arriving off the Edinburgh shuttle at Heathrow – to be met by Mara in her same old bashed-up

Beetle car – and taken directly to the gallery in Portobello Road, Eliza took me aside and told me the nature of her request.

Now, my view in these matters is that, while the State should on no account be expected to provide lesbian play centres and the like out of tax-payers' money, and that prevailing attitudes towards a self-help ethos are highly commendable, the limits of philanthropy of an individual nature should also be carefully guarded. Charity may come in the wake of a cutting back of Government support for those unable or unwilling to help themselves. But it should not, most emphatically, fall into the trap of the quixotic.

This was just how Eliza struck me last night at the Shade Gallery – and that was before the appalling revelations which followed the opening. She had a superficial air about her that I don't remember from our student days – but, I must say, she looked remarkably unchanged since then, as if the cares and wrinkles that beset the rest of us, had, magically, eluded her. She seemed a bit jittery, too, but I put that down to gallery opening nerves – and I gathered from Sir James Lister that the place has only just been renovated and launched as a picture gallery; and that it's the first time he has employed Eliza, who a few weeks ago he didn't know at all. Certainly I had a slight feeling that the young woman I'd known when a student of Art History was less in touch with the banalities of real life now than she, very clearly, had been at Oxford. (For if Mara, for example, had always had this wild, romantic side to her character – a true 'artistic personality', I suppose you could say – then Eliza, despite her good looks, was always extremely down to earth.) Her only fault, as I remember it, was generosity – she once gave her entire term's allowance to a student who was down on his luck, and worked at the Cardrona Tea Rooms to pay her way through her studies.

That, as I discovered, was the simple fact of the matter: as often happens over the years, a charming quality – such as generosity – can develop into an unattractive, even embarrassing characteristic. I'm no psychoanalyst, but it does occur to me that some

need to control the lives of others is concomitant with an obsessive need to make gifts; and an apparent need to dominate the
existence of another seemed to be uppermost in Eliza's mind as
she spoke to me yesterday in the gallery. It was, of course, not
for me to say so at the time – and our exchange was necessarily
brief – but charity should surely, in Eliza's case, permit her to
remain in her own home.

For it transpires that Eliza Jekyll wishes me to act as a convey-
ancer for her. She wishes – no less – to give her home away.

And my horror can be imagined when, in the course of the
evening at Robina Sandel's, I understood the nature of the
intended recipient.

It was none other than Mrs Hyde.

Later

London Transport has certainly worsened considerably since I
was last here and the effect of my journey to the British Library
and the long wait for the volumes I needed has been to make me
yearn for sleep.

But I think I should record here – for Paul, who will doubtless
be intrigued to listen when I return to an account of the excesses
of the sybaritic southern flesh-pots – the efforts I have made so
far on behalf of my friend Eliza Jekyll.

It has come home to me with increasing strength that Eliza
must be in some kind of trouble. Possibly she's being blackmailed
– for a distant indiscretion, which if made public now would
jeopardize her future career. (I must admit, in this age of Gomor-
rah, I cannot imagine what this could be!) Perhaps some problem
with her ex-husband has led her into a legal tangle over her
Nightingale Crescent flat.

Again, it is hard to imagine what this could be. But it's equally
hard to believe that a propensity such as Eliza's in her salad days
could have grown to a monster of such suicidal and self-sacrificial
dimensions.

I may be doubly cautious, as a Scot, when it comes to keeping
a roof over my head. But it's not been in my experience, in all my

years as a solicitor, that anyone renders themselves intentionally homeless.

No, there's something afoot here. I shall seek it out, for Eliza's sake and in the interests of justice.

And I must push to the back of my mind the preposterous thought that there was indeed at some time a relationship between Eliza and that – that literally indescribable creature I witnessed humping round the communal gardens last night.

Quite honestly, if there was or had been, necrophilia would have been the only word for it. For Mrs Hyde, as the wretched eighteen-year-old German girl put it, was as alarming and repellent in appearance as a ghost. This other-worldliness was what, I think, caused the bout of mass panic at Robina Sandel's. A woman going round the gardens in the wind and the rain. And she looked like death.

I was glad to meet Dr Frances Crane last night. And I'm only sorry that we didn't end up getting on as well as we began. After Robina Sandel – who is a bit of an eavesdropper and a busybody (always seems to be hanging around just when you think she's finally gone off to do something; and the bossiness, too, when she told me I had to move downstairs to the room off the kitchen, although I know Mara had arranged for me to have the light, airy room at the top!) – after Robina had settled us with a drink and a low table with some sort of expensive-looking candle on it, I was at last able to ask the doctor what if anything she knew about Eliza Jekyll. Mara had told me they were old friends, and it was funny timing, I said, that this relic of my student days turned out to live in the same street as Mara: that all these years Mara and I had corresponded from her 'temporary' London address in Robina's house, Eliza had been there just a few doors along.

'A lot of people seem to end up round here,' Dr Crane said, with a careful smile, as if she would guard any secrets with extreme punctiliousness. 'It's the gardens, I suppose. There isn't another area in London with such an acreage of open green spaces.'

I had the feeling I was never going to get any further than this with Dr Frances Crane. And yet she had obviously felt an instinctive liking for me as I had for her. Perhaps the wildness of Mara and the opinionated manner of Monica Purves made me appear a more restful companion for an evening's relaxation after a day's hard work than they were likely to be; possibly, recognizing a fellow professional, she felt she could count on my discretion if the time did come to let out some facts.

I was to be disappointed again, however. Dr Crane seemed more interested in the fact that Eliza Jekyll's ex-husband was in town (which of course could be of no conceivable interest to me) than in her old friend. 'I heard from a patient,' Frances said unhelpfully. 'Many of the mothers of my young charges seem to have met and fallen for Ed. I sometimes wonder if the illnesses the children contract aren't in some way connected with the mothers' infatuation.' And the doctor, seeing my surprise, went on to explain that Eliza's ex-husband was a famous charmer, an occasional film director, who led a charmed life, too, by the sound of it, living off 'projects' in development money and, often as not, the rich and famous. When in London, this paragon of virtue stays at the Portobello Hotel; and as Dr Crane has her practice in the area, she is inclined to be the first to know when he has arrived, due, as she had just explained, to the symptoms manifest in the children of single mothers living on their own, Ed's chosen love-partners.

He sounds not unlike the rapist, I thought, but kept my thoughts to myself. If I was ever going to get some insight into the unrealistic bequest Eliza Jekyll had in mind, I would do well to listen to anything anyone chose to tell me, however irrelevant.

'So he goes to see Eliza fairly often?' I said.

'Oh, I shouldn't think so,' Dr Crane said, returning my look of surprise. 'He treated her monstrously at the time of the divorce.' Frances Crane sighed, then turned to look down the far end of the room, where a new arrival was lighting a great cigar – a habit I feel strongly should be banned by Robina Sandel if she wishes to keep a pleasant establishment here.

'Eliza's attitude to life is beyond me, I'm afraid. It's a good time since we met,' were the woman doctor's last and distinctly disapproving words on the subject. And so strong was the feeling of dislike – of dread, almost – on Frances Crane's part when talking of her old friend, that I called out for a window to be opened: ostensibly to clear the room of the fumes from the cigar, but in fact to clear the sudden thundery air between us. Eliza Jekyll would yield none of her secrets through the intermediary of the doctor, that was plain. But, in one last hope that the mystery of the contract she wished me to draw up could be elucidated, I decided to ask the doctor if she had ever had dealings with a certain Mrs Hyde.

Again, I drew a blank. Frances Crane looked up from her deep leather armchair in the bay and waved at the woman who had just come over to open the side window at my request, inviting her and her young friend to come and join us. As they settled themselves, the older and taller of the two women leaning back in a low tapestry-covered seat and propping her legs on the brass fender, Dr Crane shook her head in a dismissive, almost impatient way.

'The woman who I hear was responsible for smashing the window of the Shade Gallery this afternoon,' I reminded her, 'or incited the other women to smash it.'

I suppose I must sometimes come over as an insensitive person. There has been difficulty in the past, on occasions, with particularly obdurate clients – those who were manifestly holding back information from me. I have been accused of lack of tact and sympathy with their predicament. But it is a long time since I have received a snub so direct and wounding as the one delivered to me by Dr Frances Crane on the occasion of my innocent inquiries apropos Mrs Hyde. I have my book to write, and other matters to think about than the property transfers of someone with whom I have had no contact for over twenty years. I am invited to dine – with Mara – at Eliza's on Thursday, and no doubt we will find time to discuss her request more rationally then.

Such at least were the thoughts that went through my mind after Dr Crane's glacial reply. 'I fear, Mrs Hastie,' she said, 'that I cannot satisfy your curiosity. My friendships do not lie in that domain.' And she turned to talk animatedly to the young woman, a landscape gardener, who had just come with the taller woman to sit down beside us. An argument on the merits and disadvantages of conservatories ensued: too hot in summer, according to the doctor, and encouraging sunstroke in some of her infant patients; and too cold in winter to be of any comfort.

I resolved not to sit silent and humiliated while this tedious conversation went on. It had been a long day, the flight from Edinburgh and the strain of parting from my children not to be discounted. And Mara – wandering out to the passage with that video camera in her hand – if I could just separate her from it tonight, we could have a cosy chat in our rooms before turning in.

But then, of course, we got our Lady Macbeth sleep-walking scene.

After it was over – and the argument had veered as sharply as the candle flame in the wind from the pros and cons of conservatories to the cons (mostly) of Mrs Hyde, it was appallingly late.

And I wouldn't have been able to have a bedside chat with Mara, anyway. I'd temporarily forgotten that Robina had moved all my things down to a poky, most unwelcoming basement room.

LOOKING FOR MRS HYDE

It seems unlikely that Jean Hastie's long – overlong – account of her days in the British Library could be of much value here. Yet, though her research on the subject of Original Sin was, of course, of paramount importance to her, the journal, maddeningly incomplete just where the strict and meticulous attention to detail, for which the Scottish lawyer had always been remarked, would have been most appreciated, does at the same time show an undeniable urge to seek out the evil Mrs Hyde. Jean was determined – as she rather inappositely put it – to beard her in her den.

A frustrating day on Wednesday the eleventh of February prompted Jean Hastie to leave her desk by the middle of the afternoon. The books and manuscripts she most wanted were out to someone else – and for a historian in the rich field of women's studies this might well mean a further list of scholars equally impatient to study the Gospels – and an impulse to visit the London Library with a card of introduction from Robina Sandel became, as a grey, rainy twilight descended, increasingly easy to resist. The streets, where orange shop windows beckoned with displays more extravagant and sumptuous than those to be found north of the border, seemed to lie like arms a-glitter with bangles and rings, from the vantage point of the Library window; and Mrs Hastie, as much lured by the prospect of vicarious shopping as the possibility of escape from an unfruitful period of research, went out to meet them with a sense both of purpose and relief. Soon, after a concentrated walk in the bustle and dazzle of Oxford Street and Piccadilly Circus, she found herself, by way of a No. 15 bus, approaching the less salubrious parts of Notting Hill.

Everyone has heard their own version of the impossible coincidence, the chance meeting that it is a million to one against. A favourite of mine is the case of a friend's father who, hoping to run away from his forty-year marriage in Manchester, did just that and escaped to London and the arms of a pretty young nurse. His wife, after two months of waiting for him to return, took the train to London . . . and there, two streets away from the station, walked straight into him. Well, you could say Jean Hastie's luck, on that Wednesday in February, was getting near to that kind of odds. For, within minutes of leaving the bus in Portobello Road, walking northwards, Jean had her first sighting of her prey.

There is probably as little need here to describe the streets where Eliza Jekyll's old friend Jean Hastie and her alarming new quarry Mrs Hyde were walking on that dreary afternoon as there is to transcribe Mrs Hastie's research on early Hebraic depictions of the Garden of Eden. Suffice it to say that most of the stall-holders in the market, deterred by the weather and the sparsely populated pavements, had gone home. A bread shop gave off the only warm glow, in the stretch of Portobello Road just before it ducks under the great bridge of Westway; and beyond that, by the second-hand and occult shops, a mean wind wafted nothing more satisfying than paper bags and Smartie cartons to the sleep-ing homeless by the entrance to the Tube.

Something seemed to press Jean Hastie to go on. She is not the sort of person, as we have seen, who would admit to instinct or premonition as a guiding force; but her entry for Wednesday the eleventh does own to a kind of 'drivenness', making her walk, without knowing (and almost as a foreigner to the city after all these years, and certainly a stranger in these remoter regions of North Kensington) her exact location or even compass direction as she went. Golborne Road, she says, was the last time she had any bearing on her position; yet something drew her always on, so that within five or ten minutes she was neither pleased nor concerned to find herself at the edge of a vigorously rippling brown canal.

This is where the extreme unlikeliness of Jean's prey appearing comes in. And yet it did, despite the distance from the part of Notting Hill where Mrs Hyde could reasonably be expected to be seen; and, more importantly perhaps, without the hunter knowing exactly why and how she looked there.

Imagine the scene . . . a turning down a crumbling street leads Jean Hastie to a bridge . . . a bridge with two pathways, as if those crossing over must return by the other way . . . and on the far side of the low, humped metal bridge, is a great red-brick warehouse, with words lit up in a neon glare in the surrounding winter gloom of water, asphalt and a grudging strip of tow-path: CANALOT STUDIOS. There is no sound, apart from the ripple of water. Other warehouse fronts, grey and dingy yellow, stand by the studios and front a line of water that looks as thirsty for bodies as any French river in the age of suicides. Yet no one lurks, waiting for the moment to run out . . . only Jean Hastie stands there, on the bridge, looking down. For, outside the main doorway of the red-brick giant, a woman is rustling in a rubbish bin. You can't hear her, because of the water . . . and, too, because of a blast of rock music from the studios as the main door swings open and a group of polo-necked young men come out . . . and by the time they have crossed her path and the glimpse of the white-marbled fountain and palm-filled interior has faded again with the bobbing to of the door, it is too late. The canal is as empty and as dead as ever, the quick whispering of the water no more than an illusion of depth and changingness. On the far side of the warehouses, where Jean goes as she runs over the bridge to catch the woman, Harrow Road lies in a blur of TV shops and Chinese takeaways. And here, as if luck had come to Jean Hastie and was determined to stick to her for the rest of the day, walks Mrs Hyde in a street as rough and garish and abandoned to the poor as that great warehouse behind her is a haven for creativity and wealth.

It was clear that Mrs Hyde had some messages to get – as Jean Hastie puts it. She went into a cheap butcher, and out again with a bundle wrapped in paper so thin the mince oozed at the sides; she went to a shoe-mender's bar and emerged with two small pairs of shoes, not wrapped up at all and forced to share a dingy shopper with the mince. She went – suddenly – into a betting shop and there she stayed.

Jean Hastie had, as she recalls, two choices at this point. She could go into the bookie's after the woman; or she could go home by Ladbroke Grove (for she knew well enough where she was now, the stretch of water and old windowless buildings on the canal having temporarily dislocated her) and wait for her prey to come home. No one, Jean reckoned, would go much further on an evening like this, with mouths to feed and meat soaking through the lining of a bag. But choose she must; for she had been spying; and Mrs Hyde's wasn't the only head – in an area where to be quick is a matter of survival – to have turned with the speed of a key in a lock at the sight of Jean Hastie strolling down Harrow Road.

It soon became clear that the first option was out of the question. What was she to say to this woman, whom she had seen only once, after all, in the gardens and late at night? (It's odd here, as Jean remarks, that she was so sure the woman was Mrs Hyde: it had to do with the stooping run, the air of almost palpable disintegration and of course the infamous white mac, worn now over a nondescript skirt and sweater.) The very thought of stopping such a pathetic creature – or undeserving no-hoper, depending on how you saw these things – was repellent to the solicitor and mother of two. Besides, how could she question the woman while surrounded by punters intent on changing the course of their luck? All hell might break out. Despite her provincial manner, Jean Hastie knew enough of bad areas in inner cities to desist from plunging into the heart of a better's den.

In she went, though. She wasn't sure, as she records in her diary, what decided her, in the end: it was the possible frustration, very likely, of losing Mrs Hyde again; and of waiting, unrewarded, on a corner of Ladbroke Grove while her interviewee vanished from the face of the earth (not, as Jean told Robina Sandel when she came back scared and cold from her quest for Eliza Jekyll's beneficiary, that that, or something very like it, hadn't taken place in front of her own eyes when her quarry did finally make her way back to the dilapidated houses concealing gardens and richly stuccoed crescents behind). But at least she'd got some picture of her – and here Jean shuddered again and took the hot toddy proffered by Robina gratefully. We must regret this, for the rest of the entries for that afternoon's encounter are short and stumbling, dwindling to silence after only a paragraph or two.

Mrs Hyde, apparently, had won some money on a horse,

McCubbin, the day before. (All this as related by Robina, as told her by Jean; and I think some of Robina's fanciful humour must have crept in here and there.) The woman was even joking that she'd spent the children's family allowances on the bet; and it must have been a well-worn joke, for the only person to look up, chortle, through a fag glued to lower lip, was a fat woman with some disease resembling porphyria, her purple double chins subsiding into one another as she laughed.

'Mrs Hyde?' Jean Hastie said.

A chatter of odds and races followed; the woman Jean had pursued with so much attention since hearing her old friend Eliza's commission, now looked away, turning up the collar of her sweater and pulling down her head under the mac so that for a moment she looked cowled, a medieval martyr, or a woman who has just been shriven and is being taken off to be burned. 'Can I see your face?' Jean Hastie asked.

The sound of the racing swelled, and the fat woman pushed forward. A man bumped up against Jean and obscured her from seeing anything other than synthetic tweed, ash-covered and drink-soaked from repeated efforts to lift a beer can in the jostling crowd.

And I did see her face, Jean told Robina. And I can't describe it at all. It had nothing to distinguish it.

Mrs Hyde had asked Jean Hastie why the hell she wanted to see her face. 'I thought she was going to kick me – or fly at me – then and there. But I kept my ground. The drunk was lurching his way out of the betting shop into the Harrow Road. The fat woman, like some mud wrestler – like those women in TV who are just rows of muscle under the fat – moved up to Mrs Hyde as if to protect her.'

'We have friends in common,' Jean said. 'Eliza Jekyll–' she added quickly, when the expressions on the faces of Mrs Hyde and her companion showed extreme disbelief that a woman in twinset and suit of a real tweed should have friends in common with such as these – not to mention the improbable venue of a bookie in one of the roughest streets in an already rough area, to decide to make a claim of social acquaintanceship.

'You mind your own fucking business,' said Mrs Hyde.

Jean Hastie, as she sipped her toddy – and took more without demur from Robina's big silver ladle – said Mrs Hyde had finally, after a good deal more abusive language, admitted to knowing Ms Jekyll – but not that they were friends. 'I suppose she realized this was all to do with the flat,' Jean said (for, after her unpleasant adventure, she felt the time had come to confide in her hostess). 'She didn't want to jeopardize her chances. What she didn't know,' the Scottish solicitor added with some feeling, 'is that it's over my dead body she gets that flat from Eliza. It's blackmail, you mark my words.'

The rest of the story concerns Jean's return to No. 19 Nightingale Crescent and the strange vision she suffered in the middle of the most congested stretch of Ladbroke Grove.

'I swear that woman has been "appearing" to me today,' Jean said. 'I mean, it's hardly possible that a human being can vanish from sight in front of your eyes – in swirling traffic – just dematerialize, like that!'

There was no possibility that Jean Hastie had been drinking before taking some of the punch, Robina said. She was stone-cold sober – so cold, in fact, that a hot-water bottle had been placed on her feet and a warm plaid on her knees. Robina liked her guests to feel at home.

'Yet there she was,' Jean said. 'And then – there she wasn't. I never saw her after leaving the betting shop. She could have flown home on a broomstick, for all I know. Then – just like that, the earth swallows her up–'

Robina had lit two fat candles this time and the rest of the comfortable, London-worn room was in shadow. A haze of light rose in the faces of the two women as they pondered, and drank the wine and brandy and cloves, helping themselves from a silver bowl where a thin blue flame ran in circles under the eyes of the two white wax sentinels above.

'Perhaps Mephistopheles finally came to claim her,' Robina said. And she laughed softly, as if for a time – for that evening, at least – the old tales of the Germans and the Scots might come together and be true.

Certainly, as Jean Hastie remembered, there had been a hellish aspect to the junction of Ladbroke Grove and the Crescent, as she returned from her unexpected – almost dreamlike – visit to the canal and the betting shop beyond.

Most of the street seemed to be in the process of being dug up, for one thing. Yellow diggers and dumpers moved like giant crabs in a sludge of churned earth and mud, their feelers reaching higher than the uppermost windows of the houses. Lamp-posts, facsimiles of the Victorian originals and insisted on by rich residents of the borough as replacements for the fluorescence of past decades, stood marooned on their islands of concrete as the road-widening exercise took place. The demure light they afforded – particularly as even this was shrouded by protruding rhododendron and privet from front garden hedges – had made Jean apprehensive. She was glad, she told Mara as they sat on the morning after her adventure in Mara's upper bedroom at No. 19, to have rounded the corner from the Grove; but in the main thoroughfare, at least, the lights of the roadworks had been bright enough to see where you were going.

The odd thing, Mara said, was that Jean had clearly been very much shaken by the whole thing. 'It's unlike her. She's become – well, a lot more conservative since we used to see a lot of one another. We don't have much in common now, I suppose you could say. And she's working on some theory of Original Sin as perceived in the first four centuries after Christ, before St Augustine came along and made his own interpretation of St Paul – saying, in effect, that free will is only an illusion, that we are all saddled with Original Sin: "sin that dwells in me, because I was the son of Adam".'

I couldn't see what Jean's researches had to do with it, and I said so. What we are trying to do, after all, is to piece together the events both psychological and actual of the days in what the media opportunistically like to refer to as 'Valentine's Day', or Week; and a matter of prime importance, as it now appears, is the highly improbable vanishing of Mrs Hyde under the eyes of the busy visitor from Fife.

Jean had insisted, however, on sticking to her story. The lights from the mechanical diggers were flashing; a thin drizzle was falling; here and there, like the red eye of a dinosaur, the light at the top of a crane swung into view. The roadworks had caused an appalling traffic jam, and Jean threaded her way through cars and concrete mixers to reach the pavement as it rounded and went up the Crescent towards No. 19. It was then, Jean said, that she realized that the crumbling houses of Ladbroke Grove, made even more insecure now by the sudden absence of pavement in front of them, were connected with the stucco palaces behind. For an open door in one of the most dilapidated houses, combined with a flare of brightness from the magnesium torches in the street, showed a passageway – then another door open wide – and beyond that a window, which gave out on the black, rural peace of communal gardens. At the same time, a figure of a man dashed out of the house and down the steps and Mrs Hyde, now discernible on the cordoned-off fragment of walkway made available for pedestrians in this grand scheme, came nearer, walking down from the north end of Ladbroke Grove.

There were some things, Jean insisted, which would remain in her mind a long time – and the first was by no means the descent into the ground of her original prey. No, it was the sight of the two faces at the basement window – of the house with the open door from which the man was running – the house towards which Mrs Hyde had, to all intents and purposes, been making her way – two faces, behind grimy, once-white bars, that looked up and wrung Jean Hastie's heart so that she had, in turn, to stop in her tracks and look down.

It must have been then – so Jean supposes – that Mrs Hyde 'nipped off' somewhere else. For it is, after all, impossible to go down into the bowels of the earth in the middle of a busy street in London. Yet she could have sworn, when she looked up from her anguished contemplation of these children – so different from her own bairns: so pale and underfed and miserable, such examples of an upbringing in the cruel city – that she saw, just for one split second, the figure of Mrs Hyde, as she went down. 'I know it can't be,' Jean said as Mara – and then Robina Sandel, called upstairs to hear the tale one more time – questioned her again. The man had run off, up the Grove towards Notting Hill. Jean was clear on that. But where – and you had to think of those poor children at the window – where was their mother now?

Jean Hastie had more than a few thoughts to contend with, as she left Ladbroke Grove and walked away from the bulldozers and pickaxes, towards the haven of Robina Sandel's house. Here the leather club fender and the air of battered permanence so soothing to inmates and visitors in an age of rapid change, demolition and reconstruction, would at least be the same as when she left earlier that day; here, too, she could hope to find Dr Frances Crane in a better frame of mind than before: prepared, possibly, to answer her urgent questions on Mrs Hyde and to allay some of her anxieties. She hurried on, uneasily aware that she, if not the ambience at No. 19, had certainly changed since her recent arrival. For how could it be, when she had passed nothing more alarming than a peeling house – the scaffolding proclaiming a return to mansion status; notices warning trespassers of dogs and prosecution; and then had walked right by a fine window, lit to show the terracotta hues of the room inside to the best advantage, with four or five people gathered in it, by a dark bookcase and guarded, as it seemed, by marble pilasters – that she felt, quite unequivocally, afraid? The lash of a shrub, wet and cold against her face, made her ashamed to admit that she would prefer the maelstrom of Ladbroke Grove to the sudden, suffocating silence of this residential place. Somewhere in the gardens, behind the tall houses that lean just visibly against each other in their shallow foundations, an owl hooted. And Jean Hastie, telling herself she must make some sense out of this whole puzzle, walked back past the tableau in the terracotta room, and at a greater speed past the sheeted and iron-girt No. 39. Next door was a flight of stone steps, and here Jean rang on a bell where was inscribed, under a transparent shield that was also discreetly lit from behind, the name E. JEKYLL.

'So you decided not to wait for Eliza's dinner party?' Mara Kaletsky said when Jean paused, as if trying to find words to convey what she had then seen. 'You were worried for her, right? How much you need to be I don't really know. But she seems the kind of woman who can look after herself – wouldn't you say?'

Jean said she had been worried all the same. If her old friend was actually being menaced by some kind of psychotic – well, she was in need of help and there was an end to it. If she was simply going through one of her foolish phases – then Jean would refuse absolutely to draw up any legal documents for her.

'I was let in by entryphone – actually it turns out to be video,' Jean said, with some of the naïvety of a countrywoman. 'A woman who was tidying up in there let me into Eliza's ground-floor flat. I must say, I was most impressed.'

Robina Sandel and Mara had difficulty in avoiding each other's glances at Jean's reverence for the décor installed by Eliza – a good deal more sophisticated, as Jean pointed out, than anything she would have expected of her at art school in Oxford. The front hall, Jean said, had been mirrored with old glass so that it was impossible to tell where it ended and the rest of the flat began; and when you did go through, ushered in by . . . who was it . . . Grace . . .?

'Yes. Roger Poole the gardener's wife,' Robina said, impatient already with these eulogies for a lifestyle of which she could only disapprove. 'She cleans for people round the gardens – on occasions.'

'I was lucky, though.' Jean was breathless now with her

description of the living room and its all-embracing mural, where every available surface was covered with what appeared to be ancient scenes. 'I was lucky, I mean, to be able to talk to Grace. Because she enabled me to feel that there is indeed something the matter with poor Eliza's life: that she is, certainly, in desperate need of some assistance; and that I am the one to help her – as no one else would be able to do.'

As is evident from Jean Hastie's journal, filled in the evening after her encounter with the elusive Mrs Hyde, an element of fear – of panic, almost – had begun to take root; and Jean's efforts to eradicate it and return to the world of St John Chrysostom are almost pathetic to read.

Her sense, I believe, of the 'closeness' of Mrs Hyde to Eliza Jekyll, gleaned from the meeting with Grace Poole in Eliza's empty apartment, had brought the subject with which she was concerned in her researches more close to her – for the journal, speculating on the nature of Original Sin and the irreconcilable split in each and all of us that came in the Garden of Eden, concludes that there is no hope for the human race unless we return to the position of the first Christians, viz., that we are indeed free and responsible for our actions.

No woman, however 'down on her luck', has the right to demand of another what Mrs Hyde was clearly extorting from her friend and neighbour. Neighbour! That was where the closeness came in, and it riled Jean Hastie to confess to the bad night she suffered after her visit to Ms Jekyll's flat. But confess, in the confidential pages of her diary, she did. The old clock tower at the top of St John's Gardens struck five before she found sleep. And when she woke, to a pale and watery morning, it was as if the sleep had been no more than a loan to her from the choked cemeteries of the past, so many strange and vivid figures did she see parading on exotic shores.

It would probably be easy to point out that the Pompeiian mural in Eliza's flat was responsible for these dreams of an alien world. At any rate, Jean transcribes, on waking and downing coffee brought her by Robina in her basement bedroom, the following exchange with Mrs Poole (and not before confiding that, ashamed as she is of blurting Eliza's request to the German householder, she had felt Mrs Sandel's hostility to her curiosity and now was confident that she would receive help in her inquiries on the vexed subject of Mrs Hyde).

Jean writes:

I couldn't help wondering, as I stood in that room of Eliza's – quite small, in reality, if you measured it, but so cunningly done up you could honestly feel you were in a Roman villa somewhere in the heart of the Calabrian countryside (and that in February!) whether Mrs Poole knew something of what was going on between the two women ... two women who live so close, as I thought with a sinking of the heart, that it's very likely they can hear each other through the wall or, even, have a communicating door. Not for the first time, as I asked Grace Poole whether Eliza was expected to come back soon, I felt that this proximity must force me away from the whole matter. It is none of my business, after all. Yet the very thought of having a woman such as Mrs Hyde so appallingly close made me hesitate again, when it came to walking out of the door at Mrs Poole's civil reply.

'No, Eliza [that was how she called her] has been out some time, love.'

I weighed up Mrs Poole carefully before asking her the next question. She seems a homely type of woman, a bit sloppy in her habits perhaps, from the out-of-place pockets of untidiness in Eliza's beautiful room: a wad of tissues on a low table by the marbled wood fireplace, a sweet wrapper (of all things!) on the floor by the door to the hall. But she seems straightforward enough; and was straightforwardly disappointing, too, when she said she didn't 'do' this place more than once in a blue moon – 'but there's a dinner party tomorrow night and so she asked me to come in'. By the time I got round to asking about 'the other woman' (as I feel Mrs Hyde must be, in some way, in Eliza's sexual past – unless she's an ex-employee . . . or a member of the family who's in trouble? Hardly, no) Mrs Poole was, in the politest way possible, showing me to the door. There are ruched blinds in the flat, which give an even more cocooned feel to the place, and she flicked one up a foot or so to pull the window shut before turning off the light of the central chandelier and making to go after me.

'Mrs Hyde?' Grace Poole said as we stood a second in the darkened room, lit only by a beam of light from someone's house in the gardens. 'Oh yes, she has a key. Not that I've seen her here mind you. She'll usually go in her entrance, out front.' Then, looking at me with a sudden interest: 'You a relative or something, dear? Come into town to see her, have you?'

[There was something about the whine of the London woman's voice, the obviousness of Jean's 'foreignness' in these parts and the discomfort of standing any longer in such artificial conditions that made Jean move abruptly to the window – in the opposite direction, of course, to the door to the hall and the way out. Mrs Poole made a tut-tutting sound behind her.]

I looked out of the window just revealed to me by Mrs Poole, [are Jean's last words in her entry for Wednesday the eleventh of February] and straight into the basement window of a littered pipe-clogged kitchen. The windows were filthy – and steamed over as well – but I could see who was standing at the sink, face partially obscured by one of those old Ascot water heaters they used to put in thirty or forty years ago. It was Mrs Hyde all right, and she was peeling tatties with a sharp, serrated knife that had a red handle; her hands were red too, and the water was spurting out scalding, as if she couldn't care less for the heat. The poor wee bairns were there, and now and again she'd shout at one or other of them. A black cat was on the kitchen table – if you could call a sagging strip of Formica with legs by such a name.

She looked up and straight at me. It was her bare bulb that lit Eliza's room.

Then I followed Mrs Poole back into the hall. And I nearly tripped over the umbrella stand, which I hadn't seen before! It just shows how these mirrors and trick paintings and that sort of fantabulasia can drive ye blind as a bat! Mrs Poole was quite irritated with me by now – and I with her, that I could be mistaken for a kinswoman of that monster across the way.

As I say, I tripped on Eliza's umbrella. A weird object: wood, with a parrot's head and a long, scarlet-painted beak.

I like a thing to be what it is, and no' pretend to be anything else – as my aunt Peggy used to say.

ELIZA JEKYLL AT HOME

As it so happened, Thursday, the twelfth of February, dawned bright and clear, and stayed that way all day: so cold that birds sang and then stopped, on branches etched white with frost; but with a sun that everyone in London seemed to have forgotten, so that children skated shouting on frozen puddles and their women, mothers or minders, bent down for the first crocus or stretched for the egg-yolk yellow of forsythia against a wall.

The horrors of preceding days in the communal gardens of North Kensington seemed to have been blown away along with the bad weather. The great damp blanket of rain and cloud that had lain over the city with as much persistence as the Victorian fogs of the past, had brought with it the rustle of suspicion, the stifled tread in darkness of the murderer. It was true that the Notting Hill rapist had not yet been caught – but on a day like this, he hardly came to mind. The trees were so thin you could see through them. The shrubbery, so often a menace at night when, like a locked wardrobe, it threatened to contain all manner of forgotten and execrable forms, had an innocent sparkle on deep green leaves. Tonight, too, would be bright and clear, with as fine a setting of stars as the cut-crystal, silver and bone arrangements of Ms Eliza Jekyll's dining table. There would even be a full moon, to guide those of the guests who preferred to stroll on such a perfect winter evening along the path at the back of the houses, to Eliza's garden steps.

Jean Hastie was one of these. She was, as she confesses in her journal (after a long disquisition on the bravery and freedom of the fourth century St Perpetua at Carthage) more than slightly ashamed of the 'uncomfortable feeling' to which she had owned the day before. And, although she would be loath to say that the change in the weather had been at the root of a return to her optimistic and cheerful manner, there was little doubt that the transparency of the evening and the pretty twinkling lights from the prosperous houses of Nightingale Crescent, made her feel glad to be alive – and glad, too, that she had a delightful family to return to. Like the hysteria in the gardens over the prowler, the schism in the church after St Augustine – and the subject of his own overriding lust, cause of his theory of the inherited nature of man's sin – seemed far away to an ordinary, contented housewife such as Jean Hastie. She felt sorry, certainly, for those like Mara (who trotted beside her under a moon the size of a silver pomander, the inevitable video camera slung round her neck) and their tiny, claustrophobic view of the world. All London was there, after all, for the sampling (Jean had, after a successful day in the British Library, stopped off at the National Gallery and seen the Impressionists on loan from Moscow and Leningrad). Only, as Jean dourly remarked to herself, it seemed that some women couldn't see it like that.

The women here, living as they did with a dangerous attacker in their midst, could think of little else – and their own position as women in regard to him and other men, of course. It is stultifying, Jean confides to her diary just before going to bed later that night, to find human beings restricted precisely by their need to redefine themselves, to find 'freedom'. And she swears, once this book is done, that she will take a long break from the subject and enjoy life in Fife without a further thought for Eve – or the serpent, for that matter. 'W-O-M-A-N', she says with determination, 'is a word which will be erased from my typewriter.'

It wasn't surprising that the picture of a silver pomander comes up, when we hear that the enticing smell of Eliza Jekyll's cinnamon and clove punch wafted down almost as far as the back garden of No. 19 – and was certainly in evidence as Jean and Mara, at peace with each other tonight, strolled on a path icing-white by the side of dark, churned earth prepared for spring planting. Jean said something to the effect that she'd better be careful with the toddy this time around; and Mara, laughing, agreed: as if all the hobgoblins summoned that night at Robina Sandel's had lain in a bottle of house red warmed with a scrap of West Indian spices and a floating slice of orange. But, with all the back curtains of the residents' magnificent sitting rooms drawn back – as if on a night like this, with such a high, vaulted sky and a pantomime moon, it would be criminal to shut it behind the chintzy curtains – it was little wonder that there was a feeling of benign, neighbourhood watch: a truly communal spirit in the air.

Jean saw the family she had passed on her visit to Eliza by the Crescent way – sitting still in their front bay window but visible from behind, like going into the back of the Pollock's toy theatre she had had as a child. They were listening to music – Mozart, Jean recognized – and didn't hear the scrunch of her and Mara's shoes on the pebble path. But Mara waved to them all the same. 'Jeremy Toller and his dear ones,' she said, surprising Jean with the bitterness and dislike in her voice. 'They've done *nothing* to help catch the rapist. And Toller's a local magistrate!'

Before there was time for Jean to drop the hint – something she had been longing to do all day, when it came to explaining to Mara that there was more to the world than just this garden, threatened though it might be by evil – the two old friends had come to Eliza's steps and were beginning to go up them. Neat flowerbeds, arranged in a radial petal design, lay to their left – the Toller's garden, presumably, and tended with extreme care and forethought, some of the shrubs tied, staked and protected from the winter winds by loving hands. To their right, as Jean saw with a pang of dismay, was a very different story. And, as Mara made no comment on the contrast between the two plots of land, Jean Hastie decided to look straight ahead and arrive on Eliza Jekyll's terrace in a fit mood for an enjoyable dinner party.

It was hard, however, not to look down one more time before they stood outside the curtained french window at the back of Eliza Jekyll's drawing room and tapped (a prearranged signal) to be let in. For there was something almost 'surreal – if that's the word', as Jean wrote later, before the further events of the night became known to her. A rotting pianola, reminiscent indeed of some Buñuelesque fantasy, lay in the garden adjacent to Eliza Jekyll's, its gashed keyboard and rotting marquetry long ago eaten away by rain and frost and squatted by passing cats. The garden, if so it could be called, seemed to have grown humpy, under a patchy covering of grass, as if a mass of botched graves had been attempted there; and under the window that looked out on all this lay, like a child's stick drawing of a man thrown sideways, the white rails of a broken plastic clothes horse. The light in the window was off, but Jean recognized only too well the chipped wooden sills and flaking cream paint of Mrs Hyde's kitchen. And it was with an even greater sense of resolution that she walked in through heavy, textile curtains to Eliza's painted room of trick colonnades and marble ante-chambers, among which her guests stood waiting to be introduced. She would relax as far as was possible during dinner, Jean told herself with her customary firmness. But she would have an equally firm word with Ms Eliza Jekyll before the night was out.

MARA'S FILM

Mara, proud of her 'docudrama', says that without her ever-present Video 8 camera we'd have no idea of the talk or mood of the dinner in the flat that night; and that this is true is borne out by the abrupt cessation of Jean Hastie's journal after she returned to No. 19. Her last recorded thoughts are on the beauty of the winter evening and the distressing mess of the garden that lies between the fine houses of Nightingale Crescent and the back of Ladbroke Grove, making a sort of squalid courtyard between the two. So – Jean breaks off here, which is the greatest pity, as far as our investigations are concerned – and, for this evening at least, Mara takes over.

The sound on her loaned camera is working this time, and after the regulation tour of the table (gravadlax with dill sauce on mother-of-pearlized plates, French bread piping hot, fine china and slender white candles in silver candlesticks) we see first the hired help as he comes out of the tiny kitchenette at the side of Eliza's elegant room. 'That's what they do these days, the high-fliers,' Mara says as we watch the man in a spotless tuxedo unload stores in the mirrored hall. 'They get the whole thing sent round, staff and all, on a credit card!'

The guests, as Mara then points out gleefully, could have come as some package offer as well. Sir James Lister, proprietor of the Shade Gallery and much else, looks, in his smoking jacket of plum velvet with satin facings, like an ad on TV for port or some expensive liqueur. Lady Lister, in black beaded chiffon and lace, with hair as thin spun as the strawberry meringue the hired help is at this moment unpacking from a hamper, looks as if she were herself advertising a marriage bureau of the more discreet type. Then, in trousers and leather jerkin and bottle-green dress respectively, Monica Purves and Carol Hill come into focus. A small, almost hairless man – an art critic, Mara explains – is next. They all stand near the table, for the room, despite its painted avenues, is very small; and then with a maddening deliberation that Mara speeds up for fun, they sit down.

Yes, it does seem that Eliza wants to talk to her friend Jean Hastie. She has Sir James Lister on the other side, it's true – and we hear on a loud and sighing soundtrack the tycoon's proposition that Eliza should meet him for a 'Valentine Day lunch in that little place in Holland Park Avenue?' and see her frown and then smile and agree. But it's to Jean she turns – as soon as the marinated salmon has been cleared away and magret de canard, with its exotic bilberry and cardamom sauces has been served – and it's on her face that Mara now trains her lens, so that she is in close-up, like stars in the movies used to be: Ingrid Bergman in *Casablanca* perhaps: appealing, mysterious.

Maybe one makes that comparison because Eliza Jekyll is not only looking quite outstandingly beautiful tonight, but young and – with which even Mara has to agree – surprisingly soft and vulnerable. 'High-flier' she may be, but butter wouldn't melt in her mouth. Mara would say that this is because the butter, along with every other damn thing, is brought to the door, care of American Express. (Which means, she adds, c/o Sir James Lister, who is perfectly clearly paying for all this.) 'Look,' Mara says as the camera hovers low and shows Sir James's hand on Eliza's knee. 'And look at Lady Lister's face. She's none too pleased, if you ask me!'

Despite the booming conversation conducted by Monica Purves and the art critic on the subject of *glasnost* and the future of Soviet art, it is possible to hear Jean Hastie and Eliza talk; and if Mara cannot at times resist changing the camera angles in a fanciful way, it's still possible to get the gist of what they're saying.

JEAN: Tell me, Eliza, don't you think you should reconsider? I may tell you that I feel quite worried on your behalf.

ELIZA: (*As camera pans to a Pompeiian panel of her room, this in turn replaced by a close-up of the hired butler's hands as he offers a dish of mange-touts and tiny new potatoes*) My dear Jean, I only ask you to ask as few questions as you can. You don't know how much I need and depend on that woman. I think of her very highly indeed. I owe her, you might say, almost everything.

Here we are shown the look of amazement on Jean Hastie's face. She must ask further – she has seen this unworthy recipient of Eliza Jekyll's charity in a light which, surely, Eliza should be told about: she mentions the visit to the betting shop, the children's allowances gambled away. Eliza, misty-eyed, shakes

her head. She knows it looks bad ... but doesn't Jean herself
speak and act as she does now from feelings of an old loyalty?
Imagine – so much this woman needs – life's impossible in
London now, for the poor, the single mother – how can Jean
Hastie refuse to help her?

She shall have the flat, Eliza says, and as she speaks she flinches
away from the pressure of the hand under the table – looking, as
she does so, like a bird caught in a net, fluttering, beseeching on
either side. ('They all look like that,' Mara says. 'It's the post-
feminist trick. Using the wiles of Marilyn Monroe to achieve the
aims of Stalin.')

JEAN: But one more time, Eliza. If we make over this place to –
to your friend ...

ELIZA: Mrs Hyde. Without her I would be lost, I assure you,
Jean ...

JEAN: And if something should happen to you, Eliza? Where
would you go then?

ELIZA: (*Confused suddenly*) Happen to me, Jean? What do you
mean?

It must be said that a kind of basic decency in Jean Hastie does
make itself discernible here. Worried, no doubt, by the kind of
translucent quality Eliza seemed to project that evening ('She was
like – I can't describe it – something like the sky at home before
a storm,' Jean told Robina Sandel) the Scots solicitor decided
against pressing her case any further. Suggestions that a London
conveyancing firm would be more suitable than herself for the
drawing up of a lease brought only a violent shake of the head
and something very like tears forming in exquisitely made-up
eyes. Jean, by the time the meringue and compôte of Caribbean
fruits have arrived, has agreed to Ms Eliza Jekyll's request. And
conversation becomes general, with property prices (an indignant
Monica Purves) and a sale in Somerset of netsuke daggers (Sir
James) which he and his wife will visit the next day, taking
precedence as topics on this occasion over the Notting Hill rapist.
No doubt this is because Mara Kaletsky, wandering out into the

hall to get a long shot of the dinner table, has found a door among the panels of age-stained Venetian glass and opened it to go through.

WHAT TILDA SAW

Robina Sandel tells me it took her niece some time to shake her awake, the morning after the murder.

It was the thirteenth of February – 'Friday the thirteenth', as Robina says with that wry smile which both discounts and accepts old superstitions. She'd been dreaming – tropical birds and jungles, the dream had been. Maybe it reflected the terror that stalked them each night, she said, ready to pounce like a wild beast through carelessly open window, or ventilation shaft: maybe, again, the brightly coloured birds she saw were prophetic, omens of the bloody murder to come. For Tilda was sure of one thing, when her aunt was finally propped up on a pillow, eyes wide open with the shock of Tilda's screams. It was a parrot that had killed the man – deep into his throat, with it's beak.

It took some time to make sense of Tilda's story. She was sleeping upstairs now – and sleeping better than she had been when down in the basement, with the door straight out to the shrubbery Robina never got round to trimming. She, unlike her aunt, had dreamed of war; and this time there was no need for magical beliefs to trace the origins of the dream. Twice she had woken and heard the very real sound of a police helicopter overhead. Perhaps because she felt safe in the attic she'd dozed off again without much difficulty. Everyone knew the sound was a sign of another ineffective hunt for the rapist (some said he must be a member of the police force, to evade them so often) and yet, at an unconscious level, Tilda didn't care enough to wake up or go downstairs. It was something else that had woken her finally – and she and Robina had to laugh later about 'ze birds', as Mrs Sandel termed the nocturnal visitants to her and her niece's sleep that night – it had been the cry of an owl.

Tilda got up and went over to the mansard window in her tiny, sloping-walled room. She felt cold all over, she said: was it because the owl's hooting had come after the sound of the chopper had died away, thus showing the criminal uncaught and triumphant? Or was it, as the gullible Tilda was only too prone to believe, because the 'bad karma' of that evil woman Mrs Hyde in the gardens had floated up to her in her perch above the trees and told her of the approaching crime? Poor Tilda, whichever way it was, she was the last person who should be subjected to witnessing such a scene.

Mrs Hyde was visible – when Tilda had crawled out on to the ledge by her window and looked down – because something had set off the electronic security light in the Toller's garden, several doors down.

She caught the man round the neck with her left arm. She'd come up behind him, as if she were about to overtake and wham! she'd hooked him with the left while the right brought this instrument down on the man's head. The spotlight had shown up, in its unblinking white light, the blood of the man as it spurted on the grass by the side of the path.

And the instrument – Tilda was sure of this because the scarlet paint of the beak had shown up strong in the beam – was one of those umbrellas you can get in the posh shops by Mr Christian's delicatessen at the end of the Crescent where it meets Portobello Road. An umbrella with a long, elegant handle and a parrot's head.

TWO LETTERS

Jean Hastie took the train north later that day. She was too shaken, she told Robina Sandel, to stay on at No. 19. She wanted to see her husband and children.

The atmosphere of jubilation in the gardens was more than she could stomach, too. 'I suppose I can just about understand,' she wrote to Mara, once safely ensconced in the noon express to

Waverley, with tray-table, pen and a folder of notes on the Gnostic Gospels arranged in front of her. 'If you've been at the mercy of this man for so long you must feel some sense of overriding relief that he won't trouble you any more. But surely a murder is still the taking of the life of a human being? And it frightens me that you – and those such as Monica Purves – don't seem to consider men to belong to the human race any more. This can never be the route to a saner world. And remember: it is always a case of freedom of choice. None of us (other than the criminally defective) lacks the opportunity to refuse evil. As you will discover, important new knowledge on the origins of sin and the thinking of early Christians is coming to light. The message of the story of Adam and Eve in the Garden of Eden is that we are responsible for the choices we freely make, good or evil, just as Adam was.

Mrs Hyde is a killer and must be punished for her crime.

You speak of compassion for such as she. But she is where she is as a result of choices freely made by none other than herself.

Mara, I won't go on preaching at you. I want to tell you how pleased I was to see you again. But then of course this whole thing came along and overshadowed our reunion – my work – everything.

And now I must tell you of my last, hurried meeting with Eliza before I went off to catch the train.

I felt more and more apprehensive, as you might well imagine, at the contract Eliza had requested for transfer of her apartment to Mrs Hyde.

After the appalling and violent murder in the early hours of this morning, I knew one thing at least: that neither heaven nor hell would move me to do this "favour" for her now. And I decided to go along there and tell her, face to face.

Mara, I myself feel a great sense of relief.

If one good thing has come out of this lawlessness, it is the end of the relationship between Eliza Jekyll and Mrs Hyde.

Eliza came to the door in a lovely frothy pink *peignoir*. She'd obviously been asleep and looked a little haggard, I thought, but still perfectly beautiful – in a way, quite honestly, that I don't remember in her young days at the Ruskin. She had been warned earlier, she said, by the doorbell ringing and ringing, so she knew something must be wrong, but by the time she'd reached the front door, all she saw was the back of Roger Poole as he went at speed up Ladbroke Grove. "I called him," Eliza said, "but with all that din from the roadworks, he couldn't hear me."

It had been Mrs Toller who told her of the crime.

By that time there were policemen pouring into the gardens and a TV camera crew had tried to push their way through her flat. "I told them to use the gate in Ladbroke Grove," Eliza said. She'd been quite annoyed by the intrusion, I could see.

"They tried next door?" I said – I don't know why.

Eliza flushed. Now she was getting really angry. "They think they can walk in anywhere, these people." Then suddenly she burst into tears and came to put her arm round me. "Oh, Jean," Eliza said. "I was such a fool, to allow that woman to trick me. Please forgive me for wasting your valuable time!"

I must say, I was only too pleased to hear all this, but I pretended to be very severe. "Eliza," I said, "can you give me your word that you'll never have anything further to do with Mrs Hyde?"

A sort of convulsion seemed to run through poor Eliza – I really can't describe it, except to say I suppose it's the first time I've seen a shudder like that. It was, truthfully, like witnessing someone meeting death coming towards them – and what's so terrible, they say, is that you see yourself walking towards you before you die. It was as if she was fighting something, Mara – she didn't turn round again (for now she'd gone to stand by her french window looking out on the garden in the gloom – so unlike yesterday!) but she said, in a low altered voice: "I've had a letter from her, Jean. I'll never see her again. Look, here!"

She held the letter out behind her back. She was ashamed that

I should see her crying, I suppose. And I must confess I'm not too good with over-emotional women. I went and took it.

Eliza asked me to leave, and read it at home. By which she meant Robina's, no doubt – but I just didn't have the heart to tell her that I was really going home, in under an hour. So I took the letter and left.

Oh, Mara, this is a frightful thing.

I was so relieved at first, when I sat for just a wee minute to read the letter, on Robina's fender in the club room. It's written in a childish hand, like someone who's barely learned to write or read. And it uses childish language, too, when it thanks Eliza Jekyll for all the kindness she has shown – quite honestly I wouldn't have been surprised if it had gone on to say "thank you for having me", like children are taught to write when they've been to a party! But then she went on to say that she knew she had done something wicked. That she must run. And that she would be safe, for she was going far away to a place where she would never be discovered. Nor would she ever "trouble" Eliza again – I was reminded of the language of an old-fashioned servant, just as much as a child.

I admit that, although I was sorry that Mrs Hyde might never be brought to justice, I was too happy that Eliza should be removed from her influence to care over much about it. Whatever Eliza had done in her youth, she surely didn't deserve as heavy a yoke as this woman round her neck for the rest of her life.

Robina Sandel came in and I showed her the letter.

She in turn told me about the murder weapon.

My blood runs cold as I write this. Thank God we have now crossed the border and are home. But the Christmas trees they have planted on the hills make me think of Germany – and of Robina's distinctly unpleasant laugh when she handed me back Eliza's letter.

Robina, working for the Resistance, became an expert on calligraphy. And just as much as the umbrella with the parrot's head is Eliza's – I remember it in the hall of her flat when I went looking for her that day – so is the letter from Mrs Hyde no more than a disguised form of Eliza's writing, writing known to Robina, who received a letter from her regarding a garden committee decision only the other day.

What has that wretched girl got herself into?

She must be deeper in with Mrs Hyde than ever before. Did she know her umbrella had been taken quite coolly from the hall, to commit murder?

Presumably. In which case she is doing her best to cover up for Mrs Hyde, who has killed a man and must answer for the crime.

We've crossed the border now and soon I'll be home.

When I've finished my book on the origins of sin I shall work on the Enlightenment in Edinburgh, that most wonderful of cities; and I shall study the works of Henry Cockburn, the judge whose happiness came from a childhood in these hills.

It's dark already, and I want light.'

II

IT IS AUGUST, and half a year has passed since the scandalous killing of a man in the communal gardens in what *Newsweek* referred to as 'West London's Yuppie Paradise'.

In the six months since the crime, there have been no less than 230 sightings of Mrs Hyde, from as far afield as Rio de Janeiro and Reykjavik, and – more frequently – Dieppe and the Costa Brava. Descriptions of the case as an inverted Lord Lucan are inevitable – or so the tabloids claim, painting a picture of the 'murderess' as a wronged woman, somewhere between an abandoned mistress and an underpaid drudge, who wrought her revenge on a member of the aristocracy.

For the victim was none other than Jeremy Toller, younger brother of Lord Pilsdon. A businessman, local magistrate and connoisseur of fine arts, Toller was soon removed from any suspicion of having been the Notting Hill rapist by the simple fact of the rapist's arrest while breaking in and attacking the landscape gardener Carol Hill only a few days after Toller was found dead.

Such an outbreak of violence in the gardens brought, not surprisingly, a flood of reporters and grisly crime-fans, eager to relish the atmosphere of the well-kept private park where a woman had battered a man to death. Some of these made their way to Robina Sandel's house at No. 19 Nightingale Crescent – and, in the case of the more wily and unscrupulous among them, they dressed up as Austrians, 'old friends' of Tilda's anxious to see her on their visit to London.

Robina, however, kept all callers at bay. And Mara Kaletsky

left the country on the day after the crime – too deeply shocked, it was rumoured, by the reality of Mrs Hyde's act (though championing her cause energetically in the days before it took place) to stay in the neighbourhood. And there was another reason, as became clear when it was finally possible to glean information on those confusing days round the time of the murder: on February the fourteenth, quite unexpectedly, Sir James Lister closed down the Shade Gallery and announced plans to develop the site as a club/restaurant, with multi-level cinema and health facilities. Mara had, after all her work and preparation, lost her exhibition and suffered damage to her reputation as a painter and photographer. But that, as Robina Sandel commented grimly, is what England has now become – a 'quick-change artist', is the expression she used, I think, meaning that everything this country had once represented is liable overnight to be turned into its opposite.

Apart from Robina's further comments on the recognizable tide of Fascism she saw engulfing us all, there is little else of importance concerning events on the gardens, their precursors and consequences. This is partly because Jean Hastie's brief return to London in May did not take her to Robina Sandel's but to the Bay Hotel in Westbourne Grove. As Mara was abroad, there was probably little to persuade her to revisit the scene of the tragedy. Jean's fleeting visit and return to Scotland have dictated, however, my own journey north, to see Mrs Hastie and obtain from her, if possible, an account of those days in May. Her information, unless it consists exclusively of researches concluded at the British Library, can hardly fail to shed some light on the sudden decline of Dr Frances Crane.

I leave for Fife tomorrow, August the twelfth. Six months to the day, indeed, since the killing of The Honourable Jeremy Toller by Mrs Hyde.

I should have guessed, on the 'Glorious Twelfth', that a good housewife and mother such as Jean Hastie would be out on the moors with sandwiches and flasks of soup for the guns – that is, those like her husband and other worthies of the neighbourhood whose one desire is to return with a brace of grouse for the larder. I hadn't counted on the fact of Jean Hastie's being one such herself; and I must say it came as something of a shock, after reading all the morbid details of the Notting Hill case, to find her – I'd been directed from their farmhouse to a heatherclad stretch of hill, where estate waggons and Land Rovers could be seen, parked by a ruined cottage and a small burn – looking straight down the barrel of a gun at me.

That the shoot in progress was elsewhere was Jean Hastie's first assurance; less reassuring, I thought, was her statement that she hadn't seen me coming up the hill (though I'd been only too painfully aware of the foolishness of leaving my hired Ford Sierra at the bottom and tackling a steep ascent, even causing shouts of annoyance as I put up some birds), and the succession of thoughts that then came to me, I must admit, were quite a bit to do with the likely veracity of a witness who is both shortsighted and – presumably – hard of hearing. Ask I did, all the same, first introducing myself as a friend of Dr Frances Crane; and soon I was settled in the heather next to Mrs Hastie's picnicking site. While waiting for the next drive, she told me what she remembered of the days she had spent in London in May.

'Yes, it's a terrible thing,' Jean Hastie said. A cloud of pollen rose around us as I settled myself and I saw her for a moment through a brownish haze: she looked like a woman in an old sepia photograph, distinctly Victorian then, or so I thought; and I wondered if I would ever get the whole truth from her. She could easily, for reasons of discretion, hold something vital back: she could, I reflected with some irritation, have long ago decided to see life permanently through a sweet-scented, enveloping haze.

'I certainly did go and see Frances.' Jean offered me a drink of home-made lemonade from a stoppered bottle. 'I knew we were destined to become friends – as soon as we met at Robina

Sandel's in February. It was the tension, I suppose, in the atmosphere then, that stopped us hitting it off immediately.'

'The tension caused by the rapist being at large?' I asked.

'Certainly. In my view some people had got the whole thing out of proportion.' Jean Hastie sighed, as if she alone were in possession of the secret of the important things in life, the threat to life itself – or, at the very least, to self-confidence – posed by an attack from a multiple rapist not being one of them. 'Mara Kaletsky for one. I honestly don't believe that an innocent man would have been killed if she and her – her friends hadn't incited that terrible woman to acts of violence. She'd already tried it once before, you know.'

'Who? You mean Mrs Hyde?'

'Yes. Mara told me she'd gone for Sir James Lister. He was walking down the street – to the corner of Ladbroke Grove, I think she said – and Mrs Hyde came charging at him and nearly broke his leg. With a wheeled shopper, or so Mara said.'

'Really?' I was beginning to see the vanishing murderer of Jeremy Toller in a new light; but what it was I couldn't at that moment quite tell.

'At least she's gone for good.' It was evident that Jean had pursued her quarry with the same tenacity her journals were to show. It occurred to me, slightly uncomfortably, that evil women like Mrs Hyde have a fascination for women such as Jean Hastie: as if a whole buried side to their nature, coming alive for a moment or so at the mention of the crime or whichever wicked deed, stirs pleasurably in them before subsiding again. It may account for the gigantic popularity of murder mysteries in England, I thought, and their huge female readership – for all the 'liberation' of the past couple of decades. And as for Scotland . . . we weren't far, it occurred to me, on this lonely hill, from the scene of many murders in border keeps . . . and tales, too, of *doppelgängers* and people metamorphosed to beasts or three-legged stools, somewhere in the depths of the woods.

'What *is* good about the whole thing,' Jean Hastie said, 'despite the infuriating slowness of the police in catching Mrs Hyde, is the marked improvement in Eliza Jekyll since the terrible woman has stopped battening on her. Yes, we all had dinner together – at her place – in May; and the other good thing is that Frances Crane was there. They'd fallen out over something, apparently – at least, in February they clearly weren't on speaking terms – yet in May, the seventh, I think it was, they were getting on like a house on fire. Monica Purves was there, too.'

'And Frances Crane seemed perfectly well then?' I said.

'Oh yes.' Jean Hastie shook her head in disbelief. A shout went up and a group of beaters appeared, signalling that the guns should return to their butts. Jean rose. I asked if I could go with her.

'Ye'll have to keep very quiet.' A schoolmistressy tone was employed to deliver this, and a markedly Scottish accent. I began to wonder if Mrs Hastie considered Frances Crane's misfortune to be mostly of her own making. Yet I was all the more determined to discover what Jean – possibly the last person to see her sane – had picked up in their final meeting.

The dinner had been so pleasant, Jean said, that she decided to forfeit a morning at the British Library and go and call on Dr Crane instead. She went first to the practice, in Walmer Road, where one of the two partners, Dr Bassett, said Dr Crane hadn't come in or phoned yet – and that this, while being most inconvenient for a line of waiting patients, was also most unusual. 'Then I went to her flat,' Jean said. 'No answer when I rang the bell. Of course I thought nothing of it. In fact I was quite glad to get back to the Library.'

This was the pattern of events on the eighth, ninth and tenth of May. Once the front door had been opened by a woman who said she came in to clean twice a week and that Dr Crane wanted to see no one. On the eleventh of May (and here, I must say, I had to feel grateful for Mrs Hastie's perseverance) at seven in the evening, Jean stopped in Rudyard Crescent on the way back from completing her researches and banged once more on the door.

'The shock,' Jean said. 'I'll never be able to forget it.' We were crossing the burn on a small ford of flattish stones as she spoke, and for a moment Mrs Hastie looked as if she were going to lose her footing. Instead, with nothing worse than a wet brogue to contend with, she pulled herself up on the bank, where sheep's pellets lay thick in grass entwined, at the water's edge, with wild nasturtiums. Out of breath, we panted on to the summit of the first hill, where the men had already taken up their positions in shallow dug-outs in the heather.

'She looked, literally, forty years older!' There was something eerie about the way Jean Hastie spoke, as if the memory had indeed been of seeing a ghost. The breathlessness added to the sudden, shaming sense of panic which seemed to have overtaken us both, on this calm hillside with nothing but the curlew swooping over harebells and ling.

'She was ... well, she was obviously dying,' Jean said in a matter-of-fact tone that belied her real feelings. 'She couldn't speak. She was white – and lined – and her hair – I suppose it must have been dyed or something and I'd never noticed it was growing out at the roots – was half-way grey so she looked – well, she didn't look like herself at all!'

I didn't know what to say at this point. We watched a flight of birds go over and heard a volley of shots, but Jean didn't so much as put her gun to her shoulder. When she did resume her tale, it was only to describe her terrified rush to Robina Sandel's – 'and thank God the woman was in' – and a phone call to Dr Crane's partner and then to the hospital.

'They – they came and took her away,' Jean said, 'with Robina and myself there to try and help her. But she wouldn't let us near her, you know. She was like a wild cat, hissing and scratching when we tried to come close. It took two ambulance men and Dr Bassett to pacify her. But – in the end – she went.'

I couldn't help shuddering myself. But I suppose Jean Hastie must have recovered quite a bit since then. It was four months ago, after all, and she had never known Dr Frances Crane well.

It seemed, as she returned to telling me about the delightful summer party Ms Jekyll had given on that evening just a few days before the collapse of Dr Crane, that she was definitely more interested in the 'pink candlesticks on the chestnut trees – about a month ahead of the time they come out up here, I can tell you' and the real candles in art nouveau candlesticks that had adorned Eliza's table – than in the mysterious and horrible fate of the doctor. Maybe she's not so callous as she seems, I told myself as I saw Mrs Hastie, now fully composed after her tale, swing the heavy twelve-bore sky high and bring a bird whacking to the ground. Or, even if she is, this is no moment to antagonize her.

So I tried my most deferential manner, while congratulating her on being an excellent shot; and then just happening to ask if Dr Crane had been able to communicate anything at all to her new-found friend.

'Yes, indeed.' Jean Hastie reloaded with care and deliberation. 'She handed me an envelope.'

'An envelope?' I felt like the stooge in a comedy turn. And, I reflected, there would be nothing to laugh about if only I could extract this envelope from Jean Hastie and take it to London with me.

'I'm here on behalf of Frances Crane's family and friends,' I said. 'It comes as a very great relief to learn that you have some kind of document which will clear this extraordinary matter up. Their gratitude, I can assure you . . .'

Again, I felt my words drying up. Jean was waving to a plus-foured man, her husband, presumably, who was strolling down through the hummocks of moss and heather towards us. The drive was over, then; and this was soon borne out by a posse of beaters appearing from over the top of the hill.

'I'm afraid it's out of the question for me to show it to you,' Jean Hastie said. 'Nor have I been apprised of the contents myself, I may say.'

'You haven't . . .'

This time the husband (as indeed he was) had come near enough to call out a greeting and obscure my stumbling incomprehension following a repeated request to look at the material.

'Written on the envelope,' said Jean Hastie with a cool, almost contemptuous glance over her shoulder at me, 'are the words "Not to be Opened Unless the Disappearance of Ms Eliza Jekyll makes this Imperative". I have, of course, complied with Dr Crane's wishes to this matter.'

'But why should Eliza Jekyll want to disappear?' I cried. A pitch of frustration had been reached, I knew, which would reflect badly on me with these cool, canny Scots. And sure enough, Paul Hastie and his wife exchanged quick glances. 'Those are the instructions,' Jean said quietly. 'I represent Ms Jekyll – at least I was about to until such time as, happily, she no longer required me to perform a certain conveyancing service for her – and I shall of course guard her privacy as her friend Frances Crane would have wished.'

'But where *is* the . . . paper?' I faltered.

'From the size and weight of the envelope it would seem to be a cassette,' Mrs Hastie said, with some return of conviviality. 'And it is, of course, in the safe in my firm's office in Edinburgh.'

A WINDOW IN LONDON

August is dry and lifeless, with most of the residents of Nightingale and other Crescents in the area away in Scotland – or Italy or Greece. They won't return until the school terms begin and the leaves on the chestnut trees in the communal gardens begin to go yellow and fall.

I am disappointed, I must confess, by my lack of success so far with information on Dr Frances Crane. Robina Sandel, who kindly asked me to visit her at No. 19 Nightingale Crescent pending my researches, has this to say on the matter: 'Mrs Jean Hastie is a stubborn one, and she'll never let you have the tape. Why don't you go and see Eliza Jekyll yourself and confide in her? For all you know, this is some trick being played on her by Jean Hastie – some kind of revenge, perhaps, from student days – and she'll be able to clear the whole matter up.'

I didn't relish the idea of going to call on Eliza Jekyll on my own and I said so. After all, we'd never met: surely she'd think it pretty out of order if I just went and banged on her door?

'Well, she's a friendly enough sort,' Robina said. 'Mara's coming back next Thursday, but no doubt you don't want to wait till then.' And seeing I didn't, she called her niece Tilda to walk down the street with me and introduce me to Ms Jekyll. Tilda had gone to help there with dinner parties in the past, Robina said; and although the girl had a horror of that end of the street, and particularly the garden side where she had witnessed Mr Toller's murder, she would understand my concern over my old friend Dr Frances Crane and would take me along. I thanked both Sandels for their kindness and understanding and Tilda and I set off.

Although it was only a week ago that we walked side by side down the Crescent, under heavy late-summer leaves and by the side of the now-silent road repair machines, it seems immeasurably longer – as if what was revealed to me in that time had a duration of its own, like a play, or a film – and could only exist in the memory by assuming quite different proportions. For though there seemed, on that tired August evening, to be no beginning, middle or end to the strange story of the murder in the gardens and the subsequent disappearance of Mrs Hyde and madness of Dr Frances Crane, all these components came neatly together in the days succeeding my walk with Tilda, like a spool on a tape unwinding – like the voices of two women as I was to hear them before long, speaking not to each other but into the air.

Tilda, like a horse shying away from a sudden noise, stopped all at once outside a door and refused to go on, her pale eyes and braided hair giving her the look of a lifesize German doll that someone has left propped up on the pavement. Then, with a rush and a bound, as if spirits guarded that stretch, she raced ahead; and it was as much as I could do to keep up with her.

'But, Tilda, you've gone past Eliza Jekyll's door,' I said when I managed to catch up with the girl on the corner of Ladbroke Grove; and then, having to sprint again as she ran to the gate into the communal gardens and took out a key which she fitted quickly into the lock. 'Wait a minute, that's not right, Tilda. You're going to the wrong place!'

Tilda showed no sign of answering, and was by now some way down the path on the southern side of the communal gardens, the flat, dark leaves of the big chestnut at the back of the Tollers' house almost obscuring her head as she went. If she wanted to take me out here, why didn't she go out of Robina's back garden? I thought – irritated by now, I must admit, at the air of urgency and secrecy the girl had assumed. If she's trying to tell me something, why doesn't she do so in the ordinary way?

The answer, as I now see, was plain – to Tilda, at least. She did want me to see with my own eyes – see the connection of the houses on Ladbroke Grove and Nightingale Crescent, the adjacent flats of the wicked, murderous, sluttish woman and the lovely Ms Jekyll. She wanted me, as I was to discover shortly after we had paused at the foot of Ms Jekyll's exquisite wrought-iron staircase, entwined at this time of year with geraniums and a small wall of sweet peas, to understand how close – how dangerously close the women had always been.

Ms Jekyll was sitting in the window of her flat. There was no doubt in my mind that it was she: Frances Crane had described her often enough – saying, with a laugh, that she was glad to be her friend but not her doctor (Dr Bassett fulfilled that function) as there always came a time in doctor-friend relationships when you have to refuse a request for something or other. And I wondered, remembering this, if, had Dr Crane been alive, she would have found something to be worried about in her friend's appearance today.

It's hard to define: just that, beautiful as I had expected her to be, Eliza Jekyll was even more perfect – almost impossibly perfect, with that tilt of the head and set of the neck that seem to go with beauty – and yet she seemed irredeemably sad. That old word melancholy came into my mind as I stood, half hidden by the chestnut tree at Tilda's side, and looked up at her. I remembered the photographs of Victorian madwomen incarcerated for 'eroticism', 'melancholy', even in one case 'intense vanity'. Ms Jekyll, as she sat staring at nothing in the window of her flat – she was on a sofa that had been pulled across the french windows, giving a further impression of someone barricaded in – looked as if she were badly in need of fresh air – or company.

Tilda put a foot on the first of the steps of the white iron stairs. 'Eliza!'

The face in the window turned; eyes sparkled; a charming smile appeared. 'Come out and see us!' Tilda pushed me a little forward. 'Someone here wants to meet you!'

Ms Jekyll rose, smiling and waving. (I was surprised to see that behind her, in the room, a pile of what looked like unwashed clothes and sheets threatened to topple from the table – and as if my glance in that direction had reminded her, she swung sharply round.)

I saw the back of her shoulders – we both did – convulsed with what must have been a sudden sobbing fit, or, worse, an attack of some kind that must surely need rapid medical attention. But with one hand the thick, interlined curtains were pulled to and the hunched trembling figure disappeared from our gaze. Like children at a conjuror's party, we stood, mouths open, for several seconds longer by the side of the chestnut tree.

'You know, I am very anxious for Miss Eliza,' Tilda said as we walked back slowly along the path of Robina's scruffy garden bordered by dark, unclipped shrubs. 'That woman is back – I know it. She will kill Eliza next!'

And Tilda wept, in the ragged long grass of her aunt's back garden. I thought, at first, of Jean Hastie and of summoning her down to deal with this. Jean, surely, had been here at the time of the murder. Jean alone had evidence of Dr Crane's last meeting with Eliza. Again, I realized I needed evidence myself if I were to risk calling her in her Scottish shooting party and asking her to come south and prevent further loss of life.

'I heard that woman Mrs Hyde in there the other day,' Tilda said, as if waiting for me to ask for proof. 'It was her voice. I know! She was shouting at poor Eliza!'

THE LAST EVENING

As it turned out, I didn't have to wait long to discover the truth of what Tilda said (Robina was sceptical about this, I have to say, and argued that if Mrs Hyde had indeed come back, the police of fifty countries would have been on her trail by now).

It was the following evening. Mara Kaletsky had just returned from a summer spent in gypsy caves in Hydra, and looked tanned and well; as if the whole nightmare of the killing in the gardens, and the hysteria over the rapist, had long ago gone from her mind. Robina had been kind enough to ask me round again; it was a fine evening, the gold sunlight as it poured into the long club room making even the dull of the old brass fender shine; and soon, when Monica Purves and her friend Carol Hill joined us, I saw that, for everyone, with the exception of Tilda, of course, the nightmare of the past was indeed over. I confess I had to wonder whether the girl's inflamed imagination hadn't been responsible for some of the unease I'd felt myself. It was true that Eliza Jekyll had turned away from us with a convulsive shudder; on the other hand it was possible that Tilda, who was quite an outspoken and annoying young woman, might have offended her at some dinner party to which she had been asked to come as a helper, and Eliza, with possible serious things on her mind, had turned away with a touch of intended melodrama, so as to warn us away from her window.

Whatever the truth was, an evening as pleasant as the one we were enjoying made one glad the rest of the Crescent was so empty; and a walk was soon suggested. Robina went to fetch the key to the back garden door and we all strolled out, only Tilda muttering an excuse and running upstairs to her room.

We hadn't gone far along the path when we saw the figure hurrying towards us. Monica Purves was the first to recognize the woman: Mrs Poole (for such it was) came sometimes to clean for her as she did, evidently, for Ms Jekyll. 'Oh, Miss Purves!' Mrs Poole seized hold of the stockbroker's sleeve, as if in need of something to help her keep her balance. 'There's been a terrible accident! That woman's come back and she's done away with Ms Jekyll, I know she has!'

JEAN HASTIE COMES SOUTH

I have to say at this point that I am now in possession of Jean Hastie's journals – and also the tape which Dr Frances Crane entrusted to her.

Jean may be a somewhat self-satisfied woman, but she left her family and house party as soon as she heard of the disappearance of Ms Eliza Jekyll and came south, stopping only at her firm's offices to retrieve the envelope sealed permanently unless there was a case of such a disappearance. She came straight to Robina's, after a bad night on a sleeper – and I must say she found us all as haggard as herself, sitting, as we had been all night, in the club room.

I won't go too far into the scene of chaos in Ms Jekyll's flat, once Monica had forced the french windows and we went in. Squalor needs no describing: what was worse were the evident signs of struggle, pointing almost inevitably to an attack – not dissimilar to the rapist's, as Carol Hill remarked with a grimace of strong distaste as she relived her own ordeal – and to the attacker having disposed of Eliza's body before making a getaway.

A door through the mirrored hall was open and there seemed little doubt – as dirty linen, spilled remains of junk food meals, etc., trailed from the (now equally filthy) apartment of Ms Jekyll into the run-down quarters of Mrs Hyde – of the identity of the murderer.

One mystery (for we had all learnt at the time of the Toller killing that the Hyde children had been placed in care) was irrefutable evidence of the recent presence of children. A potty had been used; and probably not all that long ago. Half-eaten fish fingers lay under a pile of broken Lego under the kitchen table. A small gym shoe, laces hopelessly knotted, had been kicked off by the door through to Ms Jekyll's Venetian-glass-panelled hallway.

'I don't know if they was back or not,' Mrs Poole said (having already given what evidence she possessed to the police she had returned to tell Jean what she had seen). 'I only know I heard a woman wailing like a banshee when I went round to give Miss Jekyll a hand with the flat. She'd not been in touch for – oh, it must have been near on eight weeks – but don't tell me that mess in there was her who done it.' Mrs Poole shook her head firmly. 'She was got at by that Mrs Hyde – wasn't she?'

'But you saw her?' Jean Hastie asked in that quiet, dry way that reminds you of her training as a solicitor.

'Oh no, love. I just heard that terrible wailing sound. Reminded me of a siren going off in the blitz, I can tell you!'

After this unexpected piece of imagery, we all fell silent.

'So you didn't see Mrs Hyde either?' Jean prompted the woman.

'I sees the kids,' Mrs Poole said. 'They was playing out by that dreadful old pianola-thing in the back garden, that the Council won't take, and I can't think why she couldn't get rid of it herself. "Funny, how'd they come to be here?" I remember thinking to myself. If I'd just gone into Miss Jekyll's that day – if I hadn't just waited one day more, but with my aunt in hospital—'

'It's not your fault,' Robina said, standing up so that we could all feel released to go in the direction of hot baths, breakfast, bed.

'The police will be searching for Eliza Jekyll everywhere. They'll find her in the end.'

'They'll have to find Mrs Hyde first,' said Tilda, appearing from her eyrie after a loud clattering down the stairs.

After a day of rest, renewed speculation and unanswered questions, Jean Hastie took the night train back to Scotland, to be with her husband and young family. She told me she had no desire to listen to the tape; and that as I had been given the brief by Dr Crane's solicitors to try and fathom the cause of the doctor's 'mystery illness' and death, she would prefer me to be its sole audience.

Mara Kaletsky invited me to come to her room at No. 19 Nightingale Crescent whenever I wanted, as home movies she had made of the opening of the Shade Gallery, etc. might be useful to me in my researches.

I have also put down as best I could my own impressions of the characters and setting of this odd tale; but if it hadn't been, once more, for Tilda, I would not now be in possession of a second, and vital, piece of oral evidence.

'The last time I saw Eliza,' Tilda said, 'on the day before we went round to call on her, she was sitting at a table by the window – she must have pulled the sofa across after that – and she was dictating a message into her answering-machine. I remember, because she was such a long time speaking, and I thought maybe she dictates addresses and phone numbers of somewhere she's going to.'

It was a weird feeling, calling the number of a person you know to have disappeared – and who, possibly, is also dead – but call I did.

Ms Eliza Jekyll's message, to whomsoever it may concern, is presented here, after Dr Crane's dictated jottings, in order to solve the mystery.

DR FRANCES CRANE'S NOTES AND MEMORABILIA

I was surprised to receive a letter from Eliza Jekyll on the day after her dinner party. May the eighth. We'd had a pleasant evening; it had been good to see an old friend in a less, I suppose one would have to say, exalted state than she had manifested on the infrequent and unsuccessful occasions of our meeting over the last year; and I must admit to a feeling of slight complacency on opening the envelope. Eliza was, in all probability, writing to thank *me* for coming to her dinner, and for openly resuming our friendship. That this was hardly the case was soon painfully evident.

I reproduce the letter in full, in the interests of medical science. And, I plainly confess, as a proof of my irremediable guilt in this grim and unsavoury business. My blindness and insensitivity as a member of the medical profession have led, in the main, to a state of affairs so appalling that no memory can encompass it without turning the corner from sanity into silence and madness.

This, as I know, is the path which is marked out for me. Yet my first reaction to Ms Jekyll's (hand-delivered) letter was that it was my correspondent who had gone mad.

Dear Frances,
I must ask you a favour. You will understand one day – and you will understand, too, the cause of a coolness between us – which came, I know from your disapproval of my way of life and general state of mind.

But for now – I really do beg you – just go round to my flat in Nightingale Crescent – Mrs Poole will let you in if you go as soon as you get this – and ask Mrs Poole to leave before you go to the little cabinet in the corner of my sitting room and open the door.

You can't miss it – the papier mâché cabinet with a scene on the door of a woman on a balcony, overlooking the sea. In the third drawer you will find a twist of white tissue paper. Take it out and wait for further developments.

This is a matter of life and death to me, Frances – please in the name of God do as I say.

Eliza

I had to move a patient to my partner Dr Bassett, all of which caused a good deal of inconvenience all round, but I went to the flat in Nightingale Crescent, half convinced, as I say, that I would have a duty to have my friend committed to a mental asylum by the end of the call.

Mrs Pool, as obviously arranged, let me in. But as far as a speedy exit from the flat went, this was not to be. I won't attempt to reproduce her speech, but the gist of what she said – and she was alarmed – considerably – I could see, amounted to a strong suspicion that violent and unpleasant scenes were taking place on the premises. There were tables overturned when she came in this morning, she said – and further signs of a struggle. That woman was back. That Mrs Hyde. And she was attacking her benefactor, who'd never in her life – and Mrs Poole knew this for a fact – done anything wrong. Miss Jekyll was hiding her somewhere here. And – this was the worst of it – when Mrs Poole had been coming back late from the pub with her husband and her sister-in-law last night, she'd heard such a sound coming out of this floor, such a sound as you couldn't for the life of you describe.

I asked Mrs Poole if she could nevertheless try. I was frightened, myself, I have to admit: and all the while we stood there talking I was keeping my eyes on this little cupboard in the corner of the room furthest from the window, with its dreamlike, oddly disconcerting picture – like a Romantic opium scene, I suppose you might say – of a girl in a ball dress with bare shoulders sitting at a desk on a great sweeping balcony and beyond, rocks and the sea. The noise had at first been just a woman weeping, Mrs Poole said. But after that – her sister-in-law had said it was like a lost soul. And Mrs Poole, as if suddenly embarrassed by herself, proceeded to inform me she had to get

263

to the shops before early closing and left the flat with all the bustle and sound of a denizen of this earth, lost soul or no.

I was both relieved and faintly alarmed by her going. But I went, steeling myself, to the squat little cabinet, knelt down, and opened the third drawer.

There, sure enough, was a twist of white tissue paper.

And there, on the back of a half-scrumpled envelope, was the name and phone number of London's most notorious doctor – a man who had deliberately allowed the deaths from overdoses of at least two world-famous rock stars; a man known to ask no questions while supplying lethal amounts of anything from amphetamine to crack, or heroin.

It wasn't hard, when I cautiously undid the twist of paper, to recognize the drug. We'd had enough patients in casualty at St Charles – young, nearly all of them, and supplied with the stuff no doubt at the clubs from which they were carried unconscious to an ambulance. So Eliza Jekyll – I must say that my brain reeled at the thought of the composed and beautiful Eliza a secret addict of the most destructive and, as yet, largely unknown in its long-term effects, substance on the black market: by name, Ecstasy.

As I still knelt there, the doorbell rang. And, as I paused, wondering what these 'further developments' were going to turn out to be, it sounded again and again, with a desperation that seemed to come right through the entryphone system and into the room.

'Yes?' I said finally into the receiver – and beginning to be properly afraid, I have to admit, for the shuffling, whimpering sounds on the other side of the door were unmistakably those of the person – or thing – with its finger jammed down on the bell.

Of course, there was no answer. I didn't press the buzzer, but went to fling open the door of the flat.

The account of what followed must not be taken as a symptom of the increasing confusion and partial paralysis of the central nervous system which has succeeded the revelations of that brief quarter of an hour in Eliza Jekyll's flat. I was able to dictate notes immediately on return to my practice – with the door locked, it goes without saying – for fear that a colleague or patient might hear this tale of the – apparently – impossible.

Mrs Hyde stood at the door. The murderer of Jeremy Toller, subject of a worldwide police search, stood in front of me, hunched, whimpering, bedraggled, hand outstretched.

'Did you open the cabinet, Frances?' said the creature (for so, to my bitter shame, I confess I saw her). And, coming into the flat and pushing the door violently shut behind her – 'I was sent by Eliza. She sent me, Frances, to collect the–'

Here Mrs Hyde stopped, as she saw the twist of paper in my hands. Before I could pull away from her she was on me. Her teeth went into my neck – there was a vile smell clinging to her clothes, which were grey and streaked with grease as if she'd been sleeping rough in a railway station, as if, almost, the smell of sulphur she had on her had come up out of the ground to envelop her filthy clothes and cardboard shoes.

She was strong, that woman. Mrs Hyde had my arm in a half-Nelson – the hand that held the twist of paper soon relinquished its burden – and she leapt away from me, to press the contents flat down on the table.

On the round rosewood dining-table where only last night we'd all sat and discussed the coming Picasso exhibition and the Impressionist treasures from the Hermitage, Mrs Hyde sifted her drug and funnelled the paper to bring to nostrils gaping and greedy for the fix.

I should have known. And yet – how could it be? For, close to fainting, I saw the body of the most hated, the most vilified, the most hunted woman transform, translate itself, and, worse, for it should not be, to a form of beauty.

As the stooping shoulders straightened, the neck rose straight to bear a head – still dirty, true, but appearing now simply muddied by some rustic idyll or purposely for a glossy magazine sitting – that in its confidence of beauty and arrogance literally took my breath away. And the smile! Eliza's sweet, taunting smile, which I had seen her use to such good effect on Sir James Lister and others, was beamed steadily, and totally unselfconsciously, on me.

'You see, Frances,' said this apparition, moving now to the hall and a line of fitted cupboards hidden in the mirrored walls. 'You have been treating me all along. But when you took me off the little helpers you first put me on so long ago, I was driven to find another to take their place. And Dr Ruby brought me back – well almost from the dead!'

I couldn't find any words. It was as if – and this was perhaps the first onslaught of the famously rapid degenerative disease which has me in its grip – I had words stuck deep down in my throat and no muscle that would haul them up. I tried to ask Eliza, as she flitted into the bathroom and reappeared gleaming-faced and bright-eyed and as she wafted from the cupboard door in green raw silk suitable for the lovely May day outside, how she could fail to give herself up to the police: how she could live with the knowledge of the guilt of her crime.

But no words came.

And, with a backward, mocking glance at me, Eliza Jekyll walked out of the flat.

Yet the ultimate blame is mine.

I treated Mrs Hyde for anxiety. Three years ago I prescribed Anxian; and on a repeat prescription that demanded no vigilance from me.

In January this year Mrs Hyde called me. She said she was desperate. I saw evidence of neglect of her children and home. She admitted to violent impulses but would not divulge their exact nature. I prescribed Mrs Hyde's withdrawal from tranquillizers and advised a healthy diet and early nights.

It is only recently that the effects of withdrawal from these drugs have become known to the medical profession – and to the public at large. Heroin withdrawal symptoms are compared favourably with the effects.

By failing to keep in touch with the most recent discoveries on the nature of these pharmaceuticals and by continuing to allow Mrs Hyde to cash a repeat National Health prescription for them, I was surely condemning her to a state of dangerous disorder.

It is hardly surprising that, doubtless after reading one of those obnoxious newspaper articles, she went to the disreputable Dr Ruby.

Nothing can ever explain the personality change: its swiftness and its absoluteness. But we, as members of the medical profession, still have much to learn on the subject of personality disorders and their causes, both physiological and social.

I will not condemn Eliza to a lifetime in prison, and leave these notes for whomsoever shall find them – but only after my own death and/or the final disappearance of Ms Jekyll/Hyde.

MS ELIZA JEKYLL'S ANSAFONE MESSAGE

This is 229 46052. I'm afraid I can't answer your call at the moment. Please leave a message and speak after the bleep.

I have one last statement to make.

I am as I am: I was brought up to believe in happiness; and my parents and schoolteachers gave me nothing but love and encouragement. I had no idea of the reality of life, of the pain and suffering which once was considered an integral part of it.

When the inevitable breakdown – for someone imbued with impossible dreams of happiness as I was – finally came, I was in no way capable of dealing with it.

My husband left me.

I became a slut. I struck my children.

My ex-husband's last visit to me was on the twelfth of February. He lives all round the world, and I live round these gardens, where I walk like a prisoner three times a day, rain or shine.

Sometimes I think of the man who comes to visit me as the rapist, and sometimes as the old rock star who owns the building and wants to tear it down and put it up again without me. Or the man who I went to see when I first took the drug and I put my hair up high and painted my nails and went out in high heels.

And he gave me the job. In the gallery.

But already the make-up wore off too soon, tired, tired.

And the meals lie round the kids' plates like a slug.

So on the nights when the birds first begin to mate, I went out in the frost and the room I'd rented and furnished on my new salary lay behind me like a Christmas decoration, and I killed the man as he came to lock up his precious family.

IT WOULD HARDLY be possible to make sense of a cursory message of this nature if it were not for Mara Kaletsky, who came to see me today and explained, after much beating about the bush, she 'had been keeping something from me all along'.

On the night of Eliza's disappearance, Mara says – before the final struggle overheard and reported by Grace Poole – she had gone round to the flat in Nightingale Crescent: first, as she points out with a trace of indignation, to demand why Eliza had done nothing to save her exhibition at the Shade Gallery; second, because she had 'a funny feeling that something was going on, and she couldn't say exactly what'. What she did see, in fact, was both surprising and intensely familiar to her, of course – for the features of Mrs Hyde, cut up and pasted down in so many of her collages, seemed, when the door of the elegant apartment was opened, to be fleetingly but unmistakably imprinted on the face of Eliza. It was like, Mara says, one of those images you get when you're half asleep – eidetic visions, she calls them (her next show will, she says, be composed of them, 'photographs from the sleeping brain') and there was an uncanny sense of unreality in Ms Jekyll's features – for a split second – as she opened the door and led Mara through into the mirrored hall. 'I've never experienced anything like it. Really – like hallucinating someone. And no wonder I thought so, because by the time we reached the window – it was a dark August day, remember, with the trees outside almost blocking the sky – and light came in on her, there was Mrs Hyde standing in front of me as plain as day.'

It was then that Mara decided to load her eternal video and shoot a roll of film. 'It's her response, one must suppose, to any situation – and perhaps Mara is no more than a presage of a world where the sole survivors are machines; where the images of people, imprinted like Fayoum portraits at the neck of ancient Egyptian tombs, speak in solitude and isolation to each other across time. Mara, it seems, has no way of answering human distress or communication other than to record it – yet Eliza Jekyll, doubled in her self and craving a true mirror image, clearly was as keen to speak into camera as any actress long starved of a part.

Mrs Hyde is speaking. It's eerie, to see the gardens framed by the french window behind her head: the gardens where the man lay dead in February. And it's shocking, somehow, to see her in Ms Jekyll's ornate quarters – though these, by now, are topsy-turvy with dirty clothes and broken plastic toy telephones, the detritus of a woman's life with children.

'I always had to tidy them away. If they offer you jobs they don't want to see a toy – a nappy – no.

'At first I pushed things under the chairs and into the cupboards. But then my big break came. I was able to rent this place – next to my own impossible flat – and I was offered a job almost straight away.

'But first I should describe what my life has been.

'I was born and grew up in London. I went to art school in Oxford and when I left school – it was there I met Jean Hastie. I'd have thought she'd have been more helpful to a woman in my circumstances. But, of course, she doesn't understand.

'I was just starting my first job, designing textiles for a big firm in the Midlands, when I met my husband. He was a journalist, doing pieces on working conditions, Trade Union legislation, that kind of thing.'

Here Mrs Hyde pauses, and Mara brings the camera right up to her. But she turns away, losing that face in the shadow from the rich, interlined curtains her new persona had put up to

impress the clients and keep out the undesirable elements of the
world. All the same, the shudder of revulsion at her appearance
remains: what is it about her except that she is clearly poor and
ground down by life? What is it, other than the mesh of lines
which seems, by catching her face so tight in its grasp, to have
shrunk her head so that she appears to be both preserved, her
head like a pygmy's head kept by a collector or hunter; and
infinitely decayed, as if she could at any time disintegrate altogether, leaving on Mara's screen a pure, blank roomscape. Or is
it just the reality of life's hard writing on her that makes her, seen
through the eyes of guilt, so alien? Aren't there a vast number
like her – persecuted by a hostile state? And facing hostility and
fear from the public too?

Speculation of this kind is, however, countered by Mrs Hyde's
succeeding statements. One can only wish, if the woman is found
and brought to trial for the murder of Jeremy Toller, that she had
not made this utterance: sympathy would otherwise surely have
been forthcoming, for her position was, after all, not an enviable
one, even if only too common.

'I may say', comes the voice of Mrs Hyde from the deep
shadows by the curtain, 'that I was charmed by my husband –
many were and still are – but I soon saw that there was no love
there for either of us and knew I would soon be on my own.

'By this time I had two babies, eighteen months apart. The flat
in Ladbroke Grove, on a fixed rent, was possible to find in those
days – and it was the area where I had grown up – though it's
changed now, of course, beyond recognition.

'I went on Social Security because there was no way at all that
I could bring up these two young children and go out to a
demanding job. I had no living relatives and only a few people
who remembered me from the past. They, too, seemed sealed off
in their worlds of trying to survive on little money and as single
parents.

'I kept the kids clean and I cooked for them. They played in
the communal gardens, but as the posh people moved in, their

children threw stones at mine. Soon they were too frightened to go out there and we were all cooped up together in the flat.

'About this time I started having the dreams. Sometimes my husband came and saw me and sometimes I saw him in the dreams, and when he came we fucked occasionally, but it was hard because of the children. One night I dreamt I saw a tear the size of a big diamond lying on my hand and I felt a terrible grief inside, as if someone I knew very well – and loved – had died.

'When I woke, every morning after that, I knew some terrible change had come over me.

'Where I had been lithe and supple, with a dancer's legs and quick movements, I became slow and plodding as a sack of potatoes being dragged along the street. My neck shrank into my shoulders and my back began to develop a dowager's stoop, as if I was in turn dragging a great load of people through the world.

'But the waking moments were the worst. I would open my eyes – woken nearly always by a scream from one of the kids – and, for the first times at least, I had to do my best to repress a scream myself.

'There would be a hand lying on the pillow next to me.

'The hand was grey and wrinkled, and it was like a dead person's hand, limp and a darkish purple where the grey skin wasn't puckered by the join of finger and thumb. And – of course – it was my own ageing, defeated, accusing hand.

'I couldn't bear it. As the dreams went on, and I woke each time to the sight of this lame, dead piece of tissue and bone – which seemed more and more to stand for all of me, to be none of me but clearly what I had become – I began to cry and lose my temper with the children, and find pleasure only in plunging my hands in soap and suds so scalding hot that the little, half-broken Ascot over the sink would practically splutter itself out at the pressure of it.

'When I'd been hitting the kids so much I knew there might be a real battering in the night – an empty cot – a social worker called (and the nosy Mrs Poole was already round when I was shouting in a voice I didn't even know, and the kids were yelling like stuck pigs) and I went to Dr Crane at the Walmer Road practice.

'Well, the Anxian just made me cry the more. The world was grey, entirely grey. I threw out the pianola, which my husband had played once and which had some kind of a hurdy-gurdy colour to it, I suppose – and I watched it going grey in the little patch of balding grass that stands for a "patio" at this end of the communal gardens. The more I cried, the more the kids screamed. I tied them in their cots, but the social worker came again – and Dr Crane said they'd have to go.

'She was kind, Frances Crane. She didn't like people's kids being taken away. She put the drug under my skin, in the flesh just below that terrible hand. Nothing much happened at first – but then the dreams began to change and so did I.

'You can't imagine what it's like when your youth comes back – and beauty, and more – and the figure and the quick step to go with it. It only happened gradually at first, but I found out that if I took the pills my friend Marge gets from Dr Ruby from time to time it had some effect on the hormone drug and I could turn – just like that – into the person I had been. Yes, into me! Eliza! Where had I gone? Who had I been? But now – when I wanted, I was me!

'For I couldn't have it all the time. It wore off, faster and faster – but of course, as you know, Mara, I was at first Ms Eliza Jekyll most of the time and I went for the interview with Sir James Lister and I got the job running the Shade Gallery in Portobello Road.

'It was a long time since anyone had fancied me, and I couldn't think at first what Sir James was doing, making those funny faces and rolling his eyes, when I sat opposite him at the interview. Then he bent down and gave me a little kick under the table, and I knew it was OK.

'I loved the power. Men would do anything for me. It was no

problem getting this flat – from which of course I could go next door to my children – and the same landlord that had been round threatening "me" only the month before, was all over "me" as Ms Jekyll. But then I was paying a "commercial" rent, wasn't I, as Ms Eliza Jekyll?

'And I liked doing up the flat and giving dinner parties. The children went into a private nursery school. But one thing I desperately needed – and that was to buy the flat, the landlord was offering the freehold to those tenants who wanted them – and I wrote to Jean Hastie, asking her to do a conveyancing job for me.

'For if Mrs Hyde was the poor poor – that is, too poor to exist without State support – and even that dwindling (legislation changed for flat-renting so as sure as anything she'd be evicted from Ladbroke Grove) – then Eliza was the "rich poor", the individual encouraged to take out a hundred per cent mortgage: which "I" could, of course, with a job at the Shade and the hint from Sir James that I'd go on to run his design business in the South West.

'Jean was very stubborn; but I couldn't ask a London solicitor, who might know who I was. And, as my fear grew that my strange condition would become known, I realized I had to find and destroy those pictures of "me" that you had taken, Mara – of both of me, that is – for fear that the pieces of the collage might be put together by some bright guy one day and I'd be rumbled. I went and hunted outside your studio, by the canal in Kensal Rise . . .

'As the fear grew, so did the rapidity with which the drug wore off. One day, coming back from Portobello Road where I had successfully been Eliza all day, I could feel myself change – and at the same time I could see Sir James Lister walking down Rudyard Crescent and coming towards me. Oh, brother! I said to myself. And – I have to tell you – the sensation of pure violence that poured through me was the most wonderful sensation I have ever had in my life. I was bow-legged by now, and my back was hunched up – and my hand, on the wheeled shopper I was pushing back with fine foods for the kids' supper was like the claw of some predator . . .

'And as he passed me I lunged at him and I ran him down. Well, I bumped into him hard, you might say . . .

'And all he saw was a poor, foul-smelling woman (for some reason these changes back to Mrs Hyde were always accompanied by a strong, unbearable smell, like escaping gas, and I always carried a raincoat with me, to cover the shrinking body and the odour of putrefaction).

' "Hey there!" he shouted.

'But he didn't think it worth his while to go after me. This man who had tried to fondle my breasts only an hour before! Who had invited me to a Valentine's Day lunch at the Pomme d'Amour restaurant in Holland Park Avenue!

'But that was a date, of course, that I was in no position to take up . . .'

'On the night of the twelfth of February – just a few days after this – I gave my dinner party. I was worried about you finding out the truth, Mara, because you had been behind me in the street when I ran at Sir James . . . but you didn't seem to think anything strange was going on whatsoever.

'I knew better. My dreams had come back again, and the night before I'd heard the birds getting ready for an almighty burst for spring.

'I was Mrs Hyde . . . unexpectedly and terrifyingly . . . more and more often; and that night I knew I was poised, like a china cup that might fall from a shelf at the slightest tremble of the earth, and go into a million different pieces.'

'The landlord had been round to Ladbroke Grove and had informed me that I must pay a large sum towards the renovation of the "common parts" of the building. I told him I wouldn't; and he told me there were a good many ways of getting me out.

'That was the day before. On the evening of the dinner, my husband – or ex-husband as he is – came to "see the kids". I wanted him out. He'd spoil my play for the big job with Sir James – and I was prepared to go all the way for it, I can tell you. Turning up just when he knows it'll wreck the chance of a new life for me – the no-maintenance fucking bastard.'

Mrs Hyde paused again. Then she stepped out from the folds of the curtain; and, as Mara records, something like the beginning of a return transformation must have been taking place, for she looked taller, handsome, almost.

'I got him out in the end,' says this new apparition. 'But it tired me, I can tell you, Mara. By the time the guests – and the food and the waiter – came, I was a wreck.

'Somehow I got through the dinner. All the talk of the rapist was getting on my nerves – especially as "I" in my persona as Mrs Hyde (who was unable to prevent myself from running naked in her terrible anger in the gale-lashed gardens) was actually a heroine now, as far as you, and most of the more radical women in the neighbourhood, were concerned.

'When everyone had gone I went out into the gardens to get some air. I could hardly believe what I had heard from Sir James – it had been couched, of course, in evasive language – but it seemed he was getting out of England altogether and setting up business in California – and the concomitant suggestion that both the Shade Gallery and his textile business would close down had been left hanging in the air between us. I walked a little; came back into the flat, and I must have fallen asleep. I woke at some dead hour of the early morning. And there ... hanging by my side ... like a dead rodent ... like something that has been dragged in and left to die ... was the hand of Mrs Hyde.

'For the first time, I had changed as I slept: the Yuppie who took a quick nap after a successful dinner party had woken the avenging slattern, practically a witch in the locality by now, hated and despised by the respectable inhabitants of these leafy crescents and squares.

'I went out into a night that had the false dawn of a London night hanging above it like a cloud from a crematorium. The birds began to strike up. Valentine's Day . . . two hearts indeed, I thought, as I saw a man walk down towards me on the path . . . two hearts, my sweetheart, beating as one in the dawn of spring.

'The rapist walked there, Mara, with the face of my husband and the landlord's long, straight legs, and the slight pot belly of Sir James.

'The rapist loomed and leered at me.

'With the parrot head umbrella Ms Jekyll carries wherever she goes I walked towards that Valentine man; and I smiled at him as if it were the most normal thing in the world to be out walking in the middle of the night, in the gardens.

'He looked worried as he passed me. I dimly saw there was a dog at his heels, a little white thing I'd grown to hate, as it bit the kids when they went out.

'He looked surprised – that was all. For, after going past him, I nipped as suddenly as the time I felt the change come on me in the gallery when I ran to heave – against my will and with all the will in the world – a brick through the window of the place – I nipped sideways and behind him and hooked him round the collarbone with that parrot on a stick with nylon wings.

'Thank God – I could change quickly back to Eliza Jekyll that night. And next day I had to stand by and watch them take Mrs Hyde's children into care.'

The film ends suddenly here. There's a run of white tape; and then a black and white fuzzy scene, as if a child was doodling with a pencil on a dirty piece of paper.

'She begged me not to follow her,' Mara says. 'And I didn't. Don't tell me I was wrong.'

I said I wasn't telling her anything.

'I gave her all the money I had,' Mara says. 'She promised to hide in the cellar. And then she climbed up from the basement and hid under the dug-up street until I gave her the all-clear.'

There was a silence.

'Where are the children?' I asked. 'And why did they come out of care?'

'Jean Hastie applied to foster them – in Scotland,' Mara replies, as if it had been dumb of me not to see that there was kindness in the Scottish lawyer, all along. 'Jean told Eliza that if there was trouble, she'd bring the children up. She guessed some of this, I think.'

Or she listened to Dr Crane's notes, I thought to myself. And, before I could imagine Mrs Hyde's children's transformation into bairns in the hands of Jean Hastie and her husband, Mara had added quietly that, although Mrs Hyde, still sought internationally for the murder of businessman and local magistrate Jeremy Toller, had briefly been sighted on a cross-channel ferry from Weymouth to Cherbourg, there had apparently been no sign of her whatsoever on board when the French gendarmerie swarmed on to the boat.

'Mrs Hyde came up into Ladbroke Grove,' says Mara. 'But by the time she was in France – well, she must have been Eliza Jekyll again.'

'Or', I couldn't help remarking, 'for all – as Jean Hastie would say – that the woman had killed and must answer for the crime, perhaps she has at last been able to find herself.'

AFTERWORD BY JEAN HASTIE

Fife, Christmas '88

It was today that I posted the manuscript of my work on Original Sin to the publishers in London and a copy to my agent in Edinburgh.

Despite my conviction, earlier in the year, that my research on Original Sin in the Garden of Eden, showing a choice for Christians up until the fourth century and the coming of St Augustine between salvation and damnation, was conclusive evidence of an innate sense of moral responsibility in each individual, I have to say here that I am no longer certain on this – all-important – point.

The case of Eliza Jekyll has caused a considerable rift in both Christian and atheist feminist thinking.

For, while it is incontestably true that the stress and discrimination suffered by a single mother in an environment growing daily more hostile in both financial and psychological terms can cause defensive violence as well as misery and frustration, it is also true that Eliza has proved to have been the harbourer of sentiments and impulses which can only be described as evil. Scribbled notes found by the bed of Mrs Hyde, in the final clear-out of her flat, attempt to give some substance to the 'bad dreams' the poor woman suffered in her phase of acute Anxian withdrawal.

That these were not dreams but murderous intentions is borne out by the knife she describes as hiding under the floorboards of the kitchen – and which was found there, under cork tiling disintegrating to the touch.

The knife was brandished at the rapist – as Mrs Hyde went out to get him that night in February, but naked, under the see-through white plastic mac.

He got away – that time. The police caught him in the end. But Mrs Hyde – will they ever catch her?

I keep hidden from her children, who stay with me here and breathe the purer air of Scotland, any news stories or headlines that crop up in the search for their mother. And I'll make sure they don't find the other side of this tragic victim of our new Victorian values: the word, scrawled across the pad under a list of household essentials –

Ajax
fishfingers
ketchup
Mother's Pride

KILL

Faustine

For Lorna Sage

I

THE GRANDDAUGHTER'S TALE

I HAVE BEEN here before.

There's a bump at the side of the road that looks as if someone, a child perhaps, had tried to build a mud hut, or make a fortification of some kind, and had then lost interest, leaving a rounded knoll, now covered with grass, that you had to swerve out into the road to avoid.

And there's the yew hedge, as tall as once I knew it, though it must have grown as I have, and been much lower then; and a jagged hole, just two feet from the ground, gapes ready, as it did before, for an exploring hand.

There's the chequered stone house, with the oak door that's gone as grey as a seal's coat from the wind and rain.

But I know I have to walk round the back, over yellow tiles two fingers wide and laid in neat late-Victorian patterns, which lie between the drive and the cobbles of the courtyard. When I am there, I will see the old coach-house, and the wing with a greenish thatch that looks as if the swans that live up-river had pecked at it for their nests.

And there I do see a couple – a man and a woman, neither old nor young, but cross, repelling – staring at me in a way that makes my feet drag and my eyes go to the intricate layout of stones on the ground. They make no motion, at my appearance, of either welcome or protest.

I stop, and we stand looking at each other. They have seen me here before.

I WAS IN the kitchen of her house in Melbourne, when Maureen Fisher, scanning the newspaper over a cup of coffee, let out one of her exasperated sighs, laid the paper flat on the table, then swung to her feet and laughed.

'Well, good luck to anyone who wants to go over there, Ella,' she said. 'One way of wasting time, if you ask me. Will there be a royal divorce? Will the police overcome the hippies at Stonehenge, or vice versa? Jesus H. Christ!'

I must say here that Maureen Fisher has never been to England.

And I – what I remember may be as invented or as real as a dream. Did I live in this place or that? Did I really see the trees in a park 12,000 miles away, straining in a great wind, and see the fear on the face of the man who was pushing me in my pram?

He broke into a run, I do remember that. And he had a dark hat, down at a sharp angle over his face. But who the man was, I couldn't say.

Maureen Fisher is a distant relative of my family on my mother's side, and, as she had with so many other children, she took me in.

Her husband, Bill, has a big sheep station to the north of Melbourne, and Maureen and I – since I was old enough to help – have been running a children's nursery in the town.

Many of the children are Malaysian or Chinese (families that come to Australia from Penang and Singapore to practise law or medicine); and I knew it would be a wrench to leave Chi-ren, my own favourite, with dark eyes and a haughty manner that makes even a disciplinarian like Maureen burst out laughing.

But, as I pointed out to her, it was time I went. Time I went to find out more about myself.

And, most of all, to find my beloved grandmother.

It's not Maureen Fisher's fault that I can't feel anything for her and never have. She's been kindness itself in her practical, no-nonsense way. It's just that she doesn't know about real love – like Muriel did.

Maureen's red hair is frizzy and looks as if it's always affected by damp weather, standing up in a carroty halo that the small children love to try and copy with their crayons and chalks. Her kitchen smells of scones, and for all her robust contempt of the British way of life, Royal Family and the lot, the calendars with scenes of sheep trials in northern glens on the walls and the line of hand-knitted Fair Isle jumpers hanging over the range seem to personify an idea of England – even if it's a vanished one – as if part of her had never really belonged to Australia at all.

Maureen never told me more about my family than it was absolutely necessary to know. My father had been killed in a car crash when I was six months old – she told me that when I was about five and had been living with her for two years. 'And your mother comes to see you when she can. She's very busy, Ella. You'll understand, one day.'

I always said, what about my grandmother?

And Maureen always replied that she knew no more than I. I got the lovely presents at birthday and Christmas, didn't I?

Wherever my Grandma was, she couldn't have forgotten me.

I WALK ACROSS the cobbles, and because the couple in the doorway are looking both at me and away from me, because they are
both hostile and deferential and I feel fear for the first time (what
if the taxi, waiting on the road, out of sight at the top of the
drive, decides not to wait and goes back to Salisbury without
me?), I deflect my gaze from them too and stare out beyond the
cobbles at the trunks of great beech trees, rooted in moss and
with branches shivering in a light breeze under a canopy of
summer green.

How beautiful it is here, I say to myself – but automatically,
like a tourist: the grass mown down to a soft bed where a few
leaves from last autumn still lie, inviting and 'tasteful', like the
pictures Maureen has on the jigsaw puzzles in our nursery in
Melbourne, pictures of a landscape none of the children has ever
known; the half-ruined outhouses, dovecot and racket court, tiles
russet with age, that are grouped around the lawn, stone walls
overgrown with roses and ivy. How beautiful it is, I say, this time
aloud. But I remember nothing now. The flash of memory has
gone. It seems improbable – ludicrous, even – that I could have
come here once. I must go back. There has been a mistake. I walk
nearer to the couple in the doorway, to apologize for trespassing
in this lovely neglected place.

A sound – a faint roar – which makes me think, inappositely,
of a football stadium at home, comes into the sheltered courtyard
where we stand. And I turn again, looking upwards this time,
past the abandoned village green and the little church with the
squat tower to the line of bright, pale blue that marks the down-
lands from the deep valley where the old house and south-sloping

garden lie. And something does come to me – a memory of a blanket, and blue-and-white-striped cups scattered in grass as short as the hair on a boy's head, strong and tufty, and a nest of eggs, blue and speckled, lying just out of my reach beyond the confines of the rug. I'm crawling . . . a firm hand pulls me back . . . I cry, trying to reach the nest with the pale eggs that look like astonished eyes fallen down from the sky.

'I'm sorry,' I begin, as the roar dies away, and the couple, who have looked apprehensively up at the line of the downs above the road, look back at me again, more steadily this time.

'I'm so sorry to come here,' I say again, and I know I sound clumsy, even slightly unbalanced, in my sudden speech. 'I'm looking for my grandmother, you see.'

And I wonder, as the man goes back into the kitchen down a couple of steep steps and his wife, looking over her shoulder at me, follows him, if they are used to strangers coming like this, barging in on their privacy, demanding answers to questions they are unable, or unwilling, to supply.

Something of the feeling that my pilgrimage isn't the first and only one – that they expect someone every minute, and grudge that too – gives me the confidence to narrow the gap between us and arrive at the back door.

The kitchen of the manor lies below me, the bright green and cream of the paint dulled by the darkness the trees throw into it, the smell antiseptic and sharp, a hospital smell. Surely my grandmother can't live here?

'I'm looking for Muriel Twyman,' I say.

I walk down the steps and the door closes behind me. I feel the stillness of the cobbles outside, and the closed face of the coach-house, and the serried ranks of trees between me and the outside world. The house lies round me, like the lair of a sleeping beast.

SO WHY DID it take me so long?

It was that day – the day in the kitchen, in the grey, rainy Melbourne winter, the day Maureen picked up the newspaper off the table and made her face of contempt for the triviality, the pettiness, the snobbery and insignificance of England – that I learned for the first time how I might find my grandmother, where to go.

It was ironic that Chi-ren came in at that moment crying; if I hadn't asked Maureen again, over the sound of his sobs (he'd lost a little red train or the like), I'd never have gone, I believe. After all, I'd left it late enough. At twenty-six – 'rising twenty-seven', as Bill Fisher used to tease me when he said he was surprised there was no husband in the offing yet – I'd have become resigned to staying for the rest of my life in Australia, gradually losing the urge to see the place where I was born. As for trying to find Muriel – herself becoming more and more of a memory turned to dust, like one of the pieces of scrap paper the kids scribble on in the nursery, stuck in a drawer by someone too sentimental (me, most likely) to throw it in the bin straight away and quite lacking in significance when retrieved at the time of a clear-out – I would have had even less energy for the search. But that day, Maureen handed it to me on a plate. Only later did I realize she must have known all along where Muriel was likely to be.

'They're using tear-gas on all those dirty hippies,' Maureen said. 'I'm not surprised. They're gypsies. They shouldn't be allowed.'

'What hippies?' I spoke purely from politeness. Chi-ren had

found the train and was climbing on my knee. He said he wanted a story, and I dug out the Beatrix Potter book Maureen always insisted on the children having read to them. I wondered, all the same, whether a child who had been on a Malaysian island for the first two years of his short life wouldn't have preferred a book with creatures and characters more recognizable to him. But then – and here I would daydream, and be interrupted by a tart remark from Maureen and a burnt slice of toast or a pool of juice upset by a toddler and in need of clearing up – what *was* it possible to remember from so early an age? Did Chi-ren see the monkeys that run in the jungle in the hills of Penang? Did I really know the dusty flat, with its big rooms and the curtains always shrunk from the washing-machine, in the noisy town where I had lived with my mother and her mother, Muriel? Did I even have, apart from the windy day in a pram in the park, any memory of home at all?

'Battle of Stonehenge,' Maureen read out. 'Mob driven back by police invade boat-house in grounds belonging to Woodford Manor, at Woodford-cum-Slape.' And Maureen, for the second time, threw down the paper with a snort and remarked that anyone foolish enough to want to go to the land of hippies, defaulting royalty and corrupt policemen, would need to have their heads examined. Then – I was used to these sentiments, which usually included a sincere hope that the undesirable elements in Australian society would be eliminated as soon as possible – Maureen said, 'Woodford-cum-Slape. Typical poncy name for a village over there, all dreamed-up with the thatched roofs and the quaint teapots, I dare say. But it rings a bell all right. Woodford Manor. That's where your grandmother lives, I'm pretty sure.'

Then Maureen, unusually for her, clapped her hand over her mouth and walked out of the room. Little Chi-ren gave a shriek of surprise when I set him down and went for the newspaper. My heart was racing – but that wasn't so odd, really, when you consider that love is a rare commodity and I knew enough about what it was like not to have it, to come over as faint as a heroine in a romantic novel when there seemed a chance of getting some of it back again. The difference, of course, was that my quest wasn't for a dashing young man (and Bill Fisher and Maureen, I'd heard them, thought this pretty weird of me). It was for an old woman. But, as I say, you can no more dictate who you're going to love than sit down and paint or write a masterpiece at the crack of a moneyman's whip. Muriel was all I had. And now I had a clue, at least, as to where I could go to find her.

I LEARNT NOT to blame my mother. If it took me a long time –
twenty years, maybe – to come to terms with her abandonment
of me, it's more a sign of my own immaturity than of Anna's
cruelty or selfishness. She couldn't manage on her own – the
mid-sixties was a time before the support of feminism, she had
neither money nor proper training for a job after my father died
– and when she brought me to Australia and handed me over to
the Fishers, I think she genuinely believed it was only for a year
or two. She came twice a year, ever after that, and she sent
the books she published, by a women's press started up on the
kitchen table of the flat that was so hazy a memory to me –
'doing it all on a shoestring,' Maureen said with pride (Maureen
is a great one for private enterprise). She sent the books, but I
never opened them. I waited – and sometimes it was almost too
painful to wait, the gap between Christmas and my birthday in
June yawned like an abyss by the time the cold weather had set
in, in May – I waited for the presents Muriel sent. And part of
me could never understand why, if my mother hadn't been able
to manage on her own, my grandmother hadn't stayed on at the
flat and looked after me as she'd done before I was sent out here.

'Things aren't like that,' Maureen had said in the cross voice
she used when a child whined or demanded too much. 'People
have other things to do, you know.'

And I suppose it was that that I didn't believe. If you're loved
as much by someone as I undoubtedly had been by Muriel, how
can they just go away and leave you?

The presents stopped twelve years ago, when I was fourteen. I think I was secretly relieved by then, for the dolls with impossibly flaxen hair and the party dresses and tutus just weren't what I wanted any more. (I couldn't say so, of course, even if I'd wanted to: the parcels came with a brief typed slip – All my love, Grandma – and a postal mark somewhere in the City of London.) But I sensed that what had seemed to be inspired by love had become automatic; and the awful thought that these items were even bought by someone else and posted off to me by a stranger became too painful to contemplate. If only she could get to know me again, I used to say, she'd love me like she used to. And nothing ever stopped me thinking that.

Maureen was as sceptical of the success of my visit to England as she had been about the presents – as they stayed the same and I got older. 'Anyone would think she didn't know you were growing up,' Maureen used to say (she was spiteful sometimes, but I suppose she and Bill both knew I couldn't care for them and they'd done a lot to give me a reasonably happy childhood). And now, when, after failing to extract any further information on the whereabouts of Muriel, I informed her that I was leaving for England the very next day, she just told me, for the umpteenth time, to go and get my head examined, for goodness' sake.

'Don't get mixed up with those hippies,' were Maureen's parting words. 'I mean, they think nothing of helping themselves to people's private property!'

Bill, before going back to the more pressing demands of his sheep, had given me a sunhat with a vulgar picture on it, 'for the hot English summer,' as he said with a wink and a nudge.

For Bill England was seaside postcards, bums and landladies; for Maureen, snooty dukes and potty druids, cavorting at the solstice and lunging at the forces of law and order.

For me it was Muriel. It seemed right that what was the old, dead time of year for us should be replaced by the young green leaves of England in June, that I should be going back to a summer which had never faded or gone stale. As I left for the plane that day, I felt as if I were going to reinvent my life all over again.

I HAD LEFT home, as I'd come to call Maureen's house over the years, and gone in search of the home I'd had before this one, on a day when squalls of rain kept Bill Fisher busy with his sheep up-country, and I'd had to take a bus alone to the airport. Maureen waved me goodbye. She was holding little Zoë, a strange child who used to bawl when her mother and stepfather came to pick her up from the nursery, and Chi-ren was standing just behind, head popping round Maureen's bulk from time to time to see if I was really going. Chi-ren was miserably hurt, I knew, at my walking off like that, and I had the honesty, even if this sounds boastful, to see the feeling I still had about my grandmother written all over his intelligent, sad little face. But people do have to go away sometimes, I'd told him again and again. And I'll be back very soon, I promise. The last part of the sentence had a hollow ring that made me think of Anna, my mother – then I did begin to hate myself for leaving him with no one but Maureen to understand his moods and smiles and tempers. Too bad, Ella, I said to myself as the bus pulled away into the foggy rain that seemed to have come down on us for good, all thoughts of sun and summer buried for the foreseeable future. Too bad, you just have to go. And I felt, with an unpleasant lurch of self-consciousness, as if I were starring in some biopic of my own making – as if someone other than I boarded the bus with the requisite hardness of heart to leave a little boy with no mother and father, only an overworked supervisor to care for him when I didn't, while knowing I might never come back at all.

The plane journey was featureless, except for the fact that I'd never gone further than Auckland before, and the size of the world, preshrunk as it has been by satellite and cable, was quite amazing to me. For all the drowsing semi-comfort, and the in-flight movie, and the junk music to be selected while nibbling at junk flight food, I knew I'd had no idea of quite how far I was going – to find this chimera, this grandmother of mine who hadn't even sent one of her increasingly unsuitable presents for twelve years. And just as the continents that unrolled beneath me seemed too enormous ever to cross back again, just as the world expanded and lay before me in all its terrifying complexity, so did the real length of span of twelve years begin to present itself. Things were always so much the same at home: Bill coming in from the sheep to the ranch-house, going behind the fifties American-style bar, mixing himself an old-fashioned with Jack Daniels, swigging it back before bothering to wash off the blood on his arms, right up to the elbow; Christmas in the stone house in Melbourne, with the decorations taken out by Maureen and carefully counted before being attached to tinsel thread and hung on the tree with its fresh, disinfectant smell. The years simply passed. How could I imagine that a woman who had in all probability put me completely out of her mind would be waiting for me in this oddly named place – a name that had slipped out only because of Maureen's hatred for the people who had come with the sixties: drop-outs, vagrants, prophets of a new age? Surely Muriel had moved on somewhere, had left the country, perhaps, for a more rewarding life in the States, had – yet I couldn't bring myself to contemplate it – died. The fact that I might not even have been informed, if this were the case, stiffened me yet again at the thought of the one meeting that would in all probability take place: the meeting with Anna, my mother. I stared from the lozenge of window at a black sky over India and saw my own face look back at me with no love for Anna printed there at all. And I knew, for all the 'grown-up' efforts I was making to picture a new life for my grandmother, I saw her in a kitchen – a warm, messy kitchen where I was allowed to make toffee whenever I wanted, and there was her knee to sit on while drinking cocoa from the mug with my name on it.

The train from Waterloo was crammed with people, and all the windows were so fogged with grime that it was impossible to see the countryside – the countryside for which I'd prepared myself for so long (with some of Maureen's resentment against a class-ridden country, and a pinch of longing too, for the spreading chestnut tree and all that Old England stuff that's oddly hard to resist).

Tourists with backpacks – a midsummer visit to the West Country, to the old stones of Avebury and Stonehenge, was, to judge by guidebooks sticking out from the rolls of sleeping-bags, a must – jostled and tripped me as I tried to make my way to the (non-existent, as it turned out) restaurant car; and I ended up in the corridor of a first-class compartment, as dirty and run-down as the rest, staring in at the passengers.

The first thing that caught my eye was the unexpected shabbiness of the people who travel first class in Britain. The women wore corduroy trousers that looked as if they had last been worn to muck out a stable; the men, pushed like dark-blue cannon fodder into pinstripe with dark tie and white handkerchief, exuded a rumpledness and lack of care for their appearance that quite went against the travel posters, everywhere to be seen in Australia, depicting a smoothly suited British ticket-holder and his cashmere-clad, complacent wife. Here was a total disregard for appearances; and a strong sense of indifference between the sexes that so often goes with it.

Except, that is, for one man – a man, I think, Maureen would term a 'gentleman' (this with a light laugh, both contemptuous and repressed), a member of a species, at any rate, that we don't have back home, however many mega-millions the Packers and the Murdochs may make or however far-flung their empires. This gentleman was wearing a suit of the deepest black – wool, I suppose – and everything that went with it was perfection too, from the 'understated' (I knew that had been a key word for the British in the old days) cut of the shirt, to the shoes, handmade obviously, which, crossed one above the other, seemed to nod with the movement of the train, as if applauding the elegance of their wearer.

My stare was suddenly returned – just as we were drawing into Salisbury, as it happened – and I was glad to be getting off, embarrassed by now at having peered so hard.

Pushing past the students and tourists, I found myself on the platform of Salisbury station with a group of hippies, or this at least was what I imagined they must be. Not at all what Maureen portrayed in her impassioned attacks; quite dashing-looking in a way, with torn velveteen trousers and jackets and long frizzy hair that looked as if the wind had been blowing through it since the days of Bob Dylan. Not like the hippies who used to camp near Maureen's sister's either, the time we were taken to the sea and then had to be taken home again because Maureen said they smelt and she couldn't stand them near her. This group – as far as I could see, they all burst out of a first-class WC at the same time, maybe having avoided the ticket collector that way – carried guitars and smelled of something strong and fusty, like the musk roses our neighbour in Melbourne tried to grow one year, and then dug out again after they bloomed. The group, about four young men and a couple of girls, had a pair of dogs that looked like large greyhounds on a string (hidden too, I suppose, on the journey in the WCs).

The hippies, once we had all passed in single line through the ticket barrier and out of the station, set off at a brisk trot down the road away from the town, the dogs bounding ahead of them. I wondered if they were going to walk or hitch a lift to Stonehenge, about six miles to the east; and whether they planned to stay up all night, to greet the summer solstice. And a part of me mourned the fact I had never had that kind of a youth, with the music and the acid and the dawn raids, that I'd never had a youth really, and if given the chance to have it all over again, would hardly know what there was to go back to that was so different from now.

A solitary taxi sat at the kerb outside the station. The train had pulled away and I was conscious of a silence; not the kind of silence you find sometimes in towns when there's a lull – on a hot day, perhaps – or at a time when most people have hived themselves off somewhere to watch a football match, but a silence that seemed to come off the stray patches of willowherb and foxglove that grew on the unused asphalt of the station forecourt. A silence all the more remarkable because at the foot of the gradual slope that led from the station to the main road, a roar of traffic could be guessed at but not heard. Tall lorries overtook each other and screeched to a halt by the roundabout. A tractor, noiseless as the rest, came into view, pulling a wagon of hay. A man at the wheel of an ice-cream van drove past and then stopped in a bay just below where I stood. The klaxon must have blared out, because a queue of five-year-olds instantly formed.

I had my hand out to open the taxi door when another hand came from behind me and opened the door instead. I had to look round. I saw the gentleman of the first-class compartment, and I thanked him awkwardly. He obviously had no desire to reply and strode off down the road – though whether he turned away from the town, like the hippies, or made for the centre, I have no idea at all.

I had the feeling, none the less, that he heard my stammered instructions to the driver to take me to Woodford Manor at Woodford-cum-Slape 'and wait a little'. It was so quiet you could have heard a pin drop on the asphalt, with the ragged flowers and the litter bin filled to overflowing with crushed Smarties packets and yesterday's newspapers. Then, as we went slowly out into the main road, the full sound of packing-up time in a busy West Country market town came in through the open car windows at me.

I OPEN THE door and walk in.

Behind me lies the kitchen, with its institution paint and square, scrubbed table where a letter lies – for the couple, presumably – addressed to Mr and Mrs John Neidpath. Then there are two steps up out of the kitchen again, and a twisting corridor, very dark and smelling of old puddings, of bad food cooked too long and left uneaten by its captive consumer. And then the door, green-felt-lined from this side, into the other portion of the house.

Of course . . . I begin to see . . . the shrine that lies before me is guarded by this man and wife; they're caretakers of the place, and with instructions to let any passing visitor come in and look around. This house is open to the public, in the way that houses of special interest were in England in the eighteenth century; to knock was to be admitted and given hospitality.

Mr Neidpath – he's an ugly man, toad-faced, with a cast in his eye that must have given me the impression, at first sight, that he was looking at me sinisterly, that he'd seen me somewhere before and had the utmost suspicions of me – steps behind me into the long, wide room. The door swings shut with a muffled thud, and then is pushed once more to admit Mrs Neidpath, whose shiny, dyed curls poke round the door first, to be followed by her unsmiling face. Then the door sighs back into the wall again, and I turn to try and thank them, for I see, I have seen at first glance, that the Neidpaths have a deep pride in Woodford Manor and its contents. And I want to tell them that I'm not a casual tripper, a sixties enthusiast who will press a note into their hands when I leave, eyes starry with excitement from having

303

been transported into the past. I came here for a specific reason, I want to say. I was searching for my grandmother, Muriel Twyman, and there is no way whatsoever that she could be here.

There's something about the place, though, that makes speech unacceptable. It's as if – and I remember that strange stillness in the forecourt of Salisbury station – the house lies enchanted, like a house in a fairy-tale, with its occupants waiting to be woken by a visitor, long-hoped-for or dreaded; and I know, of course, that the visitor can't be myself. So I walk as softly as I can on a grey pile carpet that reminds me suddenly of a visit to a grand hotel in Sydney with Maureen, the time we all went on an outing and looked at the completed Opera House. And I pause before the monuments – all to the most famous woman of her time – the pictures and silkscreen prints and lithographs and bronzes, the screens of photomontage. I walk past a bank of hydrangeas, the false pink of their petals as dead as everything else in this great, deep room with mullioned windows that look out at the back on terraces and lawns sloping down to the river. I stand by a wall of mirrors with signed studio portraits tucked in at the edges, as a teenage girl might stick snaps in her looking-glass at home; as a star's dressing-room might look, preserved for ever after a stunningly successful first night. And everywhere the signature is the same: looped and bold, with an underlying flourish that looks as if it has been taken from a parchment manuscript of an ancient deed. The signature of Lisa Crane.

'Don't ask me,' Maureen Fisher used to say, when I was at the stage of collecting autographs and pinning up posters in my room of the dead stars that were just beginning to exercise their morbid power over a world no longer able to make sense of past or present. 'Don't ask me what people see in Lisa Crane or any of the rest of them. And take those drawing-pins out of my fresh paint!'

Yet it wasn't really hard to see what Lisa Crane had had; and while some would remain faithful to the memory of Marilyn

Monroe, or even pin up Jean Harlow and Mae West in their adolescent dens, Lisa Crane had held me – and many others – partly for the reason that she had never been a star. A face as the ultimate symbol, a symbol of the meaninglessness and uniqueness of beauty, and of the potential for the endless duplication of that image, until the beauty was reduced to meaning nothing at all.

Something like that, anyway. The age of the throwaway, of the excitement of anonymity and the destruction of the bourgeois pomposity of signed art – those were the notions going around, though I was too young to know them, of course, and by the time I came to read the endless rehashes of the lives of the stars and to see the Warhol multiples in the colour supplements, the pop-art images of Marilyn and Liz and Lisa had become bourgeois collectors' items in themselves. But by then the whole glow of that era had faded anyway, and bad imitations started to appear everywhere. The age of iconoclasm and idol-worship had gone.

The faces of Lisa Crane are blurred by the printmakers' hand, lipstick smudged over the endlessly repeating smile, eyes the cheap blue of pictures that come plopping out of a polaroid or an airport machine.

I stand, observing the reverent hush, by the table, glass-topped, where more of the incunabula are laid out; and Mr and Mrs Neidpath, murmuring they'll be back in a minute, retreat into the servants' quarters of the house. I wonder – while part of me frets over the taxi waiting by the thick screen of laurel bushes at the top of the drive, and another part of me feels a dead tiredness, a sadness that my quest for Muriel has ended in a dead end – I wonder also what it would have been like to have lived then and to have been Lisa Crane.

But it's impossible to imagine. The letters from John Lennon; the coat, in violent colours, given to Lisa by Jimi Hendrix; the photos signed by Dylan. How did she feel, this star who had no need to be a star, whose wealth and power and beauty made her few appearances on screen talked about and commented on with a ferocity denied even the most famous? Did she regret the passing of time? Where is she living now?

And I realize, as I stand enfolded in that artificially re-created glow, in that exotic shrine in a plain old house in the English countryside, that I don't know whether the famous Lisa Crane is alive still or not – and why should I care to know?

The stifling atmosphere of the narcissism of another age makes me want only to fight my way out of this mausoleum into fresh air.

I know nothing of this place. I have never been here before.

THE NIGHT I arrived in England – the night of 20 June – was as unexpected in its outcome as the afternoon had been, my early half-acknowledged memories of the place becoming quickly over-laid by the contrived memories of a woman who was a monster, whether she was alive or dead. And so this tentative sense of *déja vu* was cancelled, making a mockery of my journey, reminding me yet again, if I needed reminding, that my childhood was well and truly buried and that wherever I might choose to look for myself, I would find only evidence of another life.

I suppose some stubborn wish still lingered in me, drove me up the wide flight of stairs, rather than out through the whisper-ing green door into the beginnings – at least – of the world of today, a world with telephones and a taxi sitting on the narrow road that makes a black line between the river and the downs. Some vague hope that my grandmother had lived and worked here once, at least; had left a memento perhaps, a clue as to where I might find her now, made me hold the wide, pale oak banister as I went upstairs thickly carpeted like the museum/hall below. A wish made me go, even if it were to have a gloomy answer (and I feared, for some reason, the little Norman church I had spied from the cobbled courtyard, the line of graves where Muriel might, just conceivably, be buried). I had to know, and I climbed to the top of the flight and walked as if by instinct to a door that was left ajar, a glimpse of bed and lace quilt visible beyond.

The room was succumbing, as the hall beneath had already, through the thickness of wistaria and clematis pressing against panes that were small and diamond-shaped, to an evening gloom; but here, one storey higher, the sun came in a direct shaft that

made me think of the dawn rites at Stonehenge – ahead of where
I stood and probably not more than half a mile away as the crow
flies. The orange beam of light blinded me for a moment, and I
stood feeling ridiculously defenceless in this part of the house,
to which I had most definitely not been welcomed by Mr and
Mrs Neidpath. I felt, at the same time, a presence – though
whether it was at the other side of the old manor, down one of
the landings and further flights of stairs I had seen on reaching the
top of the principal flight, I couldn't at first say. Lisa Crane was
just possibly inured here, I thought – and I cursed myself for
being a reader of trash gossip columns and not even retaining
the information I had lazily ingested. Somewhere within the walls
of the house – and thus accounting for the feeling of a lair, a
sanctuary, rather than an arranged exhibition of her life – Lisa
Crane might by lying, asleep, with the Neidpaths as her custodians. I thought, even, I could hear the quiet tread of the couple
as they climbed the stairs, and the faint clink of china and cutlery
on a tray; they were very likely bringing her evening meal and
must have considered me long gone, slipping out most probably
when they were engaged elsewhere in the house. My agitation
suddenly doubled. What if they had gone to the top of the
drive, seen the taxi, impatient of waiting, no longer there, and
considered me ensconced in it, already approaching the suburbs
of Salisbury, the spire rising to greet me and the dolmens of
Stonehenge left well behind? What then? How was I to explain
myself? So great was the power of the slumbering house, of the
past that choked any idea of the present-day or the mundane,
that I found the very concept of ringing for another taxi quite
laughable. Somehow, even if the Neidpaths in their Cerberus'
gate room to the life-in-death chamber of Lisa Crane possessed
the telephone already fantasized about and longed for in my
dangerous position here, I could barely see them lifting the
receiver and calling to a denizen of the outside world.

As it happened, a second burst of noise from the downs – the
first had caused only a flicker of interest, I remembered, but this

was much louder – stopped the footsteps on the stairs for at least a minute, if not more, and made me realize, as a police siren and wail of ambulance followed, that the road running along the boundary of the manor's grounds was the focus for all this activity. The hippies, as Maureen had eagerly informed me, were at their most disruptive at Stonehenge at the time of the summer solstice. The road would by now be almost certainly out of bounds, the taxi dismissed back to the rank at the station.

The steps resumed and, coming up to the door, paused for a moment before John Neidpath came in with a tray – as I had rightly surmised – with folded napiery and a bowl of soup and a half-bottle of a very yellow wine, glinting in the last of the setting sun.

John Neidpath – as if it were the most run-of-the-mill thing that I should be in this room (and, as I looked hastily round in the dying light, I saw it was a master bedroom, almost without doubt the bedroom of Lisa Crane herself) – set the tray down on a rosewood table at the foot of the bed and informed me in a quiet, neutral voice that my car had indeed been sent away and that the road in front of the manor's thick shrubbery was block-aded by police at both ends.

Then, apologizing for the lack of a dining-room 'at present', he made his way out of the room, flicking on an array of downlight-ers and brightly coloured sixties lighting equipment as he went.

I ate the soup and I drank the wine. It was very quiet (there was no TV or radio). I lay on the bed, with its lacy flounces, its patchwork of purple satin that hangs over the headboard like a pious reminder of those heady days of fame and drugs and rock 'n' roll. I dreamed of the great stars of the past, and the marijuana-scented picnics on the lawns outside, by the bushes of wild briar and the clumps of bamboo that hide the river and the boathouse beyond. I dreamed of the boathouse, where Maureen had said there had been an invasion of gypsies . . . of hippies with guitars and fiddles and dogs – in the long reeds by the boggy marshland there.

When I woke, it was the middle of the night. A Tiffany lamp, ruby glass with showers of droplets around the base of the shade, was trembling a little, as if a footfall had disturbed the room; or as if the equilibrium of the whole house, marooned in secrecy for years, had suffered from some unwonted intrusion. I lay with my eyes wide open. There, ahead of me, were the decorative panels, showing Lisa Crane blown-up, giant portraits, grainy and fading now, by Bailey and Donovan; there, to the left of me on a marble table inlaid with the faces of the Beatles and Lisa, all Lorelei hair floating across her beautiful face, was a pile of books. The slight shaking of the glass fringes of the art nouveau lamp subsided and the room was as quiet as before. But I was awake now – and for good. I reached out for the book on top of the pile. Were these arranged too for the maximum illusion of time standing still? Would I find the works of the new Utopians of Lisa's age, the Laings and Buckminster Fullers; the *Steppenwolf* and *Magus* of those distant years? I lifted the book. It was heavy and a sweet, oniony smell came from the pages as it fell open on the quilt in front of me. Mrs Beeton's *Book of Household Management*. My surprise caused me to read the title of the book out aloud.

I felt, at that moment – it is hard to describe, but the nearest I ever came to it, I think, was when I walked one night alone from school to home, and in the dark bushes in the last stretch of the road something breathed, or made itself known – a sense of the existence of something in the room, and then it was gone; I felt a presence hovering round me as I opened the old book of household management and stared down at the flyleaf, with its spattered trails and smears from long past.

It was the name – how long did it take me to see the name, written there in a small, neat hand? – the name, as unobtrusive and efficiently presented as a housekeeper, a keeper of the keys, was expected to be, each letter joined to the next with an almost schoolgirlish respect for form and continuity. Still, the name was as I first saw it; and as it jumped out at me, a slight flutter from the paper photo-panels, half decayed now after twenty years' exposure, made me look up again and into the eyes of Lisa Crane, magnified in the poster to lakes of darkness. But I registered the name and understood it and my heart gave a leap of joy. Muriel Twyman, read the faded script. Then, further down the page, and demonstrating, as if it were needed, the compelling urge to imprint herself everywhere, to own every scrap of paper as well as all the wealth and beauty in the world, lay the flourish and the signature of Lisa Crane.

So she had been here! My instinct was right. My memories of my grandmother always in the kitchen – the steamy air and the smell of meat stews, warmed and warmed again if my mother was late coming in; the gingerbread men that she was proud of making and I always hid in a crevice under the chair because I couldn't abide the taste.

Of course, Muriel had been a cook and housekeeper here for Lisa Crane.

She still is, very possibly.

She's away somewhere, and Mr and Mrs Neidpath have taken over until she returns.

But my heart grows heavy. The cold, antiseptic kitchen downstairs is no temporary fixture. The atmosphere of Muriel is nowhere here.

And I know I must understand that this is final proof that she is dead.

The door of the room opens and a man is standing there. He comes in, and I feel nothing but the faint breath of cool wind that seems to come in with him. I feel I have seen him somewhere before. I am too frightened to feel fear.

The man is in a dark suit. He is elegant, somewhere in his late forties. His eyebrows very nearly meet over his black eyes. His rage is cold, so cold that I'm frozen into the lacy sheets, the frivolous foam of Lisa Crane's bed.

'What in hell are you doing here?' he says.

And before I can speak, he has gone. But I see, suddenly, the man on the train, with the handmade shoes built up at the heel.

If he lives here, why didn't he come to the house at the same time as me?

DAWN HAS COME very early. It's midsummer. It's bright. There's a distant shouting from the downs, as the day of the solstice breaks at last. A creeper with bright-green leaves knocks against the window and a bird begins to sing.

I get up and go out on the landing. A blueish half-light lies over the bales of silks and gold-striped saris and straw hats Lisa must have left there on purpose, to remind her of days of travel, of Hollywood nights and dinners on mountain tops in Nepal and Kathmandu. The blue light gives them a drowsy air, as if they had already become a part of her dream and would crumble to dust if touched or picked up.

I go down to the mausoleum, which is lit with an incandescent mauve and magenta glow, and pass a little altar to Lisa's love – a red rose under a glass dome, a picture of an impossibly handsome young man, dancing, twirling, falling on his knees; a triptych of images in black and white, of Lisa and her lover together, smiling, holding hands, smothered in confetti with palm trees and the neon lights of a casino just beyond. And I push open the green baize door that takes me out on to the stone passage and choc-olate-brown and green paint of the far side of Woodford Manor. I know I must leave now. Muriel is dead and long gone. I have no place here, and never did.

Although it's so early, Mrs Neidpath is in the kitchen and the electric kettle is giving out a long plume of steam. The back door is open too, and John Neidpath is washing down the cobbles with a stiff broom and a pail of water. The air, the glimpse of trees beyond, are as sweet as freedom to a prisoner. And I think,

313

I was fortunate to escape this place, for something about it is like a web; and whether or not Lisa Crane is the spider lying at its centre, I am no fly. I resolve not even to ask who the strange man was who came into my room and vented his rage on me so devastatingly. After all, none of it has anything to do with me.

But John Neidpath, quite by accident – just by pushing his bucket over and releasing a gully of soapy, mud-coloured water – holds up my immediate flight, my attempt to walk, crawl or hitchhike back to Salisbury. He digs into his pocket for a cloth as I waver, in my thin-soled shoes, on the brink of the spreading flood.

It was then, as I turned to look out at the untenanted village green and the little church beyond, in the hope, I suppose, of seeing someone – a vicar, a parishioner, anyone who would help me from this place – that I saw a woman walking on the soft, mossy grass.

She had her back to me, but I could see that she was old.

And I recognized, with a pang, the fact that Muriel must be in her early seventies now; that I would hardly know her, very probably, if I came up against her just anywhere.

But here is where I have come to look for her. And the woman in the dull raincoat, with the headscarf and the basket with blue and red flowers from the overgrown garden at Woodford Manor, can only be one person. She is Muriel Twyman. My grandmother.

The woman walks away from me – as I run, under the curious eyes of Mr and Mrs Neidpath, over wet cobbles to the path that skirts that soft expanse of grass. (It must have been a bowling-green once, I decide, where villagers, grateful for the space allocated for their leisure by the lord and lady of the manor, played on summer evenings, the thwack of the wooden ball on the ground seeming to ring in my head from ages past. Would Lisa Crane – given that she was still there, of course – care to think of the comforts of her labourers, provide them with the amenities which once had bound owner and tenant, employer and worker, in some sort of mutual agreement? I doubted it. Lisa Crane thought only of herself.) And as I ran after the fast-disappearing figure, which turned under an arch of yew, hidden from sight by a dovecot that leant precariously on stone supports, I realized I was within a minute or so of understanding the relationship of Lisa Crane to my poor grandmother. This woman, who lay becalmed in a monstrous memorial to the years of her youth and beauty, must employ her in some way, must depend on the legendary kindness of Muriel for her continued existence in the world.

I run – and as I dodge past the dovecot, all its nesting-holes empty and abandoned now like the buildings round the village green, I see her again and I call out for her to stop.

She does. She turns and stares at me, framed in the archway like some ridiculous sentimental picture, like the Victorian Christmas cards Bill Fisher's old mother used to collect, in her bungalow in the suburbs of Melbourne.

'Grandma!' I call again. I am aware too, as she stands there uncertain, that we resemble some kind of masque – played out on an English green as a pageant at a fête – one of those morality plays where everyone dresses up as someone else and good triumphs over evil in the end.

But, as in the fairy-tales most alarming to a child (*Red Riding Hood*, perhaps, as the most extreme case of mistaken identity, of innocence betrayed), my grandmother doesn't seem too sure of who I am at all. Like the Neidpaths' odd combination of both knowing and not knowing who I am, the old lady stands irresolute under her covering of yew, while the sun streams down on her and lights up her face and – she has removed her headscarf now – her grey hair.

She comes, a step or two at a time, to meet me.

And now it is my turn to wonder if this can be Muriel. But how can one know what changes age will make, over nearly a quarter of a century? For those who weren't there to see the pre-emptive leaps, the bounds towards death, what gauge can there be of identity?

She stops. She looks as if she has seen a ghost.

'Who is it?' says the old woman, who, I suddenly know, is not my grandmother at all.

And when I say, I'm Ella, her face breaks out in a smile and she hurries now to fold me in her arms.

II

THE NURSE'S TALE

THE FIRST SHOCK is over, of finding you here. And I will tell you, only be patient and I will tell you all I can.

We are walking through more arches of yew, so long untrimmed that tall offshoots, like hair from an unruly head, rise to the sky or dip down and lash us as we go. I stare into the face of the woman who tells me she knows who I am, that I was right to come here, but that she isn't Muriel, she's not the grandmother I have come across the world to see.

I will explain, she promises. And we push through the last arch, with a battalion of nettles closing behind us after we have gone. Now, lying out in front of us, is the lawn – dotted with molehills, but still beautiful – trodden by the years, by the feet of people who have been young and grown old in this sheltered, hidden place; finer than the grass of the disused village green where I saw this woman wander, and thought she was the answer to my prayers.

At the base of the lawn, once a crippled cedar leaning sideways on its iron crutch had been circled, and clumps of bamboo have been left behind, lies the river. And there we went, Jasmine Barr and I, arm in arm as if we had always known each other; as if her proximity, through so many years, to Muriel had given her rights that no one else could claim.

The river lies glittering in the light of sunrise from the high ground up behind us, and its silver scales are echoed in the long, flat water-meadows beyond, where runnels of bright water gleam and trees stand bowed by each rivulet. The buttercups and kingcups make a gold blur, as if another kind of sun rises from the earth here, in a glow; a summer incandescence that will smoulder long after day has gone.

Tell me, tell me, I say, as we pause to stare out at the river (we have crossed a rickety wooden bridge, and now we are on a path that might have been laid down for the elegant eighteenth-century tourist to stand on and admire a chalk stream at its most magnificent: trout darting; water clear and unpolluted, as if we had indeed been returned to another age; wild water-lily weed, pretty as a garland, floating in necklaces that could knot themselves around the throat of an unwary child and pull it down).

I stand, staring at all this. And then we walk on, arm in arm on the narrow towpath, and we come to the boathouse, half-fallen, red-tile roof with gaping holes, leaning at an angle over the water, like the houses of the East little children would try to draw.

And we stop. And I begin to remember.

Yes, you came here once, says Jasmine Barr. You were nearly three years old, and you fell in the water. Just here, where you were trying to climb into the boat.

And we look down at a boat almost submerged, shored up against the black water like a body found in a peat bog – once alive, once straining against an evening wind on the river as it raced down to the weir at Slape; now murdered, garrotted, with oars broken and hull smashed into foundations of mud and brick.

I bend down to reach the boat – the young boat, freshly painted green and waiting for me, to take me out into the current – a man is at the oars. The man in the trilby hat that is pulled down over his eyes, and he's laughing; then there's a silvery laugh behind me, but to whom does it belong? And is it he who pushes me in, just for fun, so I scream and clutch at the weed that drifts by, weed that seems to have lain in wait for a slippery little victim like me?

Was I here with Muriel? I say. Where is she now?

And we walk back over the rotting bridge, through dead bulrushes white as old man's beard, then through a swamp of flag iris, yellow and brazen in the gaining strength of the sun. We reach a bench – by the line of bamboo that marks off the end of the garden from the bog the river land has sunk back into, and we sit on a line that rules the end of the demesne of the manor – a kind of no man's land. For up beyond the house again is the thin line of bright sky that demarcates the bare downs, with their straggling windbelt of larches and spruce. Pagan monuments and bleak sweeps of land and sky divide it from the valley with its little church, its ancient harvest of souls, and the medieval fields and meadows with their legends of good, evil and salvation through repentance for the damned.

Your grandmother was a happy woman when I first got to know her. At least, she thought she was happy. You see, she had grown used to her life, and maybe that's what happiness is.

Jasmine Barr looks ahead of her, and I see, in the lines of her face, an impossible enigma. Is she the person she was, before she grew old? Has her age made her what she is? Is she now interchangeable with Muriel, as anonymous in the disintegration of personality that comes with old age as she? I feel afraid, looking into the abyss of the old. I want to run, even from the possibility of seeing my own grandma, for I had never accepted that she might resemble this.

Yet there's nothing unusual about Jasmine Barr, and she's human still, certainly, for, seeming to read my mind, she touches me lightly on the arm and says she will give me the facts as briefly and as clearly as she can, and I can make up my mind about what I want to do with them.

Muriel and my mother had lived together since I was born – or, at least, since my father, a man my mother never got round to marrying, was killed in a car crash and she was left with her living to earn and a tiny baby on her hands.

As for Muriel, she had parted so long ago from her husband, Anna's father, that she thought of him very seldom; sometimes, as she told Jasmine, she thought of him when she was loading the washing-machine in the flat she and Anna shared, with its long, gloomy passage and a utility room where spiders hung from the corners and the light from the street behind never managed to get in.

She thought of him then, Muriel said, because the low-wattage light from the overhead bulb always caught the amethyst ring on her finger – it had been her engagement ring from Bert – as she shoved the baby's clothes, and Anna's cheap cotton skirts, and her own baggy shapeless dresses into the washing-machine. And she thought that the next time her ring came off would have to be if it was sawn off after she was dead – and she wouldn't be there to see it. Her fingers had swollen up so, Muriel said.

And she used to sigh and say, 'Like the rest of me.'

Your grandmother worked in an office. It was the copywriting office of a big magazine that was itself part of a big corporation, and every day Muriel had to write the sentences that describe the glossy models in the fashion pages, and their lovely clothes. (She told me, later, that she thought all the lies she had to concoct to persuade women to spend their money, and to lure men into buying clothes and jewels for the women, was in some measure the reason why she took the path she did.)

Yes, your grandmother worked . . . but she would hurry back to you in the evenings. And then she and I, as often as not, would sip at a bottle of wine together and watch TV or reminisce about old days until it was time to go to bed. She'd walk me to the bus stop – I didn't live far away.

And where was my mother all that time? I say.

Your mother worked too, Jasmine Barr says. And I look up, suddenly returned to childhood again, to try and catch some reassurance from her – as once I had done at the knee of Muriel. But why should this old woman be able to reassure me now? And anyway, I've grown up and it's far too late.

Anna was hardly ever there, I remember that. When she did come in, it was with women – always women – and they met in the front room, while Muriel read me a story and then another, until I was too tired to keep awake.

The women, Maureen Fisher told me years later, were the beginnings of the collective that was formed to start the publishing company your mother now runs.

You are very lucky to have such a mother. And Maureen would always point at the parcels of books, still wrapped and unread, at the far end of the pine table in the kitchen in Melbourne. I didn't want to see the books on the sufferings and triumphs of women that Anna sent to Maureen Fisher and to me. I wanted the pink celluloid dolls Muriel sent, with hair so impossibly blonde it made ordinary hair seem as dull as ditchwater – or as my mother's hair, as I remembered it, dull and short and brown.

What a contrast there was between Muriel's work and my mother's!

Muriel worked, I knew this even so young, so as to be able to buy special presents and treats for me. I was all she had, and she was everything to me.

Anna worked for dear life. She worked to find herself, to create a career, to matter in the world. And I knew, as small children always do, that the person she loved wasn't me. It was something frightening and far away from me: it was theory, and endeavour, and, as I bitterly felt then (for with the cruelty of the very young I knew nothing of the meaning of ideals and wanted only love), she had learned to love herself.

To my mind, Anna loved anything that wasn't me.

One day, Jasmine Barr says, the phone rings and it's Muriel's ex-husband, Bert, calling from the airport and saying he's just flown in and'd like to come round tonight for supper with Anna – and to see you, his little granddaughter, too.

Now this kind of thing always threw Muriel. For one thing, it meant keeping you up late, and you'd had a long enough day by the time you were collected from the all-day nursery – where was it? Somewhere near Knightsbridge Barracks, I think – to make you very tired by six o'clock; and then off to bed with you.

For another, Muriel always went a little bit funny when Bert turned up. I won't say that she got exactly edgy, but, as these things will, his arrival jolted her into remembering the past – when she'd been happy with him, how she'd become unhappy, all that sort of thing.

I may say – and here I'm not doing your grandmother down – that Muriel was one of the moodiest people I ever knew. Maybe that was what I liked about her – who knows? She'd be up one day and down the next, and she was very funny – we used to laugh about life together – when she was down. When I first met her, in one of those Community Centres that were springing up then (I'd been roped in as emergency sub-editor on an underground magazine), Muriel was, typically enough, there to get some copies of one of Anna's friends' unreadable autobiographical consciousness-raising pieces. Let me see, it must have been 1967; she made me laugh and laugh with her send-up of how a middle-aged woman is expected to spend her day.

– I mean, she said. Here I am, getting duplicates of a manifesto by these young women which is about how their mothers didn't give them the right kind of love and didn't bring them up to respect themselves. I ask you! They're trying to find it in their hearts to forgive us.

And Muriel laughed, throwing back her head – I could see she must have been a very attractive woman, once. Well, of course, she still was.

Jasmine Barr smiles when she says this, showing discoloured teeth. I stare at the ground, where a mole has thrown up a rich hill of bright-brown earth. I want to tunnel down, into the passages under the grass where the mole runs trapped, and then throws itself up to the surface in a last, foolhardy bid for escape.

Muriel pointed to a group of girls walking past the Centre. Where

were we? Oh my poor child, we were in Chelsea, of course.
Chelsea before the flotsam and jetsam of the sixties really brought
it to its knees . . . when there were still greengrocers, and iron-
mongers, and a shop or two that sold the new clothes.

The girls were wearing the shortest miniskirts you're ever likely
to see. Muriel looked at them and then straight at the reflection
of the two of us in the mirror by the IBM machines.

– Why should they all worry so much? she said – meaning
Anna and her friends – Why should they complain, when they
have youth?

And she made a face. It was such a funny face; it had a sort of
rueful acceptance in it, and a certain anger at our predicament,
mixed in with a bit of self-disgust as well that growing old, which
was probably the worst thing that could happen to a woman in
a free, consumerist society, should even be considered an
unpleasant fate, when compared with death and early senility in
the poor countries of the world.

Oh yes, Muriel was like that. That's what drew her to me,
really. She was so . . . understanding of every single damn thing
going on. And, as she took and paid for the sheaves of paper
that decried the feebleness of her generation, she made just that
face again, and said, Well, let's look at it like this – in the Middle
Ages we wouldn't very likely have made it to middle age at all!

That's how our friendship began, you could say.

Anyway, when Bert Twyman came over that time, Muriel rang
me and asked me to come to supper as well. We'd been friends
quite a time and I'd met him before. Well, how can I describe
your grandfather? Maybe by saying that that's the last thing he
wanted to be called. He was one of the men who stay attractive
by sheer willpower, as far as one can make out; and by hitching
up with and dropping women as fast as he can, as if speed could
outwit time, there always being a new beauty to take the place
of the last one. He was a roving tele-journalist – Muriel used to
say he had a wife in every hospitality room. No, he wanted you

to call him Bertie. As it happened, you refused to call him anything at all.

Muriel said she was asking Greg and Sammy Chen from the office too. (I know this sounds like she was afraid of being alone with Bert in some way still – afraid of him hurting her, I mean – but I honestly didn't believe that was the case.) He irritated her like hell. I mean, when he came to the flat – oh yes, the flat where you were born, my dear, was near the river in Chelsea, in one of those redbrick blocks . . . dark and dingy, but when the light came off the water, the sitting-room had quite a magical air about it, as if all the sun flashes on the walls were silver fish swimming round and round.

No, as I was saying, he irritated her, your grandfather, when he came to the flat, because he walked around like the male lion in the pride, checking glasses and plates in the cupboard, passing remarks about the carpet and cork tiles being worn, that kind of thing.

Your mother Anna didn't go for that either, as you can imagine. She often said that the only way forward was to destroy the authority of the father altogether.

No, she didn't get on with Bert very well.

It was Muriel who put herself out, almost in spite of herself. She'd had a hard day, but she still stopped off at the butcher and got chicken for a *coq au vin*. Anna told her that those attitudes to male supremacy would keep women in slavery until the day they woke up and came to terms with themselves. But then your mother was in the very forefront of the new generation of feminist women – not that that was the name they called themselves at that time.

Now I look back to that room on a river wider and deeper and more treacherous than the chalk stream that winds slowly behind us down to the weir at Slape. I look back, and I remember – Muriel was the one who made shadows on my bedroom wall with her hands: a rabbit, a fox, a silly dog with waggling ears.

Muriel was like a magician to me, for she could do anything, she could pull any surprise out of a hat, she could get me what I wanted just as soon as I asked for it.

It maddened your mother, Jasmine says, as if she is the one this time to guess my thoughts. There was Anna trying to bring you up to be self-sufficient, to go about the world with the same sense of belonging to your share of it as a boy would have: putting you in dungarees, making sure you had building bricks and counting-beads . . .

And there, I think sadly, was Muriel, coming home with dresses of spun strawberry silk, a Viennese outfit with a tiny apron and a dirndl skirt and, of course, the dolls.

But my mother it was who sent me away.

The arrangement was, Jasmine says, as a wind whips in from the downs and she pulls her raincoat close round her, that I should pick you up from the nursery and Muriel would buy the food for supper on the way home. Greg and Sammy Chen would come about seven, the same time as Bert was expected to turn up.

Now, I said that Muriel didn't exactly want to protect herself from your grandfather by having other guests, but, consciously or not, she was making sure that Bert couldn't steam ahead with his condescending remarks about her work, if the art director of *New Image* – which Greg was (Sammy Chen was his boyfriend, all very discreet in those days) – was there to lead with a few conversations of his own.

As it turned out, the whole thing was a disaster.

You must remember that Muriel had taken quite a few knocks in her time. It was insensitive of me, I know, not to see it then, but I think she was really upset by the rift that was widening daily between her and your mother.

Everything Muriel was, Anna seemed to despise more and more.

Muriel was superstitious, for instance, always consulting her stars and once even going to an astrologer. Actually, we went together – it was just good fun – but Anna was too solemn about these things. She took it all very seriously, and she actively disapproved.

– Oh come on, Anna, Muriel would say. You're the one who's likely to get an exciting new man in your life, not me. Jasmine and I just go for a good laugh.

Now there were two things there that gave Anna the pip – and anyone but Muriel could have seen what they were. One was, of course, the implication that Muriel's life was boring. It makes the young feel guilty, I think, to believe their parents are washed up. Well, it *was* boring; and so was mine (for a living I typed up manuscripts for technical or scientific authors, and it was lonely, tedious work).

And Muriel's days in the offices of *New Image* weren't much better. She used to tell me – with that rueful laugh of hers, again – that she'd had another invisible day at the office, and at this rate, they could give away her desk altogether. Not one single soul – with the exception of the gays from the art department, Greg and Sammy Chen – had so much as looked at her or said hello all day.

– Once you get to a certain age, Muriel would say, you simply cease to exist.

The other implication in Muriel's guileless remark about visiting astrologers was that Anna was on the look-out for a man. It went, I suppose, against everything Anna believed in so fervently – along with the rest of the collective, of course – that women must show they didn't live only for love, and having children (and here Jasmine looks away from me, as if she's suddenly embarrassed to find me there, to remember who I am). It suggested that Anna's new vantage point in life was nothing more than filling in time before a new man came along.

Yet the irony is, Jasmine goes on, after a pause, and a long sigh, the irony is that a new man did come along. Not, she now adds hurriedly, for she must see the conflicting emotions in my face, not that Anna let that stand in the way of the Press – not for long, anyway.

And Jasmine's voice trails off. What do I show her, in my features; and what lies behind the very thin skin, the paper that lies in folds, like a badly wrapped package, round the bones of her face? Could she still blush? She seems too bloodless for that. Yet she must have seen that I knew nothing of any new man – not consciously, at least – in my mother's life. She has opened a wound. Has she done it on purpose? And if so, why?

That evening, the evening of Bert's arrival, Jasmine says, the night of the dinner party. First, I had a work crisis at the last moment and I had to tell Muriel I couldn't pick you up from the all-day nursery. Your mother was busy, of course.

Of course, I say to myself. Anna was always busy. It's the hardest word for children to bear, this 'busy' that means they must wait another age for food/love/care.

So Muriel had to pick you up and you went to buy the food together. Now that's all I know, with any certainty, for I couldn't think what the matter could be when I came to the flat in Chelsea at seven o'clock and there was no one there to let me in.

It was one of those intercoms that's high up on the wall – the whole building looked as if it had been built for giants, Victorian giants with big demands on space, at that – and one had to stand on tiptoe and shout into the damned thing in order to get heard at all.

After I'd rung about ten times the buzzer went and I was let into the hall.

I did notice that Anna's bike was there. The freeholder, a Major Heathcote, was fairly kind about that sort of thing, and it saved having to lug it up three flights of lino-covered stairs and through a narrow door – and that followed by a flight covered in a haircord stair-carpeting that Muriel had tried to lay herself and was all bunched at the sides.

My first thought was that Muriel might have mixed feelings about Anna being there so early. I knew she rather dreaded a lot of members of Anna's all-female group turning up as well – not because Bert would mind it, I can assure you, but because he might make a fool of himself by liking it just a bit too much and making a pass at a couple of them. I mean, Bert was an attractive fifty-two year old and he needed reassurance every minute of the day that he still was just that.

Still, there was no proof that the collective was round, or planning to come round, and I walked up the three flights. To find, rather surprisingly, the flat door closed.

I heard you crying, Jasmine says, looking at me right in the eyes for the first time. And I began to worry that something had happened in there, though I couldn't think what. I banged on the door – as anyone might – but no one came down to open it.

Then I heard the doorbell, followed by the buzzer again. And Bert Twyman was right behind me, bounding up that purple lino with the white, swirling pattern – for some reason, in all the time I spent going round to see Muriel at that flat, it was the puky pattern on the floor-covering that sticks with me longest. But I don't know why.

I can tell you why, I think, but on no account say. Because there's one thing you have no control over, and that's memory. It insists. You push it away; it comes back again like a hungry dog, to gnaw at the bones you throw to make it go away.

And I tried so long not to let it in, to keep the past a place where Muriel, like the star at the top of the little tree she decorated, with my 'help' each year, was the only constant, shining thing.

The flat door was opened by Muriel in the end, and after Bert and I had made a few awkward jokes together (he doesn't like middle-aged women, they make him feel uncomfortable – that's easy to see), we followed her up the stairs into the flat proper. She was shaking and obviously in a very bad way indeed. But when we asked her – when Bert had gone with his usual stride into the sitting-room and looked around with a proprietorial air, automatically checking the positions of the sofas and chairs, going over to the drinks tray as if a loyal wife had laid it out for him after a hard day at the office, Muriel would only say it was nothing, really. She didn't know what had got into her. – It was just that the door handle broke ... the china one ... I was afraid poor little Ella would hurt herself, you see.

It just didn't seem convincing. And it didn't explain the kind of crying I'd heard from you – loud, really frightened crying. You know the kind of thing.

Yes, I do, I think, I know the sound the kids in the nursery in Melbourne make when their mums don't come and fetch them – because they're in hospital having another baby – or the sad sobbing, after an example of grown-up wickedness or selfishness has been witnessed.

Yes I do remember the door handle. Now I do.

I'm running ahead of my grandma up the stairs (she's carrying heavy shopping-bags and she's panting and groaning a bit with the effort) and she calls up after me to go to my mother's room.

– See if Anna's in, Ella darling. Her bike's in the hall, she might be. And say she's here for supper, isn't she? Here for supper. Now you can say that.

It's true, I could pass on little messages like that. Muriel was very proud of what she called my 'reading'. But on this occasion I decide not to shout it out by my mother's door. I decide to run in.

The door handle is round and white, with a blue wreath painted on it. It's probably been on the door since the artists and Rossetti types who lived in these gloomy Chelsea studios and mansion blocks first furnished the flat. That, however, is not something I know about, and I attack the knob with gusto, wrenching it from right to left until it wobbles and begins to break away from the door altogether.

I'm afraid of getting into trouble – children always are, even if someone as kind as Muriel is in charge – and I let out a piercing wail. One last pull at the handle and the door suddenly swings open, while the china knob stays in my hand like an uprooted plant, with wood shavings round its base and some of the porcelain chipped off and lying just below me at my feet.

Greg and Sammy Chen came, Jasmine says, but the dinner was completely spoiled. It was almost uneatable, for one thing. And that was very unlike Muriel, who was a very comfortable cook, if you know what I mean.

Well, something in her – what Anna would contemptuously call the 'Little Women' side of her – had made her struggle to the shops for that chicken for the *coq au vin*. And what came out of the pot tasted of – well, nothing, really. Leathery and awful.

I sometimes think, Jasmine adds in a thoughtful tone, that it was the presence of Bert Twyman that made the food go off like that. You know, like the old superstitions about menstruating women touching household utensils, that kind of idea. Except, I suppose you could say that Muriel was menopausal, and maybe Bert couldn't take it and that turned the food sour.

Jasmine laughs. Then she says with another sigh, I was being frivolous, my child. Whatever had happened earlier in the evening had ruined Muriel's powers as a cook. And I can tell you, Greg and Sammy Chen were disappointed too. All the stories about office politics fell completely flat. We all went home early.

I stand at the end of my mother's bed and I start to scream. I advance, still with my ridiculous little china door handle, right up to the side of the bed, and I try to pull him off; I try to kill him.

The man who is lying on top of my mother and pushing

himself with angry kicks right into her, while his hands are throttling her, like the worst boys do at the nursery.

But this is a man.

They don't seem to be able to see or hear me. And my mother is moaning – it takes me a long time to understand the sound, because I've never heard my mother make it before.

She is loving it. The moans are pure pleasure.

Then my grandma, searching for me, white in the face, runs into the room after me.

Muriel told me the next day, Jasmine says. On the phone from the office. She said Anna had a new boyfriend. She sounded a bit funny about it, I have to say. But I put it down to a spoiled evening, and I pointed out that any plan that concerned both Bert and Anna was bound to be a social disaster. They're both strong-willed – I call it pig-headed, I said to Muriel, to cheer her up.

But she never did seem to cheer up about it, I don't know why. And I never did know what happened that evening, while I and then Bert Twyman were trying to gain admission to the flat.

As Jasmine finishes speaking, a bell sounds from the house. It's a deep-throated bell, and I think at first it must come from the little church and be announcing a death or an impending burial.

Jasmine seems to know the sound and she rises, walking away from the bench across the lawn to the overgrown terraces at the back of the house.

I follow. I want to ask her, What are you doing here? Where is Muriel now? And who was the man who came into my room in the middle of the night?

But Jasmine has disappeared, through reeds and shrubs, into a door that leads in from a terrace with pots and a couple of ragged palm trees. I decide to follow her in.

THE LOGGIA, if that's what it is, that runs along the back of Woodford Manor is as run-down as the rest of the place, with broken lattice-work against peeling walls and a sagging ping-pong table. Last year's leaves, still unswept, huddle in corners, and a leaking pipe, with its own spoor of green fungus, disgorges an uneven drip on to the floor.

It was while I was searching for the door which must have admitted Jasmine that I saw the waterlogged bundle, on the cracked cement under the ping-pong table. And as I crawled under to retrieve the photographs – for in this mausoleum of the image, it was clear that this was what they were – I had that feeling again, the feeling I'd had in the bedroom at the top of the flight of oak stairs, in the house, the sense of being intently scrutinized, of being, even, about to be accosted by someone who was just waiting for me to let down my guard.

Then the feeling passed. I flipped through the photographs. At the same time, Mrs Neidpath, now in a green overall to match the institutional atmosphere of her part of the manor, walked along the terrace, stopped, and stared at me.

The pictures, folded like a crumpled bankroll in my hand, were all romantic in the extreme.

Lisa Crane – as if, under all the masks of a quarter of a century ago, the fancy dress of the decade of Revolution, Love and Change, there had always been a truth of innocence and beauty, unalterable by the latest fashion or fad – Lisa in these pictures danced, graceful as a swan, demurely attired as a maiden on a village green at a summer festival.

Was this the real Lisa, then? I stared entranced at the whiteness of the arms, the swooning lips, the eyes that looked naïve and hopeful. The sophisticated, world-weary Lisa who Warhol doubled and trebled, reproduced a thousand million times around the globe, was this the Lisa Crane who was said to be so rich and powerful that no one man could ever satisfy her? Who, like Catherine the Great, had retinues of suitors and diamonds the size of pigeon's eggs, and still these were never enough to satisfy her jaded appetites, so that she preferred the company of deaf-mutes, dwarves and circus freaks? This lovesick dancer in white tulle? It could hardly be.

The man (her partner, but it is so hard to see in these old photographs, where light had seeped in from the nights and days and years since that last, swirling waltz) has his back to the camera and only the svelte line of his elegantly dinner-jacketed body gives an intimation of male beauty.

Lisa had been in love, and it's always depressing to see pictures of an old love – or so I reflected. There's something of the desolation of yesterday's confetti on a station platform, when the bridal pair have long been waved off and gone.

And if she had loved like that, who could the man have been?

Mrs Neidpath stepped forward, narrowly missing the drip from the half-disconnected pipe. She had clearly come in search of me, and, stuffing the sodden Polaroids into the pocket of my coat, I tried to come forward to meet her in turn, a pleasant smile (I hoped) on my face.

For after all, what was I doing here? If I was a tourist, it was enough that the disturbances on the downs had caused me to spend the night. I should have left by now. If I was – and here I came up against a brick wall, for who else could I be expected to be? – if I was considered to be someone else by the Neidpaths, then they must wonder what I was doing here, talking to the housekeeper – for as far as I could make out, this was Jasmine's function.

It was time, I thought, that I explain properly to Mrs Neidpath the reason for my arrival, describe my need to find Muriel Twyman and hear, if she had any information on the subject, where my poor vanished grandmother could be.

Before I had time to embark on any of this, however, Mrs Neidpath, who had reached the edge of the ping-pong table, and swept off a small army of dead flies as she did so, was handing me a piece of folded paper.

She stood watching as I undid the folds and read the script, black and boldly written – as if, I thought with a sudden feeling of panic, no piece of paper could be large enough to contain the writing of this correspondent, as if the slightest encouragement would cause that great hand to spread over hill and dale, claiming everywhere as its domain.

Yet the message was simple and short. 'I'm sorry about last night. Please forgive me.' That was all. I folded the paper again and slid it into the pocket of my coat, alongside the superannuated photographs of a wealthy image-queen who had danced all night once and must be old now, if not dead.

It was as if my thoughts had been spoken out aloud, for a low laugh – or so I thought – sounded from the far end of the terrace, where an exotic garden, filled with hanging creepers and hibiscuses in urns, most of them cracked by the frosts of successive winters, had once been carefully created. Mrs Neidpath seemed to hear nothing, though, and turned to leave the roofed-over but dripping place where we now stood.

– But who is this from? I said, pulling the paper out from my pocket again, once more thinking I heard that laughter – this time from somewhere just at the edge of the loggia. Mrs Neidpath paused in her stride, and gave me an odd look.

– It's from Mr Crane, she said.

She left, walking rapidly through the hanging ferns and trailing baskets of fuchsia that constituted this half-derelict tropicana.

I didn't care to search for the door at the end of the room that was half swallowed by the garden and go in search of Jasmine, and decided to go round to the back door of the manor instead.

Something tells me I will see Muriel soon. And I will persuade her to leave with me tonight, to come to the other side of the world, where we can start up a new life together. We can open our own nursery, I said in my mind to my grandmother. And you can retire there, Grandma. And in the holidays we'll go to the beach together!

– MIND YOU, Jasmine says, they were a perfect couple.

We are in one of the tumbledown cottages that sits, interspersed with make-believe granaries and storehouses, around the village green that was the feudal fantasy of the family that once owned Woodford Manor.

In searching for Jasmine, and going to the back door of the manor once again, I have found relief and reassurance: the kitchen, antiseptic no longer, has the warm smell of baking bread, and a pleasant clutter of cooking utensils and foodstuffs, while the fat volume of Mrs Beeton's household recipes – Muriel's book – is lying there on the scrubbed pine table.

Of course she is here. Jasmine promises she will tell me 'the whole story'. And more important, she says, my grandma will come back tonight – but from where I can't, apparently, yet know.

– Come to the house where I stay, Jasmine says, as I stand looking down at the recipe book (open, rather mystifyingly, at a section on the cooking and presentation of a Christmas dinner). And I follow her across the cobbles (the Neidpaths are nowhere to be seen), resolving not to ask why she doesn't stay in the house itself – though I can't blame her if she doesn't wish to. It seems to be becoming clearer, at least, that Mr and Mrs Neidpath are the custodians of this shrine to a bygone age and have little to do with either Muriel or Jasmine's role here. I wonder, but I won't ask yet, any more than I will mention the note of apology from the intruder of last night, whether Lisa Crane did in fact disappear long ago, and Muriel and Jasmine are closing up the house prior to a sale (there's a sense of an impending end, but maybe the old trunks have always stood in the hall of the manor;

and most probably the curtains have been closed for as long as anyone can remember round here).

Then, if the sense of an ending of something does turn out to be justified, why the feast?

For, walking round from the loggia and my encounter with Mrs Neidpath, I looked in through the dark, mullioned windows of one of the rooms and saw a table laid for a meal – and a magnificent banquet at that. A long table, mahogany, I think (Maureen Fisher had teased me before I left that I'd soon be hobnobbing with lords and ladies and eating off mahogany tables, with silver and Waterford crystal by the mile); and in this case laid with gold plates and goblets of a glass that seemed to be made of ruby and diamond, so bright was the dancing reflection from the sunlight as it went in there. Six places, as far as I could see – the light was bright outside and it was dark in the panelled room, with its fusty tapestries and a tall screen covered in dark velvet. Why, I wondered, had Mr Neidpath said last night that there was 'no dining-room at present' when there very certainly was – unless of course he meant that the dining-room was out of use, in preparation for a banquet the following night?

Yet the table settings, silver platters on lacy mats, candelabra, gold and silver vine and ivy intertwined on tall gold treetrunks, each branch with its cluster of candleholders, the pepper-pots like silver chess pieces, as brightly polished as the rest – all in marked contrast to the decrepitude of the rest of the house – also seemed to suggest a presentation rather than a real meal, eagerly awaited. Didn't the stately homes of England, as Maureen had taken a distinct pleasure in informing me, 'have enough swag on the dining-tables in the state apartments – where no one ever eats, mind you', to house and clothe the horrifyingly large numbers of poor and starving on the streets of London? Isn't this board prepared for a ghostly festivity – a banquet that exists only in the imagination? Without food, wine or guests, the splendour of the table exists for the benefit of tourists only; a feast without substance or time.

Muriel will come back tonight, that is all Jasmine has said. I must content myself with that, even if it seems highly unlikely that someone like my grandma would be invited to eat off gold plates.

Your mother and Harry, Jasmine is saying.

We're in a makeshift sitting-room in the cottage on the green. It's all faded chintz and half-sagging armchairs, as if Jasmine has pillaged an old part of the manor not given over to the exhibition of Lisa Crane. For comfort's sake I'm sitting on the floor, while Jasmine sits in a low chair that looks as if it's had any number of nursing mothers sitting on it before it was thrown out (by the vain, childless Lisa?) to the general dumping-yard that is the green, with its storeroom-cum-disused racket court. Jasmine has lit a fire, and although it's midsummer – and we can hear bursts of shouting from cider punks on the downs, and see the sun on the green beech leaves outside – it's damp in here and needs the blaze of wood, some of it driftwood picked from the sides of the river, Jasmine says, blown down from the Woodford forest in a storm. It's slow to get going at first, and Jasmine tells me to fan the flames, picking up a newspaper which, I see with a now-familiar feeling of unease, is dated over twenty years ago, and which adds to the sense of an enchanted place, marooned like its owner, in time.

– Of course, I was very pleased for Anna. Jasmine has lit a small cigar, and I'm able, as she peers through smoke into the room, to look at her closely for the first time. I wonder how I can ever have thought her to be my grandmother. Muriel had something special about her – I know I'm not the only one to think or to have thought that – and Jasmine Barr must have always been extremely run-of-the-mill. Her eyes are small – 'piggy', as Maureen would no doubt label them – and her mouth has a resigned look, rather bitter but trying to appear friendly, I suspect.

But then, of course, she is old. The lines that gather round eyes and mouth seem to have trapped her – in this look of slightly irritated submission, perhaps – and it's impossible to imagine what she would have looked like when she was young.

Jasmine's hand, with its lumpy blue veins and washerwoman's fingers – puckered, and looking as if they've spent more than half a lifetime in water, whether rinsing clothes or washing crockery and pots and pans – moves jerkily with the cigar, weaving a further web of blue smoke across her face, confusing further the line where chin meets neck, and a puddingy layer of secondary chins go down to a breast the colour of plucked chicken. I know – and I know I've never thought about it with any seriousness before in my life – that I never want to grow old.

– She changed so much, after meeting Harry, Jasmine goes on, in this account (of which I feel wary) of my mother's life. Haven't I had enough, sent out to distant relatives 12,000 miles away, growing up without a mother and deprived of my grandmother, without hearing of Anna's romance? And how does it bear on the story of Muriel, which I'm told I need to hear before I'm reunited with her at supper tonight?

Nothing, it seems, will stop Jasmine, and I suspect she's one of those vicarious sex-lifers, who get their kicks from seeing the joys and pains of others.

– Anna even gave up some of her evenings that were dedicated to the collective, Jasmine says, with a chuckle which I consider to be in bad taste, even if I have little sympathy with my mother's feminist good works. Is she going to be made out now as a foolish romantic, a traitor to her cause?

– Harry even got Anna to go dancing! Jasmine says, her smile widening and the little vertical lines above her mouth gathering together and fanning out again like a concertina. And that meant, of course, getting out of those eternal jeans and wearing a dress from time to time!

Something, something I don't like at all, stirs in me at the mention of this. I can't think what it can be when the name Harry triggers off nothing in me. But then, truth be told, I don't remember

Jasmine either, and she assures me she was round countless times, even reading stories to me in bed if Muriel was busy elsewhere. I will banish this half-worm of a memory, as it crawls on to the skeleton of my infancy twenty-four years ago. I tell Jasmine I'm glad to hear Anna had enjoyed herself, but I don't remember Harry at all.

Now it's Jasmine's turn to be shocked. Can it really be true that I don't remember Harry? Surely I must.

– He was the most wonderful looking man, Jasmine says. Well, you're much too young to have gone to the movies in those days, but you've seen them on TV, even in Australia (and here Jasmine made the country where I had grown up a penal colony still, so that I sided with Maureen in my mind, resolving to tell her of the decadence of this English country house, given over to the worship of dead icons of a too-permissive age).

– Marlon Brando, Jasmine is saying, or maybe to go back a bit, Clark Gable. It was always hard to make up your mind with Harry – he looked different from one day to the next: very black, blue-black hair, such a charming smile.

– I don't remember anyone called Harry, I say.

Now Jasmine's lurking malice begins to show itself more clearly. She thinks, no doubt, that I'm playing games with her, that I can remember perfectly well the Galahad who came along and rescued my poor mother from the clutches of rabid lesbians (as Jasmine probably sees the collective), and that I'm jealous, pure and simple. I wanted her attention for myself. I resented the lover. It's all first-year sociology stuff. For the first time, I feel a slight – very slight – twinge of sympathy for Anna.

– No, you wouldn't remember him very probably, Jasmine says, as I'd seen she was going to say. I mean, he and Anna went out all the time together.

– And I was in the nursery, or tucked up in bed, I say, with some of the same bitterness Jasmine shows, with her face of one who has had to swallow neglect and humiliation – much as I have, I suppose. But I have one sacred thing: Muriel. I have her in a place no one can ever touch. In all probability Jasmine has nothing and no one like that to provide a nugget of warmth in the cold world.

– Of course, Muriel took care of you more and more, Jasmine says, and not for the first time, I feel she has some unpleasant gift of looking into your mind and seeing what's going on there.

– No more evenings out for me and Muriel, she goes on with a light laugh, and through the haze of smoke from the cheroot she leans forward and chucks a pine cone on the fire.

I stare at the burning cone, and I think of the Woodford woods ... the hippies in their circle of firelight, squatting, as Maureen would have it, on private land. Living freely and lawlessly, like gypsies, children carried on their backs.

– No, Muriel was in babysitting you every night, Jasmine says. (I feel I'm supposed to be guilty, as if it had been I and not my mother who had demanded these services.) She loved you, of course ... but she got pretty fed up with a diet of nothing but TV, I can tell you!

Colour rises in my face, and the image of the woods and the young people strumming their guitars, blowing their minds in this domain of the sixties, fades rapidly from my mind. How dare this stupid old woman suggest that Muriel was bored with caring for me, that she was anything but blissfully happy when I lay waiting for sleep in my painted child's bed, secure in the knowledge that the creak of a shoe in the next room or the rustling at the end of the passage was Muriel? I suppose all small children believe those who care for them are put in the world to do just that – and why shouldn't they? Something, uncomfortably, tells me too that this stage, in Western youth, goes on too long, that children expect to be protected and looked after well into adulthood.

– Then the TV went on the blink one night, Jasmine says. I was there. I have to say I was shocked at the state it put Muriel in. I mean, we had plenty to chat about. There was the recent visit of

Bert, which always brought the same diatribe – mind you, I agreed with her, Bert had treated Muriel shockingly, there'd been no maintenance at all for Anna when she was young – all that kind of thing. I'm glad, Jasmine says with a sudden vehemence, that I never married.

Anyway, I'd been worrying quite a bit about Muriel over the past few weeks. Since Harry started taking Anna out, you might say. True, Muriel's life had definitely changed since a man came on the scene. The cosy all-women-together, as your mother's colleagues would have put it – and Jasmine smiles, showing her discoloured teeth and very pale, spongy gums – the cosy life of what I used to call girls (here she fulfils my expectations, but desists to go further into the murky areas of what she probably would refer to as Women's Lib), the cosy life didn't go on any more.

Because Anna and Muriel did seem like a pair of sisters in a way. Before Harry turned up, I mean. There hadn't been a man around for so long that they bickered, and took turns with the washing-machine and all that – even if, I have to admit, Anna took advantage of her mother's generous nature, so Muriel definitely had the lion's share of the household chores. But isn't that what mothers are for?

I found this tactless in the circumstances and looked away from Jasmine Barr and at the window, where a fringe of leaves glowed in the sun, like a stage set. Everything is arranged and false here, it seems, and I fear the outcome, already, of Jasmine's story. It will be as melodramatic and unlike its subject – the simple, loving Muriel – as this house and garden and hidden river, with its contrived, artificial atmosphere, is unlike the true English countryside of the books I read Chi-ren at home: Beatrix Potter and *The Wind in the Willows*.

– I didn't blame Muriel for getting restless the way she did, Jasmine goes relentlessly on. It was the very worst time in history, probably, to find yourself all of a sudden middle-aged. And

Muriel – and I – well, we were both forty-eight years old at the time.

I mean, this was the great explosion of youth – the music, the miniskirts (and Jasmine looks at me with something like pity or condescension in those very small, rapidly blinking eyes). You won't know what it was like then. If one was older, with legs that didn't look so good when exposed right up to the thigh, well, you were really excluded from the world.

Not that it mattered to me, Jasmine says with a smile she must think is self-deprecating, charmingly humble. I was no Jean Shrimpton even in my heyday.

No, Muriel had been a very attractive woman, and I always told her that if she hadn't been so done up by Bert's infidelities and sudden disappearances, if she hadn't had a child to bring up on her own, she'd have met someone far better and married again. But somehow, she never did. And then, just as she was beginning to be free again, when Anna was grown up and beginning to earn a bit and so on . . .

Jasmine looks at me now. I know she is trying to be kind, she has understood her words are likely to hurt me.

. . . You came along, she says simply. Obviously there's no other way to put it. But I know Jasmine is just making trouble – for me and for Muriel – for if Muriel hadn't loved me with all her heart, why would she have dedicated herself to me in the way she did?

– There was no alternative, Jasmine says. Not enough money for an au pair, seldom enough for a babysitter. She was well and truly trapped, your grandmother, and now she was beginning to feel it. She'd come back from the office, phone me to see if I wanted a drink and by the time I got there, you'd be in the bath and the *TV Times* would be opened out on the table in Muriel's little room.

At first we talked about Bert a lot, and then about the world trip we were going to make – the Blue Rinse Brigade, we called ourselves.

And all this while Anna was really digging into her new life. Harry was the kind of man who would put himself out for someone he loved – and he didn't stop her embarking on her new career. He helped find good typesetters – I remember that because I helped a bit with my typing skills – and he helped her lay out a new magazine. When he wasn't giving a hand to her very special projects and ventures, all of which he seemed to sympathize with and know something about, he was actually encouraging her to have fun and join in with all the fun that was going on just then – pop concerts in the parks, dancing and listening to music all night long . . .

I remember, says Jasmine with a thoughtful look, that the favourite song of that summer was 'A Whiter Shade of Pale' – I think that was the name. I always thought it was a nasty, wailing sound, but it came out of doors and windows everywhere, like Bob Dylan . . . and Sergeant Pepper, of course.

And when they weren't doing any of those things, Harry and Anna were demonstrating in Grosvenor Square against the Vietnam War. It really was as if Harry had supplied a half of herself for Anna that she could never have dreamed was there.

– That's nice, I say.

– I suppose Muriel envied it, pure and simple, says Jasmine after another shrewd look at me to see if I can take what's coming next. We used to get quite drunk together, you know.

And she told me one night she thought Harry was just about the most fantastic person she'd ever met. His looks, his charm, his intelligence – I know you think I'm discriminating against women here, for after all, if Muriel had been a man and she'd found herself fancying her son's daughter, it would have been almost the expected thing to do. For women – well, it just is different, and it hasn't changed all that much yet, as far as I can see.

– She owned up to this innocent passion on the night the TV went on the blink. We'd been planning to watch a film, an old thriller by Chabrol, I think it was, and of course she was angry and disappointed to miss it.

That was what Muriel was like then, far moodier than she'd ever been like that before. Easily thrown. Irritable. Sometimes we used to joke about it together, and say hello, here comes the menopause.

In fact, Muriel had got very absent-minded and I know the doctor had put her on tranquillizers of some kind.

And Greg, who was her great friend at the Image Corporation, even phoned me at home one day and said he was worried Muriel might get the push at work, because she kept writing the same copy over and over again, and the editor – a real bitch, I can tell you – Liddy Wise was her name, was sending it back to Muriel with sarcastic comments like, 'It can't always be summer', when Muriel had written some flowery stuff and it happened to be the autumn issue coming up.

I didn't think that was the right night to tell Muriel, though, that she might be in trouble at work. I tried to steer her clear of her obsession with Harry. I mean, it was embarrassing: there he was, bringing Anna home every night, and they were making love in her room (it used to be Muriel's room, being the big double, but when Harry came into her life, Anna asked Muriel to move to the small room, down at the end of the passage, near you). All the same, she must have heard things . . . well, you're grown up now, Ella. You know!

I'm not grown up, I want to cry out. Leave me alone! I don't want to hear any of this. Muriel loved moving near to me – she told me again and again. But already my heart is sinking. Was she simply repeating, as she did the meaningless copy she had to write on beauty and fashion, the same, unmeant words?

It couldn't be true.

And now I begin to hate my mother again, for inflicting this pain on her mother and my beloved grandma. I don't care if Muriel liked Harry a lot. Why shouldn't she, for God's sake?

And I say to myself that I will leave the cottage in exactly two minutes, if Jasmine doesn't tell me where Muriel is now . . . and how I can find her before my mind is poisoned even further by her old friend.

– I don't know what happened, Jasmine says. I can't get to the bottom of it. But something happened the next day that seemed to flip Muriel – you'd almost say she went temporarily psychotic, I suppose.

The TV needed to be mended, and as it was the summer holiday break at the day nursery, Muriel took you with her to the TV shop to get it mended.

As I say, I could never piece together what happened. But when she came back from that very ordinary trip, she phoned me. And she sounded madly excited.

'It's all within my grasp now, Jasmine,' she said. 'And you can join the pension scheme too, if you want to!'

I couldn't imagine what she was talking about, and said so.

'It's just a question of signing a piece of paper,' Muriel said. 'A hire purchase agreement, a contract, whatever you like to call it. And you can get your youth back. For twenty-four years. Not bad, eh?'

'What on earth are you talking about?' I said. I must say I was surprised, with a job that consisted in the main of puffing dishonest rejuvenation treatments, wrinkle creams, collagen and all the rest – that Muriel would be taken in by some new pamphlet promising a return to youth and beauty.

But convinced she was. She even said she'd seen herself – can you beat that – on TV, looking as young and lovely as ever she did. I had to burst out laughing. But I was worried, of course, very worried. It's pretty well known that when you start thinking you're seeing yourself on TV and the like, you're in urgent need of psychiatric treatment. She'd be getting coded messages from the traffic lights soon, I thought.

So I was very gentle with her. I came over to the Chelsea flat.

I told her she needed a complete break ... and I pretended I needed one too. Why don't we go to a health farm together? I said.

I remember the TV shop.

I won't tell you, Jasmine, what I saw there, because you wouldn't believe me, anyway.

In the TV shop there were hundreds of TV sets, some small and some enormous, and all with the same cartoon playing – which made me shout out with pleasure. There was Sooty, cavorting a hundredfold across the screens.

I sat on the floor of the shop. I can see and feel the blue pile carpeting, with the dropped staples from invoices and a squashed cigarette butt I tried to pick up and play with, except that a man in a green overall came and swept it away.

Muriel must have gone into the back of the shop, with our small set that she'd lugged all the way in a wheeled shopper. At any rate, when the cartoon was over and I looked round for her, she was nowhere to be seen.

I don't remember feeling fear – Muriel had brought me up with so much affection that it would no more occur to me that she would walk away and leave me than that my mother would come into my room one night to kiss me goodnight – and I remember crawling into the back section of the shop. I could walk perfectly well by then, and I have no idea why I didn't want to.

There was Muriel – I saw her almost at once. She was standing talking to a man. That's all I thought – a man.

He had the set and he was lending Grandma another one, because he led her back into the front store, where the banks of screens were, and he was trying to persuade her to lay out for a bigger one, I think, because he leant down and patted my head as they went past and I heard Muriel say, Yes, that's my little granddaughter.

As the man walked past, I distinctly saw that he wasn't wearing socks – only built-up little boots that gave him a funny, strutting air. Being on the floor, I know I saw what his legs were like, between the turn-up of his trouser and the top of his boots. And they were black and shiny, like the coat of a pony or a goat.

Then the man had walked on, and he was saying something to Muriel, and then suddenly I heard her give a little cry of surprise. It was just a quick flash, but I know I saw it. On every screen in the shop Muriel's face looked out. But it was Muriel young and beautiful . . . and although, of course, I'd never known her then, I knew it was my grandma and I shouted out too.

Then the picture came back – an ad, I think it was, for family cereals round a table with a red-and-white-check cloth.

We went home, and it's true that my grandmother was holding a piece of paper, and she was laughing happily.

But there is no way I would tell Jasmine this, and risk an offer of psychiatric treatment, which would very likely be her response.

And I say – for my two minute deadline has passed, in my strange reverie of that afternoon with my grandmother – 'You must tell me. Now. Where is Muriel? Is she here?'

I fall silent, seeing Jasmine rise and leave her chair, and motion me to follow her out of the damp little house and across the green.

LISA CRANE IS sitting at the head of a long table. Her blonde hair, in a Twiggy fringe, is crowned with diamonds, and there is more glitter at her neck and wrists. Her dress – she rises from time to time and goes to the door to greet an especially famous or distinguished guest – is short, so short it barely grazes her thighs. Like a snake's skin, riding loosely on the shoulders as if ready to be sloughed off at a casual twist of the limbs, a resigned shrug of slender shoulders, it too is blazing with sequins and artificial gems, so that Lisa, with her look of costly brevity, could be seen to epitomize the span of a butterfly, or an exotic moth. Her eyes, blue as the glinting stones set in her sheath, seem as carefully positioned as an insect's markings; they flicker as she looks to either side and down the length of the table, gauging success, and money, and deals.

I am in the video room, as I suppose one would call it, of the old manor, a room given over to the photographic and filmic mementoes of Lisa Crane; and it's here that I've been told to stay until Jasmine finishes 'some work in the kitchen'. It's no good being impatient, she tells me. You will soon know everything.

The room is off the hall, with its rich kelims and drawn purple and mauve velvet curtains, and I feel drowsy already, for to be in here is like being lost in the depths of a cave. There are no windows at all, or if there are, they have for a quarter century been covered with the wall-hangings of Lisa's long-ago Eastern trips – carpets from Nepal and Bessarabian prayer mats – and superimposed on these are gongs and discs of beaten brass, and, of course, the big TV screen for the videos.

There is incense burning here, a reminder of both the Eastern mysticism that Lisa, like so many others then, exploited and then abandoned – and also of the nature of the shrine in which, succumbing to soporific fumes, I see myself as captive votary. And all I can think of, in this abandoned harem where Lisa Crane is both sultana and concubine, where her position of power, and her teasing beauty, seem to contradict each other to the point of making her an impossible anomaly – a monster – is how I can find my grandmother and escape with her. In this house where time is sunk like most of the once-lovely garden in the river that seems to bind us here with its twining loops across the water-meadows, there will never be a chance of finding her or of coming to terms with reality. For already, I am half seduced by Lisa Crane.

The video changes, automatically, and Lisa appears before me again, this time in a caftan of striped silks and gold thread. She is smiling. She is giving an interview, it seems, on some long-forgotten chat show, about her ambitions and aims for the Empire she owns . . . the Empire of Communications, for Lisa has bought into and runs the world's media.

I doze, and dream of the church where Maureen, not especially devout herself, but conscious of her Irish heritage, used to take me when I was four years old and not long in my new country.

We are kneeling together and a bell rings, like the little ornamental bell on Muriel's table in the place I had to leave behind . . . so far away, as far as heartbreak, in the flat my grandmother ran away from – and then my mother, so I had nowhere to go but the other side of the globe.

The incense is carried past in a swaying censer, by a boy not much older than myself. I stare at him, from low down on the worn hassock where Maureen makes me kneel; but I know nothing of the lives of other children in this so-distant place.

I am lost and I want to go home.

I open my eyes again. The video has changed. Lisa is in Manhattan, skyscrapers behind her head like a barbaric mega-billion headdress, primitive and barbaric in its glittering multi-faceted light.

Lisa is smiling into camera.

To the side of her, as the camera moves back, we see the repeating images, the Warhol look-alikes, the freaks and funnies from his sad circus of urban-deformed. Does Lisa not understand she is one of them too; that to this artist she is a sacred horror, as funny and repellent as the fat lady or the druggy young girl?

No, Lisa cannot realize this. She is money. And there's nothing pathetic about money.

Or about her beauty, more frozen now and hard, that stares back at her from mirrors in the camped-up studio – and from the likenesses of her, smudged and hasty and priceless, that hang, or lie like discarded dollar bills, everywhere you look.

Lisa is worshipped. The mask of Mammon has the exquisite features of Helen of Troy.

But Lisa owns the ships and she makes sure they never get destroyed.

On Lisa's finger, the fourth finger of her left hand, is an amethyst ring.

And I remember . . . I see a ring, left carelessly, foolishly, in bathrooms and lavatories, at motorway café stopovers.

Muriel saying, Oh damn! We'll have to go back. I've gone and left my ring there.

I'm drying my hands in the bathroom at home.

The ring lies, as it so often does, on the edge of the wash basin, next to a sliver of soap (neither Muriel nor my mother ever remember to buy soap).

The ring could so easily fall . . . into that little black hole where the water runs down in spirals (the opposite way from my new home, for everything is the other way round there, the world is upside down).

353

I don't know what makes me push the ring from its precarious resting-place on the grubby enamel ledge.

But I do.

And I hear my own screams as I run to confess my crime to my grandma, who has been away for the first time in my young life, away for so long that I knew in my heart of hearts that she was dead.

I am trying to draw attention to myself – and to punish her too, of course.

Muriel went down a black hole and I sent the amethyst down after her.

Although I know she is back – I can feel her presence in the flat – why, then, hasn't she come running to look for me?

A man comes in . . . here I hazily remember a cry of triumph and delight as he fishes it out – with a knife, I think.

The ring might have gone right down to the other side of the world, the man says with a funny laugh.

You look beautiful, he says to Muriel. What have you done to yourself?

I can hear those words, spoken all those years ago – perhaps because they frightened me. Like the story my grandma used to read to me – and I would ask for it, but then I would cry and say how much I hated it really – the story of the old woman who goes to market, and on the way back she falls asleep by the side of the road.

Like the old woman, I have been sleeping. But Lisa is still there – in a fashion shot this time – to applause, she is walking round a great hall with tall windows, like a cathedral where on the altar the rich and famous parade their clothes.

Then the picture changes again, and this time I see her hands, clasped with the hands of a dark, tall, handsome man. It's a TV news of all those years ago, and it announces the marriage of 'Lisa', the icon of the day.

And on her finger I see Muriel's amethyst ring, set, as I so well remember, with seed pearls, in a worn gold setting. There was always something comforting and grandmotherly – Victorian, I suppose I must have meant – about that ring.

In the story, as Muriel reads it to me on a dark evening by the gas log fire in the Chelsea flat, the old woman who has been to market wakes and finds she doesn't know herself at all.

Don't tell me any more, I beg Muriel. But something in me knows that the half-naked legs the old woman will see when she wakes are hers really, for all her Lawks a Mercy me, this is none of me!

What happened, Grandma? I say as I make her repeat the words again and again.

Some naughty boys, says Muriel. When the old woman was sleeping there they came along and cut off her skirts – right up to her knee.

I will expand by the end of this year, Lisa is saying to the reverent (male) interviewer, crouching like a schoolboy behind his sheaf of questions for the woman who runs the currencies of communication.

I am going into Asia, says Lisa, ruler of the world!

I'M WALKING through the garden of Woodford Manor. I go down over the lawn, where moles have thrown up their piles of bright, fresh earth. I go past the greenhouse, where glass is missing from the whole of one side and a fig, once bursting with fruit, now stands with nothing to offer but small, unripe swellings of green.

How do I know this? Did I eat a fig here once, when the greenhouse was flourishing with peach, apricot – and orchids at the far end, which I see in my mind's eye now – vulgar, flashy, the colour of the smart beige and maroon luggage that belongs to the strange lady who brought me down here in the car . . .

The lady who was, and was not, Muriel.

It all seems very close and far away, that day. Like looking into an aquarium, and seeing a world there, complete with highly coloured fish and weed in clear, waving detail; and yet not being able to touch it, sealed from it by a pane of glass.

But I must have come here. I can see the fig – it must have been the first I'd seen or tried – and the millions and millions of scarlet filaments in its flesh, like a secret light bulb that would glow at night when the lady had taken me away and no one was there to see.

I bite into the fig. I make a face. The lady laughs down at me.

It's well after noon by now and very hot. The grass yields to a kind of scrub, dotted with daisies and some swampy bits too, where my foot goes in suddenly, to mud buried under an army of apparently dry reeds.

I pull out, but my sandal has gone, and I stand there on one leg, looking and feeling a fool.

But even that is better than feeling what I really feel, after seeing Muriel's ring on the fourth finger of the left hand of Lisa Crane.

Further down the riverbank – and I hobble there, over the broken bridge where Jasmine and I walked this morning – I hear guitars playing and voices singing; and I stop, to see where the hippies encroached on Woodford land.

I'm surprised by how proprietorial I feel at the sight of these trespassers. They've done no harm, really, and yet I recoil when I see the mess they've left behind them – the rusting cans and the buckled plastic utensils, useless, garish, indestructible.

I feel like a conservationist: prim, English, shocked by any intrusion from the modern world into my idyllic rural retreat. I stoop and pick up a smashed toy train, bright and blue synthetic material of some kind, and without wheels, beyond hope of repair.

But there is nowhere to throw it and I drop it again, in the long grass by the edge of the woods where they have made a makeshift sort of camp.

And then I see him a little further on, as I limp along the bank of the river, away from the house and the relics of Lisa Crane.

I am a little higher than he is, for he's standing almost in the water and staring at the opposite bank, as if trying to decide whether to go on down to the weir and use the bridge there or walk across.

He wouldn't do that, of course. He is too smartly dressed. The black suit looks out of place here, where everything is so green and the celandines and flag iris make the only colour, under a sky of the very palest blue.

He stands out like an exclamation mark on a blank page. And yet he does not denote surprise, for me. I have seen him before.

Behind the man in the black suit, the hippies return to their camp. A fight breaks out, and empty beer cans clatter against the trees. In front of him the river swirls, at its deepest point here.

And all the effluvium, all the filth in the west of England, seems to have choked into the river now.

Where this morning the water had been as clear as the glass of a child's marble, with the blue and green moving shadows of the trees and the sky trapped in its transparency, now it is evil, indescribably filthy, ruined by the outpourings and detritus of man.

I know the stranger by the side of the river brings all this with him: the fighting, drinking, swearing louts in the woods; the foul pollution of the stream.

He turns and sees me. At that moment I know the earth is very old, and cannot much longer endure the chaos and ruination brought upon it.

The dark, quiet man pulls a gold watch on a chain from his pocket and stares down at its face.

The gold catches a fierce ray from the sun. I see a million haloes come down on the river and fly up again; and when I can see once more, he has gone.

JASMINE IS IN the kitchen, stuffing a chicken. Since I saw the image of Lisa on the screen in the room across the hall, since I saw the man who stands as patient as a fisherman on the riverbank, I have understood fragments of my past which I can fit together now, make a pattern where before there was only the blank of absence and trying to forget.

– I'll tell you, Jasmine says. She is blending sage and bread-crumbs and egg together in a Magimix and her hand goes deep into the bird, pushing in the glutinous stuff. Then two rashers of bacon go down over the back of the bird, and a blob of butter that suddenly reminds me of the way Muriel would get Sunday lunch ready. Chicken was my favourite, she always remembered that.

The bird goes in the oven and Jasmine sits at the table, motioning me to join her. There's a trug with broad beans – there must be a vegetable garden at the back somewhere, and maybe the Neidpaths are curators of that too – and Jasmine pushes a pile of them over to me. I slit my thumb along the pod, and draw the beans that look as small as a child's milk teeth from their cotton-wool setting.

Jasmine begins to speak.

– I was very worried about Muriel, as I said, at that time. So I decided to take her to a health farm I'd read about – not too expensive, you understand – it was called Summer . . . well, it's so long ago, something like Summerfield Farm.

At first it was all a big joke. Muriel still thought it was funny to start minding, at our advanced age, about our appearance –

her word, she was always laughing about the vanity of the women she worked with on the magazine, especially the editor, a tartar of the old school by the sounds of her. But we went on all the machines in the gym just for the hell of it.

I remember, we even got ourselves buried up to the neck in mud in some sort of rejuvenation treatment, and came out a few hours later looking, well, muddy.

It was so obvious that we weren't going to change into beauties overnight – and I was hungry too, I must admit; I used to smuggle in biscuits and the like – that I decided to quit after a week. Muriel was annoyed at first, because she said she'd be lonely. Then she told me to go, and to watch out for the results she'd be showing after another couple of weeks in the place.

'Suit yourself,' I said. (Truth to tell, I was very cheered up by Muriel's attitude to the whole thing. I thought – I have to admit I was wrong not to look deeper – I simply thought the poor woman had had too much work and too little play recently. That was all there was to it. What Muriel needed was a holiday. And, even if it meant a health farm with a woman friend, she'd got one.)

True, there was one night – after we'd got used to the orange juice and found we could talk freely without the usual intake of gin or wine – when Muriel started harping on about your mother and Harry again. How Anna didn't understand him. How she took him for granted, that kind of thing.

'Oh belt up, Muriel,' I said. 'He's happy – anyone can see that.'

'That's the trouble,' Muriel said.

And those, says Jasmine, rising with a colander of beans and putting them to one side, laying out a row of new potatoes that need scraping and already smell of the wild mint she gathered this morning from the riverbank – those were the last words Muriel spoke to me.

As her old self, I mean.

– I remember the dress. I find I have spoken suddenly, when a silence has fallen on the kitchen and Jasmine is washing earth from a bunch of baby carrots, immersed in the present, as if the past and Muriel's election to put back the clock to an impossible, artificial present could never really have taken place.

But I do remember the dress. I saw it earlier, in a flash of those bright psychedelic colours of the time, when Jasmine spoke of Anna putting on dresses at last, discarding the jeans and dungarees so as to look more attractive for her lover, Harry.

The dress is lying on the floor.

Something terrible has happened. There has been a fight or a scene – like an animal, I smell trouble, but alas, like a child, I run in the big flat with its shadows from the light on the water outside for my grandmother, for Muriel.

But that, it turns out, is the trouble. My mother wants Muriel too.

– Yes, Jasmine says. Your grandmother came back in the middle of the day from the health farm and went straight to the flat. There was no point in going to the office, you see; it was afternoon already.

She found a note asking her to babysit you that evening.

I only heard this much later, you understand, when I talked to her on the telephone and tried to get her to make sense. I was frightened by then – very frightened. I didn't know who to turn to, you see.

– But she didn't come back in time for them to go out, I say.

It's an evening in the middle of summer, because it's light, but I know it's late from the indigo band of cloud that moves over the Thames and lies like a basking shark in the depths of the sky opposite our window.

It's so late that Anna and Harry have missed their date. They are imprisoned here with me. They hate me for keeping them under lock and key.

After all, they're young.

But I have never known my mother in such a rage. The lovely dress she was wearing, the kinetic dress that looks like a sorcerer's robe, with moons and stars and wild cabbalistic patterns, is scrumpled up and lying on the floor, near her kicked-off shoe.

Harry stumps out of the flat and the door bangs.

Anna locks herself in her room now, sobbing into her pillow.

– I discovered later, Jasmine says, they'd been planning to get engaged over dinner.

But they did make a scapegoat of Muriel, you know. When she was there she was in the way, like mothers-in-law are conventionally meant to be. When she was out, she was no good to them because she wasn't there to look after you, so they could go out.

– I was in the way, I say.

– Still, it was bad luck that evening, Jasmine reproves me, but in a kind tone. They'd booked a table at a romantic restaurant – you know the kind of thing . . .

I don't, but I say nothing. For I remember what happened later that night. And this time I tell Jasmine how it really was.

I'm in my small bed in the room with the old wallpaper that my grandma says should be replaced with something I would really like – teddies perhaps, or cartoon characters disporting across the walls – and I've had to climb in by myself, without a bedtime story or even cleaning my teeth.

I hear the door – first the front door, at the bottom of all that purple and white swirling lino, then the door of the flat.

I know I'm not supposed to get out of bed, but I do. I stand for what seems like for ever at the door of my little room.

Then I hear footsteps. I can feel my face, all these years later, puckering into the frown I must have worn then, at the unfamiliar sound of those footsteps in the corridor outside.

At the far end of the passage the door of the sitting room opens; I can hear the creak of the hinge that Anna always says she really will get round to oiling.

I'm just about to slip down the passage too, when the two doors go again, one after the other, like a couple of shots going off.

Someone has come in angry or – I'm too young to know about this yet – drunk.

Steps come up the stairs and turn left to the sitting room.

And I, like a fool in one of the books Muriel reads to me – for there are stupid girls sometimes in the stories she chooses, and then Anna fights with her and says there shouldn't be – like a baby (as I suppose I really still was), I walk down that passage to find Harry is in the far end of the room, which is dimly lit; he's at the end where my mother's dress lay, when she hurled it from her in a rage.

Harry is standing behind a woman, and he has his arms round her, he's squeezing, he's muttering something . . .

I bang the door with my head and the noise makes them turn round.

Harry growls at me to get the hell out.

But the woman, who smiles down at me but seems a million miles away, is wearing my mother's dress and she's not my mother at all.

Harry seems only dimly to realize this as I stand there, for he pulls away from the stranger and takes a long, hard look at her.

– Well, I'm damned, says the man, whom I suddenly recall with such horrible, painful clarity. And he takes the woman's hand playfully. She smiles straight back at him, right in the eyes. Then she looks at me.

– Go on, Ella, it's time to go to bed, she says.

I run along the passage and climb for the second time alone into my bed. Then I get out again, I go into the bathroom, and it's the first time I've ever been 'naughty' on purpose. I push her cloudy blue ring over the shelf and down the little black hole. And the man and the woman come in – and the man fishes it out again and the woman smiles and says, Thank you, and gives him a kiss. The woman was my grandmother, but she was young.

I finish, and Jasmine sighs as she closes cupboard doors and runs a cloth over the kitchen table, where flour lingers from the scones she's baking in the big old Aga in the deep recess in the kitchen. Plates sizzle as she lifts covers, a pan of water goes on, and then another. I realize how hungry I am. But I also know I now fear seeing my grandmother.

Jasmine must have felt what I was thinking, for she turns now and asks me to be patient one more time.

She'll be here tonight, she says. She has promised me to . . . to go back to being her old self. She'll be so happy to see you again, Ella. Just think!

I wonder if Jasmine, who says she was so baffled at the time of the change in Muriel, can even guess at what really happened the day she came back from Summerfield. And if she could, wouldn't she refuse to believe it?

I remember:

I'm in the park. The wind is blowing the trees about and a man is running hard with me in a pram.

Thunder's coming on; people are scattering to little white pavilions.

Muriel has come back today. I'm so happy. I don't mind where we go or what we do so long as we are together.

The man sits with my grandma on a bench, in spite of lightning and big claps of thunder that are then followed by gusts of wind and rain. She is out of breath from running with him when he did his dash with the pram, and she is laughing.

I peer over the sides. I am too old to be in a pram, I want to get out and I begin to wail.

My grandma and the man pay no attention at all – because she is signing a piece of paper and he is helping her with the words on the form.

I scream like the baby Muriel now seems to think I am, and I rock the pram until it tumbles over.

My head gets a cut and the man takes a white handkerchief from the breast pocket of his immaculate dark suit. He mops my head and the white lawn handkerchief is splodged with blood.

But before I can begin to tell the tale of the afternoon I remember in the park, when the trees were blowing about and a man ran with me in my pram, against the crashing thunder and rain, Jasmine has started to whisk egg whites in a bowl, and as she whisks she talks on, in a low monotone, as if afraid, now, that someone will hear.

Jasmine says:

For a few days after Muriel was back from Summerfield, I didn't see her.

I had a very complicated job on my hands, a new book by a professor of quantum physics, with diagrams and the lot – and, don't forget, there were no word-processors in those days.

As well as that, my aunt had come to stay from the country, and after I finished work we'd go out to Bendicks for a light lunch and take in the sales – that kind of thing.

So when Muriel rang me from the office and suggested I look in that evening, I had to say no. I mean, there wasn't any point in taking poor Aunt Elsie out to a place like Anna's flat. She'd have been terribly shocked by the feminist politics – and by Anna and Harry sleeping together without being married too, I expect. So I told Muriel it would have to wait until I was on my own again. Of course, I asked her how the health farm had gone, but the whole experience had been an expensive waste of time for me, and I wasn't expecting to hear anything very different from Muriel.

– But Jas, you've got to come over tonight, she said. There's been a . . . well, it's too terrible for me to explain on the phone. There's been one hell of a bust-up between Anna and me.

This didn't sound so unusual to me – as I said before, they'd been getting on each other's nerves for some time.

– She hates me now, Jas, I know it. Muriel was practically in tears. And I don't honestly know what I've done. Please! Couldn't your aunt . . . just for one evening? I do beg you, Jas!

I went, of course. For one thing I'd never heard Muriel sound quite like that. She was . . . well, breathy, sort of startled and, well, her voice sounded younger, I suppose, is what I mean.

It didn't prepare me, though, for what I found when I got round there.

It was an evening right in the middle of summer – I do remember that very clearly, because the syringa outside that giant Victorian door in the mansion block by the river was smelling so sweet I couldn't resist picking a sprig on my way in. It smells a bit like orange blossom, you know – and I thought of weddings and young brides. I can remember that as I went up that purple and white swirling lino on the stairs I wondered whether Harry and Anna would get married in the summer, or wait until after her launch of autumn books, before going to the altar. And I thought, secretly, that it would be a good thing if they got it over with sooner and asked Muriel to move out. After all, they could bring you up together . . . and maybe if they were feeling a bit on top of one another, a nice summer wedding would be just the thing.

I sit watching Jasmine's snowy peaks of egg white. She is folding them into a tin with shallow indentations, after beating in sugar. The door of the big wide Aga swings open at her touch, like the child-sized stove in the kitchen in the forest where Hansel and Gretel wandered, lost.

The door closes. I sit still, seeing myself as a pawn, talked of, disposed of, as unwanted children always are.

I couldn't have been less prepared for what I saw, Jasmine says, after she has gone back to her seat and taken a fat onion from the vegetable rack.

It makes my eyes water, she says, handing it to me, along with a small container of cloves. Stud it with cloves, will you, Ella. I want to make bread sauce.

Not for the first time, I dread the evening meal that Jasmine prepares so assiduously. Who is coming? Why are we having all the trimmings, as if this were indeed a Christmas family celebration.

Muriel was standing at the top of the stairs, Jasmine goes on, while I still struggle to summon up the courage to ask if my mother has been invited to come tonight.

– Jas, darling, Muriel calls down to me. How d'you think I look?

Well, Ella – and here, as if determined to make her point as dramatic as possible, Jasmine drops a sharp-bladed knife to the floor and the clatter makes me jump nearly out of my skin.

I can only say that I've never seen anyone so changed – and yet, at the same time, completely themselves.

I felt as if I were being mesmerized – yes, something like that. Jasmine stoops for the knife and it comes up glinting metallic silver, like a fish tugged out of the water. She was, kind of blinding – it was as if there was some light shining round her. I could sense a gathering of people making their way towards her – you know, it's like when you see a famous film-star in the flesh, and you feel the excitement of all those she has bewitched over the years.

And, as you must know by now, Jasmine adds drily, I don't go in for believing in that kind of thing at all. OK, there's such a thing as sex appeal, I don't deny it – and here she looks across at me with, I can only say, a hostile, challenging stare. And my saying that would go very much against the grain with your mother and all her feminist cronies, I can tell you.

I mean, Jasmine goes on, glancing away now as she does every time she seems to recall my own delicate relationship with the people she describes – I mean, the whole point of Anna's relationship with Harry was that it was 'rational', they were friends as well as lovers. In those days, you know, the model was Mary Wollstonecraft and her husband, Godwin, with their separate lives and their clearly defined freedoms. Such things as chance and romance – I mean, the inequality of beauty and so on – just wasn't on.

Only Mary Wollstonecraft died in childbirth, I think to myself. And my mother didn't. She lived on, to show herself incapable of loving her child.

Jasmine goes on:

Muriel was wearing an Indian caftan, a cotton thing, and it wasn't easy to see at first whether she'd lost a lot of weight at Summerfield.

She pulled me along the corridor and into her little room. And I must say, that had undergone a transformation too.

Jasmine laughs, as if plunged suddenly into memories of a time when to be carefree was to be in the swing of things; when adult responsibilities were despised and seen as no more than symptoms of an outdated, decadent malaise.

It reminded me of how I'd felt twenty years before, Jasmine admits, mind-reading in that disconcerting way she has.

Not that dear old London could have provided, when Muriel and I were young, at the end of the war, the kind of exotica she had collected for herself in a matter of days!

There was an inflatable plastic chair with zebra stripes, there were Indian hangings everywhere, and wreaths of dried flowers, and incense burning, and posters, of course – Janis Joplin, I remember, screaming her throat out on that wall of Muriel's little room that had been so bare.

At first, I just didn't know where to look. Then Muriel, who was laughing in a delighted sort of a way, said, You see, Jasmine, I'm really going to cheer things up at the magazine. I mean, Liddy Wise is such a fuddy-duddy. If we want to attract younger readers, we must understand the new culture, don't you agree?

For the first time since I left grammar school, I felt at a total loss. I was entering a world that was incomprehensible to me, the new world of the young. And I felt damned old too, if you want to know.

Muriel stretched her hand out to me and I had to look her in the face.

I can't describe it – she had this youthful kind of power, she seemed so happy and utterly self-confident.

– Supper's ready, Anna shouted at this point from the little kitchen behind the sitting-room. And – I must say she sounded furious.

– Coming, Muriel yells back, more like a teenager than anything else, I couldn't help thinking. And – just like one of those maddening young people who don't give a damn for all the effort that's gone into the cooking of a meal, she drew me closer and showed me both her hands again.

– My ring's not there, you see, Jas, she says. My fingers have grown so much slimmer that it slipped off. I've had to send it to be tightened. Isn't it a laugh?

I just didn't know what to say. But I felt the full force of the change in her. Muriel dreamed only of herself.

So – where was I? I say. The discarded casing of the red onion lies on the scrubbed table in front of me. Tears spring as sharp as pinpricks to my eyes as I push the spear-ended cloves into the obdurate, stinging flesh.

You? says Jasmine. Oh, you came running in at just the most awkward moment. By which I mean, she says quickly, as I dodge from a spurt of onion juice and she thinks she has hurt me, has made me cry, at the very moment when a distraction was badly needed – to deflect attention from the fight that was about to break out in the flat that evening.

– Fight? I say.

Already I see the cloudy, smoky ring that Muriel had told me came from a mountain that was made entirely of this magical stone, and if you went there you could climb inside and see the city where everyone was blue and mauve.

I see the ring on a slim, elegant finger, clasping the hand of a smiling, besotted man.

By the time Muriel and I had reached the end of the corridor we both knew at once that Muriel's ex-husband Bert had called round. Clearly he hadn't taken the trouble to inform his daughter, and at first I thought the almost palpable irritation Anna was feeling was more to do with having to do a meal for so many (and it wasn't something she was used to, after all. Your grandmother always looked after the meals, in the old days).

Yes, she looked distinctly peevish that evening, your mother. She was back in her denim boiler suit again – which was definitely a bad sign. And she was all shiny in the face – lately she'd been putting on a bit of powder and rouge ... well, for God's sake, why not?

Harry was sitting at the table in what I instantly recognized as a deliberately provocative attitude. He had his legs crossed and he was smoking. Anna was saying something to him and he wasn't listening. She had to shout it at him – pass the bowl for the salad, or whatever – before he stretched lazily behind him to the dresser and took it. In doing this, he grazed the stomach of the debonair Bert Twyman, who was standing there as if he owned the place, as usual.

– Fuck off, Bert Twyman said.

Then Muriel, with me following behind, walked in. And at that precise moment you woke from some dream or other and started to bellow at the top of your lungs.

There is a silence while Jasmine goes over to the Aga and brings out the tray of meringues. She places them on the table and the sugary sweet smell fills the kitchen.

I couldn't believe my eyes at first.

Jasmine prods a meringue, the sharp, brittle exterior snapping under her thumb. Transformed from the billow of egg white that went into the fire, the thin shapes that float like swans on the tin surface of the cooking tray seem hard and unreal.

– It was the way Muriel behaved, Jasmine says. Her voice is matter-of-fact, even rather bored.

– I just didn't believe it, as I say. Not at first. Bert Twyman was eyeing up his ex-wife in a most salacious manner. And Harry didn't like it at all.

– Get off out of here, he said.

Then Anna had to go down the corridor to fetch you from your bed.

Muriel was just standing there, you see. As if she was utterly oblivious to what she would have regarded as her most sacred duty only a short time before. It was as if she didn't hear you crying at all.

Oh, I say.

Everyone concentrated really hard on cheering you up – singing songs and telling stories – and the moment passed.

But it was a relief when Bert finally left. He insisted on prising out of Muriel a time for him to come and see her next day in the office.

And I honestly think Anna would have been pleased – I mean, for your parents to come together again is a damn sight better than if they're deadly enemies – if it hadn't been for Harry's obvious interest in your mother.

She told me, you know, years later, poor Anna, that she couldn't handle the fact of Muriel's retrieved sexuality at all, at the time.

She knew how grateful she was to her mother for all the love and help she'd given her in the past – with you, of course, too – and yet as soon as 'Ma came back from that health farm', as she put it, she could only see her as a deadly rival. And that made Anna very upset, of course. It ruined all her theories of female solidarity, and sisterhood, and the like. Jealous of her own mother.

Mind you, Jasmine says, she had every reason to be.

Again a quiet falls on the kitchen, like the all-consuming hush that fell on the forecourt at the station when I arrived. I can see John Neidpath, outside on the cobbles, carrying a long wooden stave, which he places by the entrance to the green. Then he goes back for another, and another. I have the feeling that we are to be fenced in here, protected from the invading armies on the downs.

– Didn't you wonder how . . . how Muriel could have changed so much? I say. I mean, did you think the . . . that Summerfield made her like that, just on its own?

– It didn't matter for me, Jasmine snaps. I see the look of resentment and antagonism flash across her features again and then disappear into the no woman's land of old age. But it did for her. Who knows, she may have been suffering from such an accumulation of stress, over the years . . .

Caring for me, I think, but do not say. And I see how my presence affected everyone's life, and how different it would all have turned out if I had never been born.

– She was seeing devils after all, Jasmine says, into that quietness which is broken only by the steps to and fro of the man outside in the yard. And that's not a good sign. No, she came back – rejuvenated. It was what happened later that I couldn't forgive . . . well, again, not at first.

But I know. I remember what happened. And I know my grandmother's old friend is wrong.

And because I dread to know what came later, because I feel the pressure, the necessity for Jasmine to kill the dream of my childhood, trample on the only secure thing I have, I go to the back door, open it and look out. Jasmine, behind me, in the kitchen that's two steps down from the cobbles (and why do I remember that too?) bustles to the stove and takes out the chicken to baste. I can see, from the shadows of the old beeches as they fall over the roof of the stable block opposite, that it's getting late. It will soon be evening.

I make myself think of Muriel, after she came back from that long abandonment of me. I climb into her arms, kiss her face . . . I never will be parted from her again.

I remember:

I'm in the park. The wind is blowing the trees about and a man is running hard with me in a pram.

Thunder's coming on; people are scattering to little white pavilions.

Muriel has come back today. I'm so happy. I don't mind where we go or what we do so long as we are together.

Of course, says Jasmine's voice from behind me, from where she stands framed in the ugly, utilitarian colours of the staff side of Lisa Crane's house, I didn't see Muriel for quite a time after that . . . I mean, after she'd run off with Harry Crane.

And I hear my own voice:

I scream like the baby Muriel cruelly thinks I am, and I rock the pram until it tumbles over.

My head gets a cut and the man takes a white handkerchief from the breast pocket of his immaculate dark suit. He mops my head and the white lawn handkerchief is splodged with blood. And still I scream.

Why doesn't my grandma seem to care? Why, when we leave the park, me trotting along beside her this time, the dark-suited stranger gone off in the opposite direction, does she smile distractedly at me when I babble at her about my important cut on the head?

And a group of students at the park gates, seeing her come out, call and ask her to join them for a drink. Why do they laugh incredulously when Muriel calls back at them that she has to take her little grandchild home and put her to bed?

Because, as I know now, no one could believe Muriel was old enough to have a grandchild, that's why.

We are standing in the deepest interstices of the manor, Jasmine and I, in the room where the video of Lisa Crane plays night and day, tapes of her triumphs and successes, dinners and banquets, travels and receptions, succeeding each other unendingly, in a terrible travesty of life.

Jasmine is telling me Greg's tale, as he related it to her the day after Muriel's first appearance back at the office, after her 'holiday'. I stand listening to her, my head bowed. From time to time, when the music changes on the Lisa Channel, I look up – and into the video eyes of Jimi Hendrix or Bob Dylan – but mostly I stand there with the core of me drained out, as if the fame of Lisa Crane has taken away any picture of myself I might ever have had. That picture, after all, had been given me by Muriel Twyman, my grandmother. And she had long ago been replaced by Lisa Crane.

– At first Greg couldn't make out what was happening, Jasmine says. These are his words:

– You can have no idea how shocked we all were when Muriel Twyman came back from that holiday of hers – or visit to the health farm, I believe it was. Muriel looked stunning. She'd lost a lot of weight and her skin was glowing and all that, but there was something different – something that marked her out from the crowd. I can't explain it.

– You mean a *je ne sais quoi*, I joked, Jasmine says, because, after an evening like the one with Muriel and Bert and Harry and Anna, I thought the best thing was to play the whole thing down, not make too much of it – you know what I mean, Ella.

After all, the glow would fade pretty soon, after being exposed to city life and office air – so I said as much to Greg. Don't encourage her, I said. She's on a bit of a high at present. Don't let her think she's Catherine Deneuve or someone.

But how does she get away with it? Greg said.

The fashion room, as I've been telling you, was total chaos. And why? Because Muriel Twyman, a humble copywriter, has come back from her holidays and decides to fit herself out in a new dress.

No one could believe it at first. I mean, people are brought up generally to know their place in this tight little world of ours and for Muriel to go round helping herself to gowns and costume jewellery and shoes worth thousands was completely out of character. In fact, when we all looked back on it, we came to the conclusion we'd never seen Muriel in anything but a baggy cardigan and skirt.

Mind you, the fact she looked so great and could now fit into the clothes must have been a factor in her freak-out. And all the girls on the fashion floor were simply loving it. One of them had a portable record-player and soon there was music belting out – The Grateful Dead, I think it was.

Yes, 'Down Beside the Rising Tide' – my God, that song is engraved on my memory for life. Whoever it was – a young girl who was enjoying Muriel's moment of abandon, her name was Polly, I think – kept playing it over and over, and soon Muriel was dancing on the desks, in those crazy PVC boots and a mini-skirt that looked as if it were last used as a midget's cornplaster. As I say, the whole place was hopping.

We all thought Muriel was bound to get the sack. Every single one of us was waiting for the editor's door to open and for Liddy Wise to come out.

Liddy was a bit of a sour puss, as you must know.

But, as it turned out, the visit came from a different direction.

The managing director of the entire corporation, Mr New Image himself, walked into the department – and not from the elevator hall either. No, today of all days, he'd walked up the stairs and there he was, bang in the middle of us – like, like, I don't know, a sort of sprite who appears in a puff of smoke in an opera.

Mind you, I was as embarrassed as anyone. Sammy Chen and I, well we were enjoying the break too. Sammy said he hadn't had such a ball since Haight-Ashbury. And Muriel was singing by now – Oh, God, Jasmine, your toes would have curled. First she was singing along with The Grateful Dead. Then Joplin. Music came to an end and she just went on on her own. And that voice – of course, we'd all thought it was going to be a real caterwaul when she first opened her mouth, but after a few bars we thought it was just bloody great.

It's like the way she looks now, you know – it kind of grows on you. So you think there's nothing very outstanding at first, and then – wham, you can't take your eyes off her!

It must have been that that made me think something . . . well, sort of funny had happened.

What do you mean, funny? I said. The last thing I wanted was more talk of miracle rejuvenation treatments and the like, and I said so.

No, no, Greg said. It must have been that strange little man who's the head of New Image Corporation suddenly being in our midst, and Muriel dancing in that – gauzy strip and not much else – I couldn't help thinking of some magic pact with the Devil, or whatever.

For God's sake, Greg, I said. Muriel is only going through a rather silly phase. Keep your head.

– But, Jasmine goes on, weary now, as if the meaning of that day has taken the last of her strength, but Greg insisted that the effect Muriel had on the MD was absolutely devastating.

Yes, it was like a fairy-tale, a movie.

I mean, Mr Lewis – that's his name; we all know and fear it at the office, I can tell you – applauded and told Muriel she was the one to give *New Image* a real new image, a look that belongs with the sixties, with the age we're all living in now, and not a stifled echo of the past, as is dished up to us at present.

As he says this, he's eyeing the editor's door in a meaningful way. We all fell silent; we just couldn't believe what was happening. But then the door opens and Liddy Wise comes through.

And, well, Jas, I can still hardly credit my own ears. Lewis fires her then and there.

I couldn't believe what Greg was telling me either, Jasmine says. But it was true.

Muriel Twyman was that day appointed editor-in-chief of the New Image Corporation, Inc.

I look up, round the room, with its memorabilia, its cult objects of the worship of Lisa Crane. Record sleeves with her picture imprinted, and the gold disc hanging behind, on the Indian arras that muffles the room with its green-gold brocade.

The first issue of *New Image* as edited by Muriel Twyman framed in gold beside it.

And on the cover – why, of course, Muriel herself.

I think of the name, in neat handwriting, in the Mrs Beeton *Book of Household Management* up by the bed where I spent last night. Muriel Twyman. And then – and from this I look away, still – in an ornate hand, Lisa Crane.

– So, how did it happen? I say.

Jasmine has left the video room and is slowly walking away from the kitchen. But not to the main hall this time – in the opposite direction, to the bare, disused rooms of the servants' quarters. I know I will see Muriel – or Lisa – soon. Yet first, I must know.

And this time, as I walk down a dark, stone-floored passage behind the woman who was my grandmother's best friend – who cared for me, so she says, when Muriel ran off with Harry and there was no one to help out – I know she is ready to answer my questions. She can sense the impending evening as I can; the all-important moment when I will meet Muriel again and we can be together.

She has promised to change, Jasmine says.

So I hardly need to tell you all the painful details of the new, ruthless attitude of Muriel: to your mother; to you; to anyone, you might say, who crossed her path.

If you must know, it was when you went into hospital with meningitis that your grandmother so charmingly chose to take her own daughter's fiancé away from her.

Jasmine stops at the entrance to a neat little room – the Neidpath sitting-room most likely – and she makes me sit with her on a settee covered in a patterned velvet that has known better days. It creaks under our weight, and Jasmine glances apologetically around before going on.

Anna rang when her mother was in the middle of one of her most extravagant 'do's – it was a reception for General de Gaulle and the Robert Kennedys, if I remember. And I can say it cost poor Anna quite a lot to get in touch with her mother at all.

By then, Muriel had been living for almost a year in the most sumptuous flat imaginable – in Eaton Square, it was. Very unlike that purple and white lino place.

And why was she living in such splendour? Because, quite simply, everything Muriel – and in future I shall call her Lisa, so utterly unrecognizable was she, so totally unlike her old self – everything she touched turned to instant, shiny gold.

Don't ask me if she had affairs with the powerful men she seduced. I wouldn't be surprised if the answer was no, anyway. Men just did what they were told when they met Lisa.

And I never knew she had a head for business. But before long she had started a chain of companies, and made a successful bid for *New Image* and all the affiliated companies, and had set herself up as a property millionaire as well.

As I say, it cost Anna a lot to get in touch with her mother that evening. Harry was still living in the flat with her, but something seemed to lie between them now and there wasn't any talk of an engagement any more.

It's as if a kind of spell has been put on Harry, Anna said to me one day, when I'd picked you up from the nursery and brought you round for your tea and bedtime story. He's so listless – so uninterested in everything. When he used to help with the publishing, and – I don't know – he was so keen on life.

I didn't want to say anything, but I couldn't help wondering whether Harry wasn't coming down with some illness or other. However, I said nothing – and you needed your boiled egg and soldiers anyway and a cup of hot chocolate.

As Jasmine speaks, I strain to remember her when I was a child. Yet nothing comes. And it seems that, like love, memory can never be simulated or forced. I loved Muriel; Jasmine is as blank to me as if a total stranger had unwrapped me from my coat every evening on return from playschool and chopped fish fingers into bite-sized pieces for me.

It was because Anna was so terribly worried about you, Jasmine says, that she rang Muriel that night.

After all, it's at moments like those that women do ring their mothers, isn't it?

I suppose so, I say.

Lisa left the glittering reception immediately, as soon as Anna said you were ill.

I was at the hospital, holding Anna's hand, and yours too, poor little baby, except you were much too ill to be conscious of anything.

No, Jasmine, you are wrong, I say, but to myself and not to her, for something in me causes me to trust her less and less. As she rises and we walk to the end of the passage, disused sculleries and pantries leading off it, in a house that is now sinking back into a crepuscular state from which the bright blues and greens of the mid-summer day seem hardly to have distracted it, I hold back as she makes for the final room. I have a fear that she will confront me with this sleeping monster, this woman who was once Muriel and who long ago found she had no time for me – or for anyone other than herself. I am not ready yet, and I go to a window in the wall to look out at the cobbles, where the barricade erected by John Neidpath has grown tall enough to keep out an army of hippies or lager louts.

I say – to myself, for I have less and less belief in Jasmine:

You are wrong to say I was too ill to be conscious, because I remember the hospital, and the fever I had that carried me out to a country that was tiled like a great mosque and where weights like falling houses landed on my neck.

In the delirium of that fever, I remember the lady who came and stood by the foot of the bed.

She was dressed in white and she was made of frost and glass and snow. All the dripping icicles and snow ermines and frost sequins of the Snow Queen were on that lady at the foot of the bed. Yet somehow I knew that the Snow Queen was my grandmother, and I would never see her again.

Her heart had frozen. And when she turned and kissed the man who came in – just a minute before my poor, distracted mother – and she kissed him on the lips with her lips that were as red as hare's blood in her snowy face, I knew he was lost to my mother, for ever.

I was staying the night at Anna's flat, Jasmine says. To see to the laundry and generally help out.

I went back about midnight. Anna said she would sleep in the ward – there was a kind nurse there who allowed her to doss down: she was so worried about you, you see. Harry said he would stay in the waiting-room, to hear if you had passed the crisis of the illness.

– And Lisa? I say. For I know; I have seen the kiss.

About three in the morning, Jasmine says, I heard the front
door open. I was sleeping in the little room your grandmother
had – before . . .

Anyway, Ella, I thought your mother had decided to come
home, because the news about you was good.

I'm not one to meddle, so I waited until they'd gone down the
corridor before calling out to them. I remember wondering at
the time why they were nearly running. Anna, I knew, was tired
out from trying to earn her living while bringing you up without
her mother to help her – and with a relationship going sour, to
boot.

So . . . well, perhaps I shouldn't have gone right up to the door
– I don't think I ever would have, in normal circumstances . . .

– Harry and Muriel were in Anna's bed together, I say.

– Harry and Lisa, Jasmine corrects me. Then she breaks down
and weeps, puts her arm round my shoulder, and draws me to
the door of the room at the end of the passage.

– I swear to God, Ella, I tried to do all I could to stop it, Jasmine
says. But it was no good. Harry moved into the flat in Eaton
Square. They eloped – like teenagers, for God's sake – to Gretna
Green.

I see Harry and Lisa dancing, in the rain-swamped photographs
under the ping-pong table in the outdoor room where the garden
has encroached and damp cracks the paving-stones. They are
whirling, romantic, immaculate, in the midst of the age of revolution and anarchy. And it seems oddly suitable, somehow, that
their love should be so measured, calculated, formal, like a dance.

I pull the packet of photographs from my pocket and hand
them to Jasmine.

Yes, she says, with a sigh – but the sigh sounds theatrical,
unconvincing. Then:

– Give those to me, Ella. You don't need them now. And she
opens the door with a sudden brisk twist of the handle – as if

we, like the rest of the house – risked falling into a sleep from which we would never be able to wake.

– Go in there, Jasmine says.

She takes from me a wedding photo – of my grandmother and Harry Crane – which I must have missed before. A greenish smudge of damp runs, as it does in all the others, down the side of the face of the handsome man in the black suit, with his hat pulled down low over his eyes. He is staring at the camera, rather than at his bride, but his gaze appears to consist of no more than two black holes punched in the cheap Polaroid paper.

On the fourth finger of the hand of the new Mrs Crane is a new gold and diamond wedding-ring that sends out splinters of white light. Next to it, no more than a smoky blur in a modest surround of seed pearls, sits Muriel's amethyst ring.

The door ahead of me is open. Jasmine has left, walking in house slippers that give off groans and sighs, like a familiar long used to the ways of its master. She has gone to the kitchen, she says, to finish off the dinner – the dinner that will be a reunion of Anna, and her mother Muriel and their lover Harry – and me.

III

THE MOTHER'S TALE

MY MOTHER IS IN a small room, bare and sparsely furnished, that looks out on the flagstones of the unkempt terrace. It would have been the schoolroom once, I suppose, for children left to the attention of governesses and servants, and somehow I know, although I have seen her only on her visits to Australia over the span of my childhood and growing up, that Anna would choose a plain, unostentatious place like this, to talk to me in; that the flamboyant tastes of Lisa Crane are anathema to her.

She rises and comes over to embrace me. She's smaller than I remember and I feel an unexpected pang, but why is difficult to say. Her own vulnerability to the ageing process, perhaps, and therefore mine. I feel, for one moment, as our cheeks brush – hers very dry and papery – the sense of mortality which this house does everything to deny. And I realize fully for the first time how deeply embedded in a pre-adolescent state my enforced and unnatural sojourn with Maureen and her family has caused me to be. My resentments against Anna surface once more, as soon as I stand back and take note of her quiet, determined manner. The 'selfishness', which all my childhood I believed lay under that wide forehead with its businesslike fringe, manifests itself to me as it used to do on our strained outings to a tea-room in Melbourne, when all she wanted, probably, was to escape to the solace of her work rather than stay with a hostile teenager.

You've heard from Jasmine, Anna says simply, when we have sat down, facing each other across a table laid with a paisley cloth that must once have served for lessons; there are ink stains and torn places in the fabric where the pen nibs of children long ago were stuck rebelliously in.

And sure enough, Anna – publisher, writer, editor – shows as little emotion at seeing me as she had in the banished years of my youth, and every desire, as ever, to inform and instruct.

– You see, Anna begins, it took my mother to show me that the consequences of interfering with nature are potentially fatal.

Let me explain. After the first shock of your grandmother's transformation – into a woman, to put it brutally, with a future, when what was expected of her and her contemporaries was the acceptance that nothing lay ahead but memories of the past – I argued with myself that she had every right to continue enjoying her life. Rather, she had every right to improve the quality of her life after middle age.

After all, women were programmed by nature to become grandmothers as soon as their own childbearing years were finished, and for many, after a life sacrificed to continual pregnancy, childbearing or miscarriage, this enforced old age came as a well-earned rest – a relief after the struggles that had gone before.

But what of a woman of today, who, like my mother, your grandmother, has no experiences of this kind, who wants to go on living, and working and appearing youthful and attractive?

Why should she be exiled to old age and redundancy just because the laws of the Victorian age laid it down?

So, although I was bitterly hurt at the time, I understood. I couldn't bring myself to see her, of course – but I understood.

As my mother speaks in her quiet, dispassionate tones, I wonder if she really means what she is saying, or whether, for dignity's sake, she has decided to forget the anguish of a quarter of a century ago. It is she who appears a Victorian, a Jane Eyre figure, as she sits upright at the old schoolroom table, and lectures me on ecology and, as I might have known, mythology, for Anna is leaning forward now, as if trying to pull me out of the indifference and lethargy of my life – and warning me of the other perils that have beset our age. Outside, on the loggia where I earlier heard the laughter of someone I fear to meet, and who must be laughing now, at Anna's earnest efforts to save the planet before it is too late, a slight wind stirs the fuchsias that droop their gaudy purple and magenta bells into the cracked rims of the urns. Anna is talking . . . my mind wanders as she tries to lead me back from the shades of her mother's long indifference.

You see, Ella, you have come searching, like Demeter sought Persephone, but it is the wrong way round. You are the maiden who is bound to go under the earth in the autumn and return in spring, for you are the future bearer of children, the mother-to-be of humanity.

Yet, just as the myth of Demeter and Persephone represented the ancient cycles of the year, and the climate and the seasons and the fruits and crops have now been thrown into chaos by the greed of man, so the huge numbers of human beings on earth, and the invention of artificial methods of preventing their future conception, have stopped the natural progression of generations and thrown up hybrids and freaks – such as Lisa Crane, who returned to youth and then found herself unable to relinquish it.

I squirm in my seat, a restless pupil, thinking I can see an outline of a face at the window, which, like the window in Jasmine's cottage, is fringed with leaves of creeper and vine. The leaves form, as the light and the breeze run through them, an illusion of a wreath for a pagan head, a circlet of beaten gold for Dionysian curls, prancing over a face with black eyes.

And I wonder too if the presence of my mother, with her store of ancient myth and her Cassandra-like messages to the rapidly self-immolating world, has invited this illusion to come to the garden terrace outside.

– Muriel – my mother, your grandmother – tried to reverse the natural order of things, Anna says. And for these people, who deny the future of the human race, there is only one end.

I turn from the shadow play beyond the window and face my mother again.

– What is the end? I say.

But she doesn't answer, and so I ask her to tell me what she felt when I was there in the flat with her on the river, when my grandmother was still a real grandmother and I knew nothing of the dramas, other than the impressions gleaned by a three-year-old child, that were in the process of being played out.

– I went to bed early on the night Muriel didn't come back in time to babysit, Anna says. I was angry, I'll admit. You see, Harry and I were very much in love. We were going to become formally engaged that evening – he had booked a table at a riverside restaurant and afterwards we were going to come back to the flat and call our friends, and all the members of the publishing collective, of course, and tell Muriel.

I was looking forward to telling my mother the wonderful news. After all, we had lived together like sisters for so long; I knew she'd be thrilled for me. And I knew Harry would be a wonderful stepfather for you.

Harry had bought some champagne, and we put it in the fridge for when we came home.

But your grandmother never turned up. First, we drank one of the bottles of champagne. That was probably silly of us – of me, anyway. I've never had much of a head for drink.

And when it became obvious that we'd lost our reservation at the restaurant and the evening was a write-off, I did behave in a childish way, I admit. I threw a tantrum – no more, no less – it woke you up, which was the worst part of it, and Harry stormed out of the flat to go and drink with pals in the pub.

I remember taking off my new dress. I can remember to this day what it looked like – it was silver and glittered like the scales of a fish.

Anna laughs, and I begin . . . I just begin . . . to feel for her, to see her as a human being, as the young woman she once must have been.

– And there were moons and stars and suns all over it, Anna says. It was a real magician's dress.

I say nothing. In my mind's eye I see the other woman in the dress and the silver in it gleaming in the reflected lights from the river.

– I don't know what happened, Anna says. Harry came in. He came to bed very drunk.

The next morning, Muriel had gone to the office before I got up.

But when she came in, that evening . . .

– Yes, I say. How had she changed? What did you think when you first saw her walk in?

– I had a very strange feeling, Anna says. It was as if my own existence had been negated somehow.

I knew this woman – pulsing with excitement, energy – in clothes I'd never seen on her before, fashion clothes, was my mother. Obviously I did.

But at the same time she wasn't, I say. And I tell Anna how I felt the same when Muriel picked me up in her arms that night and I stared into a face that I knew and yet was strange to me.

They say that when you die all the lines of your life, made up from worry and strain and the perplexity of living, can fade away and leave you young again, Anna says. And that was what I felt about Muriel, that she had died and her youth had returned to her in this inanimate, disturbing way.

No, my mother goes on when we have been silent a while, hearing Jasmine in the kitchen just down the ugly, hospital-green corridor, at work in the kitchen, opening oven doors that release the life-giving smell of baking bread, I can't tell you much of how I felt about your grandmother and Harry. The shock was too great. The emnity I didn't know I had in me just rose to the surface, and I knew, if she didn't move away from us, I might kill my mother.

But why . . . why did Harry fall for her so easily? I say. And then I regret saying it, for Anna, as any woman would, flinches from answering.

– I'll tell you, Anna says, after a silence in which we both know we have thought the unthinkable.

I'll tell you what I thought then, and what I may, just possibly, think now. Then . . . well, I was sure in my mind there was no such thing as a woman's sexual power – not *per se*, I mean.

I saw Marilyn Monroe and the millions of other women who had had to live on their sexuality alone, as victims of an oppressive, patriarchal society. Consumerism and advertising hype persuaded men to believe they were attracted more to a 'sexy' type of woman than another.

But now I couldn't say for certain that I believe in that. And I have had to admit that the cruellest thing that can happen to a woman – her lover and the future father of her children taken from her by her own mother – had to be ascribed to something more than the stunning good looks with which Muriel came back from that health farm.

It was as if – and I don't like using the word – some magic quality now emanated from her. Jasmine saw it too. But neither of us felt it in the way Harry did.

Poor Harry, Anna adds – and by her show of compassion I feel I have misjudged her all my life, and look away at the unprepossessing brown paint of the dado in the plain little room – poor Harry, it was as if she had some kind of mysterious hold over him, you know, and he just couldn't wriggle free.

I tell my mother that I remember the scene in the hospital, where I had meningitis, and she flushes and turns to look out of the window, where the light is dull and flat; cloud has come down and rubbed out the quivering figure made by the leaves and the light outside.

And I tell her, but gently, for I know she has no need of being hurt further, that I know I have been here before – that I know why the place seems to hold a memory from the youngest years of my childhood.

– She came for you one day when you were at the nursery, Anna says in a sad voice – as if she knows I have blamed her all along for my exile to the far side of the world.

By then she had been on TV a lot – her rise to fame was certainly meteoric – and there had been profiles in the press and all that, and they were thrilled to let you go with her.

The car was a Rolls-Royce, needless to say. Anna smiles, but the smile is wan. She sent me an ultimatum from this house – that she would sue for custody of you and would prove that I was a negligent parent. She had Harry by then. I fought back. What else could I do?

I think of the boat on the river, and the man pushing me down into the water – just for the fun of it, the lady said.

Again, we sit in silence. Then Anna goes compulsively on.

– I don't know how many times I suffered humiliation at the hands of my mother, she says, glancing at me quickly and catching, I'm sure, my own flash of response, as if the same feelings have to be passed down generations of women, and no mother can ever do right by the woman who is coming up to take her place.

She said at one point that she was sorry, she wanted to change back to the person she had been in the old days. She followed me – she hounded me, really – even to the street where I'd moved to and found me one morning in the corner supermarket. I was taken for *her* mother when we were seen there together.

And when Harry, who missed me really – he was under her spell, however much it goes against the grain to say it – when Harry suggested we meet from time to time, Muriel always seemed to know where we were.

My mother shivers suddenly, as if a cold wind had crept into the house on this hot summer's day.

– Then, when I began to realize that Harry still loved me, that he had only been bewitched by my mother and I might have a chance of getting him back, she really began to persecute him with a vengeance.

They'd been together – married, I have to say it – for some years then, and one of the most sinister things was how young she went on looking, while Harry . . . well, he aged like everyone else.

It was then, Ella, that I had to admit to myself the possibility that . . . well, something else had taken place when Muriel Twyman changed into Lisa Crane. I couldn't begin to believe it, at first, but after my meeting with Harry, in a place where such a person as Lisa Crane would never go – wouldn't be seen dead, perhaps I ought to say – a fast-food joint in the centre of town – it was when Lisa came after us there that I did begin to wonder very seriously, as I say.

We were sitting together, just two ordinary people in early middle age, and I suppose we looked comfortable together, because an old lady at the next table asked where we came from, as if we were a couple, you know.

Harry put his head in his hands at that and almost sobbed. And just as he was pleading with me to extricate him from the nightmare of life with Lisa Crane – the Empress of the Air, as she was known, of course, by then – we both looked up and saw her standing at the plate-glass window, staring in.

It was so terrible – so frightening. How could she have known? She was wearing, I remember so well, a canary-yellow wool suit, and her chauffeur-driven Rolls was just behind her, parked in the midst of all the traffic as if she were royalty and no one would think of moving her on. Which, of course, they didn't.

As Anna speaks, I remember the rhymes I read the children at the nursery back home, and I remember too, because poor little

Chi-ren had been frightened by tales of Chinese devils and demons, the jingle of the woman and the devil who tried to escape from her. 'Art and cunning he did not lack,' say I, as if from a deep trance of seeing the words on the page and feeling Chi-ren's little body pulling away from the picture-book on my lap. 'But aye with her whistle she fetched him back.'

– Yes, Anna says. She always fetched him back. Harry sprang up, as guilty as a scalded cat, and made for the snackbar door. Anna smiles again, but without pleasure. It was left to me to pay for the meal, she says.

YOU SEE, Jasmine says, she was afraid.

We are in the kitchen and dinner is nearly ready. The chicken and roast potatoes come out of the oven and sit glistening on the table. Jasmine will carve here, and then put the food back until the other two guests arrive – my grandmother and Harry Crane.

Jasmine sharpens a long knife on a knife-grinder that looks as if it's been in the kitchen at Woodford Manor since the Victorian owners furbished the kitchen with the ponderous objects they made their servants use. I sit on a chair watching her. She speaks low and fast, to get in the end of her tale before my mother comes out of the little sitting room and bathroom, where the Neidpaths have invited her to get ready for dinner.

I want to imagine how Anna must be feeling – after seeing me like this, and before seeing the change in her mother that Jasmine has promised for tonight. But there isn't the time. I've seen, with all the urgency of necessity, that the days of Lisa Crane must almost be up; that it must be twenty-four years to the day since my grandmother took me to the park and was wolf-whistled on her way out by students asking her for a date, on a windy midsummer evening, at nine o'clock. Twenty-four years of unlimited power in return for the immortal soul: the pact made between Faust and Mephistopheles.

Muriel will return to her old self tonight, but she will be seventy-two years old.

– Yes, Ella, Jasmine says, and the thin, worn blade of the knife which has seen better days detaches a wing from the carcass of the bird. Yes, some years ago your grandmother did try to give

394

up the life she was leading and return to her kind, loving, unselfish self.

She missed you terribly, of course. And – for Jasmine has seen me blush and look away – she knew she had lost touch with you, that sending dolls and little girls' party dresses just wasn't the thing any more.

And she wanted to have a good relationship with Anna too. Every mother who loses her daughter is distraught at heart, I believe.

Now, Ella, shake the salad, Jasmine says as I redden further and start picking at the tablecloth, made of wartime oilcloth, on the table of the Neidpaths' unprepossessing kitchen.

And she hands me a wire basket of lettuce, indicating I should go to the back door and shake it on the cobbles outside.

– She wanted to give up the whole Harry business, Jasmine goes on as I open the door and see a big moon already down on the roof of the stable block opposite, and the beech trees round the village green magically lit up, as if for a druidical Disneyland.

I told her Anna was seeing Harry again – that they'd really been made for each other in the first place.

'You must come to terms with it, Lisa,' I said (she wouldn't let anyone call her Muriel by then). It was just a . . . an extended one-night stand with Harry, wasn't it?

Well, she was sick with rage. We were in her bloody great Eaton Square apartment, with all the Aubussons, and the mirrors everywhere, as befitted Lisa Crane, and the beautiful Meissen and Chelsea and Dresden china – and she just threw a fit and started smashing the lot. 'You just tell me where I can find the bastards,' she says (meaning Anna and Harry, of course), 'and I'll see to it, I'll see they never smile again.'

I thought the harsh reality might cure her, so I said they met sometimes in a fast-food joint right near the middle of town. A pretty squalid place, I agree, with all that scum and drug crowd hanging around, but I don't honestly think Harry and Anna cared where they saw each other. No five-star restaurants for them.

So, as I heard from her next day, she went off and saw them there. And the shock of the reality of it did work – for a while, anyway.

'I'm ready to give up, Jas,' she said to me. (We were in my modest little flat this time, and I think the surroundings helped to calm her down – or feel more that there was a possibility of becoming an ordinary person again.) 'It's time I gave over, and why shouldn't young people have a chance, for God's sake?'

I thought all this was very unlike Lisa Crane, but I didn't say anything at the time. I was too delighted, as you can imagine. She'd been made even more contrite too by haring off in search of Anna, to apologize, apparently, for the tough time she'd given her in the past, and finding her in a corner supermarket near Anna's flat. (Anna, as you know, moved from Chelsea when it became too expensive, and settled in a pretty rough district in the north of town. God knows what the manageress – or the other customers – thought when Lisa did her Rolls number and walked in.)

But Lisa was upset at being taken for Anna's daughter. 'Such bloody bad luck on Anna,' she says, 'but then, she's never been a lucky girl.'

– Yes, bad luck, I say.

– So, after that, Lisa is determined to reform. It must have been a couple of weeks before I saw her again. I must say I was terrified by the change in her. The effort to return to another way of life had driven her – I'm sorry to say – pretty well insane.

– How? I ask Jasmine, as I shake the leaves of the lettuce dry, and empty the wire basket out into the salad bowl. I see that rabbits have nibbled at the green leaves and a small slug, obstinately clinging to a leaf, has left a tiny silver trail.

– I went to see her in her skyscraper office, Jasmine says. And I thought the secretary looked nervous when I said I wanted to see Lisa Crane straight away.

She was recording an interview, the secretary said. And after that, there was lunch at the Guildhall with the Lord Mayor. But there was something else troubling the girl, I could see that.

Finally, Lisa emerged, and I took her into the first room I could find – it was an empty boardroom, as it happened. I made her sit down. 'What's the trouble, Lisa?' I said.

And she suddenly looked haggard – not a day older, mind you, but drained . . . and haunted.

'I'm having terrible dreams, Jas,' she said. 'For God's sake, help me out of this.' And she said she kept dreaming she'd found the TV salesman – the man who got her to sign the contract. She found him and persuaded him to cancel this terrible lease – but when she woke, it was to hear him laughing at her; and when she went to the mirror, there, unchanged, was her beautiful, unlined face.

– Poor Lisa, Jasmine finishes. She hasn't been well for such a long time. But tonight, in the happiness of being reunited with her family again, she will recover. You'll see.

I look at Jasmine and I realize that she arranged for me to come here, that Maureen Fisher would never have blurted out the name of this place unless she had been told to. And I begin to fear, to find myself going to the door of the kitchen again, that leads into the courtyard and the beginnings – at least – of the outside world.

But Jasmine pulls me back sharply and propels me along the passage to the green baize door.

– Tell your grandmother dinner is ready, she says.

I AM ON THE upper floor of the house.

I am wearing a dress that I found laid out on the bed where I slept – and woke, last night, to see the anger and surprise of Harry Crane.

I am walking along the landing where I passed the bales of silk and the straw suitcases of shells, from Lisa Crane's journeys of the past. I am going straight ahead, where a low arch leads to a descent of three steps and a corridor, whitewashed and innocent-looking, under eaves of thatch.

I can hear the crowds on the downs, and now, as evening falls, I can see the careless bonfires they have lit, as near as the Woodford woods, by the edge of the river as it bends in its last loop before the race to Slape weir.

The sky is pink from the glow of the fires, but I can smell nothing. I walk carefully in the dark-green velvet dress, with a fichu of lace at the throat, as if I were going into a lifetime's confinement – a dark place where I would be neither heard nor seen, the prison of old age.

The corridor ends with a door that's ajar and shows a further flight of steps, out of doors this time, with a reed roofing.

But I turn into the room on the right, just before the door to the steps, which are probably a flight down into the garden, and I stand looking across at the bed where Lisa Crane lies, asleep.

I make no noise, but she wakes up and sees me. The mirrors in the room show her face and mine – like two halves of an apple, shivering in the looking-glass doors.

I turn and leave the room. I go along the landing to the main stairs and I go down. It is time for dinner and Mrs Neidpath is crossing the hall with a tray.

I know why she thinks she has seen me here before.

IT IS GROWING dark and a line of cloud, like a bruise resting on the lid of an eye, runs along the line of the downs.

At the grey stone house lights shine from the windows, and in particular from the dining-room window, where a gold candelabra holds red candles alight in the centre of an elaborately laid table. Two women sit at the table waiting. They are Anna Twyman and her mother Lisa Crane's companion, Jasmine Barr.

The church clock in the bell tower strikes the first chime of nine.

A man can be seen to be walking slowly up the drive towards the door of the manor. He doesn't turn to go to the back, over cobbles to the kitchen door, but keeps on the road, avoiding a bump where someone long ago built a child's fortification with sand and mud.

The clock continues to chime.

In the house a young woman stands on the staircase and then begins her descent to the hall.

The hall is lit to the full tonight, a whirling strobe of colour, and sound, as all the great old hits come belting out.

In the doorway to the hall a couple, Mr and Mrs Neidpath, are standing together. Mrs Neidpath is holding a tray. They look as if they are waiting for some signal from the woman on the stairs. But she gives none, and walks on.

The clock finishes chiming nine. A hand is raised, and knocks on the oak door.

The door is opened by the young woman when she reaches the hall. A wind comes in with the visitor and blows the couple,

Mr and Mrs Neidpath, backwards into the pounding music and the light of the shrine to Lisa Crane.

Borne along by the wind, the young woman can be seen walking up the drive of Woodford Manor, her arm in the arm of the visitor, who wears black boots built up at the heel and a dark suit.

It can only be the effect of light and shade from the moon – the swirling party colours from the windows of the house – that gives the impression that an old woman, huge in the faint glow from the fires in the woods, is running up the drive after them.

IV

THE DEVIL'S TALE

I HAVE BEEN invisible, unfortunately, since the Tarot pack designed by the exquisite miniaturist Bembo. I am a blank, a white space, but, of course, many writers and scholars have chosen to fill that space with words, and if my style is fanciful, I beg forgiveness – or at least understanding, for, as Nabokov remarked when he entered the skin of that old devil Humbert Humbert, murderers are inclined to flowery prose.

I give the above example for a reason. Lolita, as we know, was the ultimate temptation for the diabolical lecher, jail-bait bargainer, harridan-hater, Humbert. And just as the libertine teen-snatcher had eyes only for his Lola, his Lo-Lee-Ta, so I, I must admit with a certain hangdog air, can experience a rising of the flesh only when confronted with the sight of its drooping, falling and withering on a member of the fairer sex.

I am – to a Centrefold world – a pervert. I love women in their middle age. How I adore to see their eyes light up with astonishment and gratitude when I pay one of the compliments I learned at the court of the Medicis. How fulfilled I esteem myself to be when an ageing beauty pouts and simpers at me. Women of 'a certain age' are – well, it's too obvious, really – they're easy prey. But one thing's certain at that age: they become invisible, like me.

Take the case of Muriel Twyman. I would stalk her as she left the riverside house where it was impossible for me to go, for fear my fire might be put out – such a damp, unsalubrious place.

I followed her as she got on the bus, got off again, walked in fashionable streets near her office, where I own so many chains of shops and boutiques that all the shopping malls in Hell can't hold a candle to them.

I went in after her, across the tessellated marble floor of the magnificent building I erected for the interglobal communications network I need to keep the cauldron of greed simmering – the pot that keeps the world on the boil and lowers it every day nearer to those regions in which no one any longer believes.

I would ride up in the elevator with her. And I would watch as she went to her desk and set about her daily task of inventing the language to worship youth, and I would see her face grow older every day, while the beautiful models on the covers of my expensive magazines stayed always, always young. And my love for Muriel Twyman grew, and so did my desire for her.

At office parties, no one saw Muriel. How my heart would ache for her, as she stood quite unnoticed against a wall while the pretty models and the lascivious men helped each other to the cornucopia of exchanged favours on offer. How I feared for poor Muriel, when she limped home on the shoes that squeezed her feet, and had straight away to care for her little granddaughter and make the evening meal.

And how I despised her daughter Anna, with her foolish, 'progressive' ideas and her blindness as to the real nature of women – which is to grab love, to feed voraciously on the affections of the children they dominate and raise, and to demand attention and obedience at all times.

Just for the fun of it, I decided to teach her a lesson – while consummating my deep love for poor, harassed Muriel, of course.

Nothing could have been easier than to infiltrate myself into that particular household. The daughter, Anna, like all those frustrated spinsters – she was a virgin at heart, although she had given birth to a peculiarly unprepossessing baby girl – was thrilled by my arrival in her life.

Within days she was buying dresses and dancing to the new music I had decided to bring into the world, to give a pounding sound to the last years of the second millennium since the birth of the Redeemer – your Redeemer, who has nothing now to redeem but the pawn ticket of eternal life.

As Anna and I danced (to be near her was pretty repellent for me, but I saw real need in the mother), my lonely, unloved Muriel was darning children's clothes and suffering the agonies of the damned, as she heard Anna and myself making love lengthily and luxuriously in what had until very recently been her own bed.

Before long my opportunity came, and I was quick to take it. In one of the chains of TV stores with which I have covered the surface of the dying world, I met the sad menopausee and offered her, at the flick of a switch, a return of beauty, youth and desire. And – after all, I'm no stinge-merchant – power and money as well. Why not? If a man, such as Dr Faustus, was offered such commodities by myself, why, as I'm sure Anna would very strongly agree with me, why not a woman, in this age of equality?

You know the rest. Muriel certainly enjoyed herself, in that decade where 'Sympathy for the Devil' was – I am glad to remind you – a recurring hit. And, after all, things had changed for ever then, or so the young thought. The machines and the lights and the music and the sound made the world a gigantic recording studio, where the movie of life, printed on an indestructible tape, would play and play.

Everyone had forgotten that unendingness is Satanic chaos. Chaos even became fashionable. This was pleasing, obviously, to the old prince of all mingling and ambiguity, my master, the one who sent me out in search of my latest convert to the cult of eternal youth.

Once or twice I was asked to account, in Hell, for the time I took over the conversion of Muriel Twyman.

Be patient, I replied. Muriel was a good woman, as these wretched specimens are known, and she has to learn to enjoy the body of a young and sexually forceful woman again, while all her memories and experiences are those of a woman whose cycle is done – in short, a hag.

Muriel had to learn the exquisite power over men that her new position and beauty afforded her. At first, as in the case of the – mistaken to my mind – need for her little granddaughter, she still lived in a past that was no longer written on her body surface.

I took great pleasure, I may say, in pushing the clinging and unattractive child out of the boat – down, down into the water.

But by then I was too enamoured of my creation, the new, heartless Muriel, to prevent her from pulling the child out again. You could say, perhaps, that little Ella was the famous Lisa Crane's Achilles' heel.

Jasmine Barr . . . well, we need handmaidens as much as ever we did. Ha! She may extricate the hairs on her chin with a tweezer every day, but there is a natural witch if ever I saw one. Envious, spiteful, gloating over the mishaps of others – she brought Muriel to me without any trouble at all, and even sent for the grand-daughter when the time had come.

Please pay no attention to those distressing 'dreams' Muriel claimed to have suffered when she made the foolish decision to try and renege on her contract with me. I only switched a few channels when she came to visit me in the TV shop to present her ridiculous plea for old age. I simply showed her, after a flash of her good self at the age she actually was – and that, I can assure you, was enough to make the silly woman turn tail – I only showed her, as I say, a few programmes that happened to be playing around the world that day. A round-up of prostitutes, if I remember, in some hell-hole like Manila's red-light district. A crashed plane, where a deal between arms dealers and govern-ments – and international finance, of course – had blown it out of the sky; weeping relatives at the airport. A few cocaine ship-ments, a burnt rainforest, and slum kids, gaunt and raiding, pillaging on Crack – that was about all really.

I can't help it if you figure in all these programmes, I said to Muriel as she stood there sobbing in my smart, newly refurbished store. And I explained to her, as simply as I could, that she had wanted a high profile, and OK, now she'd got one. What the hell do women really want?

And now you must be asking, what do *I* really want – from Muriel Twyman. After all, souls cannot co-exist with consumerism. And attempts at idealism and brotherhood between men have been proved unsuccessful ever since the well-publicized scandal of my little interventions this century, notably in the Gulag. So I can hardly have gone to such inordinate lengths for a soul.

No, I must hint merely that next time you happen to turn on the TV, or find yourself lucky enough to be in a red-light district or at the receiving end of a delivery of explosives or guns, next time you enter a casino or flick channels to the latest scandal of politicians and bordellos and lies – you will see the blonde girls, dead-eyed, who bring in the crooks and villains, the murderers, robbers and rapists, who make up the Chaos that is my legacy.

Next time you see those young women anywhere, remember, one of them could be Muriel . . . or Ella . . . or it could be you!